KISS OF DEATH

The little room was filled with psychic energy of an appalling absorptive kind; it was opaque and magnetic and colder than death. In there, something had hungered and fed and still hungered. Even though it wore the shape of a man it had metamorphosed into something altogether different.

Not a single beam of light penetrated that palpable blackness—nevertheless, I saw Victor holding her. Their bodies were lit with a flickering blue-violet halo. Only his lips were bright, drinking the final dying scarlet radiance from the four-petaled energy-flower at the base of her spine.

Then it was finished. The devouring darkness vanished and room light shone on Victor. He was fully clothed in a gray suit, but every stitch had been burned from the corpse of the woman who lay at his feet. The body was charred and crackling, and up the spine and on the head were seven stigmata of white ash, marking where he had fed.

By Julian May
Published by Ballantine Books:

THE SAGA OF PLIOCENE EXILE:

A PLIOCENE COMPANION

INTERVENTION

THE METACONCERT

BOOK TWO OF
INTERVENTION

A Root Tale to the Galactic Milieu
and a
Vinculum
between it and
The Saga of
Pliocene Exile

JULIAN MAY

A Del Rey Book

BALLANTINE BOOKS ● NEW YORK

A Del Rey Book
Published by Ballantine Books

Library of Congress Catalog Card Number: 87-4021

ISBN 0-345-35524-5

First published by Houghton Mifflin Company. Reprinted by permission of Houghton Mifflin Company.

Manufactured in the United States of America

First Ballantine Books Edition: February 1989
Third Printing: August 1992

Cover Art by Michael Herring

To Robie Macauley

INTERVENTION

Evolutionary creativity always renders invalid the "law of large numbers" and acts in an elitist way.

—Erich Jantsch
The Self-Organizing Universe

At the still point of the turning world. Neither flesh nor fleshless;
Neither from nor towards; at the still point, there the dance is,
But neither arrest nor movement. And do not call it fixity,
Where past and future are gathered. Neither movement from nor
    towards,
Neither ascent nor decline. Except for the point, the still point,
There would be no dance, and there is only the dance.

—T. S. Eliot
"Burnt Norton"

CONTENTS

PART III

THE
INTERVENTION

1

FROM THE MEMOIRS OF
ROGATIEN REMILLARD

PAUL REMILLARD, MY GRANDNEPHEW, MADE AN OBSERVATION during his first address to the Galactic Concilium in 2052, when Earth's long proctoring by the Simbiari finally ended and human magnates were admitted at last to the Milieu's governing body:

"There are two prices that must inevitably be paid by the operant mind. The first is a reluctant but certain alienation from the latent members of one's race—and its consequent is pain. The second price is less obvious, an obligation of the higher mind to love and serve those minds who stand a step beneath on evolution's ladder. Only when this second price is freely and selflessly paid is there alleviation from the pain of the first . . ."

By the time Paul bespoke those words, he was merely uttering a truism that operant human beings had recognized (and debated) for more than sixty years. It was foreshadowed in Tamara Sakhvadze's keynote speech before the First Congress on Metapsychology in Alma-Ata in September 1992, where vigorous exception was taken to it by certain factions. It was formally codified after the Intervention in the ethical formulae imparted to all student operants by their Milieu-trained teachers, but not fully

3

subscribed to by the Human Polity until our recalcitrant race instigated the Metapsychic Rebellion in 2083, learning its lesson at last as it nearly destroyed the Milieu that had prematurely welcomed Earth into its benevolent confederation.

You reading this who are immersed in the Unity take the principle for granted. It is as old as noblesse oblige or Luke 12:48. As for the operant minds who denied or tried to evade their duty to serve, they are all dead or reformed except me. For a long time I thought I was tolerated as a harmless cautionary example—the last Rebel, the sole surviving metapsychic maverick, neither a "normal" human mind nor an operant integrated into the Milieu's Unity. I believed, like other Remillards, that I had been allowed to persist in my unregeneracy because of my famous family and because I was no menace, my refusal having been grounded in bloody-minded stubbornness rather than malice or arrogance.

But now, as I approach the climax of this first volume of my memoirs, I am inclined to revise my modest evaluation of myself. Perhaps there *is* a deeper purpose in my relegation to the sidelines in la grande danse. I do bring, after all, a unique perspective to these memoirs. This may be the reason why I have been compelled—by something—to write them.

The rain seemed interminable during the summer of 1992, not only in my own section of New England but also in much of the rest of the Northern Hemisphere, as if the sky itself were obliged to share in the universal sorrow following the Armageddon strike. There was the human tragedy, the half million dead and more than two million others rendered homeless, and the suffering of the injured that would extend over so many years. But there was also the symbolic loss: The land holy to Jews, Christians, and Muslims was debarred to us for uncountable years beneath its pall of radioactivity.

The devices exploded in Tel Aviv and Dimona by the Islamic Holy War terrorist group had been crude, with a yield of about ten kilotons apiece. The fallout was intensified by the incineration of the Israeli nuclear weapons stockpile in the Dimona blast; and it was debris from this that spread northward in a wide swath, heavily contaminating both Jerusalem and Amman and rendering some forty thousand square kilometers of Israel and Jordan uninhabitable for the foreseeable future.

In the early days of that summer of lamentation, when the rain was poisoned and the whole world was shocked into incredulity, the magnitude of the disaster almost lifted it out of the political realm. Human beings of all races and all religious faiths mourned. A massive multinational relief effort mobilized while church bells tolled, mosques overflowed with bereaved Muslims, and Jews around the world sang Kaddish—not only for the dead and for lost Jerusalem, but for the dashed dream of peace.

"We could not watch everywhere," the EE adepts said. "There are too few of us, and the Armageddon strike was completely unexpected."

True; but there was still an irrational undercurrent feeling of betrayal. The miraculous "happy ending" of the metapsychic coming had proved a hollow mockery. Not only had the operants failed to prevent the calamity, but they were not even able to help locate the perpetrators. It was more than a year later that ordinary UN investigators cooperating with Interpol traced the members of the Iranian clique that had planted the bombs and brought them to trial. The psychotic Pakistani technician who had sold them the plutonium had long since blown his brains out.

After six weeks, the airborne radioactivity was almost entirely dissipated and the summer rains were clean again. Over most of the planet, the deadly isotopes were spread very thinly, and they sank with the rain into the soil or drifted to the bottom of the sea. Earth recovered, as it had from Hiroshima and Nagasaki. But the Holy Land was ruined. With the farmlands contaminated by the heaviest fallout and livestock dead or scattered, the rural population that had escaped immediate injury fled in panic to the nearest unaffected cities, triggering food riots and the collapse of law and order. The Jordanian government disintegrated almost immediately. Israeli officials set up an emergency capital at Haifa and vowed that the nation would survive; but by August, expert consensus held that the economy of the Jewish homeland, always fragile, had this time suffered a mortal blow. Surviving middle-class and professional Israelis began a growing exodus to the United States, Canada, and South Africa. Some Oriental Jews and Arab Christians resettled in Morocco. Upper-class Muslims and others with foreign bank accounts readily found haven. But the bulk of the displaced Muslim population faced an uncertain fate. Armageddon had killed more Jews, but it had left far greater numbers of Muslims homeless because of the fallout pattern. Few Christian nations were inclined to offer them asylum because the refugees were associated in the popular mind with the cause of the Islamic terrorists, and because a vengeful minority proclaimed their intention of escalating Armageddon into a full-scale jihad. Responding to popular opinion, the politicians of Europe, the Americas, and the Pacific Basin concluded that the refugees would be "unassimilable," a social and economic liability. Dar al-Islam countered proudly that it would take care of its own. However, when the speechmaking ended, it appeared that only Iran was eager to welcome large numbers of immigrants. Other Islamic countries were willing to open their doors to small numbers of homeless; but the oil glut and overpopulation had already strained their economies, and they feared the political consequences of an influx of indigents.

The displaced Muslims were notably reluctant to put themselves at the mercy of the fanatical Shiite regime in Iran. Most of them were Sunnis, of a more moderate religious persuasion than the Iranians, and they were appalled that the Ayatollah had proclaimed Armageddon to be justified under shari'ah, the traditional Islamic law. Furthermore, the refugees suspected (quite rightly) that they would be required to show loyalty to their new country by fighting in the long-standing war between Iran and Iraq. A few hundred fiery young men accepted the Ayatollah's invitation. The rest of the 1.5 million men, women, and children remained encamped in squalid "receiving centers" in Arabia and the Sinai, subsisting on charity, until China announced its remarkable proposal. When this was approved, the great airlift began early in September. By the end of the year the last of the displaced families were resettled in remote "Lands of Promise" in Xinjiang. Red Crescent and Red Cross inspectors reported that the refugees were made welcome by their coreligionists, the Uigurs, Kirghiz, Uzbeks, Tadjiks, and Kazakhs, who had lived in that part of China from time immemorial; they worked on collective farms in the oases and the irrigated deserts and adapted well—until Central Asia blew up in the course of the Soviet Civil War, and only the Intervention saved the Xinjiang population from becoming cannon fodder in the projected Chinese invasion of Kazakhstan.

The Intervention also restored Jerusalem to the human race as a city of pilgrimage. Milieu science decontaminated the Holy Land and thousands of the original inhabitants elected to return. However, since the Milieu statutes forbade any form of theocratic government, neither Israel nor Jordan were ever reborn. Palestine became the first territory governed solely by the Human Polity of the Milieu (successor to the United Nations) under mandate of the Simbiari Proctorship and the Galactic Concilium.

The rain was torrential on 21 September 1992, the last Monday of the summer, which turned out to be a very memorable day at my bookshop.

The excitement began when I unpacked a box of paperbacks I had purchased as part of a job lot at an estate sale in Woodstock the previous weekend. The spines visible at the top showed mostly science-fiction and mystery titles dating from the 1950s, and I'd bought three boxes for thirty dollars. I figured I would at least recoup my investment, since I had already spotted a moderately rare collectible, *The Green Girl* by Jack Williamson. As I sorted through the rest of that box I also uncovered a halfway decent first edition of *The Chinese Parrot*, a Charlie Chan mystery that I knew would fetch at least fifteen from a Dartmouth physics professor of the same name. I began to whistle cheerily, even though the storm was lashing the streets and the wind roared like a typhoon. There probably wouldn't be a customer all day—but who cared? I could catch up on my sorting.

Then I reached the very bottom of the box. I saw a soiled manila envelope marked SAVE THIS!!! in a pencil scrawl. There was a small book inside. I pried the corroded clasp open, let the envelope's contents slither out onto my worktable, and gasped. There lay Ray Bradbury's *Fahrenheit 451*, from the limited Ballantine 1953 edition of two hundred copies, signed by the author. The white asbestos binding was spotless.

With the utmost care, I edged the precious volume onto a sheet of clean wrapping paper and carried it to my office at the rear of the shop. Setting the treasure reverently aside, I sat down at my computer and summoned the current paperback collector's price guide, my fingers shaking as I tapped the keys. The screen showed the going rate for my rarity. Even in VG condition, it would sell for no less than six thousand dollars. And my copy was mint.

I chortled and hit the keys again for the Worldwide PB Want List, and a moment later began to scrutinize the small group of well-heeled bibliophiles who presently coveted my nonincendiary little gem: a Texas fantasy foundation; a doctor in Bel Air; a Bradbury completist in Waukegan, Illinois; the Countess of Arundel, a keen collector of dystopias; the Library of the University of Taiwan; and (hottest prospect of all) a certain wealthy horror writer in Bangor, Maine, who had just recently begun to snap up rare Bradburiana. Did I dare to start the bidding at ten thou? Would it be worthwhile to invite the Maine Monstermeister to inspect the book, so that I could try reading his mind to see what the traffic might bear? And to think I'd acquired the thing for a piddling thirty dollars!

And you should be ashamed of yourself.

I looked up with a start. Coming toward me from the front of my shop was Lucille Cartier, followed by another woman. I erected my mental barrier with haste, stepped outside the office and closed the door, and gave the pair a professional smile.

"Well, hello, Lucille. It's been quite some time."

"Five months." *You'd* really *take advantage of a poor unsuspecting widow who didn't realize how valuable that book was?*

Don't be ridiculous. The rule is caveat vendor, and I'm as ethical as any other book dealer. "Have you been keeping busy with that new Ph.D. of yours?"

"Fairly busy." *But not nearly as busy as* you *espèce de canardier!*

"Is there some way I can help you?" *And what's that crack supposed to mean?*

For starters you can BUTT OUT of my relationship with Bill

Sampson! "I'd like to have you meet my coworker, Dr. Ume Kimura. She's a visiting fellow at Dartmouth from the University of Tokyo, here under the auspices of the Japanese Society for Parapsychology."

"Enchanté, Dr. Kimura." I abruptly terminated my telepathic colloquy with Lucille, which was straying close to dangerous waters. It was very easy for me to concentrate all my attention on the Oriental newcomer, who really *was* enchanting. She was older than Lucille, and exquisitely soignée, with a complexion like translucent porcelain and delicately tinted lips. A black wool beret dotted with raindrops was pulled down at a saucy angle above her exceptionally large eyes, which had black feathery lashes and little of the epicanthic fold. She wore a trenchcoat of silvery leather with a wide belt that emphasized her tiny waist, and a high-necked black sweater. Her mind was densely screened in a manner that gave a new dimension to inscrutability.

Lucille said briskly, "Ume and I are colleagues in a new project that will investigate the psychoenergetic manifestations of creativity—"

"Working with Denis?" I cut in, raising my eyebrows in exaggerated surprise.

"Of course working with Denis," Lucille snapped. "We've been associated with the Metapsychic Lab since the beginning of the summer term."

"I haven't seen him much lately," I said. "He seems to be spending most of his time in Washington since Alma-Ata. Were you and Dr. Kimura able to attend the big congress?"

"Oh, yes!" exclaimed the delectable Ume, her eyes sparkling and her mind all aglow with a spill of happy reminiscence. "It was a most profound experience—more than three thousand metapsychic researchers, and over a third of them operant in greater or lesser degree! So many interesting papers and discussions! So much warmth and rapport!"

"So much talking and cautious telepathic chitchat," Lucille said. "So much political pussyfooting."

"It was a good beginning," Ume insisted. "Next year, in Palo Alto, the Metapsychic Congress will meet for the second time with a much expanded agenda—especially in the matter of education, the training of new operants. That must be our most urgent goal."

I frowned, remembering the media furor that had greeted the final resolution at Alma-Ata, proposed by Denis and seconded by Tamara and passed by a large majority of the Congress. Both Lucille and Ume picked up on my skepticism.

"Denis was absolutely right to push through the resolution calling for metapsychic testing of all people," Lucille said. "I can't understand the objections! We have very reliable mental assay techniques now. You'd think that after Armageddon, the necessity of finding and training all potential operants would be obvious."

"A pity," I said, "that Denis's resolution didn't specify voluntary testing."

"Oh, for heaven's sake," Lucille said. "We have to test *everyone*. That stands to reason."

I shrugged. "For an intelligent woman, you're really very naive."

Ume looked at me with perplexity. "You really believe that this will be a problem in the United States, Mr. Remillard? Such a universal testing program is quite acceptable in Japan, I assure you."

"It'll be a problem," I said. "A big one. I'd be glad to explain the ins and outs of the independent Yankee psyche to you over lunch, Dr. Kimura." My mind was still well guarded, but Ume's mental veil thinned then for just an instant, giving me an unexpected glimpse of something very encouraging indeed.

Her lashes lowered demurely. "That would be delightful. Lucille and I thank you very much."

So much for my tête-à-tête hopes! I gritted my teeth in frustration—and then had to jack up the strength of my mental shield against the renewed and insidious coercion of Lucille, who was now grinning heartlessly at my discomfiture.

She said, "You're *so* closely attuned to the social and political implications of operancy, aren't you, Roger? I can't wait to hear your opinions on the subject. But before we go to lunch, let me tell you why we came here today. I mentioned that Ume and I have a creativity project. We're studying persons who seem to be able to exert a metapsychic influence on energy—or even generate energy mentally. Denis said that you apparently experienced such a psychocreative manifestation right after the Edinburgh Demonstration. As I understand it, you inadvertently conjured up some form of radiant energy and melted a small hole in a window."

"A Kundalini zap," I said.

"Denis recommended very strongly that we check with you on your experience. I was told that it took place when you were under unusual conditions of stress." All the time she was speaking, the damn girl was skitteringly slyly all over my mind, giving little prods with some incisive faculty quite different from coercion. I found out later it was an aspect of the redactive function, a primitive mind-ream. As she crept and poked, her telepathy hectored me on my intimate mode: *What have you been saying to Bill? WHAT you sneaky undermining ratfink sale mouchard? What did you tell him cafardeur?*

I said, "I was shit-scared when I zapped the window, if you call that stress."

Ume giggled.

Lucille said: *Tu vieux saolard! Ingrat! Calomniateur! Allez— déballe! Foutu alcoolique!*

I said: *Nice to know you haven't completely abandoned your French heritage kiddo but I'm not really an alcoholic you know only an alcohol* abuser *as an experimental psychologist you should watch those fine distinctions!*

The insults flew like bats out of hell, but her outward cool never wavered. She said, "Roger, we'd like you to participate in a series of simple experiments. An hour a day over the next eight weeks would provide us with ample data to begin with. Now that you've concluded your therapy with Dr. Sampson, we can hope that your creative potential has been somewhat restored. The energy-projecting faculty is extremely rare. You'd be advancing our understanding of psychocreativity greatly by working with us." *WHAT HAVE YOU TOLD BILL ABOUT ME?*

"I'll think it over." *Nothing he didn't already suspect.*

Suspect? Suspect?

She was still on the intimate mode, smiling on the outside and raging on the inside, with enough antagonism slopping over now into the general telepathic spectrum for Ume to catch. The Japanese woman blinked in astonishment.

Lucille said suddenly, "And if you don't mind, we'd also like to take your zapped windowpane for analysis."

I have to hand it to her: She almost got me. I let out a guffaw at the incongruity of the request . . . and at that instant she shot a sharply honed and extremely powerful version of the coercive-redactive thrust right between my eyes. It was a zinger worthy of Denis himself (and I discovered later that he'd taught her the technique), and it rolled me back on my heels. If I hadn't been expecting her to try something, that probe might have turned my mind inside out like a shucked sock. But Lucille hadn't really had a close view of my mental machinery in more than a year, not since the time she's played Good Sam after the *60 Minutes* taping. If I'd cracked, she'd have gotten the whole story—Ghost and all. But I didn't crack.

I said, "You see? I *am* feeling much better. Old Sampson's a topnotch shrink. I never really thanked you properly for introducing me to him, Lucille. I owe you. You want my zapped windowpane? You got it! But I think you'd better find another experimental subject for your creativity project—for both our sakes, and maybe for Sampson's too."

"That wouldn't help. It's too late!" And then she burst into tears, and turned around and rushed out of the bookshop, slamming the door so violently that the little bell came off its bracket and fell to the floor.

"Bon dieu de merde," I said.

Ume and I looked at each other. How much did she know?

"I know more than I should, perhaps," she whispered, her huge dark eyes sad. "Lucille is my very dear friend, and she has told me that her relationship with Dr. Bill Sampson is faltering badly. She believes that you are somehow responsible. Are you, Mr. Remillard?"

What Lucille's coercion had failed at, Ume's empathy accomplished. "Yes," I admitted wretchedly.

"Why?" Ume was calm.

"I won't explain my motives to you, Dr. Kimura. It was for Lucille's own good. Sampson's, too."

"They are wrong for each other," she said, averting her gaze. "It was very obvious to all of us. Nevertheless, we did not feel we had the right to meddle in the lives of the two lovers. Lucille knew of the general disapproval of the operant group. It seemed only to strengthen her feeling toward Bill."

"I know." I went up the middle aisle to the front of the shop, bent and picked up the fallen door-chime, and hung it back in place. The rain was letting up a bit.

"You felt that you did have the right to interfere?" Ume asked.

I turned. "What I did was necessary. Lucille's badly hurt and I'm sorry. But I did have the right to interfere."

"Tell me only one thing. In your swaying of Bill's feelings— did you lie about Lucille?"

"No." I dropped my barriers just for an instant so she could see that I had told the truth.

Slowly, Ume nodded. "Now I understand why she put off so long approaching you about our project, even though Denis was very anxious for us to include you in it. Today she suddenly insisted that we come here. She has been upset about Bill for more than a week. He seems to have . . . spoken to her just after our return from Alma-Ata."

It figured. News about the extraordinary discussions there opened a lot of people's eyes to the seamier potentialities at large in the metapsychic wonderland. There was the hitherto underre- ported coercive function, for one thing, and the ominous implica- tions of the mental testing program. I'd been doing my own special number on Sampson over a period of some eight months, and the success of my subversion had been signaled when he finally punched me in the nose. Fortunately, it happened outside of office hours. When I broke off my counseling sessions in mid-July Sampson had been fully primed to doubt and fear his operant young fiancée. Alma-Ata had sparked the blowup, and now it looked like my Ghostly mission was nearly accomplished. Shit . . .

Ume put a gloved hand on the sleeve of my old tweed jacket. "Please. There is still the project. You will not wish to work with

Lucille, but would you consider working with me? The creativity studies are most important. I myself have manifested a modest projection of actinic radiation, as have certain others working in the Soviet Union. But no one has ever channeled psychoenergies in a coherent beam of great strength, as you seem to have done. Let me show you the theoretical correlation between physical and psychic energies presently being postulated by workers at Cambridge and at MIT." Would you open your mind a bit please? Thank you—

Voilà! The limpid thought-construct flashed to me inside of a split second. It was abstract as all hell and fiendishly complex— but I understood! Her transmission was to ordinary telepathic speech as a Turbo Nissan XX3TT ground-car is to a bicycle. Not that I would be able to explain the concept verbally to anyone else; but I *would* be able to remember it and project its symbolic content.

"I'll be damned," I said appreciatively. "Is that one of your new educative techniques? The ones you use in operant training?"

"Oh, yes. It is called bilateral transfer. One coordinates the output of the brain hemispheres. I would be happy to teach you this and any of the other preceptive techniques that interested you, if you would only agree to the experiments."

"I'm tempted." Oh, was I. And working with her in the lab wasn't even the half of it . . .

The winsome academic turned up her charm rheostat. I was aware that it was merely another aspect of coercion, her will acting to master mine, but what a difference from Lucille's effort! Ume said, "We would respect your desire for noninvolvement with the operant community, Mr. Remillard. There would be no pressure."

"Call me Roger."

"And Lucille will present no problem for you. I shall have a discreet word with Denis. He can assign her to other creativity studies."

"All right, Dr. Kimura, under those conditions, I agree."

"Please call me Ume." Her expression was very earnest. "I think we will be able to work together very compatibly, Roger.

And now, shall we talk about things further while we share a nice Dutch lunch?"

"I hope I won't disappoint you," I whispered. "Once I was rather good at this, but it's been a very long time."

"I can sense the latent power. It only needs to be reawakened. Sadness and repressed violence have clogged the flow of ambrosial energies."

"Violence? Ume, I'm the most harmless guy in the world."

"No, you are not. Your great reservoir of psychocreativity remains sealed up within you, and this puts you in peril, for if these energies are not used in creation, inevitably they destroy. The font of creativity lies within all human souls; in women, it is very often never channeled to the conscious level, but rather fruits instinctively in childbearing and maternal nurture. A very few men are also creative nurturers. But most—and certain women—must guide their creativity deliberately into the exterior reality by intellectual action. They must build—work. Unchanneled creativity is very dangerous and readily turns to destructiveness. The creation process is painful. One may be strongly tempted to evade it, since its joy is largely postponed until the creation is complete—and then the satisfaction is intense and lasting. Destruction brings pleasure, too, dark and addictive and nonintellectual. For the destroyer, however, process is all; he must continue, lest darkness catch up with him and he come at the end to the hell he has deliberately prepared for himself."

"Donnie . . ."

"Hush, Roger. Do not think of your poor brother now. This is a time for you to think of yourself, and of me."

Ume and I saw each other perfectly in the dark. Her aura was a rich blue, warmer close to her body and scintillating gold at the halo's edge. I glowed a flickering and shadowed citron, with an outer aureole of dim violet. My root chakra had a faint, hopeful carmine radiance, signifying that the spirit was willing while the flesh was weak.

"Don't worry. We are going to take a long time," Ume said. Her lips brushed my forehead, cheeks, and mouth as she spoke. "This is a very old way in my part of the world. In the West, it has been called carezza. It is unappreciated because of the impatience of occidental lovers, who seek explosive release rather than immersion in a pool of enduring light."

Her lips had taken on the golden glow now, and so had her eyes. The outermost precincts of both our minds had opened so that we could synchronize the pleasure; but in spite of what she revealed to me of her life, the real identity of Ume stayed that night and forever apart from me . . . as I remained hidden from her. She had brought me to the small rented house on the Ruddsboro Road where she lived alone. It was sparsely furnished, almost ascetic, with many oddly shaped ceramic vases holding arrangements of leafless branches and dried grasses and bare, gnarled roots. The rain still fell. A brook outside the bedroom window rushed over its bed of granite boulders, filling the place with pervasive thunder. Ume had been straightforward about the sexual attraction, and I in turn was honest about my abaissement du niveau psychique. Sampson's psychoanalysis really hadn't helped me all that much spiritually, aside from bolstering my courage and putting me more or less on the track toward sobriety. I'd confessed to Ume that I was very dubious about coming up with anything useful in the creativity experiments. She had countered with suggestions for a rather different style of therapy. I had doubts about that, too, but she only smiled wisely.

"We will begin very slowly and proceed very slowly," she said, kissing my shoulders, stroking my inert arms in the lightest possible manner with the tips of her fingernails. "You must not speak. Try not even to think. Simply rest in me. Resist arousal. My mind will speak to you and my body will share its creativity. You will discover things about me and I will familiarize myself with you. There will be feedback and a very slow increase of energetic potential. Very slow. Now sit here among the cushions and take me to you gently . . ."

This is Ume:

. . . A frail, strange child. The oldest of three daughters. Her home is in the city of Sapporo on Hokkaido, the rugged northernmost island of Japan. Her mother, once a schoolteacher, now cares for the family. Her father is a photographer whose business never seems to prosper. Both parents are descended from the

Ainu, the aboriginal inhabitants of the island. The heritage shames the husband and wife and they never speak of it. The oldest daughter, with her betraying fair skin and exotic eyes and the slight waviness of her silken hair, is a reproach. She is not the favored child.

. . . A little girl of six. Her father takes close-up photographs of her face for an advertising assignment. The child is obedient but impatient with sitting still. She wishes ardently to run out of the stuffy room to play with the little girl next door. This other child's face, distorted but recognizable, appears on three successive negatives of a film roll, in place of Ume's own.

. . . The father is astounded. He experiments and the miracle happens again. He begins to realize what must be happening. "Ume!" he cries. "Dear girl! You must do this again!"

. . . The child is eager to please him, to feel his love and admiration. She cooperates in her father's experiments for weeks. It is learned that she can imprint film not only while it is in the camera, but also when it is outside it—provided the film is not exposed to normal light. In the beginning her "thoughtographic" images vary greatly in clarity, depending upon whether she is summoning them from her imagination or "reading" them directly from her surroundings or from a book. Her best pictures are made with Polaroid film. All she has to do is stare into the lens and think about a subject while her father clicks the shutter. He makes many photos of Ume's thoughts. He praises her lavishly and dreams of the millions of yen the family will make when little Ume enters show business.

. . . The father's father learns of the marvel. He comes from the Ainu settlement to the city and studies the little girl. "She is possessed of an ancient demon," he says. "She will bring bad luck." The father is scornful. He has found a book. It tells how thought photos were produced by a psychic researcher named Tomokichi Fukurai in a remarkable series of experiments between 1910 and 1913. Another book, translated from English, tells how the American physician Jule Eisenbud obtained psychic photos from a hotel worker named Ted Serios. Serios also stared into a Polaroid camera. Most of his images were fuzzy and eventually his rare talent faded away. But the talent of little Ume does not.

The more she practices, the better the results. Her pictures are now superbly sharp. She can do both color and black-and-white.

. . . The great opportunity comes at last. The girl will appear on a television show featuring local amateur performers. She and her father have prepared for a whole year. But when she comes on stage before a live audience, she is devastated by sudden shyness. Her performance is a fiasco. A week later her father is killed by falling in front of a subway train in the main Ohdori station of Sapporo.

. . . The televised failure has one good result. It brings the little girl to the attention of Dr. Reiko Sasaki, a respected parapsychologist. This woman becomes a second mother to the girl. The real mother is only too glad to relinquish care of her. Under Dr. Sasaki's kind tutelage, Ume again produces thought photos. She also shows evidence of being telepathic. Helped by the good doctor, the girl receives a fine education, becomes Dr. Sasaki's assistant, and cooperates in research that shows how her thought photos are made.

. . . Unconsciously, Ume directs photons to impinge upon a selected area of photo-emulsion, creating concrete images of her thoughts. She can affect emulsion even when it is heavily shielded. Many careful experiments prove that the photons are not derived from existing sources of light. Either Ume's mind excites the emulsion atoms or air atoms to a point where photons are emitted, or else she creates the photons ex nihilo—out of another aspect of the Greater Reality, as proponents of the new Universal Field Theory would say.

. . . The strange and lonely little girl is now a woman, pursuing her own goals. Dear Dr. Sasaki is gone, and so is the girl's mother. Her two sisters do not have metapsychic talent. Ume writes to them, and to her nieces and nephews. Sometimes there are answers.

Then Ume sang a poem:

> Autumn light painting
>   shadow patterns bright and dark;
>   my mind reflects them.

Now her entire face was bathed in golden radiance, and her breasts became autumn moons, and her sex a mystery of midnight blue that I saluted as she sank down, enclosing me. Her hands seemed to weave a luminous fabric around about us, an auroral chamber that rippled in the remote sounds from the cascading stream outside.

She pressed her fingertips to my nipples, my breastbone, and my throat. My aura there kindled into lotuslike flames, no longer sickly but rose-gold and shimmering. Her fingers traced mystical patterns on my back, and I saw with my mind how the skin retained the cool blazing designs, and how they blossomed and became more intricate all by themselves after her hands had passed on.

I began to awaken. The penetration was very slow, a hesitant growth after a long, parched dormancy. She arched her body back and brought the fire-limning fingers over my shoulders. I kissed the golden roses of her breasts, reverently pressed lips and tongue to the aural mandala burning above her heart. It was incredibly sweet, and as I drank from it it throbbed and expanded, and became invested with rainbow colors. A blue brilliance now poured from her hands, becoming golden as it gushed over my lower limbs. She rose up, freeing me, and I groaned in protest.

Trust me! We have so long a time . . .

I kissed all of her turning body, now clothed in astral fire. There were pulsating symmetries of blue-white with aureate coronas at her mons, her navel, her heart, and her throat. Both breasts were blinding stars. I was fully potent again myself, burning crimson and gold. *Please!* I besought her. *Let me return!* But she only lifted my arms, that had hung helplessly at my sides, and delineated the pathway of every nerve with scarlet epidermal radiance.

I wanted to crush her, to devour her, to impale her on the incandescent blade and burn her to ashes. *No,* she said. *No. Wait my dear one wait.*

Tears of frustrated fury scalded my face. I was enveloped in a thundering inferno with her coolness flickering madly out of reach. And then she guided the star-fires to my eyes . . . and into my mind burst the most beautiful thing I had ever known, a psychocreative lotus-form revolving and ever-changing in a thousand glorious variations. A new rare energy spread from my loins, up my spine, and suffused my trunk and limbs. She was suspended in the flower's heart, her body golden and her hair and blazing écu azure. I enfolded her at last and she descended. I penetrated her so profoundly that it seemed I would pierce her heart, and there we stayed, rapt together in contemplation of our own many-colored splendor. There was never a culminating orgasm as such, but we shared joy that persisted without cloying as we elaborated upon the beautiful thing flowering between us, our personal creation. Whatever it was, we had made it together, and we worshiped it for hour after hour until we seemed to pass effortlessly into dreams, separated, but still conjoined in the memory of that fantastic night's work.

We woke the next morning contented, at peace, and the best of friends.

Ume and I were never lovers in the conventional sense. We never lived for each other or felt a need for permanent commitment. We were more like two musicians coming together in a duet of perfect harmony, delighting in a work of art that neither of us could have created alone. Sometimes sex was a part of it, and sometimes not. Coitus was always sublimated in the service of creativity—and since what we made was abstract, vanishing as music vanishes, it was probably not a true creature of love. But it was marvelous and it did us both good.

Ume's experimental work with me at the Metapsychology Lab, on the other hand, was a failure. Under controlled conditions, I could not generate the least attoerg of detectable energy anywhere in the electromagnetic spectrum—let alone produce a coherent laserlike beam. The out-spiral yoga technique only left me with top-of-the-skull headaches. (The in-spiral, on the other hand, was a great adjunct to carezza!) I spent far too much time messing around in the lab during the eight weeks of experimentation than I should have, and at the end of it I was dismissed from the creativity project as a nonstarter and my zapped windowpane was relegated to some forgotten storage cabinet.

Denis told me, "There's an off chance your creative function might become operant with practice, but I don't hold out much hope. Our educative techniques are most successful with youthful subjects. You're forty-seven and your metafunctions are encrusted with a lifetime's accumulation of neurotic dross. The more psychoenergetic powers will probably always remain latent, except possibly under conditions of great mental stress."

"No big thing," I said, glad of having escaped guinea-pig status. "I can live very well without it."

I was wrong about that. But then I've been wrong about a lot of things throughout my checkered career.

Lucille Cartier and Bill Sampson endured a stormy severance. In time—and most likely thanks to Ume's subliminal reassurances—Lucille came to understand that I had not acted maliciously. I was more to be pitied than censured, and she decided to forgive me. The peace pact was sealed during the Christmas season of 1992, when she presented me with what she said was a much-needed addition to my bookshop: a dark and shaggy Maine Coon kitten to chase mice, keep me company in morose moments, and lend the place tone.

The kitten became the first Marcel LaPlume. By the time I discovered that he was not only telepathic but coercive as well, I was too used to him to give him up.

2

EXCERPTS FROM:
FINAL CONVERSATION BETWEEN
CAPTAIN, ORBITER MODULE AND
SURFACE EXPLORATION TEAM

JOINT SOVIET-AMERICAN
MARS EXPEDITION

NOCTIS LABYRINTHUS, MARS

2 NOVEMBER 1992

GAVRILOV: What is your position now, Volodya?

KLUCHNIKOV: We are 32 meters [garble] top of the fog is perhaps 20 meters below us. It is not stable as it was yesterday but is rising as sunlight [garble] the fissure and melts [garble].

GAVRILOV: Say again, Volodya. You are breaking up.

KLUCHNIKOV: We're 32 meters down the canyon wall. Descent is easy. Top of fog bank 20 meters below but rising. Today fog bank is rising. Do you copy, Andrei?

GAVRILOV: Roger on the copy. Fog rising . . . I am scanning the other fissures of the Labyrinth of Night. Fog is filling most of them. Perhaps the small dust storm yesterday provided condensation nuclei. Is the fog hampering your operation?

KLUCHNIKOV: Not yet . . . Are you receiving any video yet, Andrei?

GAVRILOV: Negative on the video signal. Wayne, you had better give that fancy American camera a good kick.

STURGIS: Listen, I been pounding on this sucker ever since we went over the rim and she started cutting out [garble] seals on the housing when we bumped her. But if it's something else, like maybe a glitch in the power supply, I can likely fix [garble] to put our money on the ciné camera today. She's doing fine, so we'll have the record. Tough luck about your travelog, Andrei.

GAVRILOV: [laughs] Well, you fellows will just have to give me a word-picture of your descent into Night's Labyrinth. Be sure to let me know at once if you see green men with four arms.

STURGIS: Hey, you betcha. Ol' Tars Tarkas himself creeping up out of the mist [garble] but red layers of rock. We're taking regular samples. It's sedimentary and a fast eyeball scan shows no evidence of macrofossils. There's a sizable dike of blackish igneous rock a few hundred meters to the east of us. On our way back up we'll work our way over and grab a specimen.

KLUCHNIKOV: Wayne, do you see how the dust in the crevices is not so dry and fluffy anymore? It is more like coarse sand. I will take some . . . under the surface it begins to firm up even more. The outcroppings have that spongy look even more down here than on the surface. They are something like orange coral, but there is no coral structure. No regularity indicative of life.

STURGIS: Hey . . . you know? Hey.

KLUCHNIKOV: What?

STURGIS: Over here. Like a little, shallow cave. Does that look like a puddle of ice to you?

KLUCHNIKOV: It does. Sheltered [garble] from yesterday. There is no dust on it. I will chip some out.

STURGIS: Oh-oh. Here comes the fog.

KLUCHNIKOV: Helmet lamps.

STURGIS: Aye-aye, Commander . . . Helps a little. No problem climbing down [garble] goddam crunchy sand. And some of the outcroppings have sharp edges. But outside of that [garble].

KLUCHNIKOV: Wayne, do not descend so quickly. I cannot see you.

STURGIS: Sorry, Volodya, I wanted to . . . the damnedest thing. You got me in sight now?

KLUCHNIKOV: Yes. This fog, ulcers to its soul, is getting thicker than clotted cream and—

STURGIS: Hey. Hey. I don't believe this. Put your headlamp to a rock. Look. Just look.

KLUCHNIKOV: The rocks look wet.

GAVRILOV: Say again, Exploration Team? You found *wet rocks*?

STURGIS: It looks like a thin coating of ice on the rocky outcropping, with liquid water in a film on the surface. I'm taking a sample.

KLUCHNIKOV: Fog . . . it is the fog. Look—the porous rocks are all getting this—this icy rind. And if we go lower . . .

STURGIS: Now you wait for *me*.

KLUCHNIKOV: Usrat'sa mozhno. . . . This is incredible.

STURGIS: Sheesh. Oh, wow.

GAVRILOV: What is it? What have you found? What do you see?

KLUCHNIKOV: Down here there is plenty of light, you understand, but the fog turns everything to an orange haze . . . and the rocks have a glistening coating. It is much darker than the ice. In my helmet lamp it is sometimes dark blue-green, sometimes brown. Yey bogu. It changes before my eyes.

STURGIS: It's alive.

GAVRILOV: You think you have found Martian *life*?

STURGIS: Well, it's not like any chemical reaction *I* ever saw . . . but then I'm only a geologist. What this stuff is starting to look like is a gelatinous marine growth. It's swelling very slowly. It must be frozen—what's the ambient, Volodya?— but there's this glistening film of what sure as hell looks like liquid at the surface.

KLUCHNIKOV: The ambient temperature is minus seventeen Celsius.

STURGIS: Jeez—that's warm. There must be a thermal vent at the bottom of the fissure. That was one of the hypotheses about this damn Labyrinth, with the craters all connected by wormholes . . .

GAVRILOV: Life. Life on Mars. What a magnificent achievement for the Diamond Anniversary of the Revolution.

STURGIS: And Columbus sailed the ocean blue . . . 500 years ago, comrades. One for America, too.

GAVRILOV: Of course. Of course. This is wonderful.

STURGIS: Right where we half expected to find it: down in the cracks. . . . We're taking samples. Damn. That's tough. The pick ain't gonna do her, Volodya.

KLUCHNIKOV: Let us see what [garble] diamond-bit drill?

STURGIS: Yeah, that might work. Stuff's like some incredibly tough plastic. Resilient. But it'd have to be, right? To live in this godforsaken place . . . Ah. You got that micro-sabresaw handy?

KLUCHNIKOV: Here. Yes . . . That looks like it will do it. I think I'll [garble] you get that specimen packed. Here, connect the life line [garble] another ten meters or so further down. I want to check out the temperature and take an atmospheric [garble] stay here much longer.

GAVRILOV: Are you descending further, Volodya? You are garbled.

KLUCHNIKOV: The outcroppings inter[garble] . . . reconnoitre a bit farther . . . [garble] on the rocks. Not amorphous, like the other, but with a kind of jellyfish radial symmetry. Like a thick pancake perhaps fifteen [garble] and two, three centimeters thick.

STURGIS: Jee-*zuss*. It's—it's corroding the stainless steel baseplate.

KLUCHNIKOV: Fantastic . . . [garbled] . . . that stupid specimen, Wayne. Get your arse down here and *look*.

STURGIS: Oxidizing the thing like a house afire. . . . What the hell is it? God—I think the blade's going. And the drill bit—

KLUCHNIKOV: . . . are quite beautiful, with flowing structures of ultramarine blue that engulf and seem to eat the green-brown [garble] . . . with a light of their own. Like lucite lanterns.

GAVRILOV: Volodya. Commander Kluchnikov, come in. Your transmission is breaking up and fading badly.

KLUCHNIKOV: It is a fairyland. The beauty. Wayne, come down.

STURGIS: Goddammit, Volodya, will you quit [garble] so sure this stuff can't get at *us*. It could be dangerous. The acids or whatever that I released when I [garble] a fuckin' vanadium-steel blade to a rusty nubbin. Do you hear me? Commander?

KLUCHNIKOV: I am coming. You will not believe [garble] right off the rock.

GAVRILOV: Exploration Team, this is Orbiter. Come in, please. Come in Exploration Team.

KLUCHNIKOV: Zakroy ebalo, Andryusha. We are too busy to [garble] life-forms of exquisite beauty. They are hard, but resilient, and some of them are biolu[garble] of them right off its rock and into my collection bag.

STURGIS: Listen . . . listen, Volodya. Get up here fast, hear me? Don't touch those things. Anything that can live in this awful place—

KLUCHNIKOV: Now, then. What ails you, little [garble] so active. How did you [garble? scream?] . . .

STURGIS: Volodya.

GAVRILOV: Vova. Commander. Vladimir Maksimovich.

STURGIS: I'm coming. I'm coming . . .

GAVRILOV: The thing, Wayne. The thing he picked up. The Martian.

STURGIS: Hey. You okay, Commander? . . . oh . . . oh, no. No.

GAVRILOV: Wayne, what's happened?

STURGIS: . . . [garble] . . . not a user-friendly world. No. Tell 'em that, Andrei. Anyplace but Mars! Oh, Jesus. I can still [garble] fly in blue amber dissolving [garble? scream?] . . . on my suit like little drops of blue soup. Growing. Primordial soup is blue-green, Andrei [garble] . . . love you dear Ruth . . . [garble] . . .

TRANSMISSION ENDS

3

DU PAGE COUNTY, ILLINOIS, EARTH
20 JANUARY 1993

AS THE CHAIRMAN OF THE REPUBLICAN NATIONAL COMMITTEE came slowly to the point, Kieran O'Connor's attention wandered—and thus it was that he heard the unaccountable mental voice.

Desiccated embryos returned to water ... floating in aloof sadness ...

"Even though some people may think it premature to consider such a matter at this early date, let me assure you that the Nominating Committee of the Republican Party does not," Jason Cassidy said. "We suffered a devastating defeat in November. The incumbent beat our ass into the dust. He's riding high on the platform of economic prosperity that the Democrats stole from us, and he's managed to convince the voters that the metapsychic peace initiative and the disarmament program are both personal triumphs."

Floating in the lustrous sea ... letting their dry blood reconstitute ... pumping out, regaining form ...

Do any of the rest of you hear that voice? Kieran demanded.

Four of the five men sitting around the fireplace with him on that bitterly cold night strained their farsense, listening. The other man, Brigadier General Lloyd A. Baumgartner, USAF (Ret.), only sipped his Drambuie and stared at the Aubusson carpet in front of Kieran O'Connor's hearth. He wondered, in a subvocalization that was clearly perceptible to the telepaths, just when the National Committee Chairman would get to the point and offer him the 1996 Republican presidential nomination.

Jason Cassidy said, "There was a time when candidates were

27

picked in smoke-filled rooms at the nominating convention itself. Later, primaries influenced the nomination and presidential aspirants began their campaign a year in advance." I hear absolutely zilch Kier.

Len Windham said: I don't get anything but the subvocals of our male Cinderella impatient for his glass-slipper fitting. Would you look at that noble profile? Holy Gary Cooper! And the silver cowlick will be a political cartoonist's delight.

Neville Garrett said: I don't detect anybody.

Arnold Pakkala said: Nor do I... The domestic staff was given the night free as you ordered. There is no one in the house except the six of us.

"Today," Cassidy droned on, "the presidential nominating process is infinitely more complex and requires long-range strategic thinking. The National Committee has been working on that strategy ever since our November defeat, in consultation with Mr. Windham and Mr. Garrett, our Party poll and media specialists, and certain senior advisers."

Like Mr. Moneybags Kieran O'Connor! General Baumgartner said to himself. And now it's all perfectly clear. Why he acquired McGuigan-Duncan Aerospace and kept me on as CEO in spite of the losses I'd incurred in the Zap-Star debacle. Why his media flunky Garrett was so interested in my glory days as a Moonwalker—

And now the embryonic music starts... peeps and squeaks and fidgets and flowing bloodhum... a song of rebirth from death...

Kieran said: Scan the entire house and grounds Arnold. I can still hear the voice and now there's some damn music carrying over.

Yes sir.

Cassidy said, "The '96 presidential race is going to be even tougher for us than the '92 campaign. A two-term incumbent, one of the most popular presidents in history, will be able to pick his own nominee—and we know that nominee will be Senator Piccolomini."

Another self-righteous Guinea prick, thought the General.

"We could, of course, stick with our Republican candidate of last fall."

If you want to lose again, the General thought. The goddam quarterback really knows how to lose with style!

"However," the Chairman went on, "Piccolomini will be a hard nut to crack because of the success of his antinarcotics program, because of his close ties with the incumbent, and because of his undeniable personal magnetism."

So, thought the General, you can't run your bought-and-paid-for Minority Leader, Senator Scrope. He's smart but he's a nerd, and putting him up against Piccolomini would be peeing into the wind.

"We've studied a number of prospects, only to conclude that most of them do not project a suitable image. The Party will be developing a new platform for '96 in response to what we see as gathering threats to our national economy and security. The candidate we seek must exemplify that platform. He must be a man of authority, of proven courage, in tune with conservative patriotic values. A man who will confront the disasters that our experts foresee with a forthrightness unclouded by pseudoliberal globalism."

General Baumgartner straightened and frowned at the Republican Chairman. "Disasters? What kind of disasters, Jase?"

He was answered by Kieran O'Connor. "By the end of this year our Middle Eastern oil supplies will be entirely cut off by escalating Islamic wars in the Persian Gulf and Arabia. Our reelected Democratic President and the Democrat-controlled Congress will not dare send in American military forces. They have boasted that theirs is the Party of Peace. An American military action in support of the oil industry would be unthinkable." Arnold. Listen!

Sea creatures . . . holothurian and crustaceans sad and glad . . . singing and dancing in bloody water . . . a funeral dance and a birth dance . . .

Pakkala said: I detect no intruder anywhere within the perimeter of the estate. There is an aurora borealis tonight and you have been hypersensitive lately. Perhaps there is some metapsychic phenomenon operating analogous to the skip of AM radio waves—

Kieran said: No. Never mind Arnold.

"Our analysts," Cassidy said, "believe that the world is on the brink of another serious energy shortage. Thermonuclear power is still two decades away. Without that Persian Gulf oil, a major depression will affect all industrialized nations. The Third World will be pushed to the brink of anarchy. Africa is certain to blow up and Pakistan is on the verge of an armed confrontation with India."

Are they right? Baumgartner asked himself. If they are, America is heading for the biggest mess since World War II—and whoever the president is, he'll find himself in the same shoes Harry Truman wore when he had to decide whether to invade Japan or drop the bomb...Christ! No magical mystery meta-whoozis finagling can keep America safe from *this* crock of shit! Only strong leadership by a real man—somebody people could be sure wasn't trading the country off for some pie-in-the-sky utopia scheme hatched by Commies and loopy Scotch professors and fortunetelling freaks.

A dance...a water dance with embryos...I've been gestating it for more than six weeks now ever since we knew Nonno was dying...

Kieran said: Oh Christ!

The ballet is a tribute to his memory...so much more tasteful than the usual gangland obsequies...I want you to share it...If you like it I may finish my performance alive Daddy...

"The turn of the century," Cassidy said solemnly, "may turn out to be the most dangerous period in American history."

And one, thought the General, in which certain industries stand to make an unconscionable amount of money—especially if they own the White House. As if they could control *me* the way they do that sleazy little douche bag Scrope! O'Connor and Cassidy and the rest of their cabal think I'd play along...be manipulated like poor old Ike. Just let me get into that Oval Office!

"Events may accelerate," Cassidy went on, "so as to give us a good shot at winning even in 1996 if we present a candidate with a powerful, take-charge image. A man who knows his own mind."

General Baumgartner said, "You know those mentalist freaks —those metapsychics in the Psi-Eye program—could be real trouble if they got into the political arena."

"We do know that," Kieran O'Connor said. "Party strategists have been examining the metapsychic movement very carefully. Those people represent a menace to American liberty, General. We'd expect our presidential candidate to come down hard on any suggestion that metapsychics participate directly in government."

"Fuckin' A!" the General affirmed. The others chuckled.

Daddy it's for you . . . it's for Nonno . . . I won't go to his funeral tomorrow but I will mourn him in the dance . . . and you . . . and me . . .

Kieran said: Shannon!

Arnold Pakkala said: Sir—your *daughter*?

Kieran said: The goddam voice. It's her she's here screening herself threatening I think she may know—

Pakkala said: Where is she? I'll take care of it.

Kieran said: NO. I must. We'll have to finish this—*Jase*! Wind up the pitch and then get him out of here! Neville you and Len take him to your place. Jase and Arnie will help you wrap him up . . .

"Our pollsters and analysts are eighty-six percent certain that there will be a Republican president in the White House by the year 2000," Cassidy said. "The odds are longer for '96, but worth the push. The National Committee has designated a unanimous choice for the perfect candidate. That man is you, General Baumgartner."

"Gentlemen," said the General, "I'm—I'm really overwhelmed."

Escaping from his guests in the library, Kieran hurried to the nearby butler's pantry, where there was a master monitor-intercom unit. He tapped 16 and the screen lit, giving a long overhead view of the indoor swimming pool located on the mansion's lower level. The chamber was dark except for what appeared to be underwater illumination of a concentrated cobalt blue. A shape suspended within the light gyrated rhythmically. From the small loudspeaker of the intercom came the nervous, deformed sound of Erik Satie's *Embryons Desséchés* being played on a synthesizer. Kieran tapped the code that would turn on the main room lights and the underwater lamps of the natatorium. Nothing happened.

"Shannon?"

Kieran spoke calmly into the mike. At the same time he manipulated the zoom control of the monitoring camera to magnify the image of the swimmer. She was eighteen but looked more like a twelve-year-old. Her legs were long and beautifully shaped but the rest of the body was angular, the breasts small and flat, the hips boyishly narrow. She was wearing a chaste white maillot. Her long hair swirled in an inky cloud, its normal bright Titian red masked by the Cerenkov blue of her visible psychic aura. From her extended wrists curled other diaphanous filaments that her hands seemed to caress and weave as she undulated in the submarine ballet she had dedicated to her dead grandfather.

Her wrists were cut, trailing streamers of blood.

"Shannon, I'm watching. Do you hear me?"

I hear, Daddy! Holothurian larvae clinging to their purring, grotesque parent . . . break away break away, babies! . . . go free if you can and celebrate spineless triumph . . . be sure to hide from the light!

"Shannon, come out of the water." *Come out. COME OUT.*

He exerted his full coercion while zany electronic music tinkled and trilled. Sweat had broken out on his brow and he found that he was holding his breath, commanding her to hold hers. But the range was too great for his compulsion to take hold of her. He felt, to his horror, a reciprocal mind-clutch and a gentle warning:

No . . . I must finish this dance . . . come down and watch me properly, Daddy. Your creatures have gone away now . . . come and share mine with me . . . I'll help you . . . THE HOLOTHURIAN SPINS A WEB LIKE MOIST PURPLE SILK—

"Damn you!" Lashing out violently, he broke her mental shackle and erected a defensive barrier. She only laughed. The blue light was fading with the end of the first embryonic song. A ruddy glow introduced the second.

This is the dance of the edriophthalma, a crustacean with sessile eyes . . . of a mournful disposition, it lives in retirement from the world in a hole drilled in a cliff . . . Nonno! Dear Grandpa Al do you want me with you shall I retire behind my film of red water with my mind's eye turned inward?

"Shannon—for God's sake!"

The music was a lugubrious parody of a funeral march. The swimmer's limbs folded tight against her body and she became a fetal ball, pinkly throbbing, floating some six feet below the surface of the water. A measured stream of silver bubbles, flattened like coins, tumbled upward from her emptying lungs.

Kieran stormed through the formal dining room into the main hall and ran to the elevator. As he punched G and the door whisked shut, he felt a hot pounding begin in his chest. There was an irresistible urge to inhale, pressure on his eardrums, a scarlet fog seeping into his peripheral vision, a deadly stirring in his loins. God damn the little bitch! He'd delayed the bonding too long—

The elevator door opened. Kieran staggered along a passage walled with thermopane windows that cast wan light on the snowy landscape outside. The great house had been built into the east side of a hill and even now, in the dead of a winter's night, the metropolis over forty miles distant lit the sky like false dawn.

This is the third and final song . . . the lively podophthalma have eyes on mobile stalks . . . they are skillful and tireless hunters but they must be cautious—their own flesh is good to eat! . . . Eat or be eaten, Nonno. You lived in such a world and so will I twice over . . . if I choose to . . .

Jolly galloping music and a vision of a slender form darting zigzag through black water, leaving twin trails of golden blood behind. Kieran ran sluggishly, as though he himself were under water. It was impossible for him to breathe, harder and harder to move. He passed the exercise room and the spa and finally came to the open door of the natatorium. It was dark inside and there was a strong smell of chlorine. The synthesizer music filled the tiled chamber with clanging echoes. His mind screamed.

Shannon!

Deep in the pool was an upright, spindle-shaped violet glow. It brightened abruptly, then shot up like a submarine missile, breaking the surface with a great splash and a dazzling burst of white light. A parody of a symphonic finale blasted from the overhead speakers. Erik Satie's jocose treatment of marine life was coming to an end, and so was the sinister water ballet of Kieran O'Connor's daughter.

He was finally able to haul in a gasping breath. His eyesight cleared and he stabbed at the control panel on the wall beside him. Normal incandescent light flooded the room and the only sound was the slap of wavelets against the sides of the Olympic-sized pool. Above the middle of the water a girl in a white tank suit floated on her back, eyes closed, hair fanned out like strands of algae, arms extended cruciform. She was smiling.

To Nonno. To my Grandfather on the day of his entombment. With love from Shannon.

"Come out," Kieran told her.

Descending, she swam, using a vigorous backstroke. She climbed the ladder and stood looking up at him, pale and shivering, with tiny drops of water winking at the ends of her eyelashes. Her mind shone bright and it was impervious to either probing or coercion.

"I hope you liked my dance, Daddy. It was for you, too."

He took hold of her hands and raised them, studying the wrists. The cuts were not deep and she had not severed the tendons, but there was a steady flow of blood that mixed with the water of her dripping body to make a pinkish puddle on the travertine floor. He released her, turned, and walked out the door. "We can fix you up in the gym. Let's go."

She followed with complete docility. The trainer's cubicle in the elaborately equipped exercise room provided hydrogen peroxide, antibiotic ointment, and bandages. He sat her on the massage table and wrapped her in a voluminous towel before tending her wounds, closing the lips of the cuts deftly with butterfly tapes and finishing up with gauze and temporary cuffs of waterproof plastic wrap.

"Now you can take a hot shower without spoiling my first-aid job." His voice was gentle.

"Thank you, Daddy." She eyed him askance. "You won't make me go to the doctor for stitches, will you? I can heal myself easily enough. But I had to have . . . the effect."

"You had to scare the living shit out of me," he told her in a level tone, turning to rinse his hands of her blood.

"Have it your own way."

"How did you get out here from Rosary at this time of night?"

"I took Tippie Bethune's car and just drove out, then hid the car in Goldman's orchard and walked up our driveway. You were all so busy with your low politicking that it was easy to fudge your minds and sneak inside. I sang only for you. Don't you know about the intimate mode of farspeech? You can aim it at only one person."

So she knew about his plans for Baumgartner! "There'll be hell to pay when the college authorities find out you skipped."

She shrugged. "I'll take my shower now."

When she was gone, Kieran took several damp towels and went to clean up the gory traces she had left on the floor. The members of his domestic staff were well-paid psychics, bonded to him and utterly loyal; but he did not want them to know about this escapade. It was extreme—even for Shannon.

He said to her: You ought to examine your unconscious motivation for this piece of adolescent idiocy. The guilt you feel because of who/what you/we are is irrational. Seeking punishment to atone for my/your/Al's imaginary wickedness is also irrational. Attempting to dissociate yourself from me/Family/your mental heritage is not only irrational but futile. There is no rebirth for us. We are.

He put back the first-aid supplies, then lay down on the Panasonic Shiatsu lounger and turned it on. Timed waves of vibration soothed away some of the stress. It was nearly one in the morning. Big Al's funeral was today. She'd loved the old bandit deeply. She didn't think it a bit hypocritical that he had confessed a lifetime of sins on his deathbed and expired with the Viaticum on his parched tongue.

Damn her! She *would* have followed Al tonight if he hadn't

given in to her and begged . . . The suicide attempt was his own
fault. It was the culmination of a lot of things—mainly his own
neglect of her developing mind-powers. She'd grown up patho-
logically shy, introverted. There'd been suicidal hints that he had
tried to laugh off. The Edinburgh telecast had been traumatic,
intensifying her brooding. And now Big Al's death, and her
growing realization of her father's extraordinary ambition. She
would have to be bonded. The alternative was probably a descent
into madness or self-destruction.

But to bond his own daughter . . .

She was mind-humming a reprise of the crustacean dirge as
she took her shower. The musical parody was superimposed in-
congruously upon an image of Queen of Heaven Mausoleum, a
fulsome monument to Italian-American piety that would, come
daylight, receive the mortal remains of Aldo Camastra.

Kieran said: Shannon? Do you know why so many of your
Grandfather's people prefer tombs in a place like Queen of
Heaven rather than ordinary burial in the ground?

I never thought about it, Daddy.

Back in the Old Country, cemeteries may be more than a
thousand years old. Space in the earth is at a premium. When a
new grave is dug they may find old bones. The bones are taken
up and put into a kind of storage place called an ossuary, all
mixed up higgledy-piggledy with the bones of other skeletons.

How awful!

The only bodies sure to be left undisturbed are those interred
in aboveground tombs or in mausoleums. That ancient fear of not
being left to lie in peace lingers in tradition even here in America.
Tradition can be a powerful motivator. Many kinds of tradition.

. . . Oh, I *know* the twisted justification that Al and the others
in the Outfit subscribed to, Daddy—the old story about the simple peasants resisting tyranny in Sicily, then later on using the
Thing as a steppingstone to power and wealth in this country. But
it's different for you! You're no persecuted immigrant. You have
mental powers that you could use to help all humanity, just as the
organized metapsychics around the world are doing. But you
won't join them, will you, Daddy! You'd rather get rich and then
take over the country with your Mental Mafia.

Is that how you see it?

"That's how it is!"

Shannon came out of the spa wearing a white velour sweat suit, with her hair bound up in a towel. Revulsion and frustrated love radiated from her but her voice remained measured. "You're worse than Big Al ever was, Daddy, because you came deliberately into the Outfit. He and the others had their Family tradition, but you joined them because you'd analyzed the possibilities in cold blood. And you've done very well, transferring the Mob assets into legitimate business and covering your tracks. You're Big Al's son-in-law but nobody holds it against you—especially after your mind exerts its special charm."

Kieran laughed.

"Will bossing President Baumgartner be power enough for you, Daddy? Or are you bucking for Boss of the World?"

"You could be my little Crown Princess," he said.

She folded her bandaged arms and looked down on him lying in the chair. "No," she replied with cool dignity. "The embryo dance helped me decide. I'm leaving here, getting out of Rosary College and transferring to Dartmouth. I'll ask that Professor Remillard to accept me in his psychic Peace Corps thing. I won't do anything to hurt you, but I won't stay with you anymore. I've been very silly and naïve, thinking it was natural for us to—to be above normal people. The Edinburgh Demonstration was like some kind of miracle, opening my eyes. That wonderful Russian woman and her vision! And then Denis Remillard explaining his educational plan for all people with metapsychic talents—"

"He's very good on television," Kieran admitted. "Very nearly as charming a coercer as your depraved old Dad . . . but also an idealist with no notion of the way the normal world actually works. He and the rest of them are in for a rude awakening, you know."

"No, I *don't* know!" Shannon flared. "Suppose you tell me."

Kieran got up from the lounger and regarded her with concern. She had begun to shiver again and her lips were blue. He wondered how much blood she had lost. "If you're really interested, I'll explain it to you. But not down here. I could use some coffee and brandy right now, and so could you."

He headed for the door and she trailed after. "I know you think I'm only a child," she said as they approached the elevator. "Maybe I am, but you can't expect me to accept this—this scheming of yours without questioning it!"

"Be sure you ask the right questions. You've led a very sheltered, pampered life up until now, thanks to the loyalty of Bayard and Louisa. Not all of us have been so lucky. I wasn't. Neither were Jason or Arnold, or Adam or Lillian or Ken or Neville, or most of the other people you so glibly designate my Mental Mafia. I wanted to spare you the horror stories. It seems I made a mistake, denying you the history of the persecuted minority we all belong to."

The elevator door closed as Kieran pressed 3.

Shannon said, "When I saw MacGregor and his people do the Edinburgh Demonstration, I was just devastated. There they were, doing their thing just as though it were—natural. And I thought: It doesn't have to be Daddy's way, hiding the powers, using them selfishly. I could come out in the open! When more and more operant people began to reveal themselves I got so excited I thought I would die. I wanted to confess what I was, too! But I was afraid . . ."

"For a good reason."

Her eyes were pleading. "We're different, but not so very different. The normals have been so grateful about the Psi-Eye program. The sensible ones support the metapsychic testing plan, too. The opposition is just from fundamentalist fanatics and people without the education to appreciate the good we can do. When the normals learn more about what operancy really means—"

"They will try to kill us," Kieran said.

Shannon stared at him, speechless, and in that split second of appalled vulnerability absorbed the details of the peril that he projected. Then they were at the third floor of the mansion and emerged into a part of the house that had always been officially barred to her (although she had snooped through most of it when Kieran was out of town). Here were the self-contained guest suites for certain visitors; the antiseptic sanctum that housed the awesome mainframe computer with its huge data bank, connected by dedicated fiber optics to corporate headquarters in downtown Chicago; the satellite receiving station; the mysterious "recovery room" that was occupied from time to time by certain Mental Mafia recruits; and—most tantalizing of all—a locked room referred to in hushed tones by the household staff as the Command Post and by Kieran as "my study." Shannon had never been inside it. Few people other than Kieran himself and Arnold Pakkala had.

They stood now in front of its door, armor-plated steel without a knob or latch. Kieran pressed his right hand against an inset golden plate. There was a complex clicking sound and a single electronic chime. "Open up," Kieran commanded, and the door slid silently aside, admitting them.

Shannon uttered a low cry of astonishment.

Her father smiled. "Do you like my study? I do, very much. You may come here as often as you like from now on. I'll reprogram the door. But please don't attempt to operate any of the equipment until I've given you proper instruction. I can begin that now, if you like."

"Oh, *yes*."

"Sit there while I make our coffee." He opened a taboret and took out a Chambord. "I amuse myself by thinking of this room as the high-tech equivalent of the kingdoms of the world that Satan showed to Jesus from the pinnacle of the temple. If I *were* the Earth Boss, I could certainly supervise things very nicely from right here . . . Kona or Naviera?"

"Kona," she whispered. She sat on the edge of a maroon leather settee, looking very young. Her mental barriers had fallen completely. Kieran came to her, unwound the turban from her head, smoothed the damp hair, and kissed her crown. As he did so he slipped a subliminal command into the exposed psyche that would prevent voluntary closure until he released her. It was a thing he had learned to do instinctively when he bonded the first hurt minds to himself—how long ago?—before her birth.

Daddy I feel very strange.

Relax dear baby.

He handed her the steaming coffee with a splash of fine cognac, feeling his energies begin to mount. He had feared there might be an insuperable inhibition, but there was not. So, he thought, we think we know ourselves, but we don't! Perhaps all devoted fathers keep the thing repressed in the unconscious. It was as true an instinct as the other, so closely related, that bound mind to mind in perfect loyalty. He wondered if anyone else among the operants had discovered it. He thought not. The hierogamy was an old mystery that repelled the overcivilized mind, dying with the old Celtic and Greek votaries . . .

"Are you comfortable now, Shannon?"

Her smile was dreamy. "Yes. The coffee is good."

"Drink it all." He slipped off his Shetland cardigan, folded it, then unknotted the blue silk scarf he wore at the open neck of his shirt.

"I thought the coffee would wake me up. But now I feel very sleepy." The dark lashes fluttered. She set her empty cup aside and relaxed against the cushions.

"You can spend the night here," Kieran said. "I often do. It's the one place I know that I'm completely safe. The windows are armored glass and the entire room is a self-contained little fortress. Secure."

Shannon's eyes had closed. "It's snowing. I can see the snowflakes with my mind, blowing in the cold wind. Whenever I do that I feel so lonely." Her face was as white as the soft velour suit she wore.

"You aren't going to be lonely. You'll be part of our group now." Would she remember? The others hadn't—except Arnold, whose love had been strong enough to overcome the posthypnotic suggestion. You won't remember, he told the deepest part of her soul. Not unless you want to.

"I feel cold again," she murmured. "A little."

"Let me warm you," he said, and touched the switch that would turn off the lights and blind the machines.

Shannon remembered.

4

EDINBURGH, SCOTLAND, EARTH
7 APRIL 1994

WHEN THE GIRL CAME WITH THE SANDWICHES, JAMIE AND JEAN and Nigel fell to with the usual voracious appetite of the EE adept, but Alana Shaunavon didn't even seem to notice the plate in front of her. She stared out the pub window at the statue of the wee dog, faithful and melancholy in the rain. A hardy Japanese tourist focused his camera on it, took the shot, and hurried off along Candlemaker Row. Two nurses huddled under a single umbrella came into the pub for lunch, and an old man in a black trench coat moved slowly in the direction of the churchyard gate. He had a plastic carrier bag.

Alana sighed, lifted the teapot, and poured a bit into her cup. It had gone cold.

"Here now, we can't have that," Nigel said. He took the pot in both hands, squinted at it with keen determination, and grinned when steam spurted out of the spout.

"What a useful talent," Jean MacGregor observed. "With you around the house, one wouldn't even need a microwave. Or an electric blanket."

Nigel filled Alana's cup. "So I've told this lovely lady many a time to no avail."

Alana smiled absently. "You want a wife, luv, and I'm not the marrying kind."

"Piffle," said Nigel. "I won't give up, you know. Drink your tea and eat your sandwich. You'll need your strength for this afternoon's outing. It's Dallas again. Sibley and Atoka think the

Super-Stealth skin formulation may be hidden there in a fabricating subcontractor's place."

"How dreary." Alana took one bite of sandwich and one sip of tea. "We've wasted five months haring about after this silly ferrite coating process. Why couldn't the bloody stubborn Yanks simply hand the thing over to the Russians instead of daring us and Tamara's people to find it? There's so much more important work we could be doing."

"They're testing," Jamie said. "Measuring our capabilities and our resolution, and making a classic American 'Don't Tread on Me' gesture. You can bet that the formulation is in a lead box walled up in a reinforced vault surrounded by an electrified grid in the midst of an alligator pond . . . but we'll find it, whatever the rigamarole, and we'll send copies to Washington and Moscow via diplomatic pouch and tell the world press we've done it. Then we'll chalk up another triumph for globalism and wait for the next confrontation."

"Neither side really cares about the radar-invisible gunk," Alana complained. "It's only a matter of scoring off each other. They may've thrown away their nuclear arms, but it seems they're just as determined to dominate the world as they ever were—and our metapsychic peace initiative is nothing but a referee in the charade."

"Did you really expect an instant Golden Age, my lass?" Jamie's smile was ironic.

"I hoped it would be better than this," Alana admitted, looking out the window again. The old man in the black raincoat was consulting a small book and gazing about. "We don't have the specter of nuclear war between superpowers anymore, but the old East-West antagonism and suspicion are still there, and the little countries cling to their eternal squabbles. There's war in Arabia and war in Kashmir and war in Botswana and war in Bolivia . . ."

"And I'll never pray at the Wailing Wall," Nigel said, "and your tea is getting cold again, and what is so fascinating about that old chap lurking about out there?"

Alana said, "It's odd. He's subvocalizing both the words and tune of 'Amazing Grace.' I can tell he's in a great state of emotional agitation, and one would normally be able to read his thoughts like a hoarding under those conditions—but because of the hymn-singing I can't get a glimmer. I wonder if the poor old thing is lost?"

"A kind of normal's thought-screen, is it?" Jean asked. "How interesting. Do you know, I think our young Katie and David may have cottoned on to that one! There've been times when I've noticed television commercials and theme songs and other nonsense cycling over and over in their sly little brains when they were obviously up to some deviltry."

"We'd better hope the technique doesn't catch on in diplomatic circles," Nigel said.

"According to Denis Remillard," Jamie said, "it already has. But fortunately, not too many normals are able to keep it up for any length of time . . . I forgot to mention that Denis popped over via EE very early this morning. He had some important news. Dartmouth is establishing a Department of Metapsychology with some whacking great grants that've fallen down the chimney, and Denis is being promoted to full professor and will head the thing up."

"Lucky sod," groaned Nigel. "And here we are with the University casting about for ways to put us under the U.K. Civil Service! Can't you just see our metapsychic peace initiative tucked tidily away in Whitehall?" And he sang, in an excruciating fruity tenor:

"But the privilege and pleasure
That we treasure without measure
Is to run on little errands for the Ministers of State!"

"Denis had some bad news, too." Jamie spoke in a lower tone. "The bill for universal metapsychic testing of all American children died in committee. The Civil Liberties Union and the Bible-thumpers carried the day. Now the testing is to be done on a strictly voluntary basis. There was some demand that the names of the participants and the results of the metapsychic assay be made a matter of public record, but Denis is fairly certain that meta-supporters in Washington can shoot that one down by invoking the famous American right to privacy. I asked Denis if he senses any serious groundswell of antimeta sentiment building, but he thinks not. More like a blasé attitude on the part of the normals, he said—taking the mental marvels for granted the way they do space travel."

"We were all heroes," Nigel declaimed, "right up until the last nukes in North Dakota and Skovorodino were dismantled! But what have we done for humanity lately?" He lifted his beer in a mock toast.

"Denis's new book is about due," Jamie added. "He's calling it *The Evolution of Mind*. He said it may shake people up. I hope the lad hasn't said anything too reckless. Sometimes he strikes me as a bit toplofty, and I don't think that would sit well with the American public. Your Yank-on-the-street tends to follow egalitarianism right out the window, pretending that people really are all created equal and deserving of equal treatment across the board. It doesn't work out that way in actuality, of course—but God help the fellow who advocates any elitist scheme." He chomped up the remains of his sandwich and took a deep draft of Arrol's.

"We, on the other hand," Nigel said, "just love an aristocrat."

"Speak for yourself, you kosher Sassenach!" said Jean with spirit.

A number of colorful racial slurs were exchanged in good humor, and then all of them but Alana concentrated on food and drink. She persisted in her abstraction until she suddenly said:

"Will Denis's new book have an explanation for precognition?"

"Have you had a skry, then?" Jean's face was troubled. "Not another warning?"

"Not exactly," Alana said. "No firm premonition, only a kind of feeling. Just now."

Nigel regarded the young woman with a pretense of exasperation. "She's facing her weird again, that's what. So she can get out of the excursion to Dallas."

"It's no joke," Jean admonished him. "Not to anyone born and reared in the Highlands. Our own little Katie's had the Sight—and I don't mind telling you it scares me. The other metafunctions are only extensions and elaborations of our normal mind-powers, after all. But precognition seems supernatural somehow..." She turned again to Alana. "Your feeling: was it for good or ill?"

"I—I don't know. I've never felt anything like it. It wasn't frightening. No vision, no notion of an event impending. Perhaps just the opposite." She gave a small laugh and once again turned to the window. The old man was stooped over, rummaging in his carrier bag while the rain beat on his exposed neck. "He's still singing the hymn," Alana noted softly. "Still upset. Perhaps it's *his* precognition."

"Funny you should ask about the theoretical aspect of the Sight," Nigel said. "I was defending the crystal-ball effect as a legitimate metafunction to Littlefield and Schneider just the other day. It has to be a warping of the temporal lattices producing a wormhole in the continuum through the agency of the seer's own coercion. In theory, one could catch glimpses of the future or the past quite as readily as contemporaneous remote-viewings in the here and now. It's a matter of willing—coercing—a momentary plication of time rather than space."

"But how," Alana said slowly, "can you explain the *unpremeditated* glimpse of the future? The vision one doesn't ask for?"

Nigel looked uncomfortable. He swirled the last of his beer in the bottom of the glass. "It's hard to explain that through dynamic-field theory, I admit. You see, the temporal nodalities that we call 'events' require instigating forces. Causes, if you like. But if the unexpected premonition doesn't originate in the coercivity of the seer, we must ask just what the source of the coercive vector is. It could be another person. It could be the collective unconscious of humanity, if you want to accept Urgyen Bhotia's theory."

"Or it could simply be angels," said Jamie MacGregor.

Alana started. "Oh, you're putting me on!"

He was rummaging in his notecase for the Parapsychology Unit's credit card. Discovering it at last, he waved it at the barmaid. "If you eliminate the coercivity of the seer as the instigator of Sight, and eliminate the coercivity of other *people*—using the term in its broadest sense to mean 'sapient entities inhabiting our physical universe'—then you are left with an enigma. An extra-dimensional genetrix. An initiating force outside the eighteen generative dynamic fields, but nevertheless congruent to the three matrix fields."

The barmaid took Jamie's card away. Her face had an old-fashioned expression.

"Are you speaking of God?" Alana asked.

"Not necessarily," said Jamie. "The Universal Field theory doesn't define God, or the Cosmic All, or the Omega, or whatever. But if such an entity exists outside our physical universe, then it must have a method of relating to that universe. Denis Remillard believes in God and suggests that an integral sexternion—or a whole gaggle of them—operates between the All and the dimensional construct we call the physical universe. He says the sexternions already have a perfectly good name in religious tradition: angels! Word means messenger." He signed the credit-card slip with a flourish and pocketed his copy.

Alana peered at him with suspicion. "Do you mean to say you *really* believe second sight is instigated by angels?"

Jamie shrugged. They were all rising from the table and going after their raincoats. "I didn't say that. I said it was a theory, and one of Remillard's to boot. You can think as you like, lass."

"Do you still feel fey?" Jean asked Alana solicitously. "You're dreadfully pale and you didn't eat a thing."

"It's a blank," the girl whispered. She tried to smile. "There doesn't seem to be anything beyond."

"Take my arm," Nigel urged her.

Alana's eyes slid away. "I'd really rather not. Please, Nigel."

"No problem," he said easily, and held the door open.

The two women went out into the rain.

By the churchyard gate, the elderly man was now kneeling on the pavement, rooting in the plastic carrier bag and muttering. He had lost his hat and the rain soaked his thin white hair and ran down his furrowed cheeks. He looked up wildly and froze as he saw Alana.

There shalt not be found among you any one that useth divination, or an enchanter, or a witch! For all that do these things are an abomination unto the Lord: and because of these abominations the Lord thy God doth drive them out from before thee!

Alana stopped as the cry flooded her mind and tried to crowd Jean back into the pub doorway with her body, but she was not quick enough; the machine pistol that the old man pulled from his bag spat five sudden gouts of yellow fire and woke thundering echoes up and down the ancient street. Alana crumpled, her face turned scarlet and formless, dead before she reached the ground. Jean took only one bullet, but that was in the neck, and she fell back into Jamie's arms with her life fountaining onto the rain-darkened granite pavement.

The old man shouted: "Thou shalt not suffer a witch to live!" He threw down his weapon and darted into the Greyfriars church-yard.

Jamie went to his knees with Jean clasped to his breast, hearing her mind say what her voice was unable to utter:

Katie and David . . . love them . . . continue the work . . .

He bent and kissed her, with the rational part of his brain assuring him that this could not be happening. Not to her. Not to them. Their life together had been absurdly perfect, an idyll throughout the thirteen years of their marriage and professional collaboration and the rearing of their joy-bedight offspring. This sort of ending was impossible.

Jean said: I'm always with you.

He kissed her again, and was aware of a terrible howling sound. Then, shockingly, he was almost bowled over by a plunging shape and knew it was Nigel, gone after the madman, screaming at the top of his lungs.

Jean said: He mustn't. Stop him.

When Jamie continued to cling to her, she mustered up a last coercive impulse.

Go before it's too late!

He lowered her carefully to the stones. People were pushing out of the pub, babbling and shouting. Several cars had stopped and their occupants looked out, horror-stricken. Jamie dodged pedestrians and pounded through the churchyard entrance. Beneath one of the venerable trees just softening in spring leaf was a fierce orange blaze. Nigel stood over it, his scholarly face as implacable as the marble death's-heads that decorated the seventeenth-century tombs on either hand. A man writhed in the midst of the fire, making a shrill keening sound.

Jamie ripped off his coat to blanket the flames, rolling the burning man on the wet turf. Suddenly, without a word, Nigel leapt onto Jamie's back and clawed at his eyes. Jamie levered himself upright, got a grip on the wrists of the smaller man, and pried the hands away from his face. Redness tinged the vision of one eye.

"No, Nigel! For God's sake!"

"Let the swine burn!" Nigel sank his teeth into Jamie's right hand. Agonized, Jamie lifted Nigel bodily and flung him head-first against the trunk of the tree. He fell, groaning feebly, and Jamie turned again to the smoldering body beneath the raincoat.

There were people running about the churchyard now and a sound of approaching police cars. The flames seemed to be out. Jamie pulled a fold of fabric aside and saw the charred features of the fanatic—hawk-like nose, bold brow-arches of Caledonian bone, lantern jaw—a face very much like his own. The eyes in their lidless sockets seemed to retain an uncompromising gleam and the mouth, distorted by the rictus of violent death, might have been triumphantly grinning.

Jamie let the cloth drop back. He got up and limped over to Nigel, who appeared to be embracing the tree as he attempted to haul himself upright. One sleeve of his coat was torn and his bald pate was purpled with a massive contusion. Jamie extended his left hand to his colleague and pulled him to his feet. Nigel reciprocated by binding Jamie's bitten hand with a handkerchief.

Police officers came and led them away, and then there was an interval during which they were asked the same questions over and over again with irritating persistence. Dr. Nigel Weinstein was arrested and charged with culpable homicide. Later he was released on his own recognizance to attend the third Metapsychic Congress, which was held that year in Edinburgh. He did not present a paper.

In February 1995 Weinstein was acquitted when the Scottish jury brought in a verdict of "Not Proven." By then, however, with the world-wide publicity given the trial, the damage had been done.

5

SURVEY VESSEL
KRAK RONA'AL [KRON 466-010111]
SECTOR 14: STAR 14-893-042 [LANDA]:
PLANET 4 [ASSAWOMPSET]
GALACTIC YEAR: LA PRIME 1-357-627
[8 AUGUST 1994]

THE MONSTROUS KRONDAKU ARE A RACE FABLED THROUGHOUT the Galactic Milieu for their ancient wisdom, their merciless objectivity, and their composure. But there is another aspect to the great tentacled invertebrates that other polities (except the Lylmik) do not suspect.

At those rare times when they can be certain of being unobserved by exotic minds, the Krondaku are given to fooling around.

The mated pairs, especially, in conditions of absolute privacy, will cast aside all decorum and circumspection and for a brief interval submerge themselves completely in sensory input. They revel, they wallow, they become intoxicated voluptuaries—drinking in, above all, the supernal pla'akst sensation engendered by their ponderous amours. Only the Gi, those paragons of concupiscence, have a greater capacity for pla'akst than dallying Krondaku. When the passionate interlude ends, its memory lingers on and suffuses the normal Krondak phlegmatism with sunniness. For a while, the terrible monsters are awash with uncharacteristic bonhomie.

It was in just such a mood that two senior Krondak planetologists approached the Landa solar system in the 14th Sector.

Comparator Dota'efoo Alk'ai and her mate, Attestor Luma'eroo Tok, had received a most unusual assignment from the Sector Base on Molakar [Tau Ceti-2]. They were to go themselves, without the usual support crew consisting of a mixed bag of Milieu races, and perform an update assessment of the fourth Landa planet, which they had surveyed many Galactic millenaries ago. Once a promising prospect for colonization, the world had suffered the misfortune of being within a critical distance of supernova 14-322-931B-S2. As this dying star exploded, it launched a relativistic blast wave of high-energy particles, x-rays, and gamma rays in all directions. For several centuries, the normal background cosmic radiation flux through the Landa system increased by a factor of nearly five thousand, with cataclysmic effects upon the biota of the single habitable world. The blast wave had swept past Landa exactly two Galactic millenaries ago [5476 Earth years]. The 14th Sector Survey Authority decided it was now time to find out if the irradiated fourth planet had simmered down, and if it was still potentially colonizable. A full-scale resurvey was not required. Experienced fieldworkers such as Dota'efoo and Luma'eroo would be able to decide rather quickly whether or not the world was a write-off.

The Landa solar system lay on the outer fringe of the Orion Arm of the Galaxy, some 6360 light-years from Molakar. Traveling at its usual brisk displacement factor of 370, the starship of the two Krondak planetologists required 17.19 subjective Galactic days to make the trip, which was executed in eighteen consecutive hyperspatial catenaries. Twice each day, as the ship entered and left subspace by means of its upsilon-field superluminal translator, the two entities within experienced a brief moment of horrific pain, which they bore with Krondak stoicism. But in between the translations, when they were alone together in the gray limbo of the hyperspatial subuniverse, that most remote of nonlocations, the couple felt free to doff their dour racial façade and romp. They had not had a honeymoon in more than five millenaries, and its glow stayed with them as they neared the journey's end and climbed reluctantly out of the connubial vat of glycerin, imidazolidinyl urea, and iso-yohimbine.

The terminal break through the superficies was due any minute. They headed for the survey craft's control room slithering side by side, settled into their squatting pads, and waited. A small cyan indicator on the instrumentation panel flashed on as the translator mechanism spun the upsilon-field gateway. The viewport showed only quasi-dimensional gray negation . . . and then there was a unique swimming snap, a *zang* attended by incredible agony, a *zung*, and relief. They had returned to normal space, in the vicinity of the Landa system.

The smallish G1 sun was of modest mass and luminosity, unassociated with solar companions. It shone golden-yellow, exhibiting minimal flare activity and an attractive "butterfly" corona with pearly equatorial streamers and polar plumes. Five of its family of fourteen planets were immediately visible to the multiple Krondak oculi, but all of them were gas-giants of no interest to colonization evaluators.

Luma'eroo shut down the overdrive mechanism and fired up the subluminal gravo-magnetic propulsion generators. He switched the ship's navigation unit from automatic to tentacular. A crawling network of faint violet fire, the rho-field, now clothed the outer hull of the dull-black spheroid. Under Luma'eroo's pilotage, it went full inertialess and proceeded to the fourth planet, moving at a sizable percentage of the speed of light. The ship took up station in a geosynchronous orbit a few hundred thousand kilometers above a bluish-green, cloud-swirled world.

"I wish thou wouldst not hot-dog, Tok." Dota'efoo's admonition had overtones of fond languor; the aftereffects of the recent debauch were still very much with her.

"The sooner we get this evaluation over with, the sooner we can begin the trip back to Molakar." Luma'eroo's primary eyes retained a misty periwinkle color and his integument was flushed with the telltale rosy blotches of fulfillment. "This mission is hardly likely to end positively, Alk'ai, given the proximity of the poor planet to the supernova."

"I daresay thou art right," Dota'efoo said, stroking his warty dorsal prominence with absent-minded affection as she stared out the main viewport. "Just look. The cloud cover has deteriorated to only about fifty percent and there are polar ice caps now. The atmospheric ozone layer must have been zapped to a green frazzle. All-in-All pity the life-forms! . . ."

"I'm going to call up a précis of our last survey. It's been a long time—and thanks to thee, O alluring source of hyperhedonia, my mnemonic faculties are just the least bit unresponsive." He flicked a request to the computer and the abbreviated data flashed into both their minds:

EVALUATION SUMMARY—14-893-042-4

This eminently habitable world is a typical small metallolithoid with an equatorial radius of [5902 km] and a mean density of [5.462 gm/cm^3]. It has a nickel-iron core and is internally heated by natural radioactivity. The dipolar magnetic field is classed 06:2:05:9. Planet Four is attended by three interlocked moons: A is a coreless lithoid giant with a diameter 0.22 and a mass 0.01 that of the primary; B and C are lithoid midgets scarcely 1/1000th as massive as A, orbiting at the equilateral points of the giant. Planet Four has an axial tilt of 19.35 degrees and a nearly circular orbit around its sun. Its year is equivalent to 611.3 Galactic days and its day 93 time units. The planetary albedo is 39.7 percent.

The atmosphere of Planet Four is generally within acceptable parameters for Milieu races: 22.15 percent oxygen, 0.05 percent carbon dioxide, and 77.23 percent nitrogen, with the balance consisting of noble gases, hydrogen, ozone, miscellaneous trace gases, miscellaneous suspended particulates, and varying amounts of dihydrogen oxide vapor. Clouds formed of the latter shroud about 62 percent of the planetary surface.

Land areas comprise 19 percent of Planet Four, and 81 percent is covered with dihydrogen oxide oceans with an average salinity of 3.03 percent. Nearly 20 percent of the hydrosphere is epicontinental and very shallow. There are many freshwater lakes of small area. The lithosphere has a Class 4 motile-plate structure with a basaltic abyssal sea-floor and granitic continents. Two continents are of moderate size and five are much smaller. There are myriads of continental-class islands and many extensive island-arcs at oceanic plate boundaries. Continental mountain ranges have formed adjacent to the active subduction zones of the two principal land masses, and some of their peaks exceed [6000 m] in height. The continents also feature eroded highland remnants of earlier cycles of continental drift. There is moderate vulcanism in the island-arcs, along mid-oceanic ridges, and in the subduction ranges.

Planet Four has a generally warm and humid maritime climate, lacking polar or continental glaciation. Tropical conditions prevail in the equatorial belt, with full-summer temperatures exceeding [40°C] and no winter. The midlatitude continental temperature range is: summer—above [40°C]; winter—above [10°C]. Island temperatures are generally lower than continental in summer and higher in winter. One small continent near the North Pole has a summer maximum temperature of [23°C] and a winter minimum of [−5°C]. There is only one small desert, in the rain-shadow of the coast range at the equatorial region of the largest continent.

Life-forms of Planet Four are C-H-O-N-S-Fe proteinoid, predominantly aerobic. Both the oceans and the land harbor large populations of protist and multicellular autotrophs. There are some 690,000 species of photoautotrophic, chemoautotrophic, and mixotrophic plants —with green photoautotrophs making up the majority of micro- and macroflora. About 60 percent of the energy they bind is taken up by heterotrophic life-forms. Heterotrophs include some 2,000,000 species of protists, plants, and animals—marine, amphibian, terrestrial, and semiaerial. Most of the animals and about half of the protists and plants are mobile. Higher species of animals display homeostasis, bilateral symmetry, disexuality, and endoskeletal body structure, with increasing cephalization in the more highly evolved species. The most advanced life-form is a presapient ovoviviparous semierect terrestrial biped with a brain classification of 67:3:462. It is stalled in its cephalic evolution by a low birth rate and the presence in its ecosystem of six major predators, two of them aerial.

PRELIMINARY PLANETOLOGICAL RATING:
Suited for colonization, with optional ecological modification to the Fifth Degree.

WEIGHTED RACIAL COMPATIBILITY PERCENTAGE:
Simb: 89. Gi: 80. Poltroyan: 48. Krondak: 13.

"Well," Dota'efoo noted sadly, "even a quick visual scan shows that the place was severely damaged. The cloud cover's down to about fifty percent. The climate has cooled to the ice-age stage, and the concomitant lowering of sea level has exposed nearly all of the continental shelves. The greater percentage of the islands has merged into dry land."

"So much for Gi colonization. Without plenty of island trysting sites, their reproductive psychology packs up and the eggs are sterile." Luma'eroo activated a battery of monitoring devices at the same time that he sent the craft plunging out of orbit. When the black spheroid reached the planetary tropopause it came to an abrupt halt, hovering in the deep-blue sky while thin jet-stream winds hummed around it. "At least the magnetosphere has recovered to its normal value. Reversed, though."

"I was afraid of that. Is the ozone layer rebuilt?"

"To within normal parameters for the G1 sun." He twiddled with the radiation-monitoring unit, which was overdue for a refit. "Albedo's down to twenty-eight overall. UV and solar wind penetration to surface within normal range. Ditto with cosmic radiation."

Dota'efoo studied the atmosphere analysis. "Oxygen is down by a full two percent, and nitrogen is up one. Carbon dioxide has gone from .05 to .03 . . . And just look at the biotic differentiation read-out! We've lost nearly half of the plant species and an even larger percentage of the animals to hard radiation overdose, UV exposure, or general niche deterioration."

"It could have been worse, Alk'ai, and the place *was* perhaps overspeciated. Residual populations have probably expanded to fill most of the vacant niches—to say nothing of the successful mutations. The grosser supernova damage to the biota seems to have healed."

"But the world is still ruined."

He blinked his primary optics in doleful agreement. "It is no longer libidinously stimulating enough for the Gi and it is now too cold and dry for the Simbiari. It remains too warm, too deficient in oxygen partial-pressure, and too gravity-strong for us Krondaku. That leaves only the Poltroyans as potential colonizers—but the place is probably too warm for them as well, except in the circumpolar regions."

"And don't forget, we'd also have to do ecological modification of a high degree to accommodate our little mauve brethren.

This planet never did have enough sulfur springs or useful species of purple anaerobic photosynthesizers for their tastes."

"Too true," he agreed. "Shall we bother doing a surface recon? Or wouldst thou prefer that we simply mark it for a dead loss and minimize the insult to our freshly heightened sensibilities?"

She hesitated. "I would like to descend, Tok—if thou wouldst indulge me. We did spend so much time on the original survey. Besides, it's fitting to give it the utmost benefit of the doubt."

"I agree." Disdaining the instrumentation, he did a fast metapsychic farscan of the largest continent, which projected some distance into the North Temperate Zone. This part of the world, which had the most landmass, was at the onset of winter; but there was as yet no snow on the ground and the vegetation was still adequately lush. "Let us visit the eastern coast of the major continent, Alk'ai. There is a great river now traversing the old continental shelf and a rather interesting embayment."

"Very well."

The survey vessel plummeted toward the planetary surface in a straight line, shielded by its rho-field from the constraints of gravity-inertia and by a temporary sigma-field from atmospheric ablation. The region Luma'eroo had selected was just at the terminator, and so they landed just as the sun was going down behind low hills, painting a dancing golden pathway across the indigo waters of the windswept bay. There was abundant plant-life. On the hills and on the exposed headland where the ship rested were stands of trees with sturdy ligneous stems and deep-green aciform leaves. Other species of trees in the lowlands on either side of the river showed the beginning of chlorophyll degeneration in their obviously deciduous foliage, which was stained in startling coppery, xanthic, and rubineous hues.

The Krondaku emerged carefully from the ship and moved with difficulty in the gravitational field that was nearly twice their racial optimum. They slithered over a ground cover of low-growing anthophytes. Some were dried out; others, still green, bore star-shaped pink, yellow, or white sexual organs. The air tasted of terpineol, geranyl acetate, coumarin, and phenylethyl alcohol. There was also a distinctive chloride-iodide exudation from the marine organisms at the rocky margin of the sea. An offshore breeze made a rustling sound as it passed through the needle-leaf trees, and waves crashed on the seaward side of the headland. Up in one of the trees, an invisible creature voiced a complex warbling ululation having a frequency between two thousand and four thousand cycles per second. Small white-winged animals in a ragged V-formation flew low over the bay waves, heading toward the open sea.

The two tentacled monsters contemplated the scene for some time, utilizing both their conventional senses and their ultrafaculties. The sun set and the cloudless sky turned from yellow to aquamarine to purple, studded with the first bright stars. The major moon, in its full phase, came up over the blackening eastern sea like a great disk of refulgent amber. One of the twin moonlets was also in view, shining modestly silver through the silhouetted branches of a nearby tree.

"Ruined." Dota'efoo spoke with emphatic finality. "In its present state, the planet is patently unfit for colonization by any of the coadunate races of the Milieu."

"It's hopeless," Luma'eroo agreed. "Ecological engineering up to the Tenth Degree wouldn't even begin to put it back into shape." He ruminated for a few moments more. "Strange . . . it rather reminds me of *their* world." And he projected an oafish racial image that had become a notorious target of low humor among less charitable Simbiari and Poltroyan planetologists.

"By the All-Penetrant—I do believe thou art correct. Shall we go back inside the ship and check the correlates?"

"With pleasure. My plasm aches from this burdensome gravity."

The two Krondaku reboarded and went again to the control room, where the computer confirmed Luma'eroo's hunch. The weighted compatibility percentage was an amazing 98.

"And so, in the most unlikely event that they are admitted to the Milieu, our poor little orphan planet would undoubtedly be among the first worlds to be colonized by *them*." Dota'efoo called up some additional data. "Here is a noteworthy item. They recently sent an exploration team to their most hospitable neighbor planet—a dusty red frigid-desert hulk with an exiguous atmosphere. They are also constructing orbiting habitats in a futile effort to siphon off their excess population."

"Idiots. Why don't they simply limit procreation?"

"It is contrary to the prevailing ethic of certain racial segments, and others are too ignorant to appreciate the reproductive predicament of their planet. Thou must understand, Tok, that these people are even more fecund than the Poltroyans, and this poses technical difficulties for practical contraception as well as motivational ones. Their principal means of population control are famine, abortion, a high infant deathrate among Class Two indigenes, and war."

"Those amazing humans!" Luma'eroo lifted four tentacles in a gesture of puzzlement. "If the Lylmik are truly intent upon foisting them upon the Milieu, we are in for some interesting times. I think we may someday be grateful, Alk'ai, that there are numbers of solar systems on the far side of the Galaxy that await our personal scrutiny."

His mate allowed a barely perceptible risibility to enter her mind-tone. "And yet they do have a certain reckless courage. Imagine a race of their classification seriously attempting to colonize a nearly airless, frigid-desert planet . . . or worse, artificial satellites!"

"It surpasses understanding."

Dota'efoo summoned a last modicum of data from the computer. "If Earthlings *are* accepted into the Milieu, their overpopulation problem will become an asset overnight. As of now, we have 782 ecologically compatible planets within a 20,000-light-year radius of their home world all surveyed and ready for settlement." She flicked a dismissive tentacle at the viewport, with its moonlit seascape framed by evergreen trees. "And this place makes 783."

"Frightening. They'd very likely overrun the Galaxy in a few millenaries . . ."

Dota'efoo shuddered. "Let's get out of here."

Her mate activated the rho-field generator to full inertialess and sent the survey vessel screaming into interplanetary space.

6

FROM THE MEMOIRS OF
ROGATIEN REMILLARD

ON THE FACE OF IT, THERE WAS NOTHING SUSPICIOUS ABOUT THE accidental deaths of my three nieces.

The twins Jeanette and Laurette, who were twenty-one, and their sister Jacqueline, two years younger, were driving home from a ski weekend in North Conway early in January 1995 when their new RX-11 went out of control on the icy highway, crashed, and burned. Denis flew back from Edinburgh, where he had been called as an expert witness for the defense in the sensational trial of Dr. Nigel Weinstein. Once again he and Victor supported their widowed mother through the ordeal of an old-fashioned Franco-American veillée, funeral Mass, and cortège to the family plot in the cemetery outside Berlin, where the girls were buried next to their father.

Sunny was not just grief-stricken, she was devastated. Both Denis and I detected nuances of irrationality beneath the stuporous anguish that cloaked her mind, but neither of us recognized the fear. Denis had to return to Scotland immediately. He urged me to stay in Berlin for the week following the funeral to make a closer assessment of his mother's mental health. When I told him that Sunny seemed in the grip of a morbid depression, he asked a colleague from the Department of Metapsychology, Colette Roy, to come to Berlin for consultation with the Remillard family physician. Dr. Roy, Glenn Dalembert's wife, had been studying the abnormal psychology of operants and was the best redactive prober (outside of Denis) working at that time at Dartmouth. Her examination of Sunny was inconclusive and she urged that I bring Sunny to Hanover for a further evaluation at the Hitchcock Clinic. Sunny adamantly refused to go. She said she would not leave the other five children, who ranged in age from thirteen to eighteen, even when Victor offered to pay for a full-time housekeeper. The terrible anxiety that Sunny displayed at the suggestion that she leave her rather fractious adolescent brood was diagnosed by Dr. Roy as just another symptom of the depression; but in this Colette was mistaken. Sunny, the mother of two metapsychic giants, had managed for all her latency to screen her innermost thoughts with a thoroughness none of us dreamed possible.

When Denis returned to New Hampshire after Weinstein's acquittal and pleaded with her, Sunny finally agreed to a two-week course of treatment at Hitchcock, with monthly outpatient checkups to follow. She also said she would accept domestic help in the big house on Sweden Street that Denis and Victor had bought for her four years earlier. Victor interviewed and rejected a parade of Berlin applicants, and eventually hired one Mme. Rachel Fortier of Montréal, an amazonian femme de charge who came with the highest references and eye-popping salary requirements. Sunny accepted the housekeeper with apparent goodwill, and by the second week in February things seemed to be going back to normal.

So I went to a science-fiction convention.

Every year since 1991 I had attended Boskone, a sedate gathering of fantasy buffs, writers, artists, booksellers, and academics. Those unfamiliar with such meetings may get a hint of the general atmosphere when I say that I, a known operant and close relative of one of the most famous metapsychic personalities in the country, was looked upon as nothing out of the ordinary by the convention-goers. I was just another bookseller, not to be mentioned in the same breath with genuine celebrities such as the best-selling author of *Tessaract One*, the producer of the *Gnomeworld* video series, or the first artist to do on-the-spot lunar landscapes.

Sometimes at these conventions I shared a table in the dealers' room with a fellow bookseller, offering middling rarities and telling all comers about the much greater trove of goodies to be found at my shop in Hanover. Sometimes I just circulated and perused the other dealers' wares for likely items, or bought a few pieces of artwork, or attended the more bibliophilic panel discussions, or sat in on readings by my favorite authors. I scarcely ever bothered with the endless round of parties that was a feature of convention nights, preferring in earlier years to do my serious drinking in solitude. The only festivity I attended was the combination masquerade and meet-the-lions bash that traditionally took place on Friday evening. There one might legitimately scrape up acquaintance with notables, so as later to be in a favorable position to offer them modest sums for their hand-corrected proofs, typescripts (a surprising number of science-fiction writers still refused to process their words), autographed first editions, or literary curiosa of a marketable sort.

Boskone XXXII was held at the Sheraton-Boston. When the dealers' room opened on Friday the tenth I made my rounds of the tables and greeted old friends and acquaintances among the hucksters. The antiquarian pickings seemed leaner than in other years and the prices higher. Very few new books were now being published in the hardcover format; even first editions from the big houses were issued mostly as large paperbacks. Regular paperbacks, on the other hand, proliferated like fleas on a spaniel in August in response to the reading explosion of the '90s. Desktop printing technology had given rise to a host of cottage publishers of every stripe—fantasy not excluded—and limited collector's editions of every Tom, Dick, or Mary with even the most tenuous claim to fame crowded the good old stuff off the tables.

I did manage to find firsts of the G&D *Fury* by Henry Kuttner, and a fine copy of the remarkable science-fantasy *World D* in the London Sheed & Ward edition of 1935.

As I dickered for the latter with a bookseller acquaintance, Larry Palmira, I became aware of a strange hostility in his manner. At first his subvocalizations were too indistinct to decipher; but as we settled on a final price somewhat higher than I had hoped for, I heard him say:

And you won't coerce ME into going a buck lower dammitall so go try your mental flimflam on some other nebbish!

I signed the credit-card slip and gave it to him smiling. He bagged my book and said, "Always great to do business with you, Roj. Drop in when you're in Cambridge."

"I'll do that, Larry," said I, and walked away thinking hard.

I decided to test my suspicions and stopped at the booth of another dealer friend, Fidelity Swift, pretending interest in a Berkley paperback first of *Odd John*, ludicrously overpriced at twenty-five dollars. She let me beat her down a little. Then I looked her in the eye and murmured, "Come on, Fee, gimme a break. You better be nice to me, kiddo. You know what they say about not getting a metapsychic pissed . . ."

"No," she laughed. "What do they say?" In her mind was a fearsome image: Nero's garden lit by human torches.

I thought: Merde dans sa coquille! And said, "Damned if I can remember. Double sawbuck, last offer. Cash on the barrelhead."

"Sold!" Relief gushed out of her like blood from a cut artery. The nightmare picture faded but her deep disquiet was now obvious.

I handed over the money and took my prize, saying goodbye while I broadcast the most benignant vibes I could conjure up, superimposed upon an image of her that shaved off thirty pounds and ten years and arrayed her plain features in idealized sexuality.

"See you around, Roger," she breathed, all apprehension swept away. I winked and hurried out of the dealers' room.

The trial. The goddam Scottish trial!

Weinstein had been extremely lucky to win the famous "Not Proven" verdict permissible under Scots law. The lunatic clergyman he had incinerated was unarmed, and witnesses had testified that the old man had offered no threat or resistance when Weinstein ran him down. Only some fancy psychiatric footwork about diminished responsibility due to temporary derangement and Denis's testimony about the inadvertent projections of creative flame exemplified by "Subject C" and documented in his laboratory (Lucille's identity was disclosed only to the judge) brought about Weinstein's acquittal. Even then there were dark editorials about "persons of special privilege" flouting the common law of humanity. The Metapsychic Congress, held four months before the trial, had attempted to anticipate and disarm public apprehension by pointing out that only a minuscule percentage of operants

possessed mental faculties that could be classified as threatening
to ordinary mortals. There were more reassurances later. How
many normals, given Weinstein's provocation, might not have
been carried away as he was to the point of violence? In the
United States, Weinstein's immolation of the mad murderer became the most hotly argued case since a quiet electronics technician had shot four aggressive young muggers on a New York
subway back in the '80s. Behind the rational argumentation and
scholarly disputations on the dark side of the unconscious lurked
something uglier and more atavistic. The man who had slain Jean
MacGregor and Alana Shaunavon had denounced them as
witches, and quoted the Bible as justification. Of *course* intelligent modern people understood that metapsychic powers were a
natural consequent of human evolution. There was nothing devilish or black-magical about them. But on the other hand . . .

There was a simple remedy for the irrational fear of a single
individual. I had worked it myself on Fidelity Swift. But it was a
temporary thing, like a clever actor making an audience believe
in a character being portrayed. We operants would be able to
disarm the fear of some of the normals some of the time—for a
little while. But how would we convince them of our amity over
the long haul?

Sunk in the old malheur, I went up to my room to stash the
book purchases before going to supper. As I came back into the
corridor I was reminded by the number of costumed figures
prowling about that the masquerade and meet-the-pros party was
in full swing down in the hotel's grand ballroom. There would be
music and drinks and conviviality, and such a mob scene that
nobody would bother thinking twice about my sinister mental
attributes.

The down-elevator door opened to reveal a chamber jammed
with exotic fun-seekers. I spotted a squad of youths dressed in
medieval battle-gear, a nubile lass with flaming hair and a four-
foot "peace-bonded" sword, wearing what seemed to be a bikini
of silver poker chips, a Darkoverian mother with two Darkoverian moppets, a statuesque black woman in a white satin evening
gown with a little white dragon perched on her shoulder, a stout-
ish middle-aged gent clad in a conservative suit whose mundane

appearance was belied only by the propeller beanie on his head, and a large ape sporting emerald fur and illuminated eyeballs, who had neglected to use a personal deodorant.

"No room! No room!" chorused this bunch as I made to enter the elevator. The ape opened its mechanically augmented white-tusked jaws and stuck its carunculated tongue out at me.

But there is, occasionally, justice in this world. I speared the smelly ape with my most potent coercive impulse and commanded: "Out!" It complied like a lamb and I took its place to universal plaudits. We made a nonstop trip to the ballroom level.

The party had attracted nearly two thousand people. Perhaps half were in fancy dress. A live band played things like "Can You Read My Mind?," "Rocket Man," "Annapurna Saucer Trip," Darius Brubeck's "Earthrise," and John Williams's "Theme from *Gnomeworld*." In between sets the convention Toastmaster introduced the artists and writers present, and a spotlight tried to pick designated stars out of the crush. There were also parades of the more spectacularly costumed fans across the stage. Those who were particularly beautiful, humorous, or technically awesome received warm ovations.

I headed immediately for the nearest open bar. By the time I had downed three Scotches, I felt considerably cheered. I had repinned my convention badge so that my name was mostly obscured by the lapel of my suit coat. Five attractive ladies (and one flamboyantly gorgeous transvestite, whose gender I detected too late to worry about) danced with me. I introduced myself to the convention Guest of Honor, a tottering nonagenarian survivor of the Golden Age, and by dint of the most gentle coercion and a speedily fetched raspberry seltzer got him to personally inscribe a copy of Boskone's commemorative edition of his early short stories.

And then I withdrew to the sidelines for a breather . . . and had my first shock of the evening when I saw Elaine.

Even though she was now over fifty, she was still breathtaking. Her tall slender figure was clad in a long gown of some lightweight metal mesh that flowed from her neck to the floor like molten gold. Her arms, shoulders, and back were bare. The dress's collar was a wide, upstanding band of gold adorned with stones like blazing orange topazes. She had a single heavy brace-let of the same jewels. Her hair was blond now, piled high on her head in an intricate coiffure of stiffly arranged ringlets sparked with gold glints. She was dancing with Dracula.

I gulped down the dregs of my latest Scotch and pressed to-ward the dance floor. Poor Drac didn't have a prayer in the face of my coercion. For some reason the band was playing a melodic standard, "Old Cape Cod." Elaine stood there among the other dancers, dismayed by the abrupt retreat of her caped and be-fanged escort, not yet noticing me. I do not recall what my thoughts were. Perhaps seeing her after so many years had drained my brain of everything except the irresistible compulsion to be near her again.

I took her into my arms and we picked up the beat. She stared up at me, wordless. Her mind said: Roger!

"Voulez-vous m'accorder cette danse, Madame?"

"No!... Yes." Oh, my God.

"May I compliment you on your dress. It's much too chic to be a costume." How appropriate that we should meet again at a bal travesti. Do you come to Boskone often?

"No," she said. "This is my first time. My daughter thought I'd find it amusing. She's—she's a rabid science-fiction fan."

Your daughter... Don's daughter... she would be twenty. May I ask her name?

"Annarita Latimer. She's there, costumed as Red Sonja."

My eyes followed her mental indication and I was surprised to see the strapping redheaded wench in the silver-dollar bikini. She was too far away for me to scrutinize her directly for operancy, and I am unable to detect operant auras in lighted places. So I simply asked, "Did she inherit the mind-powers?"

"I—I think so." She won't let me in, Roger. There's a barrier, like a shining wall of black glass. One doesn't notice it except at very close range...

That explained my failure to spot her operancy in the elevator.

"What does Annarita do?" I asked easily. "Is she going to college?"

"She's at Yale Drama School. I think she'll be a very good actress."

"Sans doute," I murmured. "And your husband?"

The music was ending. We applauded, and then the M.C. took up the microphone to announce the costume prizes. I led Elaine to the edge of the dance floor, where Dracula waited, glowering.

Her mind told me hurriedly: Stanton died three years ago Roger now I am married to *him*. "Gil, darling! Let me introduce you to a very dear old friend of mine, Roger Remillard. Roger, this is my husband, Gilbert Anderson." The Third, she appended telepathically.

Dracula shook hands with me as though I were Von Helsing. His features, blandly handsome aside from the well-fitted orthodontic fangs, wore a pensive, well-bred little frown. "Remillard . . . Remillard. You wouldn't by any chance be related to—"

"It's really a very common Franco-American name," I said. "Thanks for letting me dance with Elaine. We haven't seen each other in years. Are you enjoying the convention?"

He uttered some hearty inconsequentialities, deftly extracted from me my modest means of earning a living, and decided I was no threat after all. "Maybe we can get together for lunch or something later on this weekend."

"Great idea. Let's try to do that," I replied with equally false enthusiasm, simultaneously reassuring Elaine that I was out of it. I asked her: What is he? Upper management? Stockbroker?

She said: VP and chief corporate legal officer.

I said: It figures given the fangs.

And then I pretended to see someone across the crowded room that I had to speak to, so I bid the pair of them adieu. Fleeing, I told her: You are more lovely than ever be happy chèrie and never never have anything to do with metapsychic operants . . .

Then I hurried out of the ballroom, wretched again, and sought a dark corner to lose myself in. I found it in one of the hotel cocktail lounges. Hunched on a stool at the bar, I ordered a double vodka on the rocks. When I had finished it my brain was as incapable of telepathic reception as any normal's.

And so he had to tap me on the shoulder to get my attention.

I peered groggily at the intruder standing behind me. It was a tall young man with dark curly hair wearing a Flying Tiger jacket, haloed by a fierce neon-red aura. Victor said, "I might have known I'd find you here getting sloshed. On y va!"

He took hold of my arm firmly and seized my mind in a grip like a pit bull's. I saw stars and lurched against him. A rude rummaging was going on in my head, punctuated with offhand thrusts of pain. I was unable to speak. Victor whispered urgently in French, trying to get me out of the bar, but my feet weren't moving. Then something inside my skull seemed to crumple and I moaned out loud and began to walk, biddable as any zombie.

"That's better," said Victor. He steered me toward the elevators. "You're all checked out. We'll go up to your room and pick up your things."

"What . . . what the hell?" I protested.

The elevator was crowded with noisy conventioneers. Victor pressed the button for my floor. I didn't know what kind of mischief he had wrought in my brain, but I was sobering rapidly and was once again able to understand mental speech. I also had a hideous headache.

He said: We're driving north Uncle Rogi up to Berlin Maman needs you and I'm taking you to her.

I said: Sunny? . . . Dieu is she all right what's happened is it serious have you called Denis—

Shut up Uncle Rogi. There is no crisis. When I said Maman needed you I was speaking generally. She needs you if she is to get well and I am to be freed from Denis's meddling.

The elevator door opened and we got out. My head was swollen with lava and the corridor rolled from side to side like a skiff caught in the trough of storm waves. Victor held me up, inserted the coded plastic key-card into the slot of my room door, and thrust me brutally inside. I staggered to the bed and collapsed on it. Muttering obscenities, my nephew relaxed his hold on me and went into the bathroom to gather my things.

Going horizontal must have helped my brain by increasing its blood supply, and I regained a measure of self-control. What the devil was going on? What did Victor really want?

He came out of the john carrying my pajamas and a pouch of toiletries. "What I want is a simple matter, Uncle Rogi. Maman has been very upset for quite some time. She has . . . suffered from disturbing fantasies. About me." He went to the closet and pulled out my seat bag and two-suiter and began to stuff my clothing into them. "Her problems have affected my younger brothers and sisters. Interfered with my plans for their future. It didn't matter so much when they were just kids, but now that they are approaching an age when they can be useful to me, I can no longer permit Maman to indulge herself by undermining my influence over them. I was very disappointed at having to write off the girls."

Slowly, I sat up. He had his back to me as he emptied a drawer of some *Operator #5* magazines I had intended to sell.

He said, "I urged Maman to go to Hanover, to put herself under Denis's care in long-term resident therapy. It would have been the ideal solution. As you know, she refused to leave the younger ones in my charge. She suspects, you see—as she came to suspect in the case of Papa."

"So you *were* responsible for Don's death."

Victor zipped up the cases with great efficiency, got my parka from the closet, and tossed it to me. "Papa killed himself, as we all know. He was a pathetic, self-destructive sot. So are you, Uncle Rogi, but you are much more intelligent and I think your death wish is probably as spineless as the rest of your character." He opened the outer door. "Let's go."

I had no choice. His coercion scooped me off the bed like a back-hoe. I teetered along after him with terrible speculations oozing out of my mind. As we waited for the elevator I asked him:

Why did you kill the girls?

He shrugged. "Ces garces, elles étaient chaudes lapines." Their rebellion took the form of promiscuity. It was disgusting. I had hoped for alliances with some of my associates. It is an excellent way of cementing loyalties you see but these sistersluts balked. They took my gifts made promises then did as they pleased. Coercion as you know has its limits. Perhaps I was too domineering during their early adolescence and fear made them reckless. At any rate it was not working and they were behaving scandalously bringing the family into disrepute. I will not have that.

"Mon zob!" I sneered—then nearly screamed out loud as he

fetched my mind a blinding wallop.

Watch yourself Uncle Rogi . . . So you find my yearnings after bourgeois respectability amusing do you? You weren't impressed by the progress of Remco Pulp and Chemicals? Perhaps you don't realize how far along I've come in the business world. Small wonder when we hardly ever see one another except at funerals. That will change.

The elevator arrived and we got in. I was so tightly controlled that I couldn't blink without the young bastard's permission. But he couldn't keep me coerced forever . . .

He said: No. And that's the problem overall. With Maman and the family and even with my notorious older brother! Unlike you Uncle Rogi I have ambitions. And they will require the close cooperation of others whose loyalty I can count upon. Yvonne is eighteen and compliant. She is not nearly so good-looking as her late older sisters but she has youth and my associate Robert Fortier will find her acceptable. Pauline unfortunately is still too young but she will mature.

Good God you're scheming up a fucking dynasty—

Tu l'as dit bouffi!

The elevator reached the lobby and disgorged us. Victor handed the two bags to me, deposited the card-key in the box at the desk, and thriftily had a clerk validate his parking ticket. Then we headed for the lower-level elevators. For the first time I began to realize what a desperate situation I was in. I still didn't entirely understand why he wanted me, but want me he did. He could coerce me into doing any number of things and lock me up incommunicado in the interim without Denis suspecting anything. Denis was, after all, distracted by matters of global importance; erratic behavior by his black-sheep uncle was only to be expected.

We descended into the bowels of the great hotel. The lowest parking level, where Victor had had to park his Porsche because of the convention crowd, was quiet, very cold, and virtually deserted. He drew me along in his wake as he strode to the sports car.

We'll take the interstates up to Hanover. Tomorrow we can

begin making arrangements for your move. By the time Denis gets wind of it you'll be settled in Berlin and they'll be reading the banns at Saint Anne's.

The banns? . . .

Of course. Don't you understand Uncle Rogi? You're going to marry Maman and relieve Denis's anxieties about her and help make certain that my surviving brothers and sisters remain under my control. And I'll find other uses for you too as time goes on.

"No!" I yelled. And from some mental reservoir I called up the power to snap his coercive lead. I flung the two bags at his head. He ducked and they skidded across the polished white hood of the car. He struck back at me and it was as though twin ice picks had been driven into my ears. I shrieked and almost fell, then recovered with a heroic act of will and tried to run. A mental thunderbolt struck me between the shoulder blades and seemed to sever my spine. I sprawled headlong, still screaming, and in seconds he was on me.

"Ferme ça, vieux dindon! Arrête de déconner!" Victor knelt on my chest and grabbed me by the hair. His eyes were like paired heliarc torches and I knew he could fry my gray matter and turn me into a drooling idiot if he chose . . . but he didn't want to go that far. He needed me and so he hesitated with his psycho-creative lobotomy, and I saw my last chance. The knot of fire ignited behind my breastbone and stark terror and prayer accelerated it into an out-spiral: around and around and around. Victor's blazing eyes dimmed with surprise and then alarm. He let go of my head and flinched, so that the ball of energy I shot at him did not strike his face but glanced along the edge of his skull just above the hairline, cauterizing a shallow furrow in scalp and bone.

He howled and fell off me. In desperation I rolled under a nearby Winnebago camper with my nerves on fire from the psychozap and most of my muscles turned to Jell-O. I knew I was a goner. I could hear Victor scrambling on the pavement and reviling me in French and English.

And then he dropped like he'd been brained with a sledgehammer.

I lay there in semidarkness, smelling the Winnie's chassis lubrication and a burnt-pork stench. Victor was utterly still except for slow, stertorous breathing.

There were measured footsteps approaching: *klok . . . klok . . . klok . . .* the sound amplified by the dank concrete walls and pillars of the underground garage, that haunt of lurking urban menace. I felt my neckhairs prickle and my guts go loose. I couldn't see the aura of the approaching operant because it was deliberately being suppressed; but I could feel it, like the horrid quavering of the nerves when you stand under high-voltage power lines.

My view of him was cut off by the rows of parked cars until he came up to where Victor lay. I saw sturdy Timberland hightops with red wool socks and black chinos stuffed into them. Arms enclosed in down mackinaw sleeves reached down to grasp Victor, taking the back of his belt in one massive hand and the collar of his jacket in the other. My nephew's body ascended out of view. The booted feet plodded to the Porsche and I heard a heavy thud, as if some vandal had desecrated the expensive vehicle by plonking a duffel bag full of books onto the roof. The car door opened and there was a softer thud. The door slammed.

The feet approached the Winnie and my two travel bags were set down next to it. The aetheric tension had dissipated and I felt enveloped in blessed relief.

A telepathic voice said: *Victor will think you did it. That was quite a commendable mental effort of yours. It provided a neat cover-up for my necessary obtrusion.*

Is that you?

Who else? . . . I don't think you'll have to worry about interference from Victor for a few years now. He'll give you up as a bad job and try to find other ways to cope with his family problems.

But Sunny—

You've probably saved her life. To say nothing of your own. Once the two of you were married, Victor would have felt free to activate his unconscious oedipal retribution fantasy, wiping out his mother's threat to his ambitions.

I don't understand.

Then I suggest you reread *Hamlet*. But not on a dark and stormy night . . . Au 'voir, cher Rogi. Until the next time.

I began to squirm out from under the camper. The booted feet walked away, their sound dispersed by the serried ranks of parked vehicles. By the time I was able to stand up, the underground garage was silent again. I could see Victor, unconscious, slumped behind the wheel of the Porsche.

Eh bien, Rogi, you long streak of piss. Saved again! Or is your psychocreativity more inventive than you suspect?

I picked up my bags. My suit was filthy and I had no doubt that my face was, too; but front-desk personnel are inured to such things during science-fiction conventions. No explanation would be required. All I had to do was say that I had changed my mind about checking out.

I went to the elevator and pressed the Up button. The damned thing took forever to arrive.

7

CONCORD, NEW HAMPSHIRE, EARTH
13 MAY 1995

JARED ELLSWORTH, S.J.: Denis! Wonderful to see you again. Sit down! Sit down! What has it been—ten years?

DENIS REMILLARD: Twelve. When I got my M.D.

ELLSWORTH: And a lot of water's gone over the dam since then, hasn't it? Brebeuf Academy is very proud of you, Denis. I shouldn't admit this, but we haven't been exactly diffident about letting endowment prospects know that you were one of our early alumni.

REMILLARD: Oh, that's perfectly all right, Jared. It makes me feel less guilty about not doing more for the Academy myself.

ELLSWORTH: Nonsense. We've appreciated your generous contributions. You'll be glad to know that Brebeuf's gimmick has been copied in other parts of the world. Now there are a dozen or so other free schools for the gifted children of low-income families. But I haven't heard that any of them harbored a really wild talent like you! Merely normal geniuses. [Laughs.]

REMILLARD: You might be interested to know that the operant population has about the same IQ spread as the normal. Just as many dummies among us as smartasses.

ELLSWORTH: That could lead to problems.

REMILLARD: It has. We don't talk about it very much publicly. A German team just completed a study, a metapsychic assay of prisoners and inmates of institutions for the criminally insane. A disproportionate percentage of the incarcerated con men and bunco artists show traits of suboperancy in the coercive and telepathic modes. The percentage of psychopaths with operant traits is also higher than expected.

ELLSWORTH: [whistles] Any theories about that?

REMILLARD: The psychos might have kept their sanity if their fragile minds hadn't been burdened with the additional load of operant function—with all the stress that entails. Mental evolution is bound to leave a lot of maladaptive souls fallen by the wayside. The operant crooks who kept their marbles adapted —but the wrong way. They used the mind-powers opportunistically. It's a big temptation, even among the high-minded. The less intelligent metacriminals got caught, probably not even realizing that they had the powers. They thought the mind reading was just keen insight and the coercion a gonzo personality. The more intelligent operant crooks would still be at large, of course. No doubt highly regarded by their beneficiaries and damned by their enemies as financial wizards . . .

ELLSWORTH: It makes you wonder about the charismatic leaders of sleazy cults. And certain great and magnetic villains of history such as Hitler and Stalin.

REMILLARD: Someday, when we know more about the genotypes for operancy, there'll be some fascinating research done. But today, we're more concerned about this—this lower stratum of operants for pragmatic reasons.

ELLSWORTH: Mm'm. I can imagine. Bound to be baddies among you, of course, as in any other human population. But it's a thing not too many normals thought about prior to Dr. Weinstein's trial—not that he could be classed among your common or garden variety of delinquent. [Takes out a pipe and begins to pack it with tobacco.] The criminal operant will pose tricky legal problems. I suppose the really powerful ones would be able to coerce juries and witnesses as well as read the minds of the prosecuting attorneys.

REMILLARD: Probably. But the real difficulty isn't in the courtroom antics. After all, the authorities can always do as the Scottish Lord of Justiciary did in the Weinstein case: bring in a watchdog operant as an amicus curiae to be on the lookout for mental hanky-panky. No . . . the problem is going to be getting the goods on operant crooks in the first place. Superior metacriminals would be able to cover their tracks in any number of mind-bending ways. Posthypnotic suggestion, for instance. This has great limitations and probably wouldn't work at all in blatant cases like first-degree murder in front of witnesses, but it might very well succeed in less emotionally charged crimes. Frauds and conspiracies and other kinds of white-collar shenanigans. You're no doubt aware that the financial world is still in an uproar over its theoretical loss of transaction secrecy. Objectively, the financiers know that the chance of a crooked operant spying on them is close to zero. *Now.* But what about later, as operants become more numerous? The global economy is in a much shakier condition than most people realize due to the impact of operancy. Not many economic analysts have written about the matter. They're afraid of making the situation worse. It was bad enough when all they had to worry about was Psi-Eye investigations of KGB and CIA bank accounts in Switzerland. This new recognition of potential operant criminality has thrown them into a real swivet. And there's no remedy yet. We'll have to wait until more operants are trained for oversight work—and are willing to take it on. It's not going to be the most popular career choice among idealistic young heads.

ELLSWORTH: Thought police! Good heavens, what an idea.

REMILLARD: [laughs hollowly] You should see my hate mail! The common folks aren't quite so sure anymore that operants belong to the League of Superheroes. Have you ever watched that Alabama TV evangelist, Brother Ernest? According to him, we're nothing less than the vanguard of Antichrist, the mystery of iniquity, with all power and signs and lying wonders . . . and the Last Judgment is only five years away! It's to laugh—until you realize how many viewers the man has. And there are other antioperant movements poking their noses out of the woodwork. That outfit in Spain, Los Hijos de la Tierra, the Sons of Earth. And the Muslim fundamentalists are fully convinced we're the agents of El Shaitan. You know, Jared, operancy will bring about a profound social revolution during the Third Millennium—but only if we operants manage to survive the Second! There's a real possibility that militant normals might opt for the easy way out of the dilemma we pose . . .

ELLSWORTH: [waving out a match and snorting smoke] Don't give me that eschatological bullshit! Defeatism? From somebody who had the finest Jebbie education lavished on him? [Gestures to photo portrait of Teilhard de Chardin by Karsh of Ottawa.] From somebody who sopped up Papa Pierre's nostalgie de l'unité and global consciousness and optimistic expectation of Omega like a thirsty young sponge? Don't talk poppycock! You swelled heads are a challenge for us normals, but we're going to work it out. This isn't the Dark Ages, and the hysterical fools don't rule.

REMILLARD: No. Thank God, they don't. You'll have to make allowances for me, Jared. I'm afraid I've always had a tendency to fall into negativism and intellectual agonizing when the going gets tough. That's more or less why I came to see you.

ELLSWORTH: And here I thought it was to atone for your shameful neglect of your old teacher all these years.

REMILLARD: I need a very specialized kind of moral advice. None of the ethicists at Dartmouth had the foggiest notion of what I was talking about. Their counsel was worthless.

ELLSWORTH: Was it really! Oh, the arrogance of the intellectual elite. Nobody has problems like *you* have problems. I always think of John von Neumann on his deathbed, deciding to convert. Is he thinking humbly about making his peace? Is he awed at the imminence of the Infinite? No. He says, "Get me a *smart* priest."

REMILLARD: [smiling] So they brought him a Jesuit, of course.

ELLSWORTH: [sighs] I'll bet it still cost him an extra half hour in purgatory. But never mind that. What's *your* bitch?

REMILLARD: There are two of them, Jared, with both universal and particular application. The first goes under the seal of confession.

ELLSWORTH: Uh-*huh*.

REMILLARD: It concerns a matter we've already touched on. Suppose I know the identity of a metapsychic criminal. But the way I found this person out was by mental intrusion: reading the secret thoughts. A deliberate violation of which our crook was unaware.

ELLSWORTH: This is your great moral dilemma? Same thing as stealing a letter that incriminates. The theft is wrong.

REMILLARD: I acknowledge the guilt. That's not the problem. If it was a letter I stole, I could send it to somebody in authority who could take action. When you steal thoughts things aren't so easy.

ELLSWORTH: No.

REMILLARD: Aside from my reading this person's mind and discovering the general fact of wrongdoing, there is no proof whatsoever of the person's guilt. He was not fantasizing, because I can see the effects of his crimes quite clearly. But the perpetrator is ordinarily an excellent screener—you know about that? okay—and most probably no other honest operant person has the least inkling what he has been up to. There is no corroborating evidence of crime, nothing that would stand up in a court of law. Some of the things he's done wouldn't even fall under our present criminal code. For instance, there's no law against mind-to-mind mayhem; at most, our courts would view it as simple or aggravated assault, with the injury not provable. So what am I going to do?

ELLSWORTH: [expels smoke slowly] Neat.

REMILLARD: I thought you'd like it. Objectively, that is. It's Shit City when you're on the inside looking out.

ELLSWORTH: This metapsychic monster of depravity. He's intimately known to you? I mean, you're close enough so that there's absolutely no possibility that you've misunderstood the situation?

REMILLARD: The person is a relative.

ELLSWORTH: Uh-*huh*. And we are dealing with very serious moral matters?

REMILLARD: The most serious.

ELLSWORTH: Obviously, you can't haul this person down to your local police station and—uh—turn his mind inside out.

REMILLARD: Obviously not. Firstly, he would probably kill me if I tried it. Secondly, even if I did succeed in wringing a confession out of him—say with the help of operant friends—it would be inadmissible evidence. In the United States, one may not be forced to incriminate oneself.

ELLSWORTH: The only logical recourse is to try to nail him with some evidence that's concrete. Do as the government snoops do: use the illegally obtained information to scratch up other stuff that *will* hold up in court. You understand—hem!—that I'm not advising you to do anything sinful.

REMILLARD: But . . . I couldn't.

ELLSWORTH: You couldn't, or you wouldn't? Do you mean you're too busy to see justice done? You've get *other* things to do?

REMILLARD: [doggedly] Yes. I have duties. Obligations to the metapsychic operant community. To evolving humanity as a whole. To find evidence against this one miserable bastard might be impossible. There might not be any. Searching for it could alert him and endanger me. Endanger my work.

ELLSWORTH: You seriously believe he'd try to kill you?

REMILLARD: Or do me grave mental damage.

ELLSWORTH: You are never morally obligated to put yourself in danger in order to do good. Caritas non obligat cum tanto incommodo. One can assume such an obligation freely, as officers of the law do, but a private individual does not have such a duty.

REMILLARD: [sighs] I thought not.

ELLSWORTH: On the other hand, Christ told us we're blessed when we give up our life for our friends. It is the ultimate magnification of love. Of course, he was propounding a behavioral ideal...The valiant thing is not always the prudent thing. As you say, you have your work, and it is undoubtedly important.

REMILLARD: I—I can't just stand by and let him get away with what he's done! He may do it again.

ELLSWORTH: You could be patient. Bide your time and watch.

REMILLARD: I'm so distracted by other things. This is...so small compared to the other problems I have to deal with. So damned personal. I pushed it aside earlier when all I had were suspicions, and that was wrong. My negligence cost lives. Now that I'm certain about him, there doesn't seem to be anything I can *do*.

ELLSWORTH: You think you're the only one who ever faced this? It's old, Denis! Old as the human race. Listen to King David: "Be not vexed over evildoers. Trust in the Lord and do good. Commit to the Lord your way; trust in him and he will act. He will make justice dawn for you like the sun; bright as the noonday shall be your vindication."

REMILLARD: This evildoer is my brother.

ELLSWORTH: Oh, son.

REMILLARD: It may be my fault he's like this. I never liked him. I never tried to show him that what he was doing was wrong. When I was a kid, I was relieved to get away from home and come here, away from him. When I was a grown man I still avoided him, even though I knew he had deliberately suppressed the mind-powers of my other young brothers and sisters. I was afraid. I still am.

ELLSWORTH: You should get your siblings away from his influence.

REMILLARD: I tried. Only one of them is legally an adult, and she won't come. He's mesmerized her. The others...I tried to convince my mother to come away with them. I know she wanted to, but she still refused. He's influenced her, too. I can't force them.

ELLSWORTH: Then you've done all you can for now. Keep working on your mother and the older sister but don't do anything to endanger them . . . You really do think there's further danger from this brother of yours?

REMILLARD: I suspect that he's killed certain individuals who were a threat to his business. I know for a certainty that he killed three of my sisters who defied him.

ELLSWORTH: Oh, my God. If I was in your shoes, I expect I'd go for the sonuvabitch with a shotgun and a bag of rifle slugs.

REMILLARD: No, you wouldn't. Neither would I. That's the hell of it . . . All right, Jared, let's table this one. All I can do is follow your advice and wait. Now this second problem is by no means as grave, so let's discuss it ex confessio—

ELLSWORTH: Don't you want your absolution?

REMILLARD: Oh . . . I didn't really think of this dialog as an actual confession. I only put you under the seal to protect you from any hazardous obligation you might otherwise have felt constrained to assume.

ELLSWORTH: The mention of grace embarrasses the learned psychiatrist! It never occurs to you to accept the forgiveness of Christ. You're like millions of other educated Catholics, Denis. You've kept the sense of guilt but not the sense of sin, and absolution without *solution* looks like a cop-out to you. It seems too damned easy.

REMILLARD: Maybe.

ELLSWORTH: But that's what grace is all about. It's a gift and a mystery. We're allowed to take it if we're sorry—even if we can't undo the evil we've done. A psychiatrist tries to offer solutions to guilt, but very often, as in your case, there *are* no solutions. That's where we priests have the advantage. We can channel the grace even if you feel you don't deserve it.

REMILLARD: [laughs softly] A spatiotemporal sexternion.

ELLSWORTH: Say *what*?

REMILLARD: God can be coerced. Never mind. It's just a dynamic-field-theory in-joke.

ELLSWORTH: You want the absolution or not? For the neglect and the violation.

REMILLARD: Lay it on me.

ELLSWORTH: [Prays in a low voice and gestures.] All right, what's the second problem?

REMILLARD: Do I have an obligation to reproduce? To have offspring?

ELLSWORTH: You're *serious*?

REMILLARD: It's been pointed out to me—by my busybody Uncle Rogi, as well as by an esteemed Soviet colleague named Tamara Sakhvadze—that inasmuch as I'm going to be twenty-eight years old next week, I should marry and father children in order to propagate my undeniably superior genes.

ELLSWORTH: Uh—the idea doesn't appeal to you?

REMILLARD: Not really. I've always been much more interested in intellectual stimulation than sex. The occasional biological urge distracted me, but it was easily squelched. I've never felt passionately attracted to a woman—or to a man, either. Frankly, the whole sexual thing seems rather a nuisance. You squander so much energy in it that could be devoted to more productive pursuits. God knows, I don't seem to have enough hours in the day for the work that has to be done!

ELLSWORTH: The Jews of the Old Testament were given the solemn duty to increase and multiply. But this part of the Old Law wasn't carried over into the New. No one is obliged to procreate now.

REMILLARD: Two persons whose opinion I value highly think otherwise. One is Tamara, who is a Neo-Marxist. The other is Urgyen Bhotia, who was a Tibetan lama and now professes an idealistic humanism.

ELLSWORTH: I can see why both of them might believe as they do. The good of society, as opposed to that of the individual, is paramount in both their faiths. Christianity—and Western civilization as a whole—gives the individual sovereignty in reproductive matters. On the other hand, having disposed of obligation, let us proceed to the more delicate matter of the most perfect choice... Let me ask you a question that's cheeky but not impertinent: Just how special *are* you?

REMILLARD: My metapsychic armamentarium has been rather painstakingly assayed. It was compared with that of known metapsychics all over the world in a study just completed by the University of Tokyo. My higher faculties exceed those of everyone else by several orders of magnitude. I am fertile, and there's a reasonable expectation that I would pass my alleles for powerful metafunction on to my offspring—particularly if my mate were highly endowed mentally herself.

ELLSWORTH: [breaks off in coughing fit and sets pipe aside] Well! In general, one might compare your case to that of certain royal alliances in the old days. When marriages were made for beneficial political considerations. Peacemaking and the like. I recall that Queen Jadwiga of Poland was deeply in love with a certain prince but married Jagiello, the Grand Duke of Lithuania, in order to unite the two countries, bring the pagan Lithuanians to Christianity, and save her kingdom from the threat of the Teutonic Knights. Her act was self-sacrificing— the more perfect choice. She had no moral obligation to do it, though.

REMILLARD: And what about me? I'm a free man, not a goddam optimal phenotype!

ELLSWORTH: You have a right to your individuality. If marriage is repugnant, you may certainly remain single. On the other hand—

REMILLARD: Well?

ELLSWORTH: Your preference for the solitary life may be selfish. Even unhealthy. You were always too cerebral as a boy, and now—forgive me—you've grown up to be a rather atypical man.

REMILLARD: Tamara and Glenn Dalembert say I'm a cold fish. Urgyen says I have an unfortunate proclivity for the inward-trending spirituality of the East, which is contrary to the loving globalism that must characterize those in the forefront of mental evolution.

ELLSWORTH: Good heavens . . . I wonder if your lama has read Teilhard?

REMILLARD: It wouldn't surprise me a damn bit.

ELLSWORTH: I won't belabor an obvious point. But much is expected of those to whom much is given. In the matter of the more perfect choice. And there is the love. Your Tibetan friend was right about that. I'm sure you feel that you love humanity in the abstract, Denis. Your sense of duty testifies to it. But a person like you . . . you need to know love in the concrete sense as well. Marriage and family life are the most usual pathway to love's fulfillment. But if you are certain it would be impossible for you—

REMILLARD: I'm—I'm not certain.

ELLSWORTH: Perhaps you're only afraid.

REMILLARD: My uncle, the matchmaker, has even suggested a woman he felt would be the perfect mate. She's a colleague of mine at Dartmouth. I laughed at him, of course. But then I checked out her assay, and it was amazing how her metafunctions were strong in areas where my own are weakest. Psychocreativity, for example. She's a brilliant woman. She's my temperamental opposite, however, and—and sexually experienced, whereas I am not.

ELLSWORTH: Oh. Does the poor girl have any notion that you're considering her as the royal consort in this grand eugenic scheme?

REMILLARD: Certainly not. I did the analysis with complete objectivity and discussed it with my closest colleagues, who concurred as to the young woman's suitability. My—my larger obligations to evolving humanity were also a subject of discussion. My genes. There is an undeniable tendency of evolution to proceed in jumps, rather than small, gradual increments. And I'm one of the jumps.

ELLSWORTH: Are you, by George! Denis, there's something terribly surreal about this conversation. You aren't a set of privileged gonads and this young woman you evaluated is not a mere source of superior ova. You can't ask her to marry you if you don't love her.

REMILLARD: Why not? Arranged marriages have been the rule among most human societies from time immemorial. She would have to agree, of course. But I presume that she would see the genetic advantages of our union as readily as my other colleagues did.

ELLSWORTH: Denis! Listen to me. You're not prize cattle. You'll have to live and work together and raise children.

REMILLARD: I don't know why one couldn't research marriage

just like any other subject. There have been intensive studies of the psychodynamics of stable, mutually satisfying conjugal relationships. The most questionable factor would be Lucille's sexual sophistication. We'd have to deal frankly with its potentially inhibitory influence upon my libido.

ELLSWORTH: Lucille! So she does have a name. And do you think she's attractive?

REMILLARD: [surprised] Well, yes. I guess she is, in a rather austere way. Funny—her character isn't austere at all. I think one might call her passionate. She has a temper, too. I'd have to—to modify some of my mannerisms. I'm kind of a snot, you know.

ELLSWORTH: [laughs] By all means, modify. Does Lucille like you at all?

REMILLARD: She used to actively despise me . . . I was a trifle tactless in urging her to join our group in the early days. We hit it off better now. She's accepted her own operancy, which was quite a problem for her when she was younger. She may still be somewhat afraid of me. I'd have to work on that.

ELLSWORTH: Denis—you've made your decision. Just let love be part of it.

REMILLARD: I'm sure we'll work very hard learning to love one another. The children will help. It'll be fascinating to analyze the penetrance of the various metapsychic traits in the offspring. And she and I would begin operant conditioning of the fetuses in utero, of course, and evaluate preceptorial techniques as we train the infants. It'll be the metapsychic equivalent of Piaget's research. Lucille should be fascinated.

ELLSWORTH: I'm going to pray my head off for your poor little kids. And for you and Lucille, too.

REMILLARD: Do better than that, Jared. Marry us. I'll let you know the date just as soon as Lucille and I work everything out. It shouldn't take long.

8

FROM THE MEMOIRS OF
ROGATIEN REMILLARD

ON THE FACE OF IT, THEIR MARRIAGE SHOULD HAVE BEEN A disaster.

Decreed by inhuman entities from another star, sordidly abetted by me, arranged in a coolly rational agreement between two mature young persons who were not even faintly fond of one another, and undertaken for the sake of an abstraction, the union of Denis Remillard and Lucille Cartier, when judged by the sentimental criteria of the late twentieth century in the United States of America, was peculiar to the nth degree.

The media came breathlessly scurrying to chronicle what they hoped was the first great metapsychic affaire d'amour . . . only to have the principals dismiss all inquiry into the romantic aspects of their betrothal and dwell instead upon the heritability of mental traits. The eyes of the interviewers glazed over as the putative lovebirds discussed assortative mating, the differentiation between penetrance and expressivity on the one hand and dominance and epistasis on the other, and the uncertainty of positive eugenics. Confronted with such esoterica, gossip columnists and "human interest" video scavengers beat a hasty retreat. A sedate article dealing with the genetic rationale of the Remillard-Cartier nuptials eventually appeared in *Nature*.

On 22 July 1995, Lucille and Denis were wed in Hanover's quaint fieldstone-Gothic Catholic church. The ceremony was attended in person by the families and colleagues of the couple, and viewed through excorporeal excursion by an undisclosed number of operants scattered throughout the globe. The bride wore a tailleur suit of pale blue linen and the groom a two-button lounge suit of navy summer worsted. They were attended by Dr. Glenn Dalembert and Dr. Ume Kimura. A wedding supper took place at the Hanover Inn, after which the bridal couple departed for a symposium on operant educational techniques being held in Brussels. The bride's diminutive bouquet of forget-me-nots and white mignonette was caught by Dr. Gerard Tremblay, the Metapsychology Department's ingenious public-relations maven, and he married an operant colleague named Emilie Bouchard later that year.

When Denis and Lucille returned from their brief academic honeymoon, they lived for some months in the Dartmouth faculty apartments. Early in 1996, at my suggestion, they bought the big old house at 15 East South Street, near my bookshop. After furnishing it to their taste and organizing what they called a Preliminary Metapsychic Prenatal Curriculum, they began to make babies with the same competence that they brought to their experimental work. Philip was born in 1997 and Maurice in 1999. A stillbirth in 2001 was the occasion of great sorrow; but the couple assuaged their disappointment by doing a revision and update of the Prenatal Curriculum and the first outline for their joint opus, *Developmental Metapsychology*. The next child, Severin, was born in 2003; two years later came Anne, then another miscarriage, then Catherine in 2009 and Adrien in 2011—at which point Denis and Lucille prematurely judged their reproductive duty to be completed. The six offspring were all metapsychic prodigies as well as healthy and scrappy Franco-American kids nurtured by parents who loved them dearly.

And loved each other.

Oh, yes. Denis had maintained all along that love could be learned if both parties were determined, and he was right. I never pried into their sex life—which one presumes they managed as efficiently as they did everything else—but I did spend many hours each month in their company and in that of their growing brood. They came to love each other devotedly as husband and wife, and each was the other's best friend—which is much rarer.

If I were asked to point out the principal factor leading to the success of their unorthodox union, I would say the *politeness*. From the beginning, they adhered to a self-imposed rule that they

would always behave toward each other with care and considera-
tion, as though one spouse were the honored guest of the other.
All disagreements would be debated logically, with as much heat
as necessary, but without personal reproaches or fits of sulking.
There would be no casual rudeness, no flippancy, no baiting or
other psychological game-playing at the other's expense, and absolutely no taking the other person for granted. In the early part
of their marriage, when they were still adapting, their relationship seemed to me to have a "more charitable than thou" artifi-
ciality—even a comical Alphonse-and-Gaston aspect. After all,
at this point in history one expected a certain breezy camaraderie
between husband and wife. Yet here were these two highly idio-
syncratic scientists—the one capable of freezing the ballocks of a
brass baboon with his coercion, the other possessed of a temper
that could literally set a house afire—conducting their domestic
affairs in an atmosphere of courtly gentility that Queen Victoria
might have thought a trifle extreme.

I called it weird; but then I had been brought up in the rough-
and-tumble menage of Onc' Louie and Tante Lorraine. I was
further amazed when Denis and Lucille carried their exquisite
civility over into their relationship with their children. Later, I
understood what a brilliant behavioral ploy the courtesy was.
(And of course a highly structured family and social system has
characterized the majority of human operants ever since the Intervention.) In a home where emotional nuances are almost continually broadcast by the minds of operant family members
(shielding requiring effort and being an art only gradually learned
by the young), there is a "crowded" ambiance that demands individual restraint and a reserved manner of action. Ume Kimura
explained to me that in Japan, which in those days had an enormous population crammed into a very small area, similar extremes of politeness prevailed. Etiquette, some wag has said, is
just an effective way to keep people from killing each other.
Strong operants such as Denis and Lucille knew instinctively that
they would have to live by more formal rules than normals, and
so would their children.

The politesse, far from putting walls between my nephew and
his wife, smoothed what might otherwise have been a stormy or

even calamitous first year of marriage. In the beginning they had only professional respect for one another, a goal mutually agreed upon, and a listing of theoretically compatible character traits that Denis wryly dubbed "Sonnet from the Portuguese, Computer-Enhanced." They were telepaths, bound to attain the deepest knowledge of each other's virtues and flaws, and so for them there was no glamour-tinged first phase of wedded life, no seeing the Beloved Other as a marvel of perfection; conversely, there was no posthoneymoon letdown. Since they were both mature and motivated, they worked hard to modify grating mannerisms and habits, made allowances for irreconcilable frailties, and strove continually to bolster the ego of the partner. From this initial effort soon came an easing of friction, and also, I have no doubt, the intense pleasure of sexual mutuality—the same as Ume and I enjoyed during our time together.

Later, when Lucille and Denis began to really know one another, there was fondness—and still later, love. They never experienced the consuming thunderbolt that struck me when I first saw Elaine; nor could their love compare in intensity to Marc's helpless physical passion for Cyndia Muldowney, or Jon's consummate metapsychic union with Dorothea Macdonald, the woman known to Milieu historians as Illusio Diamond Mask. Instead, Denis and Lucille seemed to grow slowly together. Their minds plaited, remaining individual but each supporting and enhancing the other with shared strength—almost like the mythical red brier and white brier that entwined and grew in a straight dual trunk toward the sun, blooming in arboreal splendor rather than in a tangled thorny sprawl upon the earth, as lesser roses did.

Lucille was always the braver; Denis was wiser. He was glacially efficient and just; she was fervently high-minded, with a greater creative insight. In later life he was retiring and scholarly; she became the grande dame of metapsychic society, as brilliant (and controversial) as their last child Paul, who was conceived after the Intervention and nurtured in utero on the exotic mental precepts of the Galactic Milieu.

Together, Denis and Lucille wrote six landmark studies of human metapsychology. They were personally instrumental in bringing about the Intervention itself. Denis died as a martyr to

Unity without really having known Unity. Lucille lives on in this Centennial Intervention Year, an honored pioneer and formidable clan matriarch. Their legacy is enormous, but its undoubted culmination is in their descendants—justifying the great gamble they embarked upon back in 1995. Their children became the Seven Founding Magnates of the Human Polity. Among their grandchildren were Jon, who was called a saint by both exotic and human minds, and Marc, who was called the Angel of the Abyss.

And now there are two more generations—Marc's children, Hagen and Cloud, and their newborn offspring—all carrying the precious genes for superlative metafunction as well as self-rejuvenation—which Denis never dreamt of in his wildest fancies as he and Lucille exchanged their vows.

I dedicate this memoir to all Remillards, living and dead, and most especially to the one who is both.

9

NEW YORK CITY, EARTH
6 NOVEMBER 1996

KIERAN O'CONNOR WAS OLD ENOUGH TO REMEMBER WHEN PRESIdential candidates made their victory or concession speeches on the day following the election. But here it was, only 11:45 P.M. at the General's campaign headquarters in San Francisco, and the race was decided already. The Republican candidate—Kieran O'Connor's candidate—had been defeated. But Kieran was well content.

The four quadrants of the Sony split screen on the wall of Warren Griffith's Manhattan townhouse switched from varied de-

pictions of network pundits commenting on the 292 electoral
votes safely in Democrat hands to a single image of a handsome,
silver-haired man. CBS, NBC, ABC, and SNN were opting to
telecast Lloyd Baumgartner's concession speech live.

Kieran reached for the remote control. It lay between his
stockinged feet on the littered cabriole cocktail table. When
Kieran canceled the mute, the measured accents of General
Baumgartner filled the room. He delivered his brief announcement in perfect extempore style, his eyes unwavering as he
looked directly into the cameras, his manner tranquil in defeat.
He thanked the voters who had given him a majority of the popular vote and nearly carried him to an upset victory. He thanked
the party that had chosen him as its standard-bearer, thanked his
devoted campaign staff, and thanked his gentle-faced wife Nell,
who stood at his right shoulder, smiling with tears in her eyes.
Baumgartner did not say that he would be back in the running
again for the fateful presidential race in the year 2000, but his
partisans and political opponents alike took that fact for granted.
His rival, Stephen Piccolomini, had won the presidency riding on
the coattails of the retiring incumbent, but he had not rolled up
the expected landslide; his margin was a precarious twelve electoral votes, and his party retained only a two-seat majority in the
Senate.

"Next time," muttered Warren Griffith. "Next time you're in,
General. And so are we."

The speech ended to applause and the split screen showed pan
shots as the network cameras swept over Baumgartner's campaign workers, who packed the ballroom of the famous old St.
Francis Hotel. Some of the people were weeping, but others
stomped and cheered as if for a victory, and dozens of hand-let-
tered signs waved on high, proclaiming:

THE BEST IS YET TO COME!

When the vice-presidential candidate approached the lectern
for his turn at the microphone, Kieran flicked the remote's in-
stant-replay pad, programmed it for five minutes, and watched
Baumgartner once again declare himself defeated. Then Kieran

turned off the Sony and the wall-screen went back to being an excellent counterfeit of Fuseli's *The Nightmare*, 1781 version. Griffith, who was the chairman of Roggenfeld Acquisitions and one of Kieran's principal strategists, liked that LCD projection so much that he'd had it on for nearly six months. There had been jokes about it when Kieran and Viola Northcutt arrived early in the evening for the election-night vigil.

Now Griffith got up from his chair and said, "We *still* deserve to celebrate!" He padded off into the kitchen and returned with a bottle of Pol Roger and three glasses. The two guests pretended to be surprised, just as socially proper telepaths all over the world did under similar circumstances. Griffith said, "Our candidate did not lose. He merely didn't win emphatically enough." Untwisting the wire, he eased out the cork and restrained the overflow with psychokinetic expertise. Then he made a respectful mental gesture to Kieran, calling for a toast.

Kieran O'Connor nodded and his severe features softened as he watched the bubbles rise. Catching an unvoiced hint, Warren Griffith flopped back into the wingback chair he had occupied throughout most of the evening. Viola Northcutt was curled up in the corner of the leather sofa opposite Kieran, unshod feet neatly tucked under her camel's-hair skirt. Somewhere in the townhouse an antique clock chimed three in quavery deadened tones.

I liked the placards that Baumgartner's people made, said Kieran. Let's drink to that: "The best is yet to come."

The others repeated his spoken words. Kieran sipped his champagne, but Griff and Viola tossed theirs down and went for refills.

"I'll hand it to the General," Viola said. "He was strong. A lot better than we ever dared hope."

"That viewing-with-alarm speech fingering the Meta Brain Trust's influence on the Democrats struck just the right note," Griff said. "Shot our boy up a good sixteen percent in the polls. It was a gamble, but we really proved that America's love affair with the operant clique is just about kaput. Before this campaign, I doubt that one voter in a hundred knew what metacoercion was—or redactive probing either."

"Neither did the General," Northcutt put in with a cynical

grin. She was a heavyset blond woman in her late forties, one of Kieran's earliest recruits, who had become his best operant head-hunter. Viola had vetted all the presidential campaign personnel, both operant and normal, to make certain that only loyalists would be able to exert influence on Baumgartner. Even so, the General had proved less psychologically malleable than they had hoped.

"Before we lock Baumgartner in as our millennial candidate," Kieran said, "we're going to have to make certain that he has no suspicion that his mind was manipulated during this campaign. We may have pressed too hard when he balked at the anti-Soviet speech in October."

Viola shrugged. "Len and Neville felt it was important that the General express doubt about the Kremlin's commitment to peace. We had the posthypnotic suggestion done prudently. Doc Pres-teigne handled it when the General had gas for some root-canal work."

"But it didn't work," Kieran said. "You forgot that Baum-gartner was a warm chum of the cosmonauts back in the pre-Mars days. He sincerely believes that the Russians have abandoned their expansionist philosophy. You can't depend upon a posthyp to overcome a strong conviction any more than you can coerce over the long term."

"How will we convince him, then?" Viola asked.

Kieran extracted his feet from among the mess of coffee cups, empty beer and seltzer bottles, and snack food that crowded the cocktail table. "When the hard-liners on the Politburo take charge, Baumgartner won't need convincing."

"Hard-liners?" exclaimed Griff. "Take over *when*?"

Kieran poked through a platter of ravaged deli noshes until he found a whole-meal cracker with a hard-boiled egg slice and a shaving of lox. He dabbed it artistically with mustard. "When the present General Secretary dies . . . and civil war breaks out in Uz-bekistan."

Viola and Griff stared at him. He showed them a mental sche-matic with a number of key elements blanked out.

"Jesus God," whispered Griffith.

"It's nothing you two have to concern yourselves about for a while yet," Kieran said. He popped the tidbit into his mouth and chewed it up, then downed the remainder of the champagne. "What you *will* have to deal with is Baumgartner's immediate future. Griff, I want you to find him a sinecure position on one of our foundations—say the Irons-Conrad. I want him completely divorced from the military-industrial complex and big business in the public mind. Our lad is a political philosopher now, asking questions and providing answers."

"Speaking of which," Viola interposed, "we still have that matter of Baumgartner possibly suspecting that he's being manipulated. It's going to be tricky doing a deep-scan without his cooperation, you know. We've never tried it on a person who wasn't being—actively recruited to the inner circle."

"We've got to know," Kieran insisted. "Whatever it takes. It's imperative that Baumgartner have no inkling of our own operancy. He'll only carry conviction in the next phases of our political campaigning if he firmly believes that operants are dangerous—a threat to normal humanity."

Viola was frowning as she thought. "For a proper ream-job, the subject has to be rendered unconscious for something like thirty-six hours. No way to handle that without hospitalizing him. We'll have to come up with something that will satisfy him and the PR people. Nothing psychiatric. We don't want to risk an Eagleton fuck-up."

"Eyes," said Griffith. "I had an uncle, had some kind of eye thing. Terrible headaches, then lost the sight of one eye. The docs fixed him, he was good as new."

"Sounds usable," Viola said. "Presteigne would know what the ailment is and how to simulate the symptoms. Very likely both the headaches and the blindness can be voodooed—by Greta, maybe. Baumgartner won't suspect a thing when we bring in our own eye specialist . . ."

Kieran nodded. "Work it out as soon as you can. I want to keep him newsworthy. I can see him doing lecture tours and hosting fund-raisers for the by-elections in '98. There are at least four Senate seats that could go Republican in the Bible Belt if we play our cards right and pick up on the antioperant sentiment building there."

"It'll build a lot faster," Viola muttered, "once we get good old Señor Araña on line!"

Griffith said: ?

Viola looked guiltily at Kieran, but he lifted a dismissive hand. "I was going to tell Griff about it anyhow."

"A step-up in the antioperant crusade?" Griffith asked.

"Exactly," said Kieran. "You know that my overriding concern is to insure that operants not loyal to us are barred from government service or political office. Even more important is to stir up grassroots sentiment against the metapsychic clique. I suppose you noticed the article in the *Times* this weekend about the Swiss banking group's plans to hire telepathic investigators."

"No! God—if they do it, the Japanese'll be next. And next thing you know, the Justice Department or the Treasury'll want their own Metasnooper Corps, and our organization will be up the well-known excremental watercourse!"

"Not if I can help it," said Kieran O'Connor. "Fortunately, we still have a Republican-packed Supreme Court. Next year my people in Chicago will engineer a test case to get a ruling that any form of operant screening of employees by private corporations is an invasion of privacy and unconstitutional. That will lay the groundwork for further action . . . such as the efforts of Araña. Why don't you tell Griff why we happen to be in New York, Viola?"

She grinned as she fished her suede boots out from under the cocktail table and began to put them on. "Our great and good buddy, The Fabulous Finster, has bagged us a very big fish indeed, and he is arriving tomorrow at Kennedy with this recruit figuratively tucked under his arm. The man's name is Carlos María Araña, and he is an unfrocked Dominican, late of Madrid, where the authorities were only too willing to be rid of him."

"Araña?" Griffith blinked. "Hey—didn't he start that fanatical antioperant movement in Spain? What was its name—Hijos de Putas?"

Viola Northcutt guffawed. "Come on! Hijos de la *Tierra*, Griff. The Sons of Earth. Kier figured it was time for them to open a North American branch." She stood up, stamped her feet the rest of the way into her footgear, and brushed the crumbs from her skirt. "We're going to play off Araña's fanaticism against Baumgartner's reasoned opposition to operant influence. The Spaniard wil play dirty and Baumgartner will deplore his intolerance. I mean, we don't really want to burn the confessed operants at the stake, do we? Not yet . . . Where'd you hide our coats, Griff? Kieran and I have to get back to our platonic little nest at the Plaza and get some sleep. Our cucaracha is coming in on Iberia's early flight tomorrow and poor Finster's going to need all the help he can get."

Kieran stood up, yawned, and laughed. "Don't you worry about a thing, Vi. Fabby's tamed Señor Araña very thoroughly. It was a tough assignment—perhaps the toughest he's ever had to handle. But he's delivered the goods."

"They don't call him Fabulous for nothing, eh?" Warren Griffith helped Viola on with her coat, then assisted Kieran. "I wouldn't mind meeting this Finster, Kier. If it wouldn't compromise your security arrangements, of course."

Kieran smiled. His mind touched that of his associate, giving both reassurance and warning. "Maybe another time, Griff. Fabby will be dead beat, and I have other matters to discuss with him before he leaves for Moscow on Friday."

Moscow! Kier don't tell me that's the way—

"I wouldn't dream of telling you, Griff. You're a man who thinks for himself. That's why you're part of my organization. I'll be getting in touch with you soon on the Petro-Pascua acquisition."

But Kier the man's a moderate the first reasonable Russian leader we've ever dealt with you can't—

I can. Make no mistake about it Griff if it suits my purposes and it does I can. "Thanks a lot for playing host. Don't bother to see us out. Vi and I can find our own way."

10

ALMA-ATA, KAZAKH SSR, EARTH
15 SEPTEMBER 1997

A CHILL SETTLED QUICKLY OVER THE PLAZA IN FRONT OF THE
Lenin Palace of Culture once the sun dropped behind the parched
hills. Yellow leaves, prematurely fallen in the great drought that
had plagued Central Asia that year, were swirled by the sharp
breeze around the dusty shoes of Colonel Sergei Arkhipov, who
sat on a bench near the Abai monument, waiting.

From time to time as his ulcer gnawed, Sergei would slip an
antacid tablet into his mouth. What he really needed was food;
but he could not leave his post until the first afternoon session of
the Sixth Congress on Metapsychology ended, and Donish furnished a report upon his fellow delegates' state of mind.

Finally, people began to emerge, hurrying down the palace
steps as if eager for their own suppers. Most of the longbrains
went off into the park on the left, on their way to the Kazakhstan
Hotel where the foreigners were being lodged. Numbers of
locals, heading for the buses, came straight down Abaya Pro-
spekt and passed directly in front of Sergei's bench. One of these
was a compact young man in a green windbreaker who carried a
canvas briefcase. His hair and complexion were dark and he wore
a squarish black skullcap with white embroidered designs on the
sides.

Deliberately, Sergei projected a thought as this man approached: Move faster blackarsed longbrain my poor stomach is
devouring itself I was sure you would stay in your fucking meeting all night.

"And good evening to you, Comrade Colonel!" The young
KGB agent, Kamil Donish, smiled good-humoredly and sat down

94

on the bench. "An outstanding panel on psychoenergetic projection's more benign aspects went a bit overtime. There was this Italian, Franco Brixen, who reported that his people at the University of Torino have been able to inhibit the growth of malignant neoplasms in rats—"

"Tishe!" hissed Sergei irritably. "What do I care about such trivia? Tell me the mood of the operant delegates—their feelings on the matter of the Islamic riots, especially—so that I can pass the information on to the General Secretary's aides before his speech tonight."

"They regret our use of extreme force. But you can hardly expect them to side with Muslim fanatics who label them allies of Satan."

"Don't play your longbrain games with me, Kamil. I'm not feeling well and I want straight answers. Are the foreign operants satisfied that we have acted properly? Do they accept our reassurances that the uprisings were isolated occurrences, and that the situation is now under control?"

Kamil's black eyes flashed. "Comrade Colonel, you remain obstinately a man of your time. Of course they don't! The whole world can see what is going on in Uzbekistan through the mental vision of their EE adepts. The only reason that the global news reports have downplayed the matter is that there is voluntary restraint being exercised by the operants themselves. They give their local journalists the bare details of our troubles, but without sensational embellishment that might inflame world opinion. The Soviet Union is being given the benefit of the doubt! Oh, yes— there are some bleeding-hearts among the delegates who deplore our killing of the so-called innocent bystanders during the storming of the Bukhara airfield. But most of the Congress attendees are politically sophisticated persons who realize the gravity of the situation—the danger of civil war. Most nations of the world are on our side, Comrade Colonel. They have no wish to see the Central Asian Republics explode like Iran and Pakistan."

"But do they worry about their safety here in Alma-Ata?"

"Certainly not," Kamil said. "They know that the nearest fighting is more than a thousand air-kilometers away. They are also aware that this is a modern city, with a minimal number of

Shiite fanatics among the populace. Operants who had any doubts about their personal welfare stayed at home. The majority accepted the assurances of Academician Tamara Gawrys-Sakhvadze that Alma-Ata welcomes them even more eagerly than it did in 1992. The Comrade General Secretary can make his little speech tonight without fear of any hostile response."

"Well, that's a relief. You longbrains are all the Secretary's darlings—the showpiece of his much vaunted policy of Otkroveyinost'. If he got a cold reception from the foreign delegates at the Congress, certain persons in Moscow would be encouraged in their attempts to discredit him." Sergei's mind showed an image of a tightrope-walker.

"Discredit him—and us." Somberness spread over Kamil's face. "You are not part of the Twentieth Directorate, Comrade Colonel, but you are quite aware of our critical role in the New Soviet Openhearted Society that the Secretary has championed. All loyal citizens have rejoiced in the new freedoms and the acceptance of personal responsibility for progress. But Otkroveyinost' would be impossible without the EE monitoring function of the KGB Twentieth."

"Oh, you are all certified heroes," Sergei agreed archly. "Just do your job efficiently and pinpoint the terrorist reactionaries without at the same time scaring the simple-minded to death! Especially the Muslim simple-minded."

"Some of my coreligionists are deficient in social consciousness," Kamil admitted. "This modern Age of the Mind has come too quickly for them to assimilate. According to the Prophet, magic is one of the Seven Ruinous Sins—and we operant metapsychics are accused of its practice. Furthermore, it is being said that the Last Days are upon the earth, and our appearance is one of the signals thereof. The KGB's reliance upon EE monitors inflames the reactionaries and makes even loyal Muslim citizens fearful."

"And so the powder keg at the southern belly of the USSR grows hotter each day—and I, for one, do not see any simple solution to the mess," Sergei said. "Thus far, the General Secretary has been lucky. The outbreaks have been small enough to be put down by the militia or by the KGB's own Border Regiments.

But if the antioperant paranoia grows, the jihad movement may spread from the Shiites to the vast numbers of Sunni Muslims in Soviet Central Asia. Then nothing less than the Red Army will suffice to control the insurrection—and we will all be in a very deep arsehole."

Sergei's imagination drew a portrait of Marshal Yegor Kumylzhensky, the hard-liner Minister of Defense and longtime Politburo opponent of the General Secretary. The figure had horns, wolfish teeth, and brandished a tactical missile as an erection.

Kamil giggled. "You are getting very good at that for a short-brain, Comrade Colonel. You should take the operancy exam again sometime."

Sergei swore and spat on the pavement. A pretty young woman passing by frowned at the uncultured behavior.

"She labels you a crude old fart," Kamil whispered slyly.

"I can read her mind well enough," Sergei growled. "As for you, you are an insubordinate blackarse who would have been shot for speaking to your superior in such a way back in the old days."

"Old days! If those old days still prevailed, you would be waiting for American missiles to blast your family to bits. And the Soviet citizenry would be drinking itself to death instead of reveling in Japanese VCRs and North American movies and British silver-disc music and satellite-transmitted sports programs from half the countries of the globe. Cheer up, Comrade Colonel. It's not such a bad brave new world! Who would ever have thought that the KGB would be applauded as good guys?"

Sergei shook his head and took another antacid tablet.

Chuckling, Kamil unsnapped his briefcase and took out a minicorder. "Here are my hushaphone comments on the opening session of the Congress and the afternoon panels. There is really nothing extraordinary going on that the General Secretary need be concerned about. We operants are worried about our image worldwide, and about the unreliability of our techniques for detecting clever psychopaths among us. We are concerned about the U.S. government's proposal to ban operants from seeking political office. The Congress is not, by and large, worrying about the status of operants in the Soviet Union. Our nation is looked upon by most of the delegates as a progressive place, ascending rapidly into high-tech prosperity after shelving an ill-considered political experiment. Our successful juvenile suboperant screening program is admired, as are the new schools for accelerated EE and telepathic training. The Japanese think that their operant teaching techniques are superior. Perhaps they are. Tomorrow is education day and there should be lively discussion."

"Fuck the lot of you and your discussions," said Sergei wearily. "All I care about is smooth sailing for the General Secretary's speech tonight—and then two weeks' rest cure in Sochi for my poor aching gut."

Kamil Donish arose from the bench. "Do svedanya, then, Comrade Colonel. I'll look for you in the audience tonight. Try to calm your tummy with some nice yogurt or rice pudding before you come, though. You don't want to make your sensitive longbrain neighbors uncomfortable."

Sergei threw an obscene mental menu suggestion of his own after the departing young agent. It was blithely ignored. Longbrains! What an arrogant and nonconformist lot they were— more loyal to each other and their global clique of do-gooders than to any motherland! The General Secretary was taking a colossal risk, pinning his policy to them. By far the majority of Soviet longbrains were not even Slavs! Look at Kamil—a Tadzhik, one of the fast-breeding Asian groups that now outnumbered the true ethnic Russians. The Twentieth Directorate of the KGB and the academic metapsychic groups swarmed with blackarses, Caucasians, and Mongoloid riffraff . . . but then, so did every other segment of Soviet society, operant or normal. What a hell of a world . . .

Not caring who overheard his dark thoughts, Colonel Sergei Arkhipov walked along Lenin Prospect to the Arman Café. He had only forty-five minutes to grab a bite to eat, and then he would have to go out to the Alma-Ata KGB HQ and liaise with the locals prior to the General Secretary's arrival at the air terminal. His opposite number had issued a supper invitation that Sergei had declined. He wanted to coddle his stomach in peace.

He peered into the café. There was a waiting line, of course, and many of the persons standing there wore the red and green delegate badges of the Sixth Congress on Metapsychology. Sergei pushed past them, ready to flash his KGB card, confident of being shown immediately to an empty table.

And so he was. But as he settled down with the menu he was astounded to see another man approach his table, grinning in a cocksure fashion, and pull out a chair.

Sergei opened his mouth to put the upstart in his place. It was a dapper little fellow, obviously a foreigner, whose badge read: J. SMITH—SIMON FRASER UNIV.—VANCOUVER CANADA. His two upper incisors were comically large, like those of a squirrel.

Sergei closed his mouth. He had to. J. Smith's coercion had taken control of him as though he were a wooden marionette.

"Hey there, Sergei! How you doing, old hoss?" The Fabulous Finster snapped his fingers and a waitress rushed over with another menu before he even drew his chair up to the table. "Been a few years since we pub-crawled in Edinburgh, eh? We've got a whole lotta catching up to do . . . By the way, you heard the sad news from Tashkent? The Grand Mufti of Central Asia was assassinated. Terrible thing. The poor old guy's head burst into flame just as he was going into the Barak-Khana Mosque and the whole goddam city's gone ape. They think some perverted metapsychic operant musta been responsible. I couldn't get out fast enough this afternoon, I'll tell you. I was lucky to get a plane . . . Well! Enough of that. What d'you say we order, eh?"

"Yes. Certainly." Sergei heard the voice coming from far away. Surely, he thought, it could not be his own.

Dr. Pyotr Sakhvadze regarded the enormous silver platter and its contents with undisguised consternation.

"But this is a great honor for you!" the maître d' insisted. His Kazakh mustachios bristled and he was slightly miffed. It was obvious that the kitchen staff of the big hotel had gone to considerable trouble to produce the special tribute. "You are the aksakal, the Whitebeard of the Feast! You must carve the dish and distribute it to the other guests, who have ordered this traditional delicacy in celebration of your eighty-third birthday. Bon appétit!"

He placed the carving tools in front of Pyotr and withdrew,

full of dignity. Most of the others at the table—his grandchildren, his daughter Tamara and her colleagues the Kizims, and the three foreign guests—were applauding and laughing. Telepathic jests crackled in the aether so energetically that Poytr, could almost (but not quite) understand them.

On the platter, the braised whole lamb's head seemed to stare at him with an air of jaunty mockery. One ear was up and the other down. Quail eggs stuffed with ripe olives formed its eyes, and it had a peeled ruby pomegranate in its mouth and a collar of lacy gold paper. The head perched upon a steaming bed of besbarmak, the famous Kazakh lamb and noodle stew. Poytr, as designated aksakal, was not only expected to serve this outlandish culinary triumph, but he was also obliged to accompany each portion of head-meat with a suitable witticism.

"We operants only think we've got troubles," Pyotr said to the lamb's head. "You, in your position, you *know* you've got troubles."

Everybody laughed and radiated sympathy except for his oldest grandson Valery, whom Pyotr had teased mercilessly last week for mooning over a young woman who would have nothing to do with him. Now innocence poured from Valery's mind like watered honey, but his close-set Polish blue eyes had a suspicious gleam. So! He was the one responsible for this, was he?

Pyotr cleared his throat and continued. "I am only a decrepit psychiatrist, not a faciocephalic surgeon. If I were to serve this head, I fear I would do it so slowly that we would be here all evening and miss the distinguished speakers who will honor us with their presence later in the Palace of Culture. And so it is with pleasure—to say nothing of relief—that I delegate the carving of this pièce de résistance to the founder of the feast, Valery Yurievich, whose idea it was to honor me in this unusual way. It is the custom, I know, for the aksakal to cut off and present to a favored guest that anatomical portion of meat most appropriate to his nature. But alas, I cannot give my dear grandson the part he deserves. The chef has cooked for us the wrong end of the sheep."

He bowed and sat down to uproarious laughter and clapping. Valery had turned red to the tips of his ears.

Tamara, who sat at the foot of the table, addressed her son. "I left the arrangements to you, and you play undergraduate pranks! Now how are we going to eat this monstrosity?"

The American, Denis Remillard, sitting on Pyotr's right, had his strange compelling glance fixed on the swinging doors of the restaurant kitchen. He said gently, "Allow me." And then there was a miracle. The two sturdy waitresses who had brought the besbarmak in the first place came out again, pushing a serving cart loaded with side dishes. After distributing these, they transferred the silver platter to the cart and began to carve and fill the plates of the dinner party with the besbarmak, which turned out to be delicious. Besides the meat stew with its diamond-shaped noodles, there were bowls of fragrant broth with floating herbs, feather-light rounds of bread, spicy palov, pickled mushrooms, melon rind, and a salad of cucumbers, tomatoes, scallions, and exotic green stuff. The wine, which Valery had preselected with a good deal more seriousness, was a Château Latour that brought tears of rapture to Pyotr's eyes. He forgave his grandson, and Valery led the birthday toast; and then Pyotr proposed a toast to Denis, and Denis proposed a toast to the Sixth Congress, and Tamara proposed a toast to the Seventh, which would be held the following year in Boston.

"You must go with us there, Papa," Tamara said to Pyotr. "We will celebrate your birthday in the American style."

"No feasts!" Pyotr pleaded.

"If you came up to New Hampshire," said Denis, "we could cook you a traditional ham and baked-bean supper with pumpkin pie and whipped cream."

The old man leaned toward the American. Being unable to converse telepathically on the intimate mode, he simply whispered. "I think it would be a great improvement over this boiled lamb's head. I am a Georgian, you see, and our cuisine is celebrated throughout the Soviet Union. My grandchildren have been barbarized by their residence in this way station of Marco Polo . . . My dear Professor, I am so grateful to you for salvaging the dinner. None of the others would have had the mind-power to coerce the waitresses over such a distance."

"You must call me Denis. And it was my pleasure. But I think that any one of your grandchildren, had they thought of it, would have been able to do as I did."

Valery, Ilya, and Anna protested: *Oh NO Professor!*

Pyotr did not hear, but the expressions on the young faces were eloquent enough. "It's true. They are growing up to be mental bullies, all three, too clever by half. They are—are—oy! I don't know the English word for what they are!"

"Whippersnappers," Denis offered.

Pyotr was delighted. "Yes! They think the world will leap as they snap their marvelous mental whips. You must take care, Denis, that your own new baby son does not grow up so disrespectful of his shortbrained elders."

"We attempted a simple form of ethical guidance even before the baby was born," Denis said seriously. "I'll be describing the new prenatal educational techniques that my wife Lucille and I devised for Philip in a paper I'm delivering tomorrow."

There were expressions of interest from the other academics around the table. Urgyen Bhotia said, "I find it fascinating that you would include ethics in your prenatal curriculum. Newborns are, of course, completely self-centered. And the infant human is egotistical in its evaluation of right and wrong."

"When the infant is a normal, that's acceptable," Denis said. "It may even be acceptable for the weaker operants. But"—he shrugged—"Lucille and I weren't sure just how strong-minded our offspring would be. You may have—er—read the article in *Nature*."

Alla and Mukar Kizim, who were friends and close associates of Tamara at the university, exchanged meaningful looks. "It is a matter that perplexed us as well," Alla admitted. "We have held off having children, wishing to give their young minds the best possible guidance both before and after birth. But I think we also were somewhat fearful of not being able to control them. There have been instances among our colleagues . . ."

"In America, too," Denis said.

"I don't think we've had much trouble in Scotland," said Jamie MacGregor. "Even normal Celtic parents are coercers from the word go. You hardly find a spoiled brat among us." He hesitated, then added, "There are crazies, though. And *I* have a paper on that."

"Children are very precious to our people," Tamara said. "It is always so in lands where nature is cruel and young life is vulnerable. It has been said by some psychologists that we have been too kind . . . that our children grow up lacking in initiative and inner strength because they were coddled. And when they become adults, and find how harsh life is, they either strike back and become cruel themselves or else bend dumbly to the yoke."

"Each nation," Urgyen said, "has its own strength and weakness. The roots of both are in the relationship of parents and children. I think Denis's talk of ethical training for the infant mind will be among the most significant to be delivered at this Congress. It will be my pleasure to lead a symposium on operant-nonoperant moral relationships. In light of the Tashkent tragedy, the subject is appropriate."

There was an uncomfortable silence. Finally, Annushka Gawrys said impulsively, "It *couldn't* have been one of us who did that awful thing! It's not possible!"

Jamie MacGregor said, "Lassie, I'm sorry. But it is possible. My dear friend Nigel Weinstein has had to retire from active metapsychic work just because it's possible."

"It could have been a provocateur," Tamara said. She switched to mental speech, even though it would exclude her father: *Our internal politics . . . you visitors see only the bright new face of the Soviet Union the Secretary's sweeping changes in the economy the unrestricted flow of information the new pride taken by workers inspired by Otkroveyinost' . . . but there is a faction in the Kremlin bitterly opposing the Secretary as a traitor to Marxist-Leninist ideology and they are allied with senior militarists who resent their drastic budget cuts and diminished power . . . Marshal Kumylzhensky aspires to head the Politburo himself and has deep hatred for Kirill Pazukhin Chairman KGB and General Secretary it is suspected that some of the Islamic rioting was fomented by agents Glavnoye Razvedyvatelnoye Upravleniye so as to discredit the Twentieth Directorate assassination of Grand Mufti would fit in with such a scheme . . .*

Urgyen Bhotia was incredulous: This Marshal would toy with civil war just to bring down a political enemy? He would cause the death of thousands of citizens merely to consolidate his power in Moscow?

Mukar Kizim said: It is only non-Slavic people the blackarses like us who die.

Jamie MacGregor asked: What'll stop this fool Marshal?

Tamara said: He is 73 years old... But his lackey Vadim Terekhov head of the GRU is only 56 and a Politburo aspirant. The consensus is that the General Secretary himself a man loved and respected by almost all the proletariat is the greatest bulwark against the militarists and diehard Marxist ideologues.

Denis Remillard said: I hope he has good bodyguards... especially tonight.

Tamara said: Tonight the nine of us the strongest minds I am able to trust utterly will guard him.

The General Secretary was showing signs of winding down now. He had set aside his notes to address the Congress delegates less formally, and Finster whispered, "It won't be long now. I hope those TV cameras stay on close-up for the big finale. We want this to be the zap seen round the world."

Colonel Sergei Arkhipov was incapable of vocal response. He was a skull-prisoner, no longer in control of his own body and knowing he would soon die. Nevertheless he watched the Killer Squirrel's professional modus operandi with fascinated detachment through the windows of his own eye sockets; and from time to time he even asked mental questions, which his captor answered quite frankly.

At supper, the Squirrel had given a brief account of his life—the creepy child, the third-rate entertainer and drug addict, the obscene "redemption" through bonding to the American megalomaniac, the progression from psychic spy to blackmailing suborner to specialist in wet affairs... It appealed to Sergei's mordant Russian sense of humor that the Squirrel's master, the archcapitalist exploiter O'Connor, should be the great enemy of metapsychic globalism. And in Moscow the zealous Marxist ideologue Kumylzhensky shared the identical viewpoint! If this crucial mission of the Killer Squirrel succeeded, both O'Connor and Kumylzhensky would win. Everyone else would lose. Oh, it was rich.

Four other KGB agents stood there in the wings of stage right with Sergei and Fabian Finster, and all including the Squirrel wore on their lapels the golden shield with stylized sword and red star, surmounted by the black VI of the Ninth Directorate. It was the insignia of the unit assigned to the security of top Party leaders. To any casual observer backstage in the Lenin Palace of Culture, the men—including the rather undersized one in the flashy double-breasted glen plaid—were part of the General Secretary's bodyguard.

To the subordinate four, the Killer Squirrel was simply invisible. This was a most useful faculty for an assassin to have, but Finster had explained to Sergei that there were limitations. The mental exertion required to project the illusion increased with the cube of the distance from the operant's brain. Thus it was very easy to render oneself invisible (or psychically disguised) when close to a normal observer, but relatively difficult to manage when the observer was farther away. Finster was also limited by having to retain his coercive hold on Sergei himself. Effectively, this limited his invisibility radius to less than nine meters. Thus he could not simply walk out onto the palace stage and terminate the General Secretary without being detected. Nor could he fulfill the special purpose of his assignment by means of an ambush. It was O'Connor's plan to incite antioperant feeling by making the assassinations seem to be an operant conspiracy, and so Finster had to play a part.

Sergei had been very surprised to learn that Finster was armed. He assumed that the longbrain would kill with astral fire, generated by mind-power alone. As all the world knew, this was the way that the Scottish operant had worked. But no. The Squirrel had explained that he was quite impotent in the conjuring up of mental fire. It was a knack, and his talents ran along other lines. Nor could he kill by cooking brains or stopping hearts, lethal aptitudes possessed by his master, O'Connor, among others. Finster explained that these killing methods, while tidy and much more efficient than psychocreative flaming, would not have the propaganda impact of the latter. So Finster intended to use an ingenious infernal device to *simulate* astral fire, and the General Secretary would—as the Grand Mufti before him—seem to die from the assault of an operant terrorist.

Tell me something belkushka, Sergei asked now. Were you there in Edinburgh to kill Professor MacGregor?

Yes, said Finster. But not at the press conference. By then it was too late, and I only went to provide a firsthand account of the affair to my principal. I tried to kill MacGregor six times during the months preceding his announcement. Each time I failed. He was being guarded.

By his metapsychic compères?

No . . . By somebody else. It was worrying. I never told the Boss about that bit.

This Boss. Why do you serve him? Kill for him?

Irony. I love him.

Now do not balls about with me! Why?

Why do you work for the KGB?

At first I was patriotic. Then I enjoyed the power. Then I was stuck in the shit like everybody else. Then . . . [laughter] when we were *transformed* it was just a job. Just a job . . .

You don't enjoy it now that you're respectable cops?

No.

That's where we differ then Sergei. I've always liked my job! This assignment's the biggest kick yet.

Belkushka. Little killer squirrel.

Laughter.

Out in the auditorium, the delegates were laughing, too. There was a smattering of applause for a particularly well-chosen piece of comic relief delivered by the General Secretary as he approached the end of his speech.

Finster pinched off the KGB colonel's maundering thoughts and concentrated on the matter at hand. Behind the Commie leader, seated at a long table decorated with red bunting and bouquets of autumn flowers, were ten or a dozen people—high mucky-mucks of the Metapsychic Congress with a few odd spouses and older kids. One seat was empty. The head lady, after introducing the Comrade Secretary, had gone off into the left wings. She was a plump, auburn-haired woman with a distracted overcast to her well-guarded mind, but she did not project the dangerous vibes Finster had learned to beware of. Most of the others seated on the platform seemed similarly harmless: an old guru type, four assorted Russkies, Jamie MacGregor, a Russky couple, and three kids in their late teens or early twenties who had to be the offspring of Madame Chairperson. No threat in the lot, for all their vigilance. He'd take care of them with the mind-buster, his great projection of sensory confusion.

The only potential joker in the pack sat at the far end of the table. Unlike the others, he was dressed formally in a dinner jacket and had a cold, uptight little smile on his face. Oh, yeah. Give Denis Remillard a guitar and a mike, take away the chrom-alloy bear-trap mind, and you'd have a young John Denver! Talk about a monster in wimp's clothing . . . Remillard would have to be handled. He was at extreme coercion range and probably un-coercible anyway. So stick to the mind-buster, but thicken it to max between Remillard and the podium. Then? Would the prof try a hit? He wasn't a known antiaggression freak like MacGregor or Madame Sakhvadze. Fact was, he almost never demon-strated his faculties in public, or even talked about them. Which was bad.

All right, just go for it. Speed and surprise and *fwoosh* and then haul ass for dear life to the big ZIL ticking over outside the stage door of the palace.

Ready . . .

"You have changed the course of world history," the General Secretary told the Metapsychic Congress. "In six short years you have given fresh hope and a vision of a golden Third Millennium to all nations, large and small. Thanks to you—and to others who had the good sense to understand and implement your dream—we have seen the end of the suicidal arms race and the beginning of true globular social thinking. But let us not deceive ourselves. There are still grave problems confronting humanity in many parts of the world, and some of them pose as great a threat to civilization as the late, unlamented nuclear deterrent. There is a terrible plague in Africa. There is continued bloodshed and terrorism in parts of the Islamic world. There is hunger and suf-

fering caused by extremes of weather. There is a growing shortage of energy. And, yes ... there is even controversy over the
proper role of operant persons in relation to the larger human
community. We must confront these problems honestly and
openly, and work together to solve them. We must never lose
sight of the fact that we all belong to the human family. All of us
share the wish that the future will bring to us and our children
peace, prosperity, and mutual respect. I thank you. I thank you
for *everything*."

The delegates rose for a standing ovation and Finster turned to
the four agents standing behind him. He held a silvery cylinder.
The sounds it made were nearly inaudible and its needles coated
with poison killed in a subtle way. The four agents, blinded and
voiceless, crumpled slowly to the floor.

Sergei realized that he was next. A sudden spurt of adrenalin
energized him, weakening Finster's coercive hold. Clumsily, Sergei fell against the killer and knocked the needle-gun to the floor.
Finster's arm scythed out and he broke Sergei's neck with a single karate chop. Then a swift-moving foot crushed Sergei's lar-
ynx.

Paralyzed and silenced, but with his mind free, Sergei
watched Finster take up a huge bouquet of red roses from a fold-
ing table near the proscenium arch. Out on the stage, the General
Secretary was bowing and smiling. He waved to the continuing
thunder of applause. Finster approached, his mind radiating homage and loyalty, and the leader of the Soviet Union held out his
hands to accept the flowers.

Sergei's lips moved. He managed a small, useless sound. His
eyes caught sight of Academician Sakhvadze in the opposite
wings and he *thought* at her. She started as though electrically
shocked and hesitated. Fool! Sergei raged. He thought at the
American—but, ah! Holy Mother! A mind-numbing surge of
sensation smote him, obliterating pain and darkening his vision.
Was he dead? No, not yet! He saw a flash of brilliant orange and
felt an unspoken shriek of disbelief. His nervous system—that
fragment of it still precariously connected to his brain—shrank
from another mental assault emanating not from one mind but
from thousands.

Sergei seemed to hear two titanic voices shouting *NO! NO! NO!* The formally dressed American and Tamara Petrovna had paid for their indecision and together they were trying to support a terrible headless figure. Cowards, Sergei told them. Cowards.

NO! NO! NO! the man and Tamara begged the raging audience. The anger and sorrow swelled into a vital thing; the minds of the delegation meshed spontaneously into metaconcert and focused on the hated target.

Something was running toward Sergei.

NO! NO! NO!

It was a man, brighter than the sun. A flaming angel come for him and his sins.

NO . . .

Not an angel. Only a small man enveloped in seething energy, and then tumbling bones glowing red-hot on the boards of the stage.

From each, Sergei thought, according to his abilities. To each according to his needs.

He closed his eyes for the last time, smiling.

11

LACONIA, NEW HAMPSHIRE, EARTH
7 FEBRUARY 1998

AS THE CRITICAL YEARS OF COADUNATING CONSCIOUSNESS dawned for the indigenes of planet Earth, the Milieu stepped up its psychosocial surveillance. Ever larger numbers of field-workers went planetside to track firsthand the irruptions of operancy among different population groups, gathering data on the numbers of metapsychically talented children being born, the spectrum of the various functions, and their potential strength—given optimum nurture and education.

The results of these late studies were a source of both enthusiasm and anxiety among the exotic observers. It had been known even in Earthly prehistoric times that the race had an exceptional creative component to its Mind; but the most recent samplings had begun to show just how awesome human psychocreativity might eventually prove to be. Analysts among the Krondaku were finally able to verify what the Lylmik had cavalierly stated at the inception of the Intervention scheme: humanity's mental potential undoubtedly exceeded that of any other race in the galaxy—coadunate or noncoadunate. Whether the puerile Earthlings would survive to manifest the potential was as questionable a point as ever.

Exotic field-workers on Earth were usually Simbiari or Poltroyans, since they had the most humanoid form and so required the least expenditure of psychic effort in projecting illusory bodies. Often the Poltroyans did not even bother with mental disguise. They were a trifle short in stature compared to average humans, but with wigs, a dab of Pancake make-up to lighten their purplish-gray skin, and contact lenses over their ruby irises they could pass as natives among many Earth populations.

Fritiso-Prontinalin, who called himself Fred during his sojourn on Earth, and his colleague Vilianin-Tinamikadin, who was known as Willy, were young Poltroyan psychogeomorphologists on their first assignment as xenosurveyors. Their project, a rather tedious one that had them tending automated data accumulators in widely separated parts of the world, attempted to correlate operancy in the farsensory spectrum with long-term population residence in the proximity of granitic lithoforms. The hypothesis wasn't working out too well in any sampling area except New Hampshire—and here the correlates were so high that the two researchers suspected a fudging factor. Discouraged and very much in need of a break, they decided to drive down to Laconia from their secret base camp in Waterville Valley and take a holiday. Primed for a weekend of alien thrills, they joined the crowd that had packed Laconia for the annual World Championship Sled-Dog Derby.

The sky was heavily overcast and the temperature hovered around the freezing point of a saline solution—glorious weather

for Poltroyans, who generally hail from wintry planets—and
Fred and Willy mingled happily with the mob. In recent weeks
they had done extensive field-work in Norway, and they had
brought souvenirs with them to New Hampshire—distinctive Samish "caps of the four winds"—which they wore to cover their
bald mauve skulls. Otherwise their garb was ordinary American
winter gear, comfortable enough but skimpy and drab when compared to the gem-studded fish-fur parkas and mukluks of their
home world. They told curious natives that they were Lapps.
This helped to explain away their shortness and also made them
some quick friends, since many of the mushers and fans were of
Scandinavian descent.

On Saturday morning Fred and Willy caught the first round of
Husky-drawn sled races in the hard-charging sprint classification.
When their favorite dog-team did poorly, they went around afterward to offer condolences to the driver, a petite lavender-eyed
blonde named Marcie Nyberg who reminded them very much of
certain girls they had left behind.

She was quite ready to commiserate. "Just my luck! I didn't
bring the right kind of wax for the runners, and none of the places
in Laconia stock it. It's called Totally Mean Extra Green. I don't
suppose you guys ever heard of it."

"Well, no," Fred admitted. "In Norway we use another kind."

But Willy was rummaging in the kangaroo pouch of his an-
orak and murmuring, "Wait a minute! Wait a minute!" And then,
triumphantly, he pulled out a flat container of pinkish metal with
a soft pad at one end. "Marcie, you're not going to believe this,
but I remembered that I had this defrictionizer stowed away in
here from the last time I was on—from *Norway*. I think it would
be just the thing for snow conditions today. Please try it."

Marcie examined the container dubiously. "Gee, I never saw
this kind of wax before. Is this writing on the side? I thought
Norwegians used the same alphabet as we do—"

Hastily, Willy said, "That's Samish. You know, the Lapp language. The stuff is simple to use. You just stroke it on, using the
pad end. It's not like crayon wax. It's—it's new."

Marcie grinned. "Okay, Willy. I'll give it a try this afternoon.
Thanks a whole bunch."

She had to tend to her dogs' feet then, so the Poltroyans said goodbye and went to watch a weight-pulling event. Malamute dogs, much more massive than the rangy Huskies, strained eagerly to move sledges loaded with weights up to a ton per animal. Fred and Willy were overwhelmed at the strength of the furry quadrupeds—and especially interested to note that the handler of the heavyweight Grand Prize winner had unconsciously exercised a telepathic rapport with his dog, aiding its performance.

When the contest was over, Fred went to the man and offered hearty congratulations. But when he offhandedly added a remark about telepathic encouragement, the musher let loose a blast of profanity that nearly took off the Poltroyan's quaint four-cornered cap.

"Use telepathy? Me? You accusing me of being one of them goddam cheating *heads*? Well, lemme tell you, pipsqueak, I run my dogs honest, and any guy that says different can taste a knuckle sandwich!"

He was a black-browed bruiser with a stubbly jaw and the number 22 pinned to his down jacket. Several other dog-handlers crowded around, looking none too friendly, and the prize-winning Malamute took a lunge at Willy with its lips curled back from enormous teeth. Fortunately, its owner had a good grip on its chain.

Fred quickly apologized. "I'm sorry! I didn't understand! We're visitors from Norway, you see. We didn't know that—er—that kind of thing was considered improper here."

The animosity of the bystanders dwindled and Number 22 seemed slightly mollified. "Well . . . so long as you're foreigners and don't know better, I won't take offense. But you better watch it, fella. Calling somebody a head won't make you any friends in this part of the U.S. of A."

"No, sirree," the others chimed in. "Damn tootin'!"

Number 22 squinted at the Poltroyans in suspicion. "You two wouldn't be heads yourself, would you?"

"Oh, my, no," Willy said. "We're Samish. You know—Laplanders. The people who used to herd reindeer."

"Reindeer!" humphed Number 22. "Mighta known."

"Oh, we're very interested in dogs, too," Fred said. "Ours are called spitz. They're something like small Huskies."

The Malamute handler was patently unenthusiastic and his dog, a huge gray and white creature with black eyes, continued to growl. "You see this?" The musher indicated a big round button pinned beside the cloth square with the numerals 22. "You wanta stay outa trouble, you better know what it means."

Fred and Willy took a closer look. The button was a depiction of Earth as seen from space, a blue disk splashed with white. "It's very attractive," Fred said.

The man gave an unpleasant laugh. "It means I'm one of the Sons of Earth, shorty. A normal human being, and proud of it! You ever heard of us?"

"Yes," said Willy, keeping a neutral expression.

"Well, then you know where I'm comin' from. As far's I'm concerned, God made this Earth for normal human folks—not for freako heads who break the laws of nature and try to lord it over the rest of us like they're some kind of fuckin' master race."

"Yeah!" members of the crowd affirmed. "You said it, Jer! Damn right on!"

Number 22 slackened the dog chain a fraction and the Malamute reared. "I don't know what goes on in Norway, but in *this* country we're gonna make sure that real people stay in charge of things—not freaks. You get what I'm saying?"

"Oh, yes," said Fred, backing away. There were quite a few of the big blue buttons being worn by the crowd. Neither Poltroyan had taken any note of them before.

"Well, thanks for explaining," Willy said. "And congratulations again on winning the Golden Bone. You've got a really fine dog there." And with that, Fred and Willy fled, hurried along by hostile and contemptuous aetheric vibrations. They stopped near a refreshment stand to catch their breaths.

"Half-masticated lumpukit!" Fred swore. "That was a nasty one."

"The buttons must be a new fad here in America. I certainly don't recall seeing them in New Hampshire last year at the ski jumps. It seems to me that the Sons of Earth were still a disreputable fringe movement then. Membership was quite furtive."

"Not anymore." Fred was looking about. "Love's Oath—

every third or fourth person seems to be wearing one of those buttons. We'll have to send notification to the Oversight Authority."

"They're probably aware of the situation. But we'll do it."

It was almost time for the next heat of sprints that Marcie was scheduled to participate in, so the Poltroyans decided to get something to eat and go cheer on their new friend. Willy dug in his pocket for a credit card and ordered two hot dogs with sauerkraut and mustard and two Classic Cokes. Then the exotics wandered over to the racecourse, sipping and munching. The beverage's alkaloid was invigorating even if it wasn't quite sweet enough, so they tossed in three or four maple-sugar candies to saccharify it. The delicious sulfur taste of the shredded hot vegetable mingled nicely with the speckled buff condiment's bite. Too bad that the proteinoid was too highly nitrified for really safe metabolization—but an occasional treat wouldn't kill them.

When the heats began they forgot the unpleasant incident with the Sons of Earth and reveled in the excitement of the racing. Dogs howled, mushers yelled, the spectators cheered on their favorites, and a diamond-dust snow sifted down on everything. It was glorious! And when the final times were posted, Marcie and her team had won.

Fred and Willy ran to her, shouting their congratulations.

"Your wax! Your wax!" She swept the pair of them into her arms like a mother embracing her children. "The wax made all the difference! I love you guys, do you know that?"

She was covered with crusted rime thrown up by the galloping dogs, and one could almost forget she was the wrong color and chromosomally incompatible. Fred and Willy pressed lips with her because that was what her mind told them she wanted. Then she brushed herself off and untied the vivid Day-Glo racing vest with her number, 16, and pulled it over her head.

On the jacket underneath was a big blue button.

Marcie was bubbling over as she began to load her dogs into her truck. "Listen, you guys. Tonight there's a Musher's Ball with beer and chili and a live band. I want you to come. My treat! You can meet the whole gang and tell them about the crazy wax and the whole Laplander thingypop!"

"We'd love to," Fred said sadly.

"But we really have to go now," Willy concluded. "Please keep the wax. I wish I had more, but—it's in short supply."

Marcie's face fell. "Oh, guys. What a shame you can't come. Maybe you could catch me later? The Adirondack's two weeks off—"

"We're finishing our work in the States very soon," Fred said.

"We're really sorry," Willy added.

"Well," Marcie said, "it was awfully nice knowing you. I'll always remember you two."

The Poltroyans turned and walked away. All around were mushers tinkering with sleds or adjusting harnesses and traces. The loudspeakers announced the start of another event and the dogs began to yelp, eager to be off and away.

"Let's go home," Fred said.

"I wish we *could*," Willy muttered.

"Oh, you know what I mean," said Fred.

Together, they headed for the place where they had left their car.

12

FROM THE MEMOIRS OF ROGATIEN REMILLARD

WE WERE NOT YET PARIAHS, ONLY SUSPECT.

The terrible murder and instant retribution that had taken place in Alma-Ata were played and replayed on the television screens of the world. The implications—perceived almost instinctively by every normal person—were argued in heat and in cold blood, but then rationalized away because humanity was not yet prepared to turn upon and repudiate the operants.

After an investigation that took more than a year, Soviet forensic scientists, assisted by experts from many other countries, determined that the assassinations of the General Secretary and the Grand Mufti were not accomplished by psychocreative energy at all, but by a chemical explosive device that was almost but not quite without traceless residue. That the agent provocateur had been operant himself was verified by the testimony of the delegate-witnesses there in the Lenin Palace of Culture, particularly those who had been on stage. The killer had used a quasi-hypnotic technique to stun and confuse those close to the General Secretary. Only Denis and Tamara had been able to resist the mind-paralysis; but they could not prevent the murder.

The killer's true identity was never discovered. His image was shown distinctly on the tapes of the video cameras recording the event; but the face was obscured by the large bouquet of flowers at first, and then by the miniature explosion. He had turned away as he started to flee, again hiding his face from the cameras, and his subsequent cremation obliterated any other clues to his identity.

The cremation, not the murder of the Soviet leader, was what really gave the world pause.

After months of hedging, a special investigatory committee of "blue-ribbon" metapsychologists called by the United Nations issued a lengthy analysis of the so-called Retributory Incident. Its findings can be compactly summarized:

1. The assassin of the Soviet General Secretary met his death through a process of incineration by psychoenergetic projection.

2. The energy projected came from the brains of the operant delegates who had just witnessed the assassination.

3. The energy was focused and amplified by means of a maneuver known as "metapsychic concert," in which numbers of operant brains act as one synergistically, the whole being capable of an output greater than the sum of the parts.

4. It was not possible to calculate with total accuracy the amount of energy focused upon the assassin, since its characteristics were anomalous. (For example, there were no auditory manifestations as there had been when the General Secretary's

head was vaporized by the explosive device.) Furthermore, it was
not possible to calculate the percentage of psychoenergy generated by individual delegates.

5. The metafaculty of psychocreativity, which may generate
energy, is at present poorly understood. Except for the Weinstein
case, there is no previous record of a fatality resulting from the
projection of psychic energy. Metapsychic concert is also poorly
understood. Its manifestation has been experimentally verified by
magnetoencephalography; but in no instance have researchers
ever encountered an effect even remotely approaching the magnitude of the Retributory Incident.

6. In the opinion of the investigatory committee, the Incident
was the result of an unconscious velleity on the part of the dele-
gate-minds, without true volition. In lay language, the delegates
were so shocked and angered by the General Secretary's murder
that their mutual loathing of the perpetrator generated the blast
that killed him.

7. On the advice of the committee, no action at law against
the delegate-perpetrators was contemplated by the Soviet judi-
ciary. It was felt that the principle of diminished responsibility
applied to their actions in view of the heinousness of the crime
they had just witnessed.

8. Repetitions of Retributory Incidents could not be ruled out,
given similar provocatory circumstances.

9. The committee recommended strongly that legal scholars,
ethicists, and moral theologians address themselves to the unique
problems of culpability devolving upon metapsychic operancy.
The ancient question of whether the law should take the will for
the deed would have to be reopened when, ipso facto, the will
was the deed.

Debate over the philosophical and legal implications of operancy would beget an avalanche of articles, monographs, and
books off and on over the next fifteen years, until the topic received its ultimate resolution in the Intervention. Of course Denis
did not serve on the investigating committee. (The fact of his
nonparticipation in the destructive metaconcert was proved when

the Simbiari Proctorship reopened the inquiry into the Incident in 2017, at Denis's insistence.) Lucille, who had not attended the Sixth Congress because of her confinement with her first son, Philip, *did* serve. It should be noted that she laid open her personal psychocreative case history to assist the committee in its deliberations, an action that required great courage at the time. Fortunately for her, the committee decided that it was not necessary to include that history in the public record.

You, the entity reading these memoirs, should not get the impression that reaction to the Retributory Incident was as reasoned and high-minded as this chapter may have thus far implied. On the contrary, there was a royal rumpus kicked up in the United States, where the media hashed and rehashed the affair ad nauseam, bringing the term "psychozap" into slang usage, together with the pejorative "head," applied to operants—which was perversely embraced by us and later used as an innocent appellation. As the Third Millennium approached, cranks and fanatics of every sort crept out of the woodwork—most notably the Sons of Earth movement, which claimed worldwide adherents by 1999 and succeeded in disrupting part of the Eighth Metapsychic Congress in London.

The Great California Earthquake gave new life to the prophecies of Nostradamus. Never mind that the prophet's dating for the quake was so ambiguous that it might have referred to any century following the sixteenth, with the locale of the seismic disaster unspecified. Two other pertinent quatrains from Nostradamus were dusted off and presented to the gullible as portents of things to come:

> L'an mil neuf cens nonante neuf sept mois,
> Du ciel viendra un grand Roi deffraieur.
> Resusciter le grand Roi d'Angolmois.
> Avant que Mars regner par bonheur.

> Apres grand troche humaine plus grande s'appreste,
> Le grand moteur des Siecles renouvelle.
> Pluie, sang, laict, famine, fer et peste
> Au feu ciel veu courant longue estincelle.

Which can be roughly translated:

In the seventh month of the year 1999,
A great King of Terror will come.
He will revive the great King of the Mongols.
Before that Mars will run riot.

After great human suffering, even greater comes,
When the great motive power of the Centuries is renewed.
Rain, blood, milk, famine, iron [war], and disease
In the heavens is seen a fire, a long flow of sparks.

The hysterical could equate the new, bellicose leader of the Soviet Union, Marshal Kumylzhensky, with the King of Terror. By a long stretch of the imagination, the new Genghis Khan could be seen in the insurrections flaring up in Soviet Central Asia. (No one yet had any inkling that the Chinese were watching the accelerating dissolution of the USSR with keen interest.) The continued fighting throughout the Islamic world was certainly a source of suffering, and the crazy weather that had rotted the crops in some parts of the world while parching others also seemed to fit. As to the milk, there remained the legacy of the Armageddon fallout, poisoning both milk and "blood" in a wide swath of the Middle East and the Balkans for seven years now. The fateful Seventh Month of 1999 came and went without any signal disaster; but in August, the total eclipse of the sun that was visible in Europe, the most embattled regions of the Middle East, and the Indian subcontinent wreaked havoc among the superstitious, who were certain that the end of the world had come. After that crisis had passed, there was another to be endured on 11 November, when Earth passed through the great Leonid meteor "storm," a Nostradamic fiery flow of sparks if there ever was one. But once again Earth abided, the day of wrath was unaccountably postponed, and the eschatologists went back to their original prediction of doomsday at the actual turn of the Millennium.

Sadly enough, certain of the Remillards did meet their end during those days. Their tragedy went virtually unnoticed because of the gaudier events that Milieu historians have concentrated on; but I will tell it here as part of the family chronicle.

In the months following the Alma-Ata affair, Denis brooded over the misuse of operant metafaculties. He discussed this subject at length with both Tamara Sakhvadze and Urgyen Bhotia, and was convinced that resolute pacifism was the only ethical course open to persons with higher mind-powers. There remained, however, the odious problem of Victor. Denis had told Lucille what he knew and what he suspected about his younger brother, and she was simultaneously outraged and wary. Lucille was particularly concerned for Sunny and the nonoperant siblings left under Victor's influence, and pressed Denis to do something to help them, even if it meant a direct confrontation that might end in violence. But Denis refused, countering her reproaches with both logic and his espousal of the superChristian ethic. No course short of engineering Victor's demise was likely to resolve the terrible stalemate—and Denis would not kill his brother in cold blood even to save the lives of his mother and the others.

Denis stood by, apparently impotent, while his younger twin brothers Louis and Leon, who turned twenty-one in 1999, were brainwashed by Victor and joined him in Remco Industries as nonoperant factotums. Both young men were ruthless and intelligent, and they were also completely trustworthy, unlike many of Victor's operant associates. That left only George, who was nineteen, and Pauline, two years younger, still living with Sunny. George was an unprepossessing young man, very unassertive, who was studying computer technology under Victor's orders. I had always thought him a poor stick. Paulie, the youngest of Don and Sunny's big brood, was an exquisite creature. Except for her dark eyes, she was the image of her mother as a young woman— and when I saw her that year at the family Easter get-together, suddenly matured into radiant femininity, my heart stood still.

Their older sister Yvonne had been married in 1996 to the middle-aged operant crook Robert Fortier, whose sinister mother still acted as Sunny's nominal housekeeper, all the while contriving to dominate her utterly. Over the years, by use of ingenious metapsychic variants on old-fashioned racketeering, Victor and Fortier had converted Remco into an international operation that now owned not only pulpwood harvesting companies but a large paper mill in New Brunswick, a chemical plant in Maine, and other forest-product industries in cities scattered across upper New England and southeastern Canada. Having succeeded so well in his first dynastic ploy, Victor now decided to atttempt a much more audacious variation on the theme.

One of my nephew's underhanded acquisitions was a small genetic-engineering firm in Burlington, Vermont. This outfit had perfected and patented a bacterial organism called a lignin degrader, that broke down (i.e., "ate") a common waste product of the pulpwood industry, converting it into a host of valuable chemicals that had heretofore been obtained from increasingly scarce petroleum. The process utilizing the superior bug was very nearly ready to be put into production, and it was going to be a gold mine; but Victor's Remco Industries faced a dilemma well known to medium-sized corporations—it did not have enough capital to develop a lignin-chemistry company of its own, which would reap huge profits. Rather, it would have to license the process to giant petrochemical conglomerates and settle for a much smaller piece of the pie.

Naturally, Victor balked at this. The golden bug and its principal nurturer had been stolen from a famous Michigan university at considerable risk to Victor's own hide, and he had invested a good deal of money in the perfecting of the process. Having won game and set, as it were, he wasn't going to let outsiders rob him of the match.

There was only one font of finance he felt he could safely approach for additional capitalization, a money source that had earlier approached *him*, only to be repulsed. Now, Victor decided, the time was ripe for reconsideration. And so he made a telephone call to Kieran O'Connor's Chicago office, waited patiently while his name was passed from buffer zone to buffer zone in the corporate hierarchy until it reached the Boss of Bosses, and then made his proposition.

A merger, to their mutual profit. To seal the deal, Victor would marry Shannon O'Connor and Kieran would take Pauline Remillard.

O'Connor laughed his head off at the raw Franco chutzpah of

it all. It was *primitive*. It was damn near Sicilian! Still, Kieran had kept his eye on Victor over the years and had been impressed. At the callow age of twenty-nine, Victor was worth upward of sixty-two million dollars—peanuts when compared to Kieran's own empire, but not too shabby when you remembered that the kid had started out with nothing but his drunken daddy, a '74 Chevy pickup truck, and two Jonsered chain saws boosted from a local logging-equipment supplier. And this lignin-gobbling bacterium had possibilities. Kieran's facile mind hatched a scenario in which the process could be used as a fulcrum in a scheme to corner the world's energy supply. As for Victor himself, he would either have to be made an ally or eliminated. The dynastic link-up opened the way for either option.

After their telephone conversation had gone on for some ten minutes, Kieran told Victor that he was inclined to accept the proposition. There were, however, two small matters that would have to be clarified. First, did Victor have his sister Pauline under complete control, as Kieran did Shannon? . . . and was she really beautiful and unsophisticated?

Of course!

Kieran hoped that was true, because they couldn't coerce the girl permanently. The second matter was more delicate. Kieran did not want Pauline as his wife or mistress. He would possess her only once (for reasons not explained to Victor), and after that she would be married to Kieran's close associate Warren Griffith, who had recently lost his third wife under tragic circumstances. There was, however, this thing about Griff. He was brilliant, both in coercive talent and business acumen, but he had special personal needs. Pauline, as his wife, would live in a ménage à trois, and the third party was a young man of rather stern disposition. Did Victor understand?

Different strokes for different folks, Victor said. But Kieran would have to make *damn* certain that Paulie didn't end up like the third wife.

Kieran would see to it personally.

Then there was no problem.

And so this decidedly curious arrangement was agreed upon. But Victor made the mistake of explaining the situation very carefully to Pauline while she was under his coercive hold. He talked to her for three hours one late October afternoon when the sky was clear and the trees were in full color on the hillsides surrounding Berlin, and then he left her in the back yard of Sunny's big house on Sweden Street, sitting on a rustic bench under an incandescent maple tree. When her brother George came home that day from computer college, she asked him to take her for a ride in his car along the Androscoggin River, and while they drove she told him without any emotion at all (for that was the way Vic's brainwashing affected the forcibly latentized) what was in store for her.

George thought about it in his nerdish way. And he thought about his own future as a superhacker under Vic's mental thumb, and his older brother Denis's apparent inability to help any of them. Then he told Paulie not to worry. They drove up to Dave's Gun Shop in Milan, where George bought a handsome Marlin 120 shotgun with a twenty-six-inch barrel and a genuine American walnut stock and forend, all hand-checkered, because George didn't want to wind things up in a sleazy way. After that they found a nice spot where Paulie could watch the river and the trees reflected in it and not notice a thing. There was string in the glove compartment that George tied cleverly around the trigger and guard of the gun to take care of himself.

Vic knew at once when they died and so did I; but for some reason he did not receive the farspoken truth of the affair that was transmitted to me in the split second of George's final agony. Instead, Victor went to the car and found the note, which he destroyed before calling the State Police to report the double tragedy. He was mad as hell. Kieran O'Connor took the news more calmly and said that he would think things over, and doubtless something could be worked out between them after all. He promised to get back to Victor early next year, after the Millennial hysteria cooled and the financial world returned to normal.

Sunny's link to a reality that had become insupportable was shattered by this final trauma. She smiled a great deal at the double funeral and said that Don and the five dead children spoke to her from heaven, saying she would soon be joining them. Victor now had no objection to her going to Hanover to live, so

Sunny spent her last months in the pleasant house on East South Street with Denis and Lucille, rocking newborn Maurice and reading storybooks to little Philip.

I saw her nearly every day. She remembered who I was when I would address her as Marie-Madeleine, as I had done when we first met in the Berlin Public Library thirty-eight years earlier. We often spoke about those days. At other times, her drifting mind perceived young Maurice as baby Denis, and she and I would re-enact some of the simple metapsychic teaching games I had devised so long ago. Such charades soothed her even as they tortured me, but at any rate they did not last long. She died the next spring, in March, impatient for the flowers to bloom.

13

MOUNT WASHINGTON, NEW HAMPSHIRE, EARTH 31 DECEMBER 1999

THERE WAS THE QUESTION OF WHERE TO SPEND THE TURN OF THE Millennium . . . Her father was going to an opulent masked ball in Vienna where the international set was prepared to outdo the twilight of Byzantium, and he invited her to accompany him. She declined. It wasn't her style to waltz away the fateful hours in the company of tipsy financiers and diamond-crusted media stars, and then at midnight link arms to sing "Brüderlein und Schwesterlein" and "Auld Lang Syne," awash in sentimental tears and vintage champagne.

No. She wanted something different . . . just in case the world did end, as the crazies kept predicting. Something incomparably dramatic.

Kieran laughed indulgently, but then went all serious and re-

minded her that she would have to be with him in Zürich without
fail on Monday January 3 for the signing session establishing
their new European satellite consortium, in which she was a nominal officer. Perhaps, he suggested offhandedly, she could spend
the holiday weekend skiing. She would be welcome to use
Darmstadter's chalet at Gstaad, since he and his family would be
going to the ball.

She thought about that. She was a superb skier, and her operancy gave her unusual talents that added zest to the sport. But she
would not go to Gstaad. For one thing, her father had suggested
it. For another, it was crowded and artificial and she might meet
people she knew. Her fancy painted a very different picture of the
Millennial Eve: a precipitate slope of powder snow, virgin in the
moonlight, and herself flying downhill, a streaming torch in her
hand, into the blackness below. Yes!

And then she had another great idea. The perfect place—and
an appropriate companion.

She telephoned him and invited him to be her guest in the
Bugaboos. He did ski, didn't he?

"Yes," he said.

"Then let me send the family Learjet for you and we can meet
in Banff. Our chopper and a private guide will be waiting. We'll
have to see one another eventually. Why not do it this way, without him even knowing?"

"He doesn't know?"

"He's in Europe. That's why I'm . . . free."

There was a pause on the other end of the line, and then he
said, "If you'd like something really climactic, an even bigger
thrill—"

"Bigger than skiing the *Bugaboos*?"

He told her what he had in mind and this time it was her turn
to hesitate. "Is it possible?"

"If you're black diamond . . . and if you have some PK, it's
quite possible. I've done it twice."

"I suppose it's illegal or something."

"Oh, yes, definitely." He laughed.

"Tell me where to meet you!" she demanded.

And so he had; and early the next morning she had driven out to DuPage County Airport and taken the Lear herself. It took her a little over two hours to get to North Conway, New Hampshire, from northern Illinois, since she had to detour around some bad weather over Buffalo. But when she touched down at White Mountain Airport she found bright sunshine, fresh powder, and a throng of like-minded ski nuts overflowing the resort town, all determined to await Gabriel's trump schussing their brains out. There were no rental cars to be had, but she coerced the young man at the Hertz office into giving her the keys of his own nifty little BMW sports coupe. Then she drove north to Wildcat Mountain, where she spent what was left of the day and the early evening warming up her muscles on the rather modest slopes of Upper Lynx and Lower Catapult, all the while eyeing the real challenge that loomed to the west, dazzling in its deepest snow-cover in decades.

Could they get up there without a chopper? He'd said they could, in spite of the fact that it was deadly dangerous as well as prohibited. That, of course, made it perfect.

Along about seven she was ravenous so she drove down to Jackson, to a well-known country inn on the Thorn Hill Road. There she dined alone on lobster bisque, a salad of spinach, endive, and red onions with mustard-vinaigrette dressing, veal scallops with black mushrooms and cognac sauce, potatoes rösti, and steamed baby green beans. She drank a single glass of a fine Souveraine California Cabernet and left the rest (to the scandal of the host), and finished with a pumpkin-pecan tartlet and a pony of calvados.

Then it was time to meet Victor Remillard.

Following his instructions, she drove to the deserted parking lot of the Mount Washington Carriage Road. Its gate was open and she turned off her headlights and went in, following a plowed track through very deep snow that was sometimes drifted higher than the roof of her car. The sky to the south had a warm glow from the lighted slopes at Wildcat, three kilometers away, but aside from that the only illumination was from starlight. The moon, four days past its full, had not yet risen above the eastern heights. Near a deserted ticket-taker's shack was a cleared space where a peculiar vehicle was parked. It looked like a boxy van precariously perched above four very wide tractor treads. She parked beside it and studied it with fascination.

Only a few minutes passed before he came, driving a big four-wheeler that he slewed around smartly, throwing up a plume of snow that glittered under the stars. He parked a few meters away, then got out and came crunching toward her. Pulling up her hood and slipping on her gloves, she stepped out of the BMW and went to meet him.

Shannon O'Connor I presume.
Victor Remillard . . . I know.
Hey good screen!
And yours.
Lots to hide?
Haven't you?
Touché.
Pas du tout.
Ready fun?
Believe it.
Good sky.
No wind.
Headwall powder!
Super!
PK OK?
?? Yes. ??

Sure you can drive this thing?   Homing.
Marchons!   No hands babe!   Not in SnoGo?
Ready when you are.   I'm *valuable*.   *UP* only *DOWN* XC.
Épatant!   To Papa!   Oo!
Mg fusees!!   Not you?   Treeslalom.
Torches X 2?   We'll see.   Ace hi!
Wired for stereo.   *LET'S GO!*   Mogulbomber?
Hardhat?   Yo!
And deepvision   Aerials too?
Nightvision?   Only 720&Möebius!
!Hotdog hotdamn hotdog hotdamn hotdog!
!Hotdog!

So they were off in a roar of monster twin diesels, charging up the famous road leading to the summit of Mount Washington. But they weren't going to the top; they were going, by ingenious and unlawful routes, to the lip of the Headwall of Tuckerman Ravine, a steep glacial cirque that had been scooped into the southeastern flank of the peak during the past ice age. The ravine was a natural trap for snow blasted off the Presidential Range by the hurricane winds of the region. In this final winter of the second Millennium, one of the coldest and stormiest in decades, the vast bowl of Tuckerman Ravine was filled with snow more than twenty-five meters deep. People normally skied Tuckerman in the spring, when most of the snow in the country surrounding it had melted and it was possible to hike up through the woods from Pinkham Notch to the Hermit Lake camping shelters on the ravine floor. The only way to get to the Headwall from Hermit was to slog with your skis on your back—up and up and up. At the rim of the declivity—if you got that far on the fifty-five-degree slope— you skied down. The great challenge was to schuss, to ski straight to the bottom. The feat had last been accomplished by Toni Matt in 1939. Once down the Headwall, it was possible to take the precipitous Sherburne Ski Trail back to the Notch and the highway. In the dead of winter, however, nobody skied Tuckerman Ravine. The powder was bottomless and the scene magnificent, but the upper reaches of the mountain were off-limits to the public. It was deadly up there, with some of the fiercest winter weather on Earth.

But not on that New Millennium's Eve.

"Did you lay on the Sno-Crawler just for me?" Shannon asked.

"Not on your life. It belongs to the contractor who services the weather observatory and the TV and microwave transmitters on the summit. During the winter the Carriage Road is closed halfway up and unplowed. Once a week this crawler goes up with supplies and the relief crew."

"And you can just hop into the thing and make free with it whenever you fancy a little jaunt?"

He laughed. "Not by a damn sight. But I have my methods."

They sat side by side in bucket seats, strapped in with sturdy web harnesses. Shannon had erected her heaviest mental screen, the dual-layer one with the false substrate that she used to defeat her father's probing. Victor had made a perfunctory stab at it during their initial encounter, then backed off; but she could still feel the searing power of him, like a searchlight held at steady focus against a window blind; and when they had faced each other in the dark parking lot she had seen his ghostly aura—vermilion laced with steely flashes of blue, the colors of potency and danger.

Inside the surging vehicle, studying the electronic displays on its console, Victor Remillard hardly seemed to be the black mental menace her father had described. His bare head was a mass of tight dark curls. He wore a one-piece Thermatron ski-suit with all the high-tech options—temperature control, spot massage, comunit, stereo sound-surround, and locator beacon—ready for anything. (But *she* wore her old red North Face jacket and pants with the Ski Patrol patch from Snowbird! One up.)

She said, "My father's off in Vienna, where the Third Millennium has already come. He and his plutocratic friends are at a fancy-dress ball like the last act of some Strauss operetta. Next week he takes control of the Dione satellite-engineering consortium—the one that's to build the European section of Zap-Star."

"Nice for him."

"I'm to be its nominal CEO."

"Nice for you."

"Daddy expects me to be a figurehead." She smiled, letting just a bit of her supposed scheme to seize control of the consortium seep beneath the margin of her outermost screen. Victor jumped on it, just as she knew he would, and crashed the frangible barrier for a thorough scan of what lay behind. He was sure that he'd laid her mind wide open—just as her father was always sure. But Shannon's true self was secure behind the secondary shield, letting the intruder see only what she permitted him to; and as Victor sorted through what he believed were the plans and dreams of Kieran O'Connor's daughter, he himself lay vulnerable to her . . . and she entered softly.

God—he was strong! By no means as intelligent and demonic as her father, and with ambitions predictably narrow in scope. But what a coercer, and what brutal unformed creativity was there, waiting only to be molded and directed! He would do. Oh, yes, he would do.

She finished her lightning penetration long before his scan was complete. He had noticed nothing, and when he finally withdrew, smiling in a patronizing way at her callow scheme to rule the consortium, she simulated dismay at the mental violation and then pretended to sulk.

"You'll have to do a lot better than that if you expect to put one over on your old man."

She let him wait, repaired outer barrier back in place, and then said, "I suppose *you* could think of a better plan."

"I might." His eyes were fixed on the snow-depth-and-density monitor and he throttled back. They had passed the dark bulk of the shuttered Halfway House and come into the open. There were great drifts blocking the way now, some of them six meters high. Victor studied their contour and composition and the nature of the rocky terrain buried beneath them, then geared down to clamber over. An unsecured boot-bag tumbled toward the rear of the cabin as they ascended a steep incline, zigzagged, then came back more or less to horizontal and proceeded up the invisible road.

Shannon said, "Nicely done . . . So my little plots interest you, do they? I thought you wanted to form an alliance with my father. You could report my contemplated subversion to him, you know, and score."

"Perhaps I'm playing an altogether different game. Just like you."

The powerful headlights of the Sno-Crawler lit a hairpin section of the way that doubled back along a precipice skirting the Great Gulf, another big cirque on the north side of the mountain. They had passed above the tree line now, but rime-coated scrub decorated the crags and sparkled as though it were coated with sugar. Victor accelerated, conquered a small avalanche fall, and headed up the icy Five-Mile Grade, an exposed section that had been swept clear of loose snow by the nor'easter winds. Tonight the air was still. Victor punched a control button deploying the tread spikes and the crawler chewed its way upward.

Shannon said, "My father thinks he has control of my mind. My loyalties. From the very beginning, he's used this—this technique to bond his associates to him irrevocably."

"It's pretty obvious the technique didn't work on you."

"It does when I'm with him. Then I'm like all the others, under his spell . . . Even at other times I can *belong* to him. When

I'm lonely and afraid of myself and everything else and want it all to end, then I'm caught in his vision of the Absolute, and I know Daddy's way is the only way that makes sense . . . But then he loosens his hold. Perhaps he's too caught up in other things to bother with the little satellite minds orbiting him and worshiping . . . And I remember how he bound me. The fire racing up my spine and exploding my senses and burning my resistance to ashes. It should have taken—the bonding. But it didn't, not fully. I think Daddy may have been inhibited because I was his daughter, and his will didn't finalize the personality conjunction. It took me a long time to remember. To know why my own world had died along with the honest love—daughter's love—I had felt for him. Now, when I love him, he's not my father. When I'm myself, and I know who he is and what he did to me, I hate him."

The sudden explosion of approval—of kinship—that escaped him was a profound shock to her and a revelation. He said, "Hate. That's your antidote. Mine, too. But I've known it forever."

She had the ski gloves in her lap and she pulled each finger carefully, straightening it, before rolling the gloves and tucking them into her jacket. "He'll try to bond you, too. It's the only way he'll allow operants to be associated with him."

Victor let out a harsh bark of laughter. "Y a pas de danger! . . . Or as you micks might say—in a pig's eye! I'd like to see him break into my skull—"

"He doesn't. That's not his way at all. He makes us love him. With those who aren't—aren't naturally inclined to accept him, he uses a hypnagogic drug to weaken their psychic defenses, then seduces them. If the person recognizes what's being done, he kills them. He's killed one hundred and eighty-three natural operants and bonded forty-six. He finds most suitable ones when they commit certain crimes. Scams. Conspiracies. There's a kind of suboperant signature that he recognizes. The people themselves don't realize that they have the powers. In the seduction, he shows them what they can be, with his help. It's wonderful. That's why we'll do anything for him, commit any atrocity. The man who assassinated the Russian Premier and the Grand Mufti of Central Asia was one of his. Daddy has a lot of reasons for wanting to foment war. His Zap-Star satellite defense system needs concrete global villains as targets—not just scattered groups of Islamic hotheads."

"He's got it right," Victor conceded. His knuckles tightened on the wheel as the vehicle entered the Cutoff Track, bypassing another notch that was full of deeply drifted snow. "He's done a damn good job consolidating power. My operation is small potatoes in comparison. But it won't stay that way."

"If you oppose him directly," Shannon said, "he'll kill you. If you try to join him, you'll end as I have. Bound."

He was silent for several minutes, guiding the big machine through a chaos of compacted white ice blocks. Despite the strut suspension that dampened the worst of the lurching, the cabin bounced and tilted and flung its occupants against their seat harnesses like rag dolls until they finally exited the Cutoff and came back onto the buried Carriage Road proper.

Victor said, "They all want to bind us, Shannon. Starting with our parents, of course, at the very beginning. They say they love us and then make conditions. They try to hold us back, to keep us from climbing above their own puny level. They want to live through us—on us!—like some kind of psychic vampires. That's what love is. At least your father's version makes no bones about it."

"I never thought about it that way."

"Well, *start*. Your unconscious mind knew and you started to hate and you started to free yourself. I've always hated them all and I've never been bound. I take the little empty ones and use them, and crush the mind-fucking lovers. I'll crush your father someday, and my brother Denis, who's even worse."

"Daddy'll get you if you let him near you. I know what your scheme is. You think you can marry me and hold him off long enough to take what he has. But you won't be able to help yourself. I can sense it in your soul. The—the attraction. Daddy wouldn't have to drug you. You'd find him irresistible."

He was scowling, punching up snow-depth read-outs as the vehicle crept through looming blue-white corridors. "Maybe I'd bond him to *me*! Suppose you tell me just how he works it."

Shannon opened her mind instead and showed him.

Merde et contremerde! Loathing spilled from Victor's mind before he sealed off.

She said: The bliss of it and the welcome pain are long gone and now the Absolute is formless and dry and all that drives me is the need to bring him down to take the power away and have him *know* that I did and for that I need your cooperation.

Victor swore again in French. He superimposed the snow-condition analog on the true-terrain display and discovered that the blip of the crawler was off-course. Somewhere they had missed the Alpine Garden Link just above the Six-Mile Post of the road. It was only a simple hiker's track cutting in a southerly direction across the windswept upper shoulder of the mountain. The crawler reversed, growled slowly backward in its own tread-prints. The headlights withdrawing made the snow-plastered crags seem weirdly artificial, like stage sets fading out.

Shannon said: You *must* help me. I warned you in time. I saved you from him.

Shut up! Let me think!

He saw the way on the right, rough as hell but open, along a gentle slope below Nelson Crag. He began to smile, retracted the ice-spikes, and deployed the flanges. The Sno-Crawler roared as he gunned the engine. "Only two kilometers left to go . . . Tell me: how much is your old man really worth?"

"I don't know. I doubt that he does. He controls more than a hundred big corporations, a TV network, two airlines, a major oil company, five big aerospace contractors—and that's only in North America. He has links to conglomerates in Europe, Japan, and Korea."

"What about this political thing? Does he really control the Republican party?"

"Not the whole thing. That'd be impossible—even for him. He does own four Senators and nineteen Representatives from key states. The politicians aren't operants, of course. Some are bought and paid for, some know they're the tools of special interest but don't realize that their strings are pulled by Daddy, and a few believe they've managed to retain their integrity even though they've accepted Daddy's help. Like the President of the United States."

"President Piccolomini? My ass!"

"President *Baumgartner*. He'll win the Millennial election next fall. Daddy's troupe of media consultants and PR hotshots and political-action committee fronts have it all worked out. Baumgartner is a forceful spokesman for law and order. He's hawkish on the Arab countries that have cut off our petroleum supplies and he's wary of Russia and China. He's willing to accept Daddy's antioperant strategy in order to exploit the backlash against President Pic. You know how antsy the normals have been getting, worrying about operants turning into thought police and that kind of malarky. The Sons of Earth thing was started deliberately in this country by Daddy's agents just to work up tensions for the upcoming election."

"Your old man is antioperant? I don't get it."

"Daddy sees Pic's Brain Trust and all the public-spirited operants as a personal threat. And they are, Victor. If there is ever any organized metapyschic education program in this country and operants become numerous and powerful, Daddy is bound to be exposed as an operant himself. A maverick one. He'll be ruined. Not financially—he's beyond that. But his edge will be lost. His source of power."

They drove on and on, over a surface that was now much smoother, tumbled granite rubble almost completely buried in deep, crusted snow, and wind-scoured slabs of rock that had been planed by the ice-age glaciers. In the hollows and in the lee of the occasional crag were drifts. Glittering spicules of ice danced in the crawler's headlights. On their left, the whiteness fell away to black and they began to skirt the top of Tuckerman Ravine at last. They could see the Headwall itself, a precipitous apron of untouched silver under the waning moon, which had risen above the crest of Wildcat and Carter Dome.

Victor decelerated, changed course to avoid a dangerous cornice of snow, then headed for the rim again. A moment later they stopped. He cut the engine and extinguished the exterior and interior illumination. Side by side, still imprisoned in their harnesses, they sat looking over the drop-off. There were sparkling strings and clusters of tiny building lights in the Wildcat Ski Area and along Pinkham Notch, where houses and roadside establishments lined the highway. Only a few cars and trucks were abroad. Most of the drivers had evidently found some congenial place to wait the Millennium out.

Victor unfastened his straps and hers. They went into the back of the cab to put on their ski boots and other equipment. Shannon unpacked the flares and checked her wristwatch. It was four minutes until midnight. Together, they climbed onto a rippled ice crust, carrying their skis. Victor had left the keys of the crawler in the ignition and now he slammed the door shut without locking it.

"Are you just going to leave the thing here?" she asked.

He gestured toward the summit. The antenna complex and other small structures were barely visible against a velvet sky dusted with incredible numbers of stars. In one of the buildings shone a little yellow light.

"Somebody from the weather station will put on fangy snowshoes and come down for the machine in the morning. It's a good thing the weather's calm. Some of the windblasts across this rock pile could blow our little ten-ton ice-buggy clear to Massachusetts."

They bent to their bindings and put on hard hats with heated visors. Neither had poles. Psychokinetics, whose minds are able to exert motive power affecting their own bodies, rarely have need of them.

Shannon peeled the wrapper from her magnesium flare, activated the ignitor, and held the smoky white light aloft. In an instant it cleared and blazed brightly. Over to the east, fireworks were exploding above Wildcat's slopes and a river of golden luminescence had begun to flow downhill. The new year had arrived and skiing torchbearers celebrated the date that popular acclamation had designated as millennial.

Shannon said, "Happy New Millennium, Victor."

He lifted his unwrapped cylinder. The tip lit with a loud concussion, activated by his own psychocreativity. "Happy postponement of doom, Shannon. For a little while, anyway."

She said: Will you help me? Not merely to kill him you understand he must be taken down at the peak of his hopes when he thinks the black Absolute is within his grasp.

When?

It's years away . . . but I'll let you know. Go your own way for now never act to threaten Daddy directly and you'll be safe from him. He's afraid of you at the same time that he's attracted. He'll wait. I have a plan of my own worked out. I'll explain it at the bottom of the slope after the schuss going back through the woods . . .

All right.

They maneuvered to the lip of the chasm. The descent was not vertical, it only seemed to be—a perfect expanse of powder, unimaginably deep, fresh, and clean.

GO.

Their minds pushed them off. They were on their way, flares held high, trailing twin plumes of nebulous white like a pair of comets on straight parallel paths into the dark.

14

STOCKHOLM, SWEDEN, EARTH
10 DECEMBER 2003

TRUMPETS PLAYED A FANFARE AND THE ORCHESTRA BEGAN THE national anthem. Queen Victoria Ingrid and her entourage entered the assembly hall of the Konserthuset and the audience, including Lucille Remillard and Gerard Tremblay up in the loges, rose to its feet. The ceremony had begun and the honors would be bestowed, too late to do any good.

Lucille's dark-green velvet gown was heavy, and she adjusted its folds unobtrusively with her PK. The metafaculty also served to hoist the tops of the wretched long white gloves, which persisted in slithering unmodishly down toward her elbows. Her feet, crushed into high-heeled pumps, ached in spite of her distrait attempts at self-redaction and so did her full breasts, deprived of baby Severin's milking for this one day of vain celebration. Some of her discomfort must have been evident, for Gerry Tremblay took her left arm to steady her, projecting his usual solicitude.

Oh Gerry never mind I'm all *right*.

None of your bitching darling I can tell when I'm needed your faithful esquire at your service m'lady Prop-Ups & Resuscitations Our Specialty.

Will you at *least* stay on the intimate mode or do you want every meta in the place to know the laureate's wife has sore feet and bursting boobs? There! Her Majesty's seated and down we go . . . *aah*.

Pauvre de toi.

Oh shut up . . . Goodness what a lot of diamonds! And furs do you suppose that's a *sable* it must be good grief what a difference from the ceremony for Jamie and Tamara at Oslo last year so friendly and modest—

—excepting the bomb scare!

Oh for heaven's sake you know what I mean even the King was as friendly and downtoearth as anyone but *this* crowd LordLord ostentation to the eyeballs I've never seen anything like—mate-moi ça! Can those be real emeralds let me deepsee . . . goodGod they are I see the inclusions and they're like *walnuts*!

There goes the brass section again darling afraid we'll have to rise again for the entrance of the heroes—

"No, madame and monsieur," came a whispered voice. "That will not be necessary."

Lucille turned in surprise. The seat on her right, which had been empty during the entrance of the Queen of Sweden, was now occupied by a distinguished-looking older man in white tie.

"This time," he continued softly, "only the Queen rises to honor the laureates as they enter. On this night, you see, they are mental royalty. Her equals."

"How charming," Lucille murmured. The music swelled as the laureates, paired with members of the Swedish institutions who had voted them the honor, entered the auditorium. To Lucille, the scene was unreal: the gilded hall with its statuary, rich drapery, sconces, and flags, the young Monarch in her sparkling white dress and tiara, standing at stage left giving anachronistic homage, and, above all—her husband. Yes, there was Denis, looking insignificant beside the Valkyrie splendor of a female professor of psychiatry of the Karolinska Institute, who would introduce and laud him. She scarcely noticed the other honorees of the evening; but behind them were seated rows of laureates from years past—including Jamie MacGregor and Tamara Sakhvadze, who had received the Peace Prize in 2002. Lucille would never have intruded her mind upon Denis at that moment; but she did not hesitate to call out to Tamara and Jamie on their intimate modes. Both looked up toward the loges where relatives of the laureates and other dignitaries were seated. Tamara smiled and projected understanding and comfort. Jamie projected an image of a winking eye and a species of mental cartoon, in which a rather tatty figure with a Nobel medallion hung about its neck sat on a snowy street corner proffering a beggar's cup; behind it was a sign: BROTHER, CAN YOU SPARE A GRANT?

The laureates and the others bowed their heads respectfully to the Queen and took their seats as the music played on, and then there was applause, and the Nobel Foundation chairman approached the lectern to give his salutatory address.

The man beside Lucille said, "It is an occasion for metapsychic operants to celebrate, is it not? There is your supremely talented husband, finally receiving the recognition he has long deserved, and his two great colleagues among the previously honored laureates, and the Prize in physics goes to Professor Xiong Ping-yung, for his formulation of the new Universal Field Theory incorporating life and mind into the mathematical fabric of the universe."

"And he's probably asking, just like we are," Gerry Tremblay put in, "whether anyone but a handful of academics and this overdressed Swedish mob scene cares."

The old gentleman chuckled quietly. "Things are that bad in your country?"

"And in most others," Lucille said. "It's a grand gesture being made here tonight, but one would appreciate it more if the pickets outside the Concert House went away."

"My country is a free one, as is yours, madame. But very many of us welcome you wholeheartedly." He bent minimally over her hand. "I am Dr. M. A. Paulson of the Karolinska. You are known to all, Madame la Doctoresse, and also the famous Dr. Tremblay."

"Not so famous as some," Gerry said, with a light laugh.

"It is well known that you are an eminent colleague of the Remillards, Doctor. Your own researches into coercivity are a foundation-stone upon which other researchers have erected many a scholarly edifice. Including tonight's Laureate in Medicine. Professor Remillard has been unstinting in his praise for your work, and his debt to you."

"We're members of the same team," Tremblay said. "Everything I am, I owe to Denis." His eyes were on the platform. "I'm the one who feels honored that he was able to make use of my findings."

Lucille said, "Gerry and Professor Glenn Dalembert have worked with my husband almost from the beginning, Dr. Paulson. And there've been many other colleagues at Dartmouth making their own invaluable contributions to the field of metapsychology." She smiled. "Even I."

"But the synthesis," Paulson whispered. "That is always the critical matter, is it not? So many workers, all adding their share to the growing body of knowledge—and then the one brilliant mind fashions of the bits and pieces a coherent whole."

"That's Denis, all right," said Gerry Tremblay. "And tonight he's finally being honored for it. It's a scandal that it's taken this long."

"Some of us on the Committee think so, too, Dr. Tremblay," the Swedish scientist said. "But the Karolinska, especially, is a most conservative body. We do not honor persons for a single discovery so much as for a continuing career of excellence."

"Oh, come on!" said Gerry archly. "It's all politics, and you know it. Denis's seminal work was *Metapsychology*, and that was published thirteen years ago. Since then he's just been elaborating on the theme. We all know why you waited so long, even though he's been nominated a dozen times—and we know why the Norwegians took ten years to cough up the Peace Prize for Jamie and Tamara. *They're* the real scandal. Everybody in the whole damn world knows they deserved to get the Nobel years ago, but the petty politicians hesitated to set a precedent by honoring superior mentalities. That's been Denis's problem, too—and even old Xiong's. He's been plugging away at his theory for damn near twenty years out there in Wuhan University. He was even nominated in 1988! But when the operants acknowledged their powers publicly, he did, too. Just a bit of telepathy and creativity, hardly enough to bother about when the rest of his brain—the conventional part—has Einstein beat six ways from Sunday. But that was enough to put your Royal Academy of Science in a snit, wasn't it? Old Professor Xiong wasn't playing fair—he was a superbrain!"

Heads were turning as Tremblay's passionate whispering became more and more audible. The elderly Swede listened with his head bowed. A burst of applause signaled the end of the Nobel Chairman's address and Gerry sat back, lips tight. Lucille's gloved hand stole over the armrest and squeezed Gerry's hand.

Simmer down Don Quixote . . .

And the Committee only coughed up the Prizes out of guilt *now that the metas are being persecuted now that the normals have turned on us . . .*

Gerry. You're off intimate again and there must be other metas in the audience. Please.

"What you have said is sadly true, Dr. Tremblay," Paulson admitted. "But we have tried to make amends, as the Norwegian Nobel Committee did in the case of Professor MacGregor and Academician Sakhvadze. We are dismayed by the disgraceful enmity that operants have had to suffer. Much of it has been due to fear and misunderstanding. Can you believe that normal-minded persons of goodwill have come to appreciate your predicament more fully with the coming of public demonstrations of intolerance?"

"We would like to believe it," Lucille said softly.

Down on the stage, a member of the Royal Academy of Science was proclaiming the merits of Xiong Ping-yung in Swedish. When he concluded his remarks, he addressed a few sentences of recapitulation in Chinese, addressing the old mathematician directly. Then the laureate rose from his seat, crossed the stage to the Queen, and bobbed his white head. Unlike most members of the glittering assembly, Xiong was dressed only in a simple black suit with a high collar. With their far-senses, Lucille and Gerry Tremblay could perceive the exchange of remarks between the laureate and the young Queen.

"I bow to you, Queen Victoria Ingrid, not as one who kowtows to royalty, but to honor the beautiful living symbol of a great nation that has honored me."

The Queen shook his hand, a glint of humor in her eyes. "I congratulate you, dear Professor Xiong. Here is your citation, and your medallion. Later, when you sit beside me at dinner in the Stadshuset, you must explain your Theory to me. If you can help me to make head or tail of it, I will gladly bow again to *you*."

The old man laughed delightedly, made a second obeisance, and returned to his seat amid applause.

"In years gone by," Dr. Paulson whispered, "the poor old chap would have had to go down off the stage via a flight of stairs to greet the monarch—then go up those stairs *backward* in order to show the proper respect! Our late King Gustaf abolished the custom. We Swedes do progress, you see, but slowly. It is the same all over the world. Old ways make way for the new, but often only after precarious and tentative transitions."

The winners of the Literature Prize and the Chemistry Prize were proclaimed, but Lucille watched and listened with a distracted mind. Paulson was right, of course. Right about the dangerous transition period. But could he also be right about the normals beginning to understand? The metapsychic backlash had only intensified since President Baumgartner took office. His abolition of the Brain Trust and sponsorship of the Benson Act prohibiting operants from seeking public office or serving on law-enforcement bodies was a savage piece of prejudice that the Supreme Court was debating even now. Of course the law was unconstitutional! It had to be . . .

Chin up Luce darling illegitimis non carborundum.

I'm sorry Gerry I know it's stupid of me to be brooding *here*.

The Nobel Prizes are going to give operants increased status you know help us to face down Baumgartner and the witch-burning yahoos the Court will rule in our favor it's got to we're citizens and the Benson Act is de facto disenfranchisement.

Of course it is. Why can't the normals get it through their heads that operancy is only relative? Its seeds are in every human mind! We can't go back to the Dark Ages operancy IS and it will continue to be. The trait has evolved and now it's becoming manifest in the population and you might as well try to outlaw brown eyes!

That's becoming plainer and plainer to them but they still hold the power and are afraid of losing it . . . And we're going to do something about that too.

? Gerry ? Is this another one of *her* great notions?

She has a name. You'll have to use it eventually when she becomes my wife I know you disapprove of her ideas but she's right the only way to avoid being oppressed is to have clout. Power.

. . . You are serious about her then.

Emilie agreed to a no-fault divorce last week. I didn't want to distract you or Denis with it. You were so excited about Stockholm. We're doing it as amicably as possible. Em will keep the house in Hanover and the kids and continue her part-time work at the Department. As for me . . . I didn't want to bother you with *that* either but I'll be leaving Dartmouth. Leaving academia. Shannon and I will be moving down to Cambridge. When the Benson Act is struck down, I'll run for Congress.

My God!

We operants have a lot to offer to normal society. But we're imbeciles if we sit by like pacifistic fools and let them set up the scaffolds. Massachusetts! Home of that old American custom burning witches! It's going to be our rallying point—

Another of Shannon O'Connor's ideas?

She's operant too . . . even if only a little bit.

Sometimes I wonder about that! . . . Gerry please don't present this to Denis as a fait accompli leave your options open for just a little while longer discuss it with him with Glenn and Sally and Mitch and the others we NEED you—

Not anymore you don't. What I had to give Denis took. And good luck to him.

!! . . .

"I have the honor to present now our Nobel Laureate in Medicine, Professor Denis Remillard of Dartmouth College in the United States of America."

The elderly Swedish doctor was nudging her gently, breaking her out of her distraction and pointing to the glittering stage. Denis was advancing toward the Queen, bowing in the graceful Japanese fashion, from the waist, as Ume Kimura had taught him, speaking to Her Majesty with smiling lips and grave, shadowed eyes. He received the leather box with the medal and the portfolio containing the citation, bowed again, and returned to his place. Lucille applauded wildly, realizing that she hadn't far-sensed a thing her husband had said to the Queen.

The ovation continued as the final honoree of the evening retired, and then a few brief words from the chairman closed the ceremony. The trumpets blared for the last time, the Queen withdrew, and the musicians played a sprightly Hugo Alfvén piece as a recessional for the laureates and the others on stage. Cars would be waiting outside to carry them, their relatives, and other honored guests to the gala dinner at the City Hall.

Lucille realized with a start that her cheeks were wet. "Gerry, wait for me while I go to the powder room. I'm a mess."

She fled, leaving Tremblay standing in the aisle behind the loges with Dr. Paulson.

"Will you be going to the dinner?" Tremblay inquired politely.

"No, I have had quite enough excitement for tonight. I will bid you adieu, Doctor. But before I go, please accept a bit of advice from an old man."

Gerry tried to look receptive.

"You feel in your heart that Denis Remillard wronged you by not granting you sufficient credit for your work. Whether he did or not is immaterial. Do not let your envy and disappointment drive you to a reckless course of action that may bring disaster upon you and all of your operant associates."

"I don't know what the hell you're talking about," Gerry laughed. "And I'm afraid you don't either."

"It is hard to work with genius. I really cannot blame you for fleeing. You know that in the laboratory you will only be competent and so you turn the beacon of your ambition in another direction. Be careful. You think falsely that Remillard used you. He did not—but certain others will."

Gerry Tremblay's face was immobile. He looked into the old man's gray eyes, probing with all his power, and met stone.

"I didn't think you'd change your mind," Paulson said. "But I thought I would make the try as long as I was here tonight anyway. It has been an evening to remember. Please give my fondest regards to Madame Remillard . . . and it may be some small consolation to you to know that even the great Xiong Ping-yung owes something of his monumental formulation to the thoughts of others. The germ of the Universal Field Theory was suggested to him by none other than I myself! But that was long ago and far away, and I have long since forgotten most of my higher mathematics. À bientôt, Dr. Tremblay." He walked off.

A nut, Gerry told himself. A salty old Swedish nut! He probably creeps out of the woodwork every year and makes a pest of himself at the Prize ceremony.

Forcing himself to believe this, he went off to find Lucille.

15

CHICAGO, ILLINOIS, EARTH
27 FEBRUARY 2004

KIERAN O'CONNOR: Come in, Gerry. I'm glad you could get here on such short notice. I wouldn't have torn you two lovebirds apart so soon after the honeymoon if it wasn't important . . . Shannon getting settled in the new place?

GERARD TREMBLAY: The house is crawling with interior decorators and carpet-layers. I'm glad to be out of the war zone for a little while.

O'CONNOR: Got your offices all set up in Cambridge?

TREMBLAY: Pretty well. Still trying to find the right staff.

O'CONNOR: Don't be in a rush. Where are you recruiting? My old Alma Mama, Harvard?

TREMBLAY: [laughs] I'm running as a Democrat, sir.

O'CONNOR: I understand there are still a *few* liberals lurking in the ivy . . . Sit down, for heaven's sake, man. And don't call me "sir." If you can't manage "Dad," try Kier. How about a drink? Cheer the cockles on a cold afternoon.

TREMBLAY: Thank you . . . Kier. [Looks around in awed admiration.] My God, what a view from this office! On a clear day—

O'CONNOR: You can see Milwaukee. Less smog than there used to be. One good by-product of the energy shortage, at any rate . . . Scotch? Sherry? Campari?

TREMBLAY: Campari and soda would be fine.

O'CONNOR: Did you enjoy Nuku Hiva?

TREMBLAY: It was fantastic, sir—Kier. I don't have the EE faculty, you see, so I've never been able to indulge in mental

145

globe trotting. Or the regular kind, either, on an Associate Professor's salary!

O'CONNOR: That'll change.

TREMBLAY: I'm looking forward to it.

O'CONNOR: No false pride, eh? That's a healthy sign.

TREMBLAY: Shannon and I understand each other. Her money will be a means to an end. An end that both of us feel is infinitely worthwhile.

O'CONNOR: That end of yours is the reason I asked you to come here to confer with me. We don't know one another very well yet, Gerry. That is . . . you don't know me. I've been interested in your political aspirations, and I'll confess that I watched you there in New Hampshire even before you and my little girl worked together on the Millennial Democratic presidential campaign. Both of you have made friends in the Party who'll do you a lot of good now that you've decided to seek office yourself.

TREMBLAY: I have Shannon's good advice to thank for any success I might have had as a campaign aide. And of course, she funded our caucus's effort. That took a lot of courage when the whole country knew *you* were for Baumgartner.

O'CONNOR: Shannon is a grown woman with a right to her own opinions and political loyalties. Having metafaculties herself—even though they're very modest ones—she was very upset when Baumgartner's campaign took on an antioperant stance. She broke with the Republican people here in Illinois over the issue and decided to go all-out for Kennedy. And what better state to do it in than New Hampshire?

TREMBLAY: It was great for a gesture. But to really *do* something in the political arena, one needs a state with a bigger population base.

O'CONNOR: [laughs] More clout! You don't have to tell me. I was born in Massachusetts. You made a wise change of domicile, Gerry, and I wish you good luck in your campaign . . . But wishes are a penny a peck, right? I want to help you in a concrete fashion as well. Not with money, because Shannon's got more than you need, but with people. I want you to accept the services of two of the finest political advisers in the country—Len Windham of Research/Market/Data, and Neville Garrett, whose agency handles media liaison for top people in both parties.

TREMBLAY: Kier . . . I don't know what to say!

O'CONNOR: Just say yes. They'll send people up to Cambridge tomorrow to begin coordinating your campaign.

TREMBLAY: Well, of course! My God, I never dreamed . . . a conservative like you . . . but *why*? It can't be because I'm your son-in-law. I'm not a fool . . .

O'CONNOR: Can't you read my mind, Gerry?

TREMBLAY: No, sir! For a normal, you're one of the most opaque mentalities I've ever run across. And we operants don't read minds with the facility that normals credit us with. That's just one of the myths—the misunderstandings that have got to be cleared up if this antioperant hysteria isn't to balloon into a national tragedy.

O'CONNOR: Exactly my own feeling. Partisan politics and fundamentalist bullshit shouldn't dictate national policy on an issue as sensitive as metapsychic operancy. Dammit—my own little girl is a *head*! I can't stand by while fanatical assholes call her and people like her freaks or servants of Satan! This is the United States of America, not some benighted camel-jockey theocracy run by ayatollahs! I was deeply disturbed by the antioperant position Baumgartner took in his last campaign and by his support of the Benson legislation. We can thank God that the Supreme Court tied a can to *that* piece of madness.

TREMBLAY: But Senator Benson has been one of your protégés for years—

O'CONNOR: No more, by Christ! Man's turned into some kind of religious nut in his old age. A senile Gray Eminence. I blame *him* for pushing the antioperant position on Baumgartner. I don't believe that the President sincerely espouses the vicious canards being circulated about you people. I think he's uninformed, and he's been influenced by bad advice.

TREMBLAY: His antioperant stance helped win him the Millennial

election. Whether Baumgartner acted out of conviction or
from expediency—

O'CONNOR: Yes, yes, I see what you're driving at. But what *I'm*
trying to say is that Baumgartner's not a lost cause! Gerry, I
don't believe Kennedy has a hope in hell of unseating the
President this fall. We're going to have another four years of
Baumgartner, for better or worse. But with you in the House
of Representatives, you'll be in a legitimate position to
counter the antioperants. Baumgartner's my friend. When I
talk, he listens! I'll admit he hasn't been listening lately . . .
but we have a good chance of changing that now that the
Supreme Court has struck down the Benson Act. Baumgartner's no fool. He'll change if it seems politic to do so.
Your job—our job!—is to upgrade the operant image so he'll
be forced to repudiate the fanatics.

TREMBLAY: And bring back the Brain Trust?

O'CONNOR: Mm'mm . . . have to go slow on that, Gerry. The old
Trust was dominated by academics who were totally out of
touch with the prevailing mood of normal voters. There was
an elitist smell to them that didn't sit well with the American
psyche. It was ridiculous for Copeland to plump for Cabinet
status for what was merely a presidential advisory commission. And downright suicidal for Ellen Morrison and those
Stanford people to persist in lobbying for universal metapsychic testing when it was plain that the mind of the country
was against it. Once the nuclear menace was out of the way,
the Psi-Eye program began to seem more of a threat than a
benefit. *You* know! An American equivalent of the KGB's
Twentieth Directorate . . .

TREMBLAY: When I'm elected, I'm going to push for programs
that will use operants in ways clearly beneficial to the normal
majority. No elite corps . . . no thought police . . . concentrate
on *good* powers . . . how about redaction, f'rinstance? Psychic
healing works! But wha'd you hear about it? Nothing. EE got
all the funding . . . yeah, and now *none* of the meta programs
got funding . . . my field, coercivity . . . take delinquent kids
and turn them around . . . funny . . . kind of dizzy . . .

O'CONNOR: Are you feeling all right, Gerry? You look a bit pale.

TREMBLAY: Maybe . . . maybe I'm coming down with a bug. Feel lightheaded.

O'CONNOR: And I called you halfway across the country when you belong in bed! Gerry, you should have told me.

TREMBLAY: Felt . . . felt all right this morning . . . funny . . .

O'CONNOR: Easy, my boy. Give me the glass. Good. Just relax. Close your eyes for a minute or two. Close your eyes. Rest. Rest, Gerry.

TREMBLAY: Rest . . .

O'CONNOR: Rest, Gerry. [Touches intercom.]

ARNOLD PAKKALA: Yes, sir?

O'CONNOR: Dr. Tremblay and I will be here for a while longer, Arnold. But there's no need for you and the rest of the staff to wait.

PAKKALA: Whatever you say, sir.

O'CONNOR: [after an interval] Gerry. Can you hear me? No? *Can you hear me now Gerry?*

TREMBLAY: Yes.

O'CONNOR: *Good. Relax Gerry. Relax with your eyes closed. I'm going to turn off the lights and then I want you to open your eyes and look at me. Do you understand?*

TREMBLAY: *Yes . . . God! The colors the colors singing purple and gold sungold bittersweet cloud the liquid depths the colors and the perfume and the ambrosia O God . . .*

O'CONNOR: *Fly away into it Gerry let me lift you fly away.*

TREMBLAY: *BeautifulbeautifulGodsowonderfulamazing . . . God! J'ai besoin de toi . . .*

O'CONNOR: *Of course you need me and I need you. Fly Gerry, Fly.*

TREMBLAY: *Who are you what are you don't leave me . . .*

O'CONNOR: *Je suis ton papa ta maman ton amour ton extase!*

TREMBLAY: *Extase!*

O'CONNOR: *Look closely at me. Beyond the colored light.*

TREMBLAY: *Bright too bright the light hurts my eyes Papa . . .*

O'CONNOR: *There my son close your poor pained eyes see how comforting the black. But I had to see all of you Gerry how special you are so much better than all the others the mind elaborated into full trained operancy sensitive and subtle an educated mind a psychologist with professional insight into secrets hidden from small minds yes my son my beautiful one you'll understand I'll have so much to show you and it will bring joy to you as you serve.*

TREMBLAY: *Papa why are you black now?*

O'CONNOR: *The Absolute is black and I reside there. When there was neither sun nor moon nor earth nor planets nor starry universe there was the dark and in it was calm and an end and there will be again.*

TREMBLAY: *Black the deep black the inaccessible black from which all things come and to which they go . . .*

O'CONNOR: *Yes! Clever son beautifulbrained son to see in the dark the form of the Formless the meaning of the engima yes yes the source of life is death and all light finds its end in deep night in the negation of the Absolute.*

TREMBLAY: *God?*

O'CONNOR: *He is light we reject him and his burning.*

TREMBLAY: *No no no LIGHT CREATION LIFE GROWTH DIF-FERENTIATION COMPLEXIFICATION MENTATION COA-DUNATION UNITY LIGHT . . .*

O'CONNOR: *A sham a joke a cruel hoax they lead only to pain. Creation groans! He is a God of pain we are born in it live in it die in it he wills it for all his creatures for all growth is pain inescapable. But there is a secret way I know a way I share with my beloved ones in a great antithesis! We do not create we destroy the dark is our birthright our Black Mother whose belly is a void that takes us in . . . dam dham nam tam tham dam dham nam pam pham . . . to consummation.*

TREMBLAY: *Papa Papa I don't understand I'm afraid of the dark!*

O'CONNOR: *Darkness is fearful only when viewed by the fleeing turn around accept it embrace it know it love it.*

TREMBLAY: *But how?*

O'CONNOR: *Make your own darkness behind closed eyes follow me along the Left-Hand Path an old neglected way but one that annihilates the corrupting Light the painful Light follow me into the Black and together we will know a moment of ineffable beauty the one perfect and final joy: leading all into the void.*

TREMBLAY: *I understand. It's true. I'm tired of pain. Show me. Papa show me . . .*

O'CONNOR: *Come.*

O'CONNOR: . . . Gerry? Can you hear me, boy? Gerry?

TREMBLAY: God. Kier? What happened. Jesus, did I pass out?

O'CONNOR: Seems like it. How do you feel now?

TREMBLAY: A little woozy. But I think I'm okay. Dammit, there's this flu thing going around back East . . .

O'CONNOR: I'm going to take you out to the house and we'll have Doc Presteigne check you out.

TREMBLAY: Listen, I'm feeling okay. Really! . . . Now, this lobbying you wanted me to do on President Baumgartner. You realize that a freshman Congressman's influence on a President of the opposition party is going to be just about nil—

O'CONNOR: Not so. He's going to like you, Gerry. And listen to you! *He will do as you want as I want just as you will . . .*

TREMBLAY: You want me to coerce him.

O'CONNOR: That's an ugly word. *Persuade* him! . . . And the message you'll be getting across is a very important one. We were discussing it just before you dozed off on me, boy. Do you remember? We want Baumgartner to *keep pressing for antioperant legislation.* The Benson Act is dead, but we can lobby for other laws that will be in our best interests. Laws restricting operants. Who is in a better position to warn the country about operancy's dangers than you, Gerry? You've seen them conspiring to take power . . . You know what mischief ambitious or evil-minded heads are capable of . . . Don't you Gerry? *Don't you?*

TREMBLAY: Yes.

O'CONNOR: President Baumgartner has begun to get soft. We put him in the White House and now that he's a shoo-in for a second term the bastard's forgotten who his friends are! His mind is normal, but he's a tough nut, Gerry. He was an astronaut and a corporation president, you know. Nobody's patsy.

TREMBLAY: Your other people can no longer handle him . . .

O'CONNOR: So *you're* going to work on him. Subtly. Using post-hypnotic suggestion and subliminal hints most of the time and saving direct coercion for critical situations. He must never have the remotest notion of what you're up to. You'll have to be artful in the presentation of your public persona as well. On the face of it, you'll be a liberal Democrat championing the rights of operant metapsychics and other minorities.

TREMBLAY: Yes.

O'CONNOR: *You see my overall plan, don't you Gerry? The rightness of it the brilliance the inevitability?*

TREMBLAY: *Yes yes oui oui mon cher Papa . . .*

O'CONNOR: Fine! Now let's get our coats. The rush-hour traffic on the East-West Freeway should be past now, and we'll have an easy trip out to the house. [Touches office-garage key-pad.] Frankie? You want to bring the Bentley around? Thanks a lot.

16

WASHINGTON, DC, EARTH
20 JANUARY 2005

WITH HER WAY CLEARED BY THE SECRET SERVICE BODYGUARD, Nell Baumgartner rushed into the Capitol Rotunda. To be late for her husband's second inauguration! Oh, please, God, she begged. Not that . . . And the *news*! How would Lloyd react? Should she tell him now or wait until after the swearing-in ceremony?

Agent Rasmussen, holding her arm, said, "It's going to be okay, Mrs. Baumgartner. The Chief Justice is just coming up to the platform. You're going to make it."

The huge white-marble chamber was chilly even though it was packed with people—members of Congress, White House staffers, influential Republicans, and personal friends and relatives of the First Couple. Outside a blizzard was raging, and so the inauguration was being held indoors for the first time since 1985. The blizzard had delayed the First Lady's dash from Reagan Jetport. She had landed in Washington only a half hour earlier after flying from the bedside of her two-year-old granddaughter, Amanda Denton.

The Marine Band finished playing as Agent Rasmussen and the First Lady reached the platform. She composed herself, took a deep breath, and smiled radiantly at her husband. His returning smile echoed relief. The child was going to be all right.

She was dimly aware of people standing close by—the Vice President and his wife; the Senate Majority Leader, Benjamin T. Scrope; the Speaker of the House, Elijah Scraggs Benson; and there was the Party Chairman, Jason Cassidy, and beside him their old friend and long-time supporter, Kieran O'Connor, with his daughter Shannon and his son-in-law Congressman Tremblay. Shannon Tremblay's eyes were wide with concern. Had she heard about little Amanda's crisis? Nell Baumgartner gave the young woman what she hoped was a reassuring wink. An instant later she forgot Shannon as a Bible was placed in her hands—the one she would hold while the President took his Oath of Office.

The Chief Justice of the Supreme Court stepped forward, her face solemn. The President placed his left hand upon the book, which was opened to Psalm 8, the prayer he had recited years ago when he first set foot on the Moon. He raised his right hand.

"I do solemnly swear that I will faithfully execute the Office of the President of the United States and will to the best of my ability preserve, protect and defend the Constitution of the United States."

Then the band was playing, and he was moving to the lectern where he would deliver the Inaugural Address, and she only had seconds to tell him, and she thought, *Should I*? And it seemed that a voice was warning her to forbear, to let it be . . . but she knew what was in the speech Lloyd was about to deliver and she could not let him go ahead without knowing—

The music was drawing to a close. Swiftly, she stepped up to him and touched his sleeve. He turned.

"Little Amanda is all right, Lloyd," she whispered. "The neurologists at Johns Hopkins say it isn't epilepsy at all. Lloyd—our granddaughter is going to be a metapsychic operant. It was the spontaneous breakthrough from latency that caused the convulsions."

The President said only, "They're certain?" And Nell nodded, then stepped back.

The music stopped. All eyes in the Rotunda were on the President. He folded the sheets of paper he had just moments before placed in front of the microphones, and put them into his inside breast pocket. "My friends," he began, "the Inaugural Address I had prepared no longer seems appropriate. In order for you to understand why, I'm going to share with you some very startling news that my wife Nell has just brought to me . . ."

He paused, passing his hand across his forehead, and there were murmurs of amazement from the audience. But then he straightened and spoke resolutely for ten minutes, and at the end there was a shocked silence, and then subdued applause with a rising undercurrent of voices that the Marine Band finally drowned out with "Hail to the Chief."

Shannon O'Connor Tremblay said: Well Daddy?

And her father replied: It will be up to Gerry and he damn well better not let us down.

17

FROM THE MEMOIRS OF ROGATIEN REMILLARD

HALLOWEEN 2007.

I have a zapshot here before me to jog my memories of that day. It shows three cunning little devils—my great-nephews Philip, Maurice, and Severin, aged ten, eight, and four at the time—

costumed as imps for the holiday, in a blatant piece of typecasting, by their long-suffering nanny Ayeesha.

Thanks to Ghostly confidences, I knew at the time that the boys would grow up to be Founding Magnates of the Concilium. Thanks to Ghostly compassion, I did *not* know that one of them would perish in the Metapsychic Rebellion of 2083, fighting to extricate the human race from the Galactic Milieu . . . But that is another story that must wait to be told. I will write now of events that led to the Intervention, and my own peculiar role as a bit player in them . . .

All that day, my bookshop had been under siege by poltergeists, for by then Hanover crawled with the offspring of operant metapsychics. Every Halloween, in the old American tradition, local merchants endured an endless stream of costumed youngsters extorting treats, the donation of which was supposed to render one immune from tricks. In my youth, trick-or-treat escapades were tame: soaped windows, upset trash cans, demounted garden gates, toilet-paper festoons on shrubs and—in the case of notorious neighborhood ogres—walks and porches defiled with smashed jack-o'-lanterns and rotten eggs. In the new Age of the Mind, however, Halloween had become the one day in the year when operant youngsters could release their inhibitions more or less with impunity. Reined in by parental coercion the rest of the time, the kids tended to go bananas once they put on their costumes and set out to pillage and plunder. By unwritten law the deviltry was restricted to those under the age of twelve, and no property was to be destroyed or rendered so befouled or bollixed as to require expensive repairs. Aside from that, the sky was the limit.

My bookshop, as I have mentioned, primarily suffered the onslaught of poltergeists. The books on the shelves would dance and tumble to the floor; the window displays (of expendable volumes) were in a perpetual state of manic frenzy; the little customer reading area in the front righthand part of the store had chairs and ashtrays dancing and rag rugs curling and writhing on the floor. Poor Marcel LaPlume, my huge Maine Coon cat, had retreated to the basement storage room after being harassed one

time too many by hailstorms of Cat Chow levitated from his dish
and mind-generated static charges that set his fur crackling. I had
a big bowl of Snickers candy bars as tribute to the invaders, but
as often as not the operant children would thank me for the treat
—then pull off the trick anyhow on their way out of the shop.

Another unwritten rule was that the depredations should cease
by 2200 hours. My shop was not ordinarily open so late on
weekdays, but only a madman would have closed up early on
Halloween and left the premises unguarded. That year, as the
evening of pranks came to a close, I wondered why I had not yet
been visited by Denis and Lucille's children. As it drew on toward quarter to ten, I concluded that they were saving me until
last, and had planned some particularly gross piece of mischief
for poor old Uncle Rogi.

My farsense tingled. I looked up from the catalog I had been
perusing and caught a glimpse of disappearing horns and red
grease-painted small faces outside. My deep-vision identified the
lurkers and I braced myself.

The door opened by itself and the chime rang eerily. Three
telepathic voices sang:

> Did you ever think, as a hearse goes by,
> That you might be the next to die?
> They wrap you up in a long white sheet,
> And bury you down about six feet deep!

Giggles, instantly squelched, came from the mind of four-
year-old Sevvy. The songsters paused . . . and I saw coming in the
door and inching along the polished floorboards a flood of white,
slimy little things—hundreds of them—glistening as they looped
and squirmed into my shop. And the inevitable chorus of the old
children's song:

> The worms crawl in! The worms crawl out!
> The worms play pinochle in your mouth!
> Your body turns a mossy green,
> And pus runs out like thick ice cream!

The three juvenile devils, shepherding their obscene cohort, came bounding in, squealing and laughing.

Trick or treat Uncle Rogi!

The books danced a fandango. The drawer of my antique cash register flew open with a jangling crash and the bills and loose change fountained up, then rained down into the midst of the wriggling maggoty mass on the floor.

"Call them off!" I bellowed.

Promise to teach us dirty French!

"Jamais!"

The worms crawl in the worms crawl out . . .

"That does it," I intoned ominously. "There's only one way to deal with this situation." I reached into my trouser pocket. "Beware! Beware, all you alien invaders! Beware the power of the *Great Carbuncle*!"

I held up my key chain, with its dangling fob of a red-glass marble caught in a little metal cage. Using an old trick of creativity that had long delighted the children, I made the thing glow. At the same time, I smote the three young minds with my adult coercion, freezing them in the midst of their capers and cutting off the PK motive-power of the lolloping larvae.

The boys screamed. Their tongues protruded and their eyes bugged out of their grotesquely painted faces, and one after another they fell to the floor—at a safe distance from the now motionless mélange of icky lucre and nameless white things.

I waved the Great Carbuncle over the lot of them in a coup de grâce, then laughed and canceled the coercion. The boys jumped up shrieking with mirth and I told them to wait while I loaded my still-video camera with a fresh floppy disk. They posed, grimacing, while I took their zapshot.

"Let's see it! Let's see it!" they shouted, and would have raced into the back room of the shop where the computer and video-printer were if I hadn't once again stopped them in their tracks.

"Who," I demanded sternly, "is going to clean up this disgusting mess?"

Little Severin grinned up at me winsomely. "It's only cut-up spaghetti, Uncle Rogi. Didn't it make *great* worms?"

"Great," I sighed, wondering how many of my fellow merchants on Main Street had been similarly victimized.

"Let's print the picture!" Philip said.

"Do it quick, Uncle Rogi," Maury added. "Mom'll kill us if we don't get home by twenty-two."

I took a plastic sack and three pieces of cardboard out of my wrapping supplies. "First you take these, and scoop up the worms and the money. When you get home tonight I expect you to sort the money out, wash it, and bring every nickel of it back to me tomorrow after school."

The telephone rang. Admonishing the imps to get cracking, I answered. It was Denis, not wanting to trust my telepathy.

"We've had some bad news." Immediately he added, "Not any of the family. But I want you to come over to the house. This new development makes the damn Coercer Flap look like a practical joke."

"The kids are here. I'll bring them." I hung up. "Leave that! Bas les pattes, kids, we're going home."

Their minds caught my serious intent instantly and they changed from devils into obedient operant children. I turned off the shop lights and we hustled out and around the corner and down South Street a block and a half to the family home. There were only a few costumed children still abroad. We hurried past the library, where the collection of pumpkins carved by Hanover youngsters and displayed in the forecourt was a predictable shambles. I was surprised to see five cars parked in front of Denis and Lucille's place. As we tramped up the front steps the door opened and the nanny, Ayeesha Al-Joaly, who was strongly suboperant, shooed the children upstairs and indicated to me mentally that I should join the others in the living room.

Most of the Coterie was there. Glenn and his wife Colette, Sally and Tater McAllister, and big Eric Boutin, who had taken over as Denis's chief PR person with the defection of Gerry Tremblay, were gathered around a bound atlas open on the coffee table, talking in low voices. Denis, Tukwila Barnes, and Mitch Losier were seated on dining-room chairs, side by side, with Lucille hovering behind them. All three were in a state of EE trance. The TV set on the wall had its audio turned off and the picture showed a murky aerial view of some city on a plain with a considerable mountain range in the background. Many of the city buildings were in flames and others, broken and devastated, poured out clouds of black smoke.

"My God, what's happened?" I cried.

Lucille hurried to me, her finger to her lips, mentally indicating the excorporeals who were obviously in the process of far-sensing the disaster. She said:

Alma-Ata. And other places as well. It looks as though full-scale civil war has broken out in Soviet Central Asia, abetted by outsiders. They targeted Alma-Ata especially because of the operant educational facility at the university.

Tamara—?

Safe! After the Congress in Montréal she and the three children and Pyotr stopped off on the way home to stay for a time with Jamie in Edinburgh . . . You knew that Tamara's middle son Ilya and Katie MacGregor announced their engagement last week?

No.

Well they did. And the pair made a trip to Islay to see Jamie's old grandmother who's 96 and they took their time because you know how grim things have been in Alma-Ata this year with the fighting so close by. They were to leave for home two days from now it's some kind of miracle they escaped but the *others* the best of the Soviet academic operants the cream of the researchers oh Rogi the PEACEMAKERS so many of them concentrated there the top minds God the university area is a fire-storm Tucker is scanning the situation but we're afraid we're so afraid . . .

What time is it in Alma-Ata?

Early morning. Everyone was on the commute in the streets students and teachers and all the university people the planes came from Peshawar in Pakistan over the high ranges Stealthed of course and Soviet Muslim sympathizers sabotaged phased-array radars in Pamirs and a key detector-satellite relay of course Moscow scrambled their interceptors but it was too late suicidal Muslim pilots screaming Din! Din! Din! certain they were on their way to Paradise—

Tukwila Barnes, the Native American who was probably the

most talented EE adept in the Coterie, opened his eyes and made a small moaning sound. Lucille turned away from me and rushed to help him. He was ashen and trembling and his black eyes spilled tears. He began to twitch and flail his arms involuntarily then, as though he were falling into some kind of epileptic fit. I strode over and helped Lucille hold him while Colette Roy gave him a shot of something. When the medication hit him he crumpled, but he was a lightweight and I caught him easily and carried him to one of the couches. Somebody brought an afghan to cover him and Colette propped his head with cushions. We all stood there waiting for him to pull out of it. When he did, there was no need for him to speak. From his shocked mind poured images of holocaust, broadcast at an awful psychic amplification. From elsewhere in the house I heard the little Remillard boys shriek out loud and the baby, two-year-old Anne, begin a panicky wailing.

"Shit," whispered Glenn Dalembert. He knelt beside Tucker and placed a hand on his forehead. He was the most powerful coercer in the group aside from Denis, and as he took hold of the EE adept's mind the cataract of nightmare sensations chopped off.

He said, "Got him. Colette, you and Lucille see to the kids."

Slowly, Barnes responded to the sedative. His eyes calmed and when he finally said, "Okay," Glenn turned him loose. Sally Doyle proffered a glass of water. Tucker shook his head. "Not now . . . might barf . . . God, I don't see how any of them could have escaped."

"Did they drop nukes?" Eric Boutin asked.

Barnes shook his head. "Conventional high explosives—but top-of-the-line. Alma's not *that* big a city. Eleven planes got through and it was enough. The university is just gone."

Nobody said anything. Nobody even seemed to be thinking anything.

Finally, Glenn said to Tucker, "Just lie there. We're still waiting for Denis and Mitch to get back. Denis is overviewing and Mitch went to check out the Kremlin. Soviet news says that the whole goddamn Central Asian region erupted in simultaneous armed revolt. They claim to be on top of things—but about twenty minutes ago CNN reported that there had been a big Iranian attack on the Soviet oil fields and refineries around Baku on the Caspian Sea."

"Supported by a ground insurrection," said Denis.

Everybody turned around.

He had risen from his chair, and although his face was pinched and pale and his eyes seemed to peer from deep inside his skull, he was in full control of both body and mind. He went to the fireplace, where a blaze had been kindled in honor of the holiday, and warmed his hands. Colorful gourds, pumpkins, and corn dollies were displayed on the mantel.

"First I did a broad scan, roughly below the forty-fifth parallel," Denis said. He watched the leaping flames. "I tried to far-sense massive stress emanations from among the normal populace. There seemed to be a dozen or more distinct foci between the Tien Shan and the Caspian: Alma-Ata, Frunze, Tashkent, Dushanbe . . . Let me see that atlas." He went to the coffee table and bent over the map, stabbing with his finger. "Here, here, here—all these cities east of Tashkent where the Uzbek revolt was concentrated. Up for grabs again." He turned to another page showing the Caspian region. "I did a closer scan in here, around Baku and up the west coast of the sea. This is the Azerbaidzhan Republic, a tough bunch of Turks with a history of resistance to Moscow rule. What evidently happened was that a flight of B-1Ds from Tehran came in at near water-level and bombed hell out of Baku itself, its two big pipelines and the railroad and highway links to the west, and the other pipeline and refinery complex up the coast at Makhachkala. The local insurgents simultaneously set off blasts in just about every refinery, pumping station, and airfield from Makhachkala south to the Iranian border."

"Christ," said Tater McAllister. "Coupled with the oil losses from the Uzbek fields, this new strike really puts the Soviets in deep shit."

Denis said, "The Azerbaidzhan region will be very hard for Moscow to pacify using ground forces. They've already sent in paratroops and gunboats from the naval base at Astrakhan on the Volga, but the Uzbek revolt left the Red Army short of reliable infantry and armor units. This new flare-up may be more than

Kumylzhensky can handle without heavy air-strikes against the insurgent cities—or even the tactical use of neutron bombs . . ."

I said, "The damn country's falling apart!"

"Not quite," Denis said. "It can cut its losses by abandoning the Central Asian republics and concentrating on regaining the really critical Azerbaidzhan region . . . It's only a matter of time, I'm afraid, before Moscow declares war on Iran and Pakistan." He glanced at Mitch Losier, who was still sitting in his straight chair, lost in the EE aether. "When Mitch gets back, he may have some information about that."

Lucille and Colette returned from dealing with the children, and Denis flashed them a detailed recap of his discoveries. We all found places to sit down. (I was on the floor in a corner, keeping my mouth and mind shut now as became one who was only an honorary member of the Coterie.) Eric Boutin deftly served coffee and tea from the Krupps unit built into the low table. The conversation fragmented.

Lucille told Denis that the children had been calmed and a redactive wipe-job performed upon their trauma, which was fortunately shallow. Ayeesha had taken a tranquilizer and was saying her worry beads. Tukwila Barnes declared that he was famished and brought in the basket of candy treats that had been left in the front hallway to serve the neighborhood urchins. Tater, Glenn, and Colette discussed the latest developments in the Coercer Flap, starring the black sheep of the Coterie, Gerard Tremblay. The Congressman from Massachusetts now stood charged with the crime of aggravated assault upon the President of the United States and interfering with a federal official in the performance of his official duties. Justice Department lawyers were wrangling over what other charges might apply in the case. Gerry had done the dirty deed on Monday. This was Wednesday. One might wonder what other surprises the week had in store . . .

And one would not have long to wait before finding out.

Mitch Losier coughed, opened his eyes, and sighed. He was the most solid and comfortable-looking of the Coterie, which ran to ectomorphic cerebral types. His tonsure of graying hair gave him the air of a kindly pastor or a country doctor. With the attention of the group now riveted on him—for he had excursed to

Moscow—he stood up, stretched, and went to the table to accept a cup of tea from Eric. He added sugar and then made his contribution to the roster of catastrophe.

"Moscow has declared war against each and every Islamic nation of the world. While reserving the right to retaliate in response to today's attacks, it will forbear force of arms temporarily and attempt to resolve the conflict through peaceful means, in consultation with the heads of state of Iran, Pakistan, Turkey, and the Kashmiri Republic."

"Thank God!" Lucille cried.

"That's the good news." Mitch stirred his tea and sipped. "The bad news is, that motherfucker Kumylzhensky has arrested every metapsychic operant in the Soviet Union. In the light of today's surprise strike, he feels their loyalty to the nation is deeply suspect. They are to be interrogated and held in custody until the state of internal emergency has passed, and then put on trial for treason."

In those dark days, when even persons of goodwill were soul-burdened with the malign aetheric resonances of hatred, fear, and suffering, there were many people in the United States who watched the disintegration of the Soviet Union with righteous triumphalism: the godless Commies had finally got what was coming to them. For the Sons of Earth movement, however, the Soviet misfortune had an ironic twist. To the Sons—who had very nearly become respectable among the American underclass by that time—all operants, including most especially the Soviets, were involved in a conspiracy to destroy religion, freedom, and the sovereign rights of individuals. Yet here was the Red military dictator himself denouncing the superminds as "the greatest menace the Communist Revolution had ever faced." As Kumylzhensky thundered on about the alleged misdeeds of the Twentieth Directorate, it became evident to world observers that the KGB as a whole had been acting to bring about the downfall of Party and military right-wingers, and restore the impetus toward an open society in the Soviet Union that had been so tragically reversed following the death of Kumylzhensky's predecessor. Excorporeal excursions by outsiders into the cells of the purged operants revealed their motivation to the world. The EE adepts of dozens of nations became witnesses for the defense—at least in the forum of public opinion. Even the most naïve and fearful normals eventually came to believe that the imprisoned Soviet operants had been a force for good, not evil.

In America, the hard-core membership of the Sons of Earth would eventually talk their way around this ideological paradox; but the movement had lost much of its momentum, along with any semblance of a moral base for its antioperant position. All over the world religious leaders—even some Muslims—made resounding statements in favor of operant civil rights. The Pope finally got around to issuing an encyclical, *Potestates Insolitae Mentis*, affirming that human metapsychic powers are a part of the natural order, by no means devilish, and as "good" in the eyes of God as any other part of his creation—provided those powers are not abused.

It was a watershed time, even though we operants did not realize it. From then on, even in spite of the Coercer Flap and other operant high crimes and misdemeanors, the surge of blind antioperant prejudice began to decline. The reversal was not an overnight affair. Pockets of antioperant fanaticism remained in the United States and would be exploited on the very eve of the Intervention. But the majority of otherwise worthy people who had been infected by fear and the prejudice of ignorance slowly experienced a change of heart that would bear unexpected fruit just when the most valiant champions of operancy faced their darkest hour.

18

BAIE COMEAU, QUÉBEC, EARTH
5 FEBRUARY 2008

"WE HAVE ALL WAITED A LONG TIME FOR THIS!" VICTOR REMIL-lard was speaking his Yankee version of Canuckois into a loud-hailer. "And it seemed as though the damned process was never going to work right, and some of us were tempted to abandon the project, and dump the holy bacteria and their dedicated keepers into the Saint-Laurent . . . I know *I* was tempted."

The bundled-up audience of refinery workers and gaugers and tanker crew members yelled and whistled their appreciative un-belief, and their thoughts were plain to read: You, boss? Give up? Tu te fiches de nous! Don't try to kid us!

Victor gave a comical shrug and joined in the laughter. He was wearing an old mangy raccoon coat and a long knitted muffler and a white hard hat like those of the workers—only dirtier and more dented. Standing beside him, Shannon O'Con-nor could not have been more of a contrast, swathed in ankle-length arctic fox and holding an empty silver champagne bucket. It was her tanker waiting at dockside to take on the cargo.

"When we conquered the production problems, we discovered we had distribution problems," Victor declaimed. "And we solved that, too. And today this refinery of ours is ready to ship its first batch of lignin-derived gasohol fuel to energy-starved Europe!"

Everybody cheered.

"I know you're wondering why we're standing out here freez-ing our pétards off, while inside the plant all those pampered germs are gobbling pulpwood in nice warm vats and shitting liq-uid gold. So I'll cut the speechmaking short and show you just what we've been waiting for—and what Mme. Tremblay's tanker's been waiting for!"

There were more cheers while Shannon handed him the silver bucket in exchange for the hailer. Victor positioned the container under a huge flexible hose that had been jury-rigged for the occasion and yelled, "Dupuis—open 'er up! But easy, for the love of God!"

The Chief Chemical Engineer of the facility, who was stationed at a redundant manual valve manifold outside the control shed, gripped a big wheel. He turned it a fraction of a centimeter and pinkish liquid dribbled into the champagne cooler. An acrid organic odor spread through the frigid air.

"Yo!" Victor hollered, and the flow ceased. He carried the bucket over to a venerable black Mercedes, his official vehicle during his supervisory visits to the Baie Comeau plant of Remco International. The car had been decorated in honor of the day's festivities with Canadian and American flags and bunches of multicolored balloons. The manager of the refinery slipped a plastic funnel into the fuel tank. Victor poured the liquid to loud applause.

"And now, my friends—we come to the moment of truth! Have we really manufactured a revolutionary new fuel . . . or is it only bug pee after all?"

While the workers were laughing he slipped behind the wheel. The engine started up with a roar, and the renewed cheers were drowned out when the tanker that towered above the pumping station sounded its great diaphone horn.

Everybody knew that the car had been all warmed up and primed to go but the symbolism was all that counted. Victor jumped out, leaving the engine running, opened the other door for Shannon, and bowed her in during a final bout of clapping. Then they drove off the quay and the ceremony was over. The crowd dispersed and the hose-handling derrick on the ship lowered its cable to begin the cargo-loading process.

They drove out of town toward the new airport, for she would have to go directly to Washington to confer with the eminent criminal lawyers who were preparing Gerry's case. Victor slowed the Mercedes and pulled off the road into a deserted log-scaling yard where trees hid them from passing traffic. He stripped the decorations off the car, dumping the flags into the trunk and letting the helium-filled balloons waft away into the leaden sky. Then he got back in and they sat there.

"Why did your father let you do it?" he asked.

"He thinks he's fattening you for acquisition. He's been watching your situation very keenly in spite of the fireworks in Washington. The way you weathered the capital crunch— squeaked through without losing control of the process—impressed him no end. Beware of sharks trolling bait."

"Just let him try . . . Is this scandal of your husband's some of your doing? Are you using him to set your father up?"

Shannon laughed, a throaty, appetite-laden sound. "Why don't you read my mind?"

"I've done that already."

He pulled her toward him and his icy lips and tongue possessed her hot mouth. Her white fox toque fell from her head and the long auburn hair flamed against the pale fur of her coat. His hands tightened, cupping her skull, and she moaned, her mind crying her need. Victor's other hand nearly encircled her neck. The fingertips against her upper spine seemed to be drawing energy from her supercharged pelvic nerves, draining—

No please Vic not that way damn you not that way let's try it for once my way please *please*!

No.

It's not love you you fool there's no real loss no bonding why won't you there's nothing of *him* only me why not please oh do it—

I'll give you your pleasure I owe you that but in my own way . . .

Bastard! . . . Oh God how I hate you how I hate you . . .

Hold on to that. Guard it very carefully until you're ready to exchange him for me.

"At least he's human," she wept aloud. "But you . . ." She screamed then as the orgasms began, and was lost to warmth.

19

FROM THE MEMOIRS OF
ROGATIEN REMILLARD

NOW I SHALL HAVE TO TELL YOU ABOUT GERRY TREMBLAY, ONCE a valued member of Denis's Coterie, whose spectacular disgrace was one of those backhanded blessings that seem to prove God's sense of humor.

The Pope's encyclical dealt frankly with the great sources of temptation that must accompany powerful operancy—a sinister fact of life that the American metapsychic establishment, in particular, had long tried to sweep under the rug. This ostrich attitude, a tendency to discount the possibility of disaster until it smacks you in the teeth, was probably quintessentially American. Even in the worst of times, we were a people who hoped for the best and believed that good intentions covered a multitude of sins. Because we were a young nation, because we skimmed the cream of the planetary Mind, and because our land was unarguably the richest and most fortunate on Earth, Americans had the arrogance of the golden adolescent upon whom fate smiles. We thought we were invincible as well as stronger and smarter than everyone else. We suffered a periodic comeuppance but bounced back as triumphalistic as ever. Even today, citizens of the Human Policy of the Galactic Milieu who are of American extraction tend to display a tiresome smugness about their heritage.

At the turn of the twenty-first century, the American metapsychic establishment shared the national flaw. It had deplored the Nigel Weinstein affair, but explained it away as a piece of temporary insanity. The atrocities of the Flaming Assassin were more patently criminal—but they, too, could be attributed to a madman. In other parts of the world, where there were fewer cultural inhibitions against the public avowal of operancy, there had been crimes committed in which metapsychic powers were used with obvious malice aforethought. In America—for reasons that became clear only after the Intervention—few such crimes were ever prosecuted; and none of them, until Tremblay's, had the aspect of a cause célèbre. American operant leaders had tended to sidestep the ethical aspects of their gifts and concentrate instead on the scientific and social applications of them. The few persons, such as Denis, who knew of the existence of evil and exploitative operants found themselves hamstrung by gaps in our legal system. American law, with its reverence for individual rights, makes no provision for the *mental* examination of suspected criminals. The very idea is contrary to the Fifth Amendment to the Constitution, which says that no person shall be compelled in a criminal case to be a witness against himself. However, if this principle holds, certain types of operant criminal activity can never be proved beyond a reasonable doubt. The Scottish jurors had come to this conclusion in the Weinstein case. It seems likely that Kieran O'Connor and Representative Gerard Tremblay (D-Mass.) counted upon escaping retribution in a similar manner when they conspired to coerce the President. O'Connor's role in the affair was never proved. Poor Gerry got what was coming to him—and forced a fundamental revision of operant ethics at the same time that he became the ultimate cause of Kieran O'Connor's undoing.

As I have stated earlier, I never really liked Gerry Tremblay. One might credit prescience or redactive insight—or perhaps just the old Franco instinct for smelling a rat. Psychoanalysis would doubtless point out that it was Gerry's deep-seated insecurity and envy that laid him wide open to O'Connor's peculiar brand of sorcery. He was certainly besotted with his wife Shannon, who pretended to mold Gerry to her father's specifications at the same time that she was planning the ruination of both of them.

After Gerry was elected to his first two-year term in 2004, he served on the House Special Committee on Metapsychic Affairs, where his unique position as the only operant congressman assured him of continuing publicity and growing influence. The stance he took was surprisingly conservative, dismaying the operant establishment. He helped kill a measure that would have set up federally funded training schools for operant children. In a speech that was widely televised, he pointed out that this very sort of program—which was being followed in a number of liberal countries such as Japan, West Germany, Great Britain, the Netherlands, and the Scandinavian nations—was leading to the formation of elite groups of operant children, the same kind of group that had tried and failed to take political control of the Soviet Union. While the Soviet operants had evidently worked on the side of the angels, could one assume that all operants would inevitably be so highminded? Representative Tremblay, an operant himself, counseled great caution. He declared that Americans should remain aloof from any schemes that would distance operant youngsters from normals and foster unhealthy illusions of superiority. While he was not in favor of having obstacles put in the way of operant training per se, he hoped that it would always be seen as an adjunct to regular public or private schooling—with operant and normal children educated together. This was the American way, avouched the Gentleman from Massachusetts, and the *best* way—for the sake of the young operants themselves and the nation as a whole.

Gerry's speech was a smash, and he was well on the road to the big time. Progressive operants tried in vain to point out that federal funding of their programs was vital. In those depressed times, the states had no tax revenues to spare for operant training; private facilities for operants, except at institutions such as Dartmouth, MIT, Stanford, and the Universities of Texas, Virginia, and California-Davis, where there were long-standing Departments of Metapsychology—were too expensive for the majority of gifted children. Minds would be wasted, the operants warned.

Not so, replied Tremblay. In time, when the nation could afford it, Congress would reconsider funding a generalized operant education program. But these were perilous days. America was threatened not only by unemployment, inflation, and shortages, but also by the escalating Holy War of the fundamentalist Muslims, which now had spread further into Africa, India, and the East Indies; and China had taken a mysterious turn toward isolationism that alarmed both its neighbors and the United States.

Tremblay told his fellow operants to be patient—and to ask not what their country could do for them, but what they could do for their country.

As the agent of Kieran O'Connor, Gerry Tremblay was given two important assignments. The first was to influence both the President and Democratic members of Congress in favor of O'Connor's military-industrial contractors, especially those connected to the Zap-Star satellite defense system, the new ON-1 Space Habitat, and the proposed Lunar Base. Gerry was successful in this area because Baumgartner was committed to a strong military posture and to the American space program, and liberal Democrats who favored the latter could rather easily be made to see the high-tech side benefits of the former.

Gerry's second assignment was to discourage Baumgartner from granting special privileges to operants, thus denying a power base to the operant establishment. The defeat of the Operant Education Bill was a great start for Gerry . . . but immediately after that he realized that O'Connor's second mandate was a no-hoper.

The factor that disrupted the carefully laid scheme was a small one: the President's grandchild, Amanda Denton. Baumgartner's antioperant feelings, never too firmly grounded in personal conviction, were shaken by the religious leaders' statements on the matter—and then utterly shattered by the little girl. She was a resident in the White House, along with her parents and two older brothers. Ernie Denton, the husband of Baumgartner's only daughter, served as a presidential aide; and whenever the Chief Executive felt depressed, he'd send Ernie off to fetch Amanda. The child was both charming and good for what ailed the President. (She grew up to be a Grand Master Redactor, a superlative metapsychic healer.) And with Amanda cavorting about the Oval Office, Gerry Tremblay didn't have a prayer of reinstituting the antioperant mood that had characterized Baumgartner's first term.

This was a serious worry to O'Connor. In 2006, Gerry was re-elected to the House . . . but so were seven other operants from liberal states. Bills were introduced to reorganize and upgrade the EE Service of the Defense Department, which had been starved for funds during the past four years. The FBI, concerned that

Islamic terrorists might once again target American cities, pressed for the recruitment of operant agents. There was a predictable outcry from conservatives; but such agents were widely used now in other countries and had proved effective—if unpopular.

And then came the greatest threat thus far to O'Connor's schemes. He had been grooming his creature, Senator Scrope, to run for president in 2008, since Baumgartner was restricted to two terms by the XXII Amendment to the Constitution. But the country now perceived the charismatic Baumgartner to be the Man on a White Horse who would save it from the maelstrom engulfing the rest of the world. In spite of all O'Connor's lobbying efforts, Congress passed a repeal of Article XXII in May 2007, and by the middle of October the necessary three-fourths of the state legislatures had ratified it. Baumgartner was free to run again, if he chose to do so. And if he did, the next four years boded ill for O'Connor and his secret operant cabal.

On 27 October, a delegation of the Republican National Committee (not including Chairman Cassidy, who had lost control of the organization) was scheduled to call on the President and formally request him to run for a third term. O'Connor's instructions to Gerry Tremblay were explicit. There could be no more subtlety. Gerry was the only O'Connor partisan with free access to the West Wing having the mental muscle for a full coercive thrust. He was to arrange for an appointment with the President immediately following that of the delegation, so he could station himself in the Oval Office's anteroom. From there he would eavesdrop telepathically, and at the critical moment compel the President to say that he believed the repeal of Article XXII to be an unwise and dangerous move—and that under no circumstances would he run again.

It was a desperate scheme and it might have worked, for Baumgartner would have contradicted his own public image of firm decisiveness if he repudiated the statement—and to charge that he had been coerced would put him in an even worse position. He would know his mind had been tampered with; but he would not know who had done it—or when it might happen again—and O'Connor was certain that subliminal follow-up thrusts by Gerry over the next few weeks would demoralize him and force him to accept the inevitable. At worst, Baumgartner would seem to be suffering a nervous breakdown and his allegations of mental compulsion would be unprovable.

The day came. Gerry arrived early for his appointment and was shown into the anteroom to wait by a White House usher who fell victim to his more subtle coercive wiles. Gerry watched as another usher shepherded in the delegation, together with a single minicam video journalist who would record the historic moment. Gerry suffered a brief qualm when he recognized an operant among the delegates, Dr. Beatrice Fairweather of the University of Virginia; but there seemed to be little danger of her detecting the coercive impulse. Her metafaculties were not strong, and she would have no reason to suspect that Baumgartner was being mentally manipulated.

The door to the Oval Office closed, leaving Gerry seated as close to it as he could get. Two oblivious aides worked at desks on the opposite side of the room. He exerted his farsenses and summoned a close-up image of the President.

There was a spate of greetings and preliminary chitchat, and then the delegation spokesman, the former Governor of Delaware, got to the heart of the matter.

"Mr. President, we have brought to you a request of the most critical importance, dictated by the Republican Party and also by millions of American citizens who have flooded our offices with their letters, videograms, and phone calls. The Twenty-Second Amendment to the Constitution was repealed for one reason and for one reason only—so that you would not have to step down from the presidency at this time when our beleaguered nation needs your continuing guidance so desperately. So I put the question to you frankly. Will you accept the nomination in 2008?"

Gerry took hold of Lloyd Baumgartner's mind in that instant. He saw from the President's eyes, heard with the President's ears, spoke with the President's mouth and vocal cords.

"Ladies and gentlemen, this is an extraordinary honor that you offer me, and I want to assure you that over the past week I have been thinking and praying over it—"

WHAT ARE YOU DOING TO MY GRANDPA?

"—so that this decision I give you today represents my carefully considered judgment, what I believe will best serve the needs of our great nation. I must decline—I must decline—"

GRANDPA! GRANDPA! YOU LET GRANDPA OUT OF HIS HEAD!

Through the President's eyes, Gerry saw the door of the Oval Office fly open and Amanda, like a pinafore-clad avenging angel, dash directly toward the desk where her grandfather sat. Far behind her, out in the anteroom, Ernie Denton stood gaping at the enormity of his five-year-old daughter's presumption.

"—I must decline—"

Baumgartner was fighting the hold. And the damn child was slashing at him with all her raw infant strength. Gerry's sight of her and of all the others inside the office dimmed as the captive mind began to slip away.

Gerry lurched to his feet, knowing that if he could only manage eye contact with the President he could reassert control. The little girl screeched and pointed at him standing there in the doorway. The six members of the delegation and the goddam cameraman, too, turned to look at him. The child cried out loud:

"That's not Grandpa talking. That's *him*! He's inside Grandpa's head. Uncle Gerry is making Grandpa say things he doesn't want to say!"

The Secret Service men materialized out of nowhere, pinioning Gerry's arms. In a last-ditch effort, he forced Baumgartner to say, "Decline . . . decline . . ."

Then the linkage broke. Dr. Beatrice Fairweather, a little old lady with a kindly face, stepped up to Gerry and put her fingers on his forehead and opened his faltering mind like a sardine can.

"Oh, dear," she said. "I'm afraid the child is right."

The President slumped back into his big leather chair. He said hoarsely, "You bet your sweet ass she's right! Arrest that man!"

Gerry Tremblay relaxed then, and even managed a rueful little smile for the camera as the Secret Service agents led him away.

In July 2008 Tremblay went on trial. The evidence of Beatrice Fairweather was disallowed under the statutes prohibiting self-incrimination, but little Amanda Denton was a telling witness for the prosecution. Her testimony, together with that of the President, was sufficient to convict Representative Gerard Tremblay of aggravated assault and battery, and interfering with a federal official. A count of kidnapping was thrown out. Tremblay's appeal of the verdict eventually reached the Supreme Court, which upheld his conviction. He was impeached and expelled from the House of Representatives and served two years and six months of a concurrent three-to-twenty-five-year sentence.

In 2012, both houses of Congress passed the XXIX Amendment to the Constitution, which would permit defendants in criminal trials (operant or not) to be cross-examined mentally by a three-person group of forensic redactors—one for the defense, one for the prosecution, and one acting as amicus curiae. The Amendment was submitted to the state legislatures but had not been ratified by the requisite three-quarters of the United States by the time the Intervention took place.

Upon his parole in 2012, Gerry Tremblay became an officer in Roggenfeld Acquisitions, a firm specializing in the leveraged buy-outs of aerospace contractors. Five months after his release from prison, his wife Shannon presented him with a baby girl, Laura, who was destined for a spectacular role in the private life of a certain Magnate of the Concilium forty years into the future. Tremblay complaisantly acknowledged Laura as his own.

He never learned—unlike his father-in-law, Kieran O'Connor—that it had been Shannon who sent little Amanda to visit her grandfather on 29 October 2007, and also arranged for Dr. Fairweather to join the nominating delegation at the last moment.

20

OVERSIGHT AUTHORITY VESSEL
SADA [SIMB 220-0000]
PODKAMENNAYA TUNGUSKA BASIN
USSR, EARTH
20 JUNE 2008

THE HUGE SIMBIARI AUTHORITY FLAGSHIP AND ITS ATTENDANT fleet of twenty-six smaller observation vessels descended slowly and openly, in broad daylight, over the event site. By order of the Lylmik Supervisors, the commemoration was to be deliberately conspicuous, reminding the populace of this war-torn Earth nation of a truth they had once championed—that human beings were not alone in the starry universe.

On the bridge of the Sada, Captain Chassatam, his Executive Officer Madi Ala Assamochiss, and Senior Oversight Magnate Adassti watched the view-screen, which was in terrain-proper mode, as the wilderness of verdant bogs and conifer thickets drew closer and closer.

"Approaching stasis altitude," said the Exec.

"Very well," said Captain Chassatam. A fast farsight sweep told him that the formation was perfectly organized, and seconds later it hovered motionless some six hundred meters above the taiga. One level of his mind commanded the attention of all crews, while another signaled the Simbiari chaplain stationed in the topside bubble to organize and energize the solemn metaconcert aimed at coercing God.

O Source and Sustainer of Life! Our minds and the Mind of the Simbiari Polity in all the far-flung reaches of the Galaxy praise you this day at the site where your martyrs, the crew and

176

survey personnel of the Observation Vessel Risstimi, did one hundred planetary orbits ago choose to sacrifice themselves rather than bring great harm upon the innocent people of a world placed under their care. Help us to understand and appreciate your martyrs' extraordinary act of love. Console the bereaved among us who lost kin and dear friends in the event. If it should be your will, give us the courage to emulate their selfless action freely and without fear, confident as they were confident that you will receive our undying minds into the Great Mind even as our bodies perish. We trust that you will welcome us one day as you welcomed them into your Divine Milieu of unending peace and light, love and joy. Praise to you, Author of the Universe and exemplar of perfect Unity! Praise throughout all space and time! We Simbiari say this with one Mind.

WE SAY IT!

"A chopper approaches from Vanavara," the Exec noted, inserting its image into a corner of the view-screen. All three Simbiari scrutinized the tiny craft with their farsight and did a surface probe of the humans within. Lettering on the body of the helicopter indicated that it belonged to the local reindeer-herders' collective.

"I'd hoped for a higher-status set of eyewitnesses than this," the Magnate said rather peevishly. She mopped green mucus from her face. As the senior personage present it had been her duty to express ritual sorrow during the prayer.

"They've closed down the air bases at Ust'-Ilimisk and Tura," the Captain said. "They'll have to send jets from Krasnoyarsk."

"Military observers always receive higher credibility ratings from Earthlings," Magnate Adassti said. "I hope they're not asleep at the switch down there at PVOS."

The Exec said, "The chopper carries a pilot and the local stringer for the Evenk People's Video Net. The journalist has remembered to load his camera and take off the lens cap, and he's framing a fair shot of the fleet."

"Thanks be to sacred Truth and Beauty," the Magnate sighed.

The small craft came whop-whopping over the spruces, following an erratic course. The Magnate turned her thoughts to higher things, reminiscing out loud in what she hoped was a comradely fashion.

"My sainted Auntie Bami Ala was among the Tunguska martyrs. I recall her clearly, even though I was a mere toddler when she left on her first exotic assignment. She was only a TechOne with the Taxonomical Service, but very keen at the thought of bringing Milieu enlightenment to a suboperant world. Dear Auntie . . . She showed me my first visuals of humans. I had to fight to keep from gagging at the first sight of them—those horrid dry skins, like Poltroyans only ranging in pigmentation from dusty black to fish-belly pink. She explained their strange physiology and shocked me to the toe-webs. No algae symbionts in the epidermis, so they were constantly eating and excreting through a hypertrophied gastrointestinal tract—even making a *ceremony* of foodtaking. And I had thought that the Gi were uncouth! Auntie told me about the primitive state of human technology and psychosocial development, and then scandalized me even more by admitting that the Lylmik had the highest hopes for Earth. But I'll tell you, Captain, that even now I can hardly imagine a more unlikely candidate-world for coadunation of the local Mind."

"I don't know," the Captain said. "They may give us a run for the money in the high-tech field. Their rate of advancement has been little short of stupefying." He waved a hand at the wealth of ingenious mechanisms that crowded the bridge of the Sada. "Give humanity a few more decades and they'll have most of this. With their elaboration of the Universal Field Theory, they've been able to begin work on gravo-magnetic propulsion. And it's only a fluke that they haven't tamed fusion yet. Fooling around, wasting their resources on manned-satellite schemes. If they only knew that we have nearly eight hundred worlds for them!"

"Captain," the Executive Officer warned, "the exotic aircraft is venturing too close to the rho-field coronal zone. Shall I push it off?"

"Do so. We can't have the thing dropping out of the sky like a zapped mosquito . . . That's better. Neat work with the pressor, Madi Ala. We'll give him just a few more minutes and then send him off. The emotional tone of the pilot is turning flaky."

"The journalist must make an explicit record of our presence," Magnate Adassti averred. "The Lylmik were emphatic on that point."

The Captain sipped carbonated water from his platinum flask with a certain air of disdain. "Does the Supervisory Body *really* believe this manifestation will divert the Soviets from their internal conflicts? Frankly, with the way things are going down in Transcaucasia, I doubt that a mere fleet of starships over the Stony Tunguska will even make the evening news."

"Vulgar cynicism is hardly called for, Captain." The Magnate was somewhat starchy over his minor breach of decorum. Rehydrating oneself among equals or in informal situations was certainly acceptable. But the Captain had not even bothered to ask her permission before drinking, and the Executive Officer was a subordinate! Flight crews were a roughhewn lot, regrettably egalitarian.

The Captain only chuckled at her subliminal rebuke. "It looks to me as though the Soviet Union is only a half skip away from complete disintegration. Cynicism seems quite justified."

"Nonsense. The nation may be battered, but its economy and governmental structure are still basically intact. The reports of our presence here will be sent to Moscow and eventually disseminated throughout the planet. As to what good the manifestation will do . . . we can expect benefits to accrue over the long term."

"Earth hasn't got a long term. If the Lylmik hold off Intervention much longer this whole Second Oversight Phase will be a wasted effort. We'll find ourselves with a suboperant world again! The normals are starting to kill off coadunating minds down there, you know."

"Unfortunately, this is true," the Magnate admitted. "If only the imprisoned Soviet operants had embraced a pacifistic stance, as their colleagues in other countries advised them. Poor misguided ones! The military dictator in the Kremlin was badly jolted by the mass escape attempt of the aggressively empowered adepts. Nearly fourteen hundred minds lost to the overall coadunation effort . . . I fear that an ethic of nonviolence is a tough bolus for many Earthling operants to swallow."

"The bunch at Darjeeling stayed peaceful—until the Muslim

mob tore them to pieces. On this planet, metapsychic operants may be in a no-win situation. It's happened on other worlds."

"The Lylmik still hold out hope. On the other hand, the revised schema postulates that Intervention must occur within the next five years here, or it probably will not occur at all . . ."

"Captain, the helicopter is retreating," said the Exec.

"Yes, Madi Ala, I see. The poor pilot's had enough. He's frightened nearly out of his mind. He didn't have nearly as much to drink today as the journalist."

A telltale blinked an alert and the Exec said, "Now we are being scanned in the infrared by a Soviet satellite surveillance system as well as by the phased arrays at Krasnoyarsk. Is this allowable?"

The Captain passed the buck to the Magnate, who said, "Affirmative. But obscure any attempt at configuration fine-scan of the Sada by light-amplifiers. I don't want us to be too blatantly on the record. We'll remain in position for a few more minutes and let EuroSat ZS spot us on its next sweep. Three sightings should provide modest credibility and give the Earthlings something to think about besides killing one another."

"Very well," said the Captain. He was watching the view and slurping from his flask again, radiating overfamiliarity. "You ever been landside in Siberia, Magnate Adassti?"

She gave up on any attempt to maintain a refined atmosphere and hauled out her own water supply, indicating to the Exec that she should also feel free to imbibe. "No, most of my work here has been administrative. I have gone abroad during the past five orbits monitoring the Metapsychic Congresses . . . Montréal last year after they decided not to risk Moscow; Paris, Beijing, Edinburgh—all large cities. And before that I attended the session held in a quaint rural hostelry in Bretton Woods, New Hampshire. Bizarre! . . . I presume, Captain, from your reference to mosquitoes, that you yourself *have* visited Siberia." She shuddered. The insects were insanely fond of Simbiari body fluids.

"I went down once, not long after the martyrdom. One of my academy mates crewed on the Risstimi. What a sight it was! The burnt trees just beneath the blast zone were standing upright, but all around them was this vast elliptical area of trunks smashed flat and radiating outward. Not a single Earthling was harmed. But if the crew of the Risstimi hadn't hung on to the failed control system mentally, the ship would have continued right across the continent and impacted on Saint Petersburg, where nearly two million people lived at the time."

"Truth!" exclaimed the Exec. "I didn't know there were that many."

"I wonder if this damn planet will ever appreciate what we've done?" the Captain mused. "Not just what the Risstimi crew did, but all the rest of it. Sixty thousand years of watching and guiding and cosseting, all the while praying that the silly clots wouldn't botch it."

Magnate Adassti had a grim little smile on her emerald lips. "If Intervention does take place and we undertake the proctorship, we'll make *sure* the Earthlings are properly grateful. Shaping up minds as barbarous as these for full Concilium participation is going to require heroic psychocorrectional measures. After what they've put us through—"

"Captain," said the Exec. "We have a wing of MiGs zeroing in on us from Krasnoyarsk."

"It's about time," the Magnate snapped.

The officer hesitated, then blurted out, "Farsense Monitoring reports that the Soviets think we may be a Chinese secret weapon."

"Chinese?" blared the Captain. "*Chinese*? Can't the flaming idiots recognize a flight of UFOs when they see one?"

Magnate Lashi Ala Adassti dripped green heedlessly over the shiny instrumentation console as she swallowed great gulps of charged water. "Up the Cosmic All!" she blasphemed. "The nincompoops!"

"So much for *that* brilliant Lylmik ploy," the Captain told her. "Your orders, Magnate?"

"Get us back into orbit and invisible. We'll be hearing from the Supervisory Body soon enough."

21

FROM THE MEMOIRS OF
ROGATIEN REMILLARD

THE FLIGHT OF FLYING SAUCERS DETECTED OVER SIBERIA MADE A very minor news splash. The videotape of the event—which was sold to Western news agencies for an enormous sum by the Soviet government—was exquisitely detailed, so much so that it was deemed a masterpiece of special effects by the ciné wizards of Industrial Light and Magic. NASA analysts said that no spacecraft propulsion system known to science could account for the movement of the alleged saucers. They simply defied Newton's Laws of Motion. These adverse judgments, coupled with the suspicious date of the sighting, on the anniversary of the Tunguska meteorite fall, led most authorities to dismiss the tape as a hoax.

Over the next couple of years there were other saucer reports from different parts of the world—none quite so spectacular as the Siberian affair, but nevertheless impressive in the aggregate. Alas! The world was so preoccupied with mundane troubles that the notion of extraterrestrial visitors caused no excitement at all. So the saucers were back again? Big deal. So was the rain in Spain, the Dust Bowl in Oklahoma, and Killer Smog in London and Tokyo.

Feeling very low one dreary November evening in 2008 (I had just finished composing a long and querulous videogram to Ume, who had moved back to Sapporo the previous summer), I sat in my apartment above the bookshop, reading and drinking. The book was an old favorite, a peerless historical novel by H. F. M. Prescott called *The Man on a Donkey*. The booze was Laphroaig, a lovely dusky malt that Jamie MacGregor had brought over on his last visit. Sleet rapped at the storm windows, the fire was low in the Franklin stove, and my stockinged feet rested on the warm shaggy belly of my cat Marcel, who was asleep on the claw-shredded ottoman.

The doorbell rang. It was after 2300. Reluctantly, I sent my farsight down into the street entryway, where I saw Denis. Setting the Prescott aside with a sigh, I extracted my feet from their cozy shelter and padded over to the buzzer.

Come up, I told my nephew. Is anything wrong?

Yes and no. I just want to talk to you if you don't mind.

I am not quite blotto.

I'll redact you sober.

You do and I'll sic Marcel on you . . .

I opened the hall door and he came in, dripping.

"I walked from the lab," he said, taking off his raincoat. "What a rotten night."

I got another tumbler, splashed in Scotch, and held it out to him. Denis rarely indulges, but it didn't take telepathy to know what he needed. He flopped down on the sofa, took a belt, and sighed.

"The President called me earlier today."

"He should be feeling pretty high," I opined. "The landslide victory to end all landslides. He's got his third term—and probably a fourth and fifth if he wants them—"

"Uncle Rogi, do you remember when I was a kid, and just learning to do long-distance scanning? We didn't call it EE then. It was just mind-traveling."

"Sure, I remember. You'd drag me along. Only way I ever got very far out of Coos County, mentally speaking."

"What we were doing was a farsensory metaconcert, a mind-meld. I didn't know *that*, either. You know, it's a funny thing. I've never been able to go metaconcert with anyone except you and Lucille. Glenn says I'm too wary, too jealous of my mental autonomy to be a team thinker. Lucille thinks I may just be afraid to trust . . . Whatever it is, it's there. And I want to excurse tonight with a partner—someone who will magnify my own sight.

Luce is out. Now that she's pregnant again I want to keep her as tranquil as possible."

The implication was dire. "And this EE's likely to be anything but, eh?"

"I tripped out myself earlier this evening, right after the President's call. He told me that the Secretary of Defense had the wind up over something his Psi-Eye people had spied. He asked me to check it out."

I poured myself another finger of Scotch and downed it before Denis could stop me. "What happened? A nuke on the Kremlin?"

"It's in China . . . whatever it is. I couldn't get any more of a handle on it than the Washington pEEps. That's why I need you. Minimal though your solitary output is, when it's yoked with mine I should experience a magnification up to threefold through synergistic augmentation."

"Your humble servant," I muttered. Minimal!

Denis dragged the ottoman over to the couch, displacing Marcel, who hissed bitterly at the imposition and slunk off to the kitchen. "Sit here beside me. We can put our feet up and it'll be nearly as good as the barber-chairs at the lab. I suppose I should have asked you to come down there, but—"

"You knew I wouldn't, and it doesn't make a damn bit of difference where we do it."

"No. It doesn't."

The body contact was unfamiliar and disquieting. Good God, was I afraid of him? His mind was utterly silent. Wide open. Waiting. I closed my eyes and still saw the living room through mind-sight, but I made no move toward him. I turned the kitchen wall transparent and saw the cat opening the breadbox to steal an English muffin. I had forgotten to fill his food dish. I kept on going out through the house wall and saw the oddly unshadowed streets slick with freezing rain and cars going up and down Main Street with tires and wiper blades crunching.

Denis said: Come.

I said: All right all right it's just been a hell of a long time since you were in my skull and you were only a kid then and now tu es un gros bonnet the Biggest Mindshot of the lot and I *do* want to help you but what you ask of me ah Denis a Franco father cannot stand naked before his son—

No no it won't be like that metaconcert among adults isn't that kind of merging please don't worry. This will not be like your experiences with Ume or Elaine those were an altogether different type of mental intercourse believe me trust me I am only Denis the same little Denis et tu es mon vrai père! Ça va Uncle Rogi?

Ça va ça va mais allez-y doucement dammit!

He took me away...

I am not much of a head. I use telepathy without a qualm, of course, and do everyday things such as deep-scanning letters before opening them and tracking potentially light-fingered customers around the shop and anticipating the moves of idiot drivers. But the larger faculties I use grudgingly (except with the ladies!) and there is almost always a sense of uneasiness after the fact, as if I had indulged a secret vice. Excorporeal excursion is ordinarily very difficult for me. I can "call" over fairly long distances, but to "see"—much less use other ultrasenses—is an exhausting piece of work when it is not completely impossible. I had braced myself for the joint trip with Denis, expecting the usual exertion. But what a difference! I hardly know what to compare that mind-flight to. There are certain dreams, where one does not really fly but rather takes giant steps, one after the other, each one covering the proverbial seven leagues. Long ago, when I had eavesdropped on the mind of little Denis as he slowly scanned New Hampshire for other operants, I had seen on the eerie mindscape the jewel-like clusters of "light" that mark the positions of living human brains—the latents glowing dimly, the operants blazing like tiny stars. There was something of this effect as Denis and I loped westward across the continent, each heroic bound covering a greater distance and attaining a greater height than the last, until at the Pacific Coast we soared up without pausing and described a vast arc above the mindless dark of the northern ocean. But *was* it mindless? There were none of the starlike concentrations, but there was something else: an intricate whispering coming not from below but from all around me, as if millions upon millions of infinitesimal voices were carrying on conversations—or even singing, since the sensation had a rhythmic pulsation to it, a tempo that was ever changing and yet somehow orchestrated . . .

It is the vital field of the world, Denis said. Life and Mind interacting. The biosphere forms a latticework that is entire but the noösphere the World Mind permeates it only imperfectly as yet and so the field is sensed by our minds only as a whisper.

I asked: When this World Mind finishes weaving itself together what will there be?

And my nephew said: A song.

We came to Japan and touched its shimmering arc. But there was no time for me to seek Ume, although I thought of it; and a moment later we were decelerating over China, flying low above the great Yangzi River basin, one of the most populous regions of the world. It was full daytime there, of course—and the minds blazed. The perception was overwhelming to me and I lost all sense of direction and differentiation; but Denis bore me onward, his goal now in view, and in another instant we were poised above the metropolis of Wuhan and ready to get down to business.

Denis said: Now we must do the real metaconcert Uncle Rogi. The flight was only a peripheral linkage a kind of piggyback ride. What I want you to do now primarily is relax. We are going to fuse our wills so that we have a single purpose. That's what metaconcert is. ONE WILL one vector for the channeled faculty in this case the close inspection of a *thing* inside a small laboratory in a modest building of the university. When I ask it you must help me to penetrate using all the strength you have. Do you understand?

Yes.

You may feel yourself fainting don't be concerned I'll hold you the vision will be mine even if you fail but hold out as best you can for as long as you can.

Yes.

Now.

It seemed that the sun rose. What had been drab was fully

colored and what had been merely bright now became supersa-
turated with a brilliance that would be intolerable to physical
eyes. At that time there were some six million people living in
close proximity in the Wuhan tri-city area, and about ten thousand of them had some degree of operancy. Naturally most of
these were concentrated in the university district, which lay east
of the Yangzi near a small lake. We seemed to plummet out of the
sky. Abruptly the mind-constellation effect was gone and we
were *there*, wafting along a modernistic concourse where crowds
of students and academics streamed in and out of buildings, rode
bicycles, or lounged about under leafless trees soaking up a bit of
late-autumn sunshine.

Denis knew where to go. We passed through the white-stone
outer wall of a smallish structure, entered offices where people
worked at computer terminals or shuffled papers, much as they
do in any university, and then we reached the lab. There were
three men and two women inside, and from the paraphernalia I
knew at once that it was a metapsychology establishment. The
so-called barber-chair, with its apparatus for measuring the brain
activity of a "performing" operant, was virtually identical to similar devices at Dartmouth. Around the chair on the bare concrete
floor was a ring about three meters in diameter, studded with
little gadgets all wired together, the whole attached by several
heavy cables to a bank of equipment racks. Some of the front
panels were demounted and electronic guts hung out, which the
scientists tinkered with.

Denis said: When I was here earlier I examined this stuff and
recorded the gross details of the circuitry. Now I want to try
microscrutiny. Hang onto your hat Uncle Rogi. I'll try to be as
quick as I can . . .

He zeroed in, and I felt as though my eyes were being torn out
of my skull—but of course my physical eyes had nothing to do
with the ultrasensory scan; the pain was somewhere in my nervous system where farsight impulses only partially belonging to
the physical universe were being amplified in some terrible eso-
teric fashion by my nephew's supermind. The brightness was
awful. In it detailed pictures of God knew what were flickering

like flipped pages in an old-fashioned book. I saw them distorted, sometimes whole and then fragmented like jigsaw puzzles. They made no sense and the rapidity of the image-change was indescribably sickening. I think I was trying to scream. I know I yearned to let go of Denis, to stop the agony, but I'd promised. I'd promised...

It ended.

Somewhere, somehow I was weeping and racked with spasms. I knew that—and yet another part of my mind stood aside, upright and proud of itself for having successfully endured. The suffering faded and my farsight once again perceived the Chinese laboratory.

Denis said: That was very good. The test subject has arrived. I'm going to break concert for a moment and check her out.

The supernal vividness of the scene faded to a washed-out pastel. I saw that only one of the scientists in the room was an operant. His aura was a pale yellowish-green, like a firefly. And then the door opened and in came a young woman with an aura like a house afire, stuffing the last of a sweet rice cake into her mouth and licking her fingers. She wore a smart red leather jumpsuit and white boots with high heels, and greeted the scientific types in a bored fashion before plopping down in the barber-chair. One man hooked her up while the other researchers completed their equipment adjustment, closed the panels, and went out—leaving the operant alone.

Denis re-established the metaconcert. Once again every detail of the place was extravagantly clear and I noticed for the first time a parabolic dish hanging above the operant's head. It looked something like a lamp reflector with a complex doodad at the center.

In an adjacent control room, the crew was powering up. The operant leader gave a telepathic command and the test subject began to count steadily in declamatory farspeech. The brain-monitoring systems were all go.

On the count of ten a mirrored dome sprang into existence, hiding the woman in the chair from view. Simultaneously, her telepathic speech cut off. The dome was approximately hemispheric, shaped like the top half of an egg and apparently as slick as glass. It did not quite touch the hanging reflector, but the ring of small components on the floor had been swallowed.

Before I could express my astonishment, Denis said: One more push Uncle Rogi. The best that you can do . . . through that mirror surface!

Our conjoined minds thrust out, and this time I did lose consciousness, after enduring only the briefest flash of mortal agony. When I recovered my senses, I found I was sitting on the sofa in my apartment in Hanover, my head throbbing like the legendary ill-used hamster in the classic dirty joke. I heard the sound of retching in the bathroom and water running in the sink. After a few minutes Denis came out, toweling his wet hair and looking like the living dead.

"Did we get through the goddam thing?" I whispered.

"No," said Denis.

"It was a mechanical mind-screen, wasn't it . . . The thing they said couldn't be made?"

"*I* never said it." Denis went slowly to the coat closet and dragged out his Burberry. I had never seen him look so terrible, so vitiated. His emotions were totally concealed.

"D'you realize they can stop Psi-Eye with a thing like that?" I nattered. "The Chinese can do anything they damn well please behind it and the EE monitors would never know! If *you* can't punch through it, then no meta on Earth can . . . Is there any way at all to open it up?"

"Destroy the generator," Denis said. "Aside from that—I don't know. We'll have to build our own and experiment." He opened the outer door. "Thank you again for your help, Uncle Rogi."

"But we're back to square one!" I cried. "The Chinese are paranoid about the Russians and vice versa. They'll start the arms race all over again or even pull a pre-emptive strike!"

"Good night," my nephew said. The door closed.

I spat one obscenity after him on the declamatory farspeech mode and damned if Marcel didn't stroll out of the kitchen and eye me with sardonic humor. He leaped to the gate-leg table where the half-full bottle of Laphroaig still stood, and cocked his great whiskers at it.

"Best idea I've heard all night," I told him; and I settled down to finish off the Scotch while the icy rain lashed the window and the cat took his place again at my feet.

22

NEW YORK CITY, EARTH
4 MARCH 2012

THERE WERE A HANDFUL OF OPERANTS AT THE SLOAN-KETTERING Institute, so Dr. Colwyn Presteigne had kept his mental shield at maximal strength during the entire three hours of the consultation. The strain—to say nothing of the emotional trauma resulting from the diagnosis—hit him in the taxi. He only regained consciousness at his destination, with the panicked cabbie yelling at him over the intercom and the doorman of the Plaza peering anxiously through the open door.

"Oh. for God's sake, it's all right," Presteigne growled. "I only dropped off to sleep for a moment." He pushed his credit card through the slot in the armored barrier. "Take fifteen."

"May I help you, Dr. Presteigne?" The doorman solicitously raised his umbrella and extended a white-gloved hand.

"Never mind." The physician retrieved his card, climbed out, and strode into the hotel. Arnold Pakkala was waiting in the lobby.

He said: ?

Presteigne's features were set again in their habitual cast of thoughtful benevolence. His mind was impenetrable beneath the outermost social level. He said: Tell Kier I'm on my way up.

Arnold said: ???

Presteigne turned his back on the executive assistant and headed for the elevator. He braced himself to resist any coercion; but Arnold only stood there trying without success to forestall the escape of inarticulate grief, then turned away toward the house phones.

Adam Grondin opened the door to the suite when the physician exited the elevator. More diffident than Arnold, he made no attempt to seek information. "The Boss is in the sitting room."

Presteigne nodded, slipped off his topcoat, and took the folder out of his briefcase. "See that Kier's things are packed up. He'll have to go in right away."

"Shit," Grondin whispered. "Shit shit shit . . ."

"Put a call through to Mrs. Tremblay and ask her to wait on hold. I think he'll want to tell her himself."

"Okay, Doc."

Presteigne went into the sitting room and carefully closed the door behind him. Kieran was standing at the window in his dressing gown, his hands locked behind him.

"Sit down, Col. Take a drink. Don't bother to say it—just open wide."

Mute, his vision blurring with tears, the physician obeyed.

Kieran O'Connor looked out over Central Park. Rags of mist infiltrated the budding trees. A policeman on horseback stopped at a bench where a vagrant lay covered with newspapers and began speaking into his walkie-talkie.

"It's interesting," Kieran said, "that it should have hit me this way. One could make an interesting case for divine retribution—if it weren't for the fact that I won't let this stop me."

"But, Kier, it's metastasized. Both the lymphangiography and the bone isoenzyme tests show—"

"I don't *need* that much longer."

"I've made arrangements to have you admitted immediately under a fictitious name—"

"No."

"But you've got to!"

Kieran laughed. "You doctors . . . so accustomed to controlling life-and-death decisions." Don't be a fool Col what do I care for your damned palliatives your brain-weakening chemicals I've lived with pain all my life I'll accept this too and keep my power until the Black Mother takes me in and all the rest as well it's perfect it's even appropriate Her jest at my expense Her proof that I'm the one loved most just as She always said where's your faith where's your love I'll *redact* the damn thing fend it off mind over matter you know it can be done you know other operants have done it why not me?

Kier you don't assay that highly in the redactive metafaculty. Some minds are good at healing and some aren't and self-redaction is the least-understood aspect of the metahealing process all bound about with unconscious factors that can enhance or inhibit—

Kieran turned around, halting the doctor's expostulations with a gentle impulse. "Enough, Col. I agreed to your tests because—because I was interested. I guess I always suspected something like this would happen as I got down to the wire. It's just another omen."

"Without any sort of treatment the pain will become unbearable."

"I can bear anything, for good reason." *Except disloyalty...*

Presteigne lowered his head in capitulation. "You're the Boss." He hesitated. "I asked Adam to put in a call to your daughter. I thought you'd want her to know. I'm sorry if I presumed."

Kieran's face stiffened. A wraith-image of Shannon, strangely distorted, flickered across his adamantine mental screen. And then it was gone and he was smiling. "Col, assuming your worst-case scenario—that any attempt at self-redaction on my part will be ineffective—how much longer will I be able to raise it?"

"If you're capable now it's some kind of fucking miracle! Please excuse the morbid pun."

But Kieran was chuckling in appreciation. "All right, that's plain as the proverbial pikestaff! I think the best thing to do then is to get back to Chicago. You go out and tell Shannon that all this was a false alarm. That I'm fine."

Presteigne sighed. "You're the Boss," he said again.

Still laughing quietly, Kieran turned back to the window. "Poor little girl. She'll be so relieved."

23

EXCERPTS FROM:
THE NEW YORK TIMES "SCIENCE TIMES"
1 MAY 2012

Sigma-Field Seen as the Key to Cheap and Reliable Fusion Power

Application also seen in development of mechanical mind-screen.

By BARBARA TRINH

Special to The New York Times

PRINCETON, N.J.—The long-awaited breakthrough in the development of small nuclear-fusion power systems was confirmed with the demonstration last week of MIPPFUG at Princeton University's Institute for Energy Research. MIPPFUG (the acronym stands for Miniature Proton-Proton Fusion Generator) differs from conventional fusion reactors in that it utilizes a "bottle" formed out of a sigma-field to contain the intensely hot fusion reaction, rather than currents of electromagnetism.

For more than 50 years, scientists have been frustrated in attempts to tame fusion by the inherent limitations of the electromagnetic confinement system, which requires massive radiation shielding and elaborate safety precautions. Fusion power-plants have remained uneconomical up until now not only because of their complexity, but also because a typical deuterium-tritium fusion plant produces only about one tenth the power of a nuclear fission reactor of the same size.

The new sigma-field confining system is fail-safe—unlike the magnetic one, which stores up enough energy to possibly destroy the reactor in a split second in case of a malfunction. The sigma-field system has the additional advantage of absorbing the gamma radiation produced in the proton-proton fusion process utilized in MIPP-FUG. Where this absorbed radiation "goes" is still one of the great mysteries of the booming new branch of science known as dynamic-field physics.

According to Dr. George T. Vicks, who developed the sigma-field mechanism for the MIPPFUG project, the "bottling" of fusion energy is only the first of what may eventually be a host of valuable applications of the sigma.

"A sigma is basically what the science-fiction writers like to call a force field," Vicks says. "It's a six-dimensional thing bound into the spatial dimensions of our space-time continuum. That sounds complicated—and it is! But you can understand rather easily what a sigma can do if you think of it as a kind of invisible wall. There are different kinds of sigmas. The one for MIPPFUG acts as barrier to the enormous heat of nuclear fusion."

Other types of sigma-fields, Vicks says, can block out other types of energy—or even matter.

"Sometime in the future," Vicks says, "we'll be able to design sigmas that act as roofs or meteor-barriers or shields against radiation or weapons. A sigma-field might even make a good umbrella! It could form the basis for those tractor beams that science fiction has spaceships use to push or pull or grab things out in the void."

An even more exotic application of sigma technology would be in the world's first effective mechanical thought-screen.

"So far," says Carole McCarthy, an associate of Vicks at Princeton, "no one has been able to come up with reliable barriers to telepathy or EE or other mental powers. This is because thought doesn't propagate in the four dimensions we call space-time, as sound and other forms of energy do. Mental impulses propagate in a six-dimensional entity we call the aether. The sigma-field, which also has six dimensions, might just be able to mesh with the aether in a way that would stop thought impulses cold."

This type of thought-screen was suggested by the late Nobel Laureate, Xiong Ping-yung, shortly before his death in 2006. Xiong was honored for formulating the Universal Field Theory, upon which sigma research is based. There has been increasing speculation in the West that China may be already working on such a device secretly, in connection with its increasingly defensive posture vis-à-vis the Soviet Union.

24

DU PAGE COUNTY, ILLINOIS, EARTH
4 AUGUST 2012

THE MUGGY MIDWESTERN AIR HIT VICTOR REMILLARD LIKE A HOT barber towel as the door of the Remco jet opened. Shannon Tremblay was waiting at the foot of the steps, her white cotton caftan billowing in the wind. Pregnancy became her, heightening her color and adding needed flesh, but aside from these changes her condition did not show. Victor could not resist scanning the perfect tiny body of the fetal girl. It was only five months alive and even now its mind showed certain familial metapsychic traits. It was damned spooky.

Shannon felt his touch and laughed. "Laura's going to be the clincher, you know. The factor to force Daddy to bring you into the organization—even without bonding. He's really very superstitious. She's an omen to him. A symbol. He may even think of her as a superior version of *me*, to be used . . ."

They hurried over the tarmac to the small airport's parking lot. The temperature must have been far over 40° Celsius and the sunlight was like blazing bars thrust through rising masses of purplish thunderheads.

"Have you told Gerry?" Victor asked.

"Of course. Why not? I think he may be relieved. Daddy was always pressuring us to have children . . . especially a girl. He was disappointed when nothing happened and blamed me, since there's no doubt that Gerry's fertile. Of course, you know why I wouldn't. Not until now. Laura will be *our* celebration, Victor—not Daddy's."

Her black Ferrari Automa was running at high revs, keeping

cool. She touched the lock, opening both doors, and said, "You drive. The guidance system is preset for most of the way."

He nodded and slid onto the icy leather seat with a sense of relief. It had been difficult to control his sweat glands. He could handle either the heat or the fear-excitement reflex, but it was hell bucking both of them at once. He checked the routing on the dash map-display, put up the spoiler, and eased the Ferrari out of the lot onto the airport frontage road.

"When is Gerry due out?"

"Next week."

"Is your old man going to stiff him?"

"Certainly not. Gerry's valuable, even if he's tainted." Her lips quirked. "He's valuable to us, too, so don't let me hear any more divorce bullshit. Not until we've won."

"Suit yourself." As they came onto the ramp for Route 64, he punched in the automatic guidance, took his hands from the wheel and his foot from the accelerator. Cruise control took over, merging them neatly with the eastbound traffic flow. On a second-class highway like 64, with only two pilot-stripped lanes in each direction, their speed was held down to 120 kph with no left-lane prioritizing; but in a few minutes they turned onto southbound 59, a three-laner, and the priority function of the guidance system began to communicate with transponders in other vehicles, sweeping them out of the Ferrari's way. They accelerated to 200 and in moments they were swinging onto the East-West Expressway and roaring toward Oakbrook, well spaced among the other privileged cars in the innermost of five eastbound lanes.

"I wish to hell we had pilot-strips in my neck of the woods," Victor groused. "It's still all manual in northern New Hampshire, except on the Interstates, and no priority speeding anywhere. New Hampshire doesn't believe in it."

"Illinois is glad of the licensing fees—but then, they have a lot more bills to pay. We all know that New Hampshire keeps costs down by giving its welfare clients bus fare to Massachusetts."

Victor chuckled. "An old Yankee custom. No taxes, no frills, and devil take the hindmost."

"He just may," Shannon murmured, "unless we're very, very careful. But I had to have you *see* what Daddy's got, Victor."

The console beeped to warn them that they were approaching their exit and the termination of programmed cruising. Victor took the wheel again as they went onto the Midwest Road ramp. He had never been to Kieran O'Connor's mansion, but the blip on the dash-map showed the way. The Ferrari slowed to a sedate ninety and made its way through rolling wooded hills where white-painted paddock fencing or weathered split rails delineated the boundaries of large estates. They turned into an unmarked lane and went another half kilometer, then came to a halt before massive gateposts of red brick surmounted by bronze lanterns. Wrought-iron gates four meters high swung open when Shannon zapped them with a hand-held beamer. Victor saw that the thick bank of blooming shrub-roses surrounding the property had concealed an inner double barrier of chain link and electrified mesh. More fencing bordered the drive and behind it bull mastiffs and Dobermans watched the Ferrari's progress with silent alertness. A short distance further along they came to another perimeter of charged chain link topped with razor-wire. On the other side of a reinforced steel gate was a guard kiosk with cameras, spotlights, windows of one-way glass, and several unobtrusive gun-ports. A rustic sign at the barrier said:

WELCOME. STAY IN YOUR VEHICLE.
OBEY INSTRUCTIONS PROMPTLY.

"Sweet shit," muttered Victor.

Cameras swiveled, inspecting the car and its occupants. An electronic voice said: "Good day. Please state your name and business."

Shannon rolled down her window, leaned out, and waved. "It's me, guys! And a friend of mine. Call off the dragons."

"Yes, *ma'am*," said the loudspeaker. "You may proceed to the house." The gate opened and tire spikes that had protruded from the roadway sank back into metal receptacles. The Ferrari drove along a winding landscaped drive.

"God help the poor bastard who has to read the water meter," Victor said.

"Don't be silly. That's all done remotely in Illinois."

"Where does he hide the antiaircraft batteries?"

"In a wing of the stable."

"You're serious?"

"Don't talk like a fool," she snapped, "or I may just regret bringing you out of the New Hampshire boondocks and stick with Gerry after all."

Victor stomped on the brakes, turned, and seized her by her upper arms. Coercion smote her like a cannon shell and she cried out with hurt and rage. He ripped aside her outer mind-screen as if he were tearing paper and blasted her strong inner shield to painful shards that swirled like a dizzy kaleidoscope while she cowered, furious and delighted. He saw her true. Saw the hate for Kieran O'Connor overarching every other conviction in her soul and her need of *him* and him alone tightening the knot of purpose.

"Bitch," he laughed, setting her free.

They drove on, and the house came into view. It was a modernistic pile with cantilevered balconies, built partly into the eastern side of a hill and heavily shrouded with gnarled white oaks and Scotch pines. Protruding from one part of the roof was a structure like a blind control tower surmounted by antenna arrays. Victor could see at least three other big steerable dishes lurking among the trees at the crest of the hill.

"Is that where it is?" Victor asked, mentally indicating the tower.

"Yes. He calls it his study. To the rest of us, it's the command post. In the beginning it was only a glorified communications and data-retrieval center. Over the years Daddy kept modifying and adding to the equipment. He built a redundant control center in the subbasement, too—and there are underground cables connecting his equipment with three commercial satellite uplinks, in case anything happens to the antennas here on the grounds."

They pulled up to a side door and Victor switched off the engine. Shannon's window was still open. A hot wind smelling of roses and freshly sprinkled grass mingled with the last cool gasp of the Ferrari's air conditioning.

He said, "Your father would have to be an idiot not to know that our relationship isn't a simple matter of business."

"He knows," she said calmly.

"He knows I'm here today?"

"I'm supposed to be converting you to his point of view. Since my little white body has thus far proved to be a less than irresistible inducement, I've been ordered to tempt you with more exotic thrills."

Victor laughed. "Let's get on with it."

Inside, the mansion was silent and apparently deserted. Shannon explained that with her father out of town, the domestic staff did only routine housekeeping chores. The domestics, the security people, and the grounds keepers were all bonded operants who by temperament, intelligence, or education were not suited to executive positions in O'Connor's organization. They lived in comfortable homes of their own in what was called The Village, in a distant corner of the estate. Shannon told Victor that some of the staff had belonged to the ménage for more than twenty years.

They went up in a big service elevator to the third floor and passed down a carpeted hallway. From the vantage point they could see the sky darkening as the storm approached.

"Let me explain the background of what you're going to see," Shannon said. "You know that Psi-Eye inspired the superpowers to end their nuclear arms race. But most of the small nations that had tactical nukes stashed away balked at giving them up—especially after Armageddon showed that the network of EE surveillance couldn't possibly prevent terrorist-type attacks by small forces. The little nations such as South Africa and India didn't give a hoot whether Psi-Eye publicized their arsenals or not. They rather welcomed letting their enemies know they were in a position to retaliate."

"Especially after the Jihad got rolling in Asia and Africa," Victor acknowledged. "Can't say that I blame them."

"Some defense analysts in America and the Soviet Union

worried about the situation and proposed a worldwide coopera-
tive satellite defense system. In the States, so long as the Democrats controlled Congress and the White House, there was talk
but no action. The Russians got a system on the drawing boards
when Pakistan and Iran started sponsoring revolts in their Central
Asian republics—but their civil war broke out before they could
carry the plan further."

Outside the windows, the oak trees were showing the bottoms
of their leaves in the rising wind. A sepulchral rumble was barely
perceptible through the thick walls of the house.

Shannon said, "When President Baumgartner was elected in
2000, there was a clear and pressing need for satellite defense.
Everybody knew that South Africa had medium-range ballistic
missiles with neutron warheads all emplaced to stave off any
black invasion from the north. And everybody also knew that it
was only the fear of more fallout that kept the Jihad forces from
using regular nukes on Russia. The Jihad didn't have neutron
bombs yet, but it seemed only a matter of time. And with deliv-
ery systems becoming cheaper and more easily available, virtually any little nation would be in a position to commit nuclear
blackmail inside of a decade or so."

They stood in front of the armor-plated door that lacked a
knob or a latch. Shannon pressed her right hand against the inset
golden plate and a chime sounded.

"For years now, Daddy's agents have abetted terrorism and
acted as provocateurs, just so this satellite defense system would
be built. His people helped the Armageddon fanatics get their
bombs. They triggered the civil war in the Soviet Union and
aided the Jihad movement in Africa. When Daddy's candidate,
Baumgartner, won the White House, it was politically acceptable
for him to resurrect the part of the old Reagan Strategic Defense
Initiative that was most workable—the ground-laser satellite-
mirror system called Zap-Star."

Shannon addressed the door's voice-print identifier. "Open
up!" The metal panel slid aside and the two of them entered
Kieran O'Connor's sanctum. An enormous banked control console took up one entire five-meter wall. "When Zap-Star is com-

plete in another year or so, it will consist of 150 battle-mirror satellites and twenty ground batteries of multiple-excimer lasers. UN peace-keepers will control the system from a new command center being built on Christmas Island in the Pacific. The Zap-Star system is being financed primarily by the United States, Europe, Japan, and Korea. China has built its own part of the network independently, twenty mirrors and two ground bases . . . but all the other satellites utilize guidance systems manufactured by Daddy's multinational aerospace conglomerate. And each one has built-in override." She indicated the console. "Zap-Star can be accessed from here, cutting out the Christmas Island syscom."

"Good God!"

Shannon sat down at the computer. "None of the weaponry is on-line yet, of course. When it is, the access code will be Daddy's great secret—the one I presume he'll offer to sell you in exchange for your soul." She laughed. "Would you like to see how the thing works?"

She spoke into a command microphone and summoned graphics to a big liquid-crystal display. "The white blips on the map represent the UN's worldwide emplacement of excimer laser batteries. The green blips are the Chinese bases. Notice the two red blips! . . . Those are Daddy's insurance policy—one in Saskatchewan and one in the Maldive Islands south of India. His own ground bases, in case the others should be destroyed—say, by the Chinese."

"What do the ground lasers do—beam death-rays to the battle-mirrors?"

"It's not quite like that. In case of a nuclear-missile launching or other hostile action, the excimer fires bursts of coherent light at the high-orbit relay mirrors. They're the large blue blips. These transfer the beams to smaller, highly maneuverable battle-mirrors that have already locked on to targets. Depending upon the nature of the beam—and it can be varied from moment to moment—the target can be pierced or fried or simply have its electronic or electrical equipment rendered useless. The last option is the most versatile! A certain type of beam can mutilate the microcircuitry of chips and turn them into useless junk. It can deactivate missiles, aircraft, ships, Asats—anything at all with computer guidance. And it can do more! It can short out auto ignition, radio, video, even light bulbs and hearing aids and solar-cell watches and calculators. The Zap-Star system is virtually the perfect defense against any sort of modern warfare."

Victor said, "Or the perfect offense."

"Oh, yes. Just imagine a modern city deprived of all electrical or electronic equipment. It would be the literal return of the Dark Ages—the end of modern civilization."

Victor gestured at the mass of equipment. "What's to prevent us from blowing the whistle on this setup?"

"You'd never be able to prove that it's anything except a horrendously expensive control system for some kind of satellite link. None of the incriminating details—the target cities, for instance—are accessible. There's no law against having descriptions of Zap-Star in your data bank—especially when your companies manufacture the guidance systems for the satellites. As for the uplinks . . . they could control *any* kind of satellites—weather-eyes, surveyors, comsats, relays. Daddy owns at least forty-six."

"When will the Zap-Star system be completed?"

"Late 2013. A very unlucky year—or lucky, depending upon your point of view."

Victor was frowning, thinking furiously behind his mental barrier. "There are at least a dozen holes in your father's scheme for using this thing to conquer the world. The most blatant, of course, is the Chinese connection. They control their sats and they have their own excimer batteries. Suppose they were able to use that sigma-field thing as shielding—"

"Daddy doesn't want to conquer the world."

"Then what—"

She whispered into the microphone. The screen went black.

Victor felt his heart constrict. "But that's lunacy!"

"It's his vision of the Absolute," Shannon corrected. "He'd tell *you* that Zap-Star was a tool for world domination and offer it to you in exchange for your help in destroying the operant leadership. He knows that they must be onto him." She paused, then got up and smoothed the skirts of her white dress, smiling slightly. "He may even suspect who has betrayed him. But he's trapped by his love. He still hopes to convert me to the way he's chosen. And the child . . ."

"Love!" Victor made the word an obscenity.

She turned away from him. "I don't come to this room very often. Just when I need to remember, to strengthen my resolve. He did it to me here . . . And always, when it's time to go, I'm afraid. What if the door won't obey my voice and open? Or what if it does open—and I find him standing outside, waiting, asking me to reaffirm the bonding? Could I deny him? Have I already accepted?

No! he said; and she clung to him, letting the fear and fury drain into ice-glazed oblivion.

In time, she did open the door. And of course the corridor was empty. Through the window they could see that the grounds of the mansion were being wracked by a violent thunderstorm.

"My Ferrari!" she wailed, all the rest of it forgotten. "I left the window open!"

They ran for the elevator together, laughing.

25

LEWISBURG, PENNSYLVANIA, EARTH
6 AUGUST 2012

THE SUPERINTENDENT OF THE FEDERAL PRISON OPENED THE DOOR to a small bare room with a metal table and two chairs. "Will this do, Professor Remillard?"

"Is it bugged?" Denis asked in a level tone.

The superintendent chuckled. "Oh, no. There's the usual window in the door—but Agent Tabata has already made it quite plain that no observers will be required during your consultation with the prisoner. Shall I have him brought in now?"

"Please," said Denis. He put his briefcase on the table and opened it. When the superintendent left the room he quickly took out four objects that looked like featureless gray business cards and placed one in each corner of the room. If there *were* bugs, they were now deaf and blind.

Denis had had to explain to the President that there was no way that a redactive probe could be accomplished at long distance. In EE, it required arduous effort to overhear declamatory telepathy—the "loudest" kind—passing among persons being observed. Probing their innermost thoughts, a virtuoso trick even with the examinee at arm's length, was totally impossible. The only way that Denis could check out the amazing accusation of Gerry Tremblay's wife would be to probe him in person. The probe might or might not succeed, depending upon the psychological tone of Tremblay. As to the ethics of the situation . . . Denis had given the matter careful thought. Since legislation that would permit mental cross-examination was in the process of being ratified, Denis would accept it as de facto—with the understanding that none of the information he obtained would be used as direct evidence in any case, nor would Denis himself be called to testify as to his findings.

The President had complimented him dryly on his prudence and perspicacity. Denis had responded that those qualities had taken on survival value, given the present mood of the country toward operants. The President had earnestly assured him that the mood was changing for the better, to which Denis had replied sadly that he, personally, had seen scant signs of improvement in operant-normal relations—and if Mrs. Tremblay's accusations of a massive conspiracy by secret operants could be proved, the Sons of Earth and other bigots would have a field day, and the operant image would be tarnished almost beyond redemption. The President had laid a big hand on Denis's shoulder and urged him to have courage. After the November election it would be possible to take action in a number of important areas. But right now . . . Tremblay! Denis had promised to do his best, and report his findings only to the President.

The door opened, and Gerry Tremblay came in.

"Hello, Denis." Here I am and yes I know I look like hell I've lost ten kilos and my colitis has turned my ass to a disaster zone and I'm even starting to go fucking *bald* and my wife is knocked up with some operant's brat and my father-in-law says All's Forgiven What the Hell You Can Be an Arbitrager! and why the devil did you have to come NOW four days before I get out of this fucking hole? . . .

"Gerry, I'm sorry to bother you. I know how you feel. We all do. But I must ask some important questions."

SUREyoumust! WhatthefuckgotintomedidI*really*thinkIwassavingAllOperantsfromBAUMGARTNERTHEARCHFIEND? The arrogance! The lunacy! ThefriggingdipshitBOOBERYofit . . .

It was Denis's almost invariable custom to veil his eyes from those he engaged in conversation. His direct gaze tended to paralyze normals and throw operants into a state of near panicky screen-slamming. Even his family could be shocked into speechlessness when he inadvertently let the power flood out instead of reining it back behind the social mask that the real superminds were still learning to wear. As Gerry Tremblay's mental speech babbled on, all fouled with self-pity and mortification, Denis looked at the table top. He had placed a pen and a jotting pad there, useless props. The ranting continued and he picked up the pen and drew a square. Then he drew a star, and a circle, and a cross, and three parallel wavy lines.

Gerry said, "Oh, hell. The Zener cards!" And then he was laughing and half crying, remembering the very beginning of their relationship, thirty-three years ago, when a weird twelve-year-old kid had come slogging down into a dusty granite quarry in Barre, Vermont, and asked him to put down his jackhammer for a few minutes and take a little test that could be really important . . .

Denis said: We used those cards. The old-fashioned ESP pack that Rhine had made famous. And you called them one hundred percent Gerry and nearly wet your jeans because you had no idea. None at all.

Yeahyeahyeah! And the test wasn't for your benefit it was for me so I'd come away to Dartmouth with you and Glenn and Sally and Tucker and the rest of the Coterie . . . Oh God Denis how did it turn to this *shit*?

"Listen to me, Gerry. There's still something important you can do. If you like . . . do to make up."

Gerry stiffened. "What I did—I did because I thought it was right. That's what I'll say until I die, Denis. I won't disgrace us. It was a hell of a dumb move, maybe even crazy, but no disgrace to operancy."

Denis lifted his eyes.

Gerry Tremblay's mouth opened in an unvoiced scream. He covered his face with his hands and his shoulders began to shake.

You know you know God you know—

I don't know all of it Gerry but I must. Shannon has confessed a lot of it. First to Nell Baumgartner and then to the President himself. Is it true that Kieran O'Connor is a powerful operant?

Of course not.

Is it true that he's been misusing his powers for years breaking every law in the book to build up a personal fortune manipulating politicians even coercing Baumgartner to run and then when he saw his puppet slipping away in desperation he—

NO NO NO!

Is it true that Kieran O'Connor has set up a clandestine control center for Zap-Star?

. . . whattheHELL???

So you didn't know. Gerry sit up. Take your hands away from your face. *Do it.*

Yes.

I'm going to probe you. To get the truth of it as you see it. There will be no follow-up at all as far as you're concerned. When I've finished I'll wipe out every trace of this visit so O'Connor will never suspect what's been done. We'll nail him through conventional investigation. He can't have covered every trace of his manipulation if it's as massive as Shannon says. Will you consent to the probe? You know it has to be voluntary.

I—I—

I know O'Connor's done something to you Gerry. I can see it a kind of command-inhibition compelling absolute loyalty. But I think I can crack it. I'll be as careful as I can.

I—I—Denis I love him. I love him and he's a filthy swine a madman—

Be calm Gerry.

Can—can you wipe *that* out too?

I could try. There's a chance that he'd know and it would be risky for you because you wouldn't remember any of this. But I think I could retain a semblance of the bondage. I'll try.

Thank you Denis thank you all right DO IT God do it help me get him out of me—

"Gerry, I'd like you to sit back in your chair and relax. Take deep breaths."

"Okay."

"Close your eyes now. If you like, you can farsense these Zener figures I've drawn on the pad. But see nothing but them. Think of nothing else."

"All right."

Gerry Tremblay closed his eyes and summoned up the familiar old markings.

Only a moment or so later, when he opened his eyes again, a guard was at his side and he was walking back toward his cell. He wondered whether he was losing his marbles. For the life of him he couldn't remember why they'd fetched him out of his cell.

Oh, hell. What difference did it make? Come Friday he'd be out of here for good, and he could pull his shit back together and make a brand new start.

26

FROM THE MEMOIRS OF
ROGATIEN REMILLARD

I WENT TO THE HANOVER POST OFFICE TO DO MY REGULAR FIRST-thing-in-the-morning pickup. It was just across the street from the bookshop and, in those days, provided more convenient service than electronic mail or parcel express—as well as being considerably cheaper.

It was 24 September 2012, two days after the calamitous Metapsychic Congress in Oslo. Because it was a Monday the box was full of letters and cards and junk mail, as well as several videograms and the inevitable "Please call at the window for package" notices. I joined the long line of patrons and began to sort my stuff, at the same time carrying on half a conversation with Elijah Shelby who was standing just ahead of me. He ran a desktop publishing company out of his home on River Ridge Road and patronized my shop fairly often.

"Tough about the way things fell apart in Norway," Shelby said.

"Serves the heads right for scheduling a symposium on operant political activism," I said. "They asked for a reeraw and they sure as hell got one. I warned Denis not to force the issue."

"Reckon your nevvy'll be coming home with his tail between his legs. Media kinda made mincemeat of him, didn't they?"

"Denis is no coward," I said shortly. "Takes balls to stand on your principles . . . and you don't want to believe everything you read in the newsplaques, Lije."

"Mf!" said Shelby. My mention of the great innovation in communication struck a sour note with the publisher. The pro-

grammable liquid-crystal reader-plaques had already spelled the
doom of printed periodicals and paperback ephemera; and the
newer large-format plaques with improved color-imaging that had
just come out of China were bound to take a nasty bite out of
conventional book publication.

One of the videograms addressed to me was from a plaque
outfit. They were haranguing booksellers, urging them to install
the latest top-of-the-line state-of-the-art super-glamorous reader-
plaque recorder-dispenser unit—priced at a mere $189,000.00 if
you hurried to take advantage of this one-time-only special offer.
I deep-sixed the expensive advertising piece in the post office's
waste bin, along with the rest of the junk mail.

The second videogram, a jumbo floppy, was from Denis, origin Oslo, transmission time last Saturday. He always conscien-
tiously sent me the proceedings of the Metapsychic Congresses
even though most of the papers and panel discussions were far
over my simple head. I rarely bothered to play them—but I'd
play this one, all right, and bring plenty of popcorn.

The third and last videogram was from Ume Kimura, origin
Sapporo, transmission time 1915 hours tomorrow...

No!

I clutched the little disk in its flimsy envelope with both
hands, letting the rest of my mail tumble to the floor. *You didn't.
You couldn't. Not because of what happened at the Congress* ...

"Hey, Roj?" Elijah Shelby was picking up my stuff and eyeing
me askance. "You okay? You look like you seen a ghost. Bad
news?"

But momentary hope burst over me and I thought: Ghost!
Ghost! Stop her stop her you can stop her—

All around me the banalities of a small-town post office
crowded with patrons, and the good old gaffer now radiating
anxiety as he realized that something was really wrong, and I
walked away still mind-shouting, pushed open the door, stood
outside in the early morning sun yelling around the world into
tomorrow's night.

Then I ran, through the parking lot and across South Street to
my bookshop, and fumbled with the old-fashioned key, and

tripped on the sill, nearly dropping the precious disk. To the back room. Power up the player. (No. I couldn't print it. I never could.) Slip the videogram into the slot and fall into my old swivel chair. No longer shouting to the Ghost but pleading to the kind-eyed naked-hearted Jesus whose picture had hung on Tante Lorraine's bedroom wall. Don't let her! Don't let her! But I knew she had.

Her image smiled at me. She wore a plain Japanese robe and sat on her heels in front of a painted paper screen set in some outdoor courtyard or atrium. A small maple tree with spidery maroon leaves was visible behind the screen and there was a tinkling of falling water. Ume spoke to me with formality after the initial smile and bow of her head.

"Roger, my dear friend . . . I have just returned from the Congress in Oslo. You know by now that there is a serious division among the operant leadership, brought about, by our increasing despair over the unending violence that afflicts the world. The dream we once shared of leading humanity to permanent peace now stands revealed as mere arrogant presumption. How did we operants dare to think that we would succeed, when all throughout history well-meaning persons have tried again and again to foster peace, only to fail?

"We tried to show humanity a fellowship of the mind, a new society where suspicion and fatal misunderstanding could be banished from political relationships, fostering a climate where peace might flower. But instead of this, we opened a chasm wider than before—a gulf between operant and nonoperant. There is no fellowship, only envy and fear. There is no peace, only ever-spreading war.

"You know how previous Congresses of operants would reaffirm, at the start of the proceedings, the ethic of love and nonaggression exemplified by the illustrious martyr, Urgyen Bhotia. This philosophy, together with its correlate—that operant minds have an obligation to love and serve selflessly those minds who stand a step beneath on evolution's ladder—was never seriously challenged during the twenty years of Metapsychic Congresses preceding this one.

"O my friend! Now the challenge has been made.

"It seemed so innocent, didn't it, when the symposium on political activism ended in an implacable deadlock! On the one side were Denis and Jamie and Vigdis, championing nonaggression, and on the other side, insisting that operants must now defend themselves and their countries with mental as well as physical force, were Tamara and Zhenyu and—the shame!—Hiroshi. My own countryman! And Tamara, the mother of us all! My soul turned to ice as these three revered ones opened their minds to the assembly and showed the reasoning that had led them to abandon the precious heritage of Urgyen.

"Yes . . . one may see the logic. The Soviet operants have suffered more terribly than any. Now that the dictator is dead and the Politburo begs them to return and unify their collapsing nation, how can they say no? They are offered great political power. Once before they were betrayed and they vow it will not happen again. One may see the logic!

"But from it flow the consequents.

"China fears the Soviet Union. It is rich in food and technology and its great northern neighbor starves for both as the civil war drags on in spite of the capitulation of Iran and the coup in Pakistan. And the rest of Asia contemplates with horror a conflict between the giants. What can save us? The Zap-Star net is unfinished. Now its defenses may be turned into weaponry! The EE adepts of every nation will survey the great laser batteries with increasing trepidation, wondering which country will first dare attempt the conversion . . . Japan fears that China may already possess this capability—and that it will be used as a preemptive strike against the Soviets . . .

"Like an avalanche in my Hokkaido mountains, it has begun with a tiny slippage downhill. Soon it will be an unstoppable monster. We operants will lend it momentum. Yes. It was already happening in Oslo as we raised mental walls against one another, feeling the former mood of trust and goodwill begin sliding into an abyss. All of us, seeing the logic; forgetting the love and the dream.

"I am saddened and shamed. In my pride I had cultivated

tsuki-no-kokoro—the mind as calm as the moon. I tried to lead and teach. I never coerced. But I cannot create within myself that selfless power, that Center of vision that my people call the hara, that would give me courage to continue. I am a proud and foolish woman who long ago turned away from her own family, and again and again my mind shows me a small girl bringing humiliation upon her father. I must escape this girl and her shame.

"O my friend! The pleasure we shared was good. The comfort we gave one another must be your remembrance of me, and not this image of pain. Burn the disk, Roger. Nakanai de kudasai. Sayonara."

She knelt silently then. There was no mat beneath her, only polished flagstones. She closed her eyes and her body tensed and I knew she was summoning the psychocreativity from what she called her Center.

There was only a split second of flame before the video recording went to black.

She had told me to destroy the disk: I could not. She had told me, in Japanese, not to cry: I did. But I did obey her request to remember our sharing; and I remember it now and possess, for a little while, my own tsuki-no-kokoro.

27

PITTSBURG TOWNSHIP, NEW HAMPSHIRE, EARTH
31 JULY 2013

"YOU WANTA WAIT HERE ON THE DECK, MR. O'CONNOR, VIC should be back from his swim in a jiff. Coolin' off nicely out here now that the sun's down. Varmints be comin' down to the water. You might like to catch a scan of 'em. Visitors often do."

"Thank you, Mr. Laplace," Kieran said. "That might be interesting. What kinds of wildlife do you have in these parts?"

"Moose, bear, panther—Vic even reintroduced woodland caribou couple years ago, when he first closed off Indian Stream Valley to the public. These north New Hampshire woods'll soon be back the way my ancestors knew 'em. Damn good thing, too."

"You're descended from the voyageurs?" Kieran inquired politely.

"Them—and the Abnaki. Figure I got my long-sight from the Redskin side of the blanket and my coercion from the Canuck." The gray-haired caretaker nodded toward an impressive instrument mounted on one of the deck railings. "Now some heads— uh—some operants like to use the spotterscope for spyin' wildlife if their long-sight gets a mite bewildered by the woods and the lake and all. Feel free. That there's a light-amp with optional warm-body targeting adjustable to the 'proximate size of the varmint you wanta scan. Try around four to six hundred kilos for moose, seventy to one-twenty-five for whitetail deer or bear . . . or a man."

Limping slightly, Kieran went to examine the scope. "Does Victor Remillard find much use for this?"

Laplace let out a pitying guffaw. "You gotta be kidding!" Then the mien of exaggerated civility was back in place and he said, "Well, you just make yourself t'home while I take care of a few things. Like I said, Vic'll be along soon."

He turned and started to shamble away, then turned to say, "Not that I wanta give you a hard time, since Vic *did* say he was expecting you. But you had your orders from Mr. Fortier. Those heads of yours in the limo—they were told to go all the way back to the main Pittsburg road and wait. They ain't done that. I think you better flash 'em your telepathic high-sign."

Kieran said, "I'll do that, Mr. Laplace. A misunderstanding."

This time the operant yokel's deadpan expression was clearly contradicted by the contempt of his mental undertone. "And while you're at it, give a shout to them four fellers pussyfootin' this way through the woods along the south shore. Tell 'em to get their asses and their arsenal back the way they come from before they fall into a bog . . . or somethin'."

Imbeciles! Adam Arnie damnyou didn't I tell you I'd handle this on my own get out and call off those piss-artist commandos!

Kier we only wanted to maximize our options in case—

GET OUT! "Well, I'm sorry about that, Mr. Laplace. An overzealous subordinate took it upon himself to countermand my explicit instructions."

"A damn shame. But no harm done, I reckon. I try to see to that, Mr. O'Connor. We're just a little two-bit lash-up compared to your organization—but we get along."

"I appreciate that. We might say that's why I'm here this evening. I've transmitted to my people direct orders for withdrawal. I intend to fulfill Mr. Remillard's conditions to the letter. You will let him know that?"

Laplace smirked and spat over the rail into the lake. From somewhere out on the water came an eerie warbling cry like demented laughter.

"An owl?" Kieran asked.

"Nope. Loon. Alias the great northern diver, *Gavia immer.* Kinda relic of the late Neogene avifauna. Been yakkin' it up in these parts purt' near five, six million years. Long time to hold on to a sense of humor, but I reckon it helps a critter survive. Be seein' you, Mr. O'Connor. You be sure to tell Vic I was on the job."

"I'll do that," Kieran said dryly.

The gangling old fellow clumped off into the lodge's interior and Kieran let out a long sigh of pain. He closed his eyes, summoning the soothing black momentarily, and let it cradle him. Serene, he banished suspicion and anxiety and the gnawing in his groin; and when he opened his eyes he saw four bulky shapes wading out from a small heavily wooded cove a hundred meters or so down the shore to the right.

He flicked on the spotterscope and swung the barrel. A cow moose and her nearly full-gown triplets were feeding on water plants. He watched them for nearly ten minutes. The sky had gone to deep purple and the loons were cackling excitedly over toward the northern reaches of the lake, so Kieran aimed the light-amplifying device in that direction after programming the infrared mode to detect bodies in excess of ninety kilograms mass. The driving mechanism took over and Kieran kept his eye to the scope as it scanned the opposite shore, about twelve hundred meters away.

The target-grid flashed on. Gotcha! And Kieran zoomed in and found himself looking at another moose. But this one was one of the most uncanny beasts he had ever seen, an enormous male standing half concealed among the dense second growth of balsam fir. His color was not the usual dark brown but burnished gray, like pewter; and the great rack of antlers, still dangling shreds of velvet, was whiter than bleached bone at the pronged edges and translucent with startling blood-veins in the broad, palmate centers and toward the base. The moose rubbed his fantastic skull adornment vigorously against saplings to scratch what must have been a colossal itch. Then he glared at Kieran from eyes like smoldering coals.

"I've named him Glaçon. Rather frivolous for such a massive brute, but it fit when he was a calf. He's a special pet. Genetically engineered albino. I always wondered what one would look like."

Kieran continued his calm survelliance through the eyepiece. His farsight superimposed the image of Victor Remillard's face in the black forest portion of the visual field. "Glaçon . . . that means ice cube, doesn't it?"

"Or a cold-hearted devil of a person," said Victor Remillard.

Kieran lifted his head from the scope. "He's beautiful. In this forest preserve of yours, he might even live to a ripe old age." He didn't ask Victor if he would like to use the instrument. In farsight, the younger man was clearly his master. But that was not the metafaculty that mattered . . .

They faced off, the burly forty-three-year-old at his physical and mental prime and the dying old man. Kieran O'Connor's once olive skin was now sallow and deeply furrowed beside the thin-lipped Celtic mouth. The eyes were sunken, having the same insatiable ardor as Shannon's eyes; the mind behind them, however, had none of her fire but instead a beckoning well of unending night.

Come to me, said Kieran.

To me! Victor commanded.

Neither man moved.

The whooping of the loons reflected the laughter that flooded the aether. They disengaged and stood back.

Kieran shrugged. "We had to try. But it isn't really a standoff, you know . . . You've won."

Victor was wary. "Explain."

"I must sit down," Kieran said.

They moved to a couple of bogus Barcelona chairs and Kieran lowered himself with exquisite caution. "You know my physical condition. I will continue to survive on will power, however, until it suits me to end what I began. You are also probably aware that both the FBI and the Justice Department are rooting feverishly through my data banks, using methods both licit and illicit, determined to find or fabricate evidence that I am guilty of treason, conspiracy, racketeering, grand theft, and multiple counts of murder."

Victor nodded.

"Do you know that your older brother Denis is responsible for this embarrassment of legal activism?"

"No . . ."

Kieran smiled sourly. "He and his partisans are also behind the recent spate of bills introduced into Congress that will empower operant investigators to meddle in the affairs of persons like you and me. The amendment permitting mental cross-examination was only the beginning, you know."

"I know. All these years, they couldn't touch us. Denis knew what I was doing, but there was never any way he could prove it. He couldn't even prove I was operant—much less that I used the powers to take what I wanted."

Kieran said, "A mechanical aura-detection device—ostensibly for use in identifying and classifying the faculties of operant newborns—is undergoing tests at the University of Edinburgh. Professor Jamie MacGregor will be demonstrating it at this year's Metapsychic Congress."

Victor said nothing. But his mind transmitted both a query and an image of an intricate control console emplaced in a blind tower in the countryside west of Chicago.

"You want an explanation of that." Kieran smiled and nodded almost absently. The pain was far away for the moment. "I should have thought it would be obvious. It's the key to ultimate victory. Once the victory would have been mine. Now I'm offering it to you."

Kieran spoke on, slowly and simply, clothing the ludicrous notion of ruling the world through the Zap-Star's threat with a glowing plausibility, but at the same time making certain that Victor recognized the scheme as the fever-dream of an aging megalomaniac. The crude brain of the self-centered entrepreneur would be immediately aware of the gaping flaws in logic. He would visualize other ways of using Zap-Star, feasible ways. He would humor the madman, intuitively accepting Kieran's genuine need of him, but never grasping the hidden motive. As to the goal of the Absolute . . . its apprehension was as far beyond Victor Remillard as were the stars that had begun to twinkle in the summer sky of New Hampshire.

"It can all be yours. I've completed the instruments of transfer—of merger, actually, granting you control of everything I own. Once I'm gone, the feds have nothing. My corporations exist as independent legal entities and they're as legitimate before the bar of justice as any American business. All you need to do is help me finish off our mutual enemies."

"Denis? His Coterie at Dartmouth?"

"*All* of them," Kieran said. "The metapsychic leadership of the world. The operant meddlers. They'll be right here in New Hampshire in mid-September having their annual confab. Even the breakaways from Russia and the Orient have agreed to send delegates for one last meeting. I can't touch them . . . but you could. I could show you how. Help you. My agents will see that the local chapters of the Sons of Earth are armed and equipped. You and your people—completely unknown to the government agents—provide the leadership and then disappear, leaving the mob to take the blame."

Victor said, "And then?"

"I die. And you take everything I have. I've worked out the details in a way that should satisfy you. Three of my closest associates—the men who were with me from the beginning—are prepared to brief you on the entire operation, beginning to end, mind-screens down. You have as many of your people sit in as you like."

"When can these associates of yours be here?"

"They're in the limousine that brought me," Kieran said, "the one that your efficient long-sighted caretaker made certain I sent back to the Pittsburg Junction before you put in your appearance."

Victor laughed. "Pete Laplace is the best farsensor I've got. Loyal as a Labrador retriever. With him and his old twelve-gauge hanging around, I'm as safe out here as a baby in a cradle. It's just a damn shame that his IQ's only around eighty-six."

"He seemed sharp enough to me... Well, Victor—what's your answer? Will you put those spoilers away for me and let me die happy?"

"Kieran, I'm only sorry I didn't think of the idea first! Let me get on the phone and get a few of my boys up from Berlin. It won't take more than an hour. Your bunch can follow them back in here. Meanwhile, you might like to join me in a little snack."

Kieran closed his eyes. Sequestered behind impregnable walls, safe in the secret depths, he gave thanks to the Black Mother. *In the end is the beginning. In death the source of life. Let Thy belly the void take us in. Dam dham nam tam tham dam dham nam pam pham...*

"Pete?" Victor was shouting. "Pete, you rapscallion—where are you hiding? We've got company coming and I need—oh, for God's sake! Kieran, you want to come in here and get a load of this? He's out like a light on the sun-porch couch, with the Browning tucked under his cheek and an empty bottle of Wild Turkey clutched to his chest! I guess I'll have to do my own cooking."

28

FROM THE MEMOIRS OF
ROGATIEN REMILLARD

In August 2013 I encountered the Family Ghost again—at the White Mountain Resort.

The sprawling white-stucco wedding-cake hotel at the western foot of Mount Washington seemed hardly to have changed at all from the days when I had worked there as its convention manager. It was as ridiculously posh and Edwardian as ever and served the same sumptuous meals, and in spite of America's depressed economy it was still crowded with virtually the same type of clientele—upscale young families, hiking fanatics with sybaritic base-camp tastes, and herds of nostalgic oldsters on expensive guided tours. The latter now arrived by X-wing airbus instead of the diesel motor coaches of my day; but they still wore lapel badges, and they were still escorted by pretty young women, and the old ladies still cheeped and tittered eagerly while the old gents looked glum and resigned.

I had come to the hotel on business, to consult with the youngster who occupied my erstwhile position, one Jasper Delacourt. Ten years earlier the Twelfth Congress on Metapsychology had been held at the resort and Denis had roped me into making the arrangements. "Who," he had asked me reasonably, "could do a better job of it?" And so I did, and the hotel's Olde New England kitsch had charmed the socks off the foreign scholars, who found it a refreshing change from the modern university locales that had characterized most of the other Congresses. The cog railway had been a big hit, and the more able-bodied operants tramped around on Mount Washington during their spare time, marveling over the relict ice-age flora and oddly portentous ambiance around the summit.

This year's Congress (which many people at Dartmouth feared would be the last) was also scheduled to be held at the resort, and so it was only natural that I should do a reprise of my 2003 duties. I had made most of the arrangements by phone and data-link months earlier; but as September approached I drove over to wrap things up in person.

Jasper Delacourt bounced up from behind his desk as I entered his office and wrung my hand. The hotel was extremely happy to be hosting twenty-eight hundred delegates during the somnolent post-Labor Day season.

"Roger, you old sonuvagun! God, you look great. Ten years, you haven't aged a day, my man!"

"You look pretty fit yourself," I lied. "The Congress committee over at Dartmouth is really very pleased that you could accommodate us, given the more modest budget this go-around."

Jasper sighed. "Things are tough all over. I can level with you because you used to sit in this seat, right? I have to hustle my ass off scratching up tours and conferences and sales meetings to keep this hulk topped off. If we had to depend on straight vacationers, we'd belly-up."

I chuckled. "It wasn't all that different in '90, when I left."

He studied me narrowly and I could see his mind doing calculations. "Jeez—that long ago? But I thought— How the hell old are you, anyhow?"

"In a week I'll be sixty-eight."

"Holy moley," Jasper groaned. "What—d'you get your seltzer from Ponce de Leon's fountain, man? I'd of said forty-five ten years ago and say the same now. I mean, you got that lived-in look and Miss Clairol never made a dime off those silver curls— but *sixty-eight*? No shit?"

I shrugged. "Kind of runs in the family. I reckon I'll fall to pieces all at once at seventy . . . But don't let me waste your time. I know you've got a lot to do. Mainly, I want to noodle with you on the matter of our big Saturday night banquet on the twenty-first. Our attendance will be a couple of hundred short of last time, but you remember how we had tables packed cheek-to-jowl in the Grand Ballroom, and out in the hall, and even filling up the Fern Salon. There were closed-circuit TV monitors spotted around so the speeches could be heard by the nonfarsensitive. But, Jasper . . . metapsychic operants want to experience the full nuance spectrum when somebody sounds off! Conventional sensory input *and* ultrasensory. Is the speaker delivering with a straight tongue and mind—or is he or she peddling tosh? Listening to a TV just doesn't cut the mustard with an audience of heads. We've got to think of something else—and I *don't* mean a buffet."

"Roger! Roger!" he chortled. "I'm way ahead of you, my man."

With a flourish, he produced a folder bound in fake leather and smacked it open on the desk, pressing the upper right-hand corner. Ta-dah! A twenty-by-thirty plaque, playing a full-color loop showing a series of lap dissolves of a luxurious mountaintop restaurant: exteriors at sunset, in sun-drenched daylight, in a majestic snowy night; interiors showing the place tricked out as a cabaret, hosting a bar mitzvah, wining and dining some affair of the New England Medical Association; close-ups of Lucullan feasts and après-hike fireside cheer. The book-plaque even had background music, for God's sake: Edward MacDowell's *New England Idyls*.

"The Summit Chalet!" Jasper declaimed. "Dine in opulent grandeur far above New Hampshire's White Mountains. Visit the fabled haunt of the Great Spirit, where even today flying saucers have been seen wafting through the crystalline air!"

"I remember now," I said. "When they demolished the obsolete antenna farm and transmitter complex four or five years ago, they granted the hotel a concession to build the chalet. Is it paying its way?"

"Not yet," Jasper confided. "We went way over budget on the environmental adaptations. You know—to keep it from blowing off the mountain when the wind's three hundred kloms an hour. The engineers finally licked it, though. A tornado couldn't budge that thing now. And what a showplace! Those globetrotting heads of yours'll eat it up, Roj."

I was dubious. "We're talking about moving nearly three

thousand people up there from the hotel, Jasper. In maybe an hour. And then getting them back down after the banquet."

"No problem. We bring in ten X-wing shuttle buses, make three trips."

"Who eats the transport costs?"

"Goes with the deluxe dinner package: prime rib or lobster, BP and veggie, sabayon dessert, nonvintage champers, gratuity included—ninety bucks a head."

I whistled. "Jasper—the budget! Do you realize that Dartmouth is so strapped that they're remerging the Department of Metapsychology with Psychiatry again? My nephew, the Nobel laureate, is getting shucked of two thirds of his staff! The research grants are gone, the endowments are gone, and this will probably be the last time the Congress meets for Christ knows how long."

Jasper leaned toward me. "Then make it a whangdoodle. Take 'em out in *style*."

"I don't see how I can justify—"

"Do me one favor. Go up and look the place over."

A van trundled me half a klom to the X-wing pad, which was tucked behind a sound-baffle wall hidden amidst greenery. In less than five minutes the versatile aircraft that combined the speed of a fixed-wing with the limited-space landing requirements of a helicopter whisked me to the top of Mount Washington. We landed in a bowl newly cut on the eastern shoulder of the summit. I recalled that environmentalists had bitterly protested both the landing facility and the new restaurant, demanding that the old Sherman Adams Summit Building, a graceless structure built in the 1980s, be retained as a historical monument and the rest of the summit be left "in a state of nature." However, since virtually the entire top of Mount Washington was covered with trucked-in rubble, and had been humanly modified in one way or another beginning in the 1820s, the natural-staters hadn't had much of a leg to stand on.

The Summit Chalet was designed to blend with the lichen-crusted granite and dazzling hoarfrost that characterized New England's highest point. The building was trifoliate, the three lobes having armor-glass windows all around, providing maximum windowside seating. Its rock-strewn roof was surmounted by a wide turret with an observation deck and open balcony, mobbed with tourists on that balmy summer afternoon. On the level below the restaurant were boutiques, souvenir shops, and a small museum, together with more open balconies. A covered tunnel led to a new sheltered terminus of the little old cog railway, which was exactly as I had remembered it. After a short inspection tour I was admitted to one of the lower balconies by the chalet's manager and left alone to think things over.

One of the primitive steam locomotives was toiling up-slope from the vicinity of the White Mountain Hotel, pushing its coach. The trails crisscrossing the summit had the same yellow-paint blazes. The grasslike sedges were desiccated, but here and there tufts of alpine herbiage grew green and indomitable, speckled with tiny flowers.

. . . The shivering boy standing at my side, pointing, his mind detecting the first empowered mind not of our own family.

. . . Hikers ascending in a line from behind the cog track, and little Denis's farsight lending me a glimpse of the second miracle: Elaine.

It had all begun right here. It would be an appropriate place for the farewell.

The wind was stiff that day, blasting in from the west, and my eyes misted over. I felt again the strange aetheric vibrations and an eerie sense of looming presence. The mountain that was sacred. The mountain that had killed so many. The mountain that had heard foolish dreamers crying out to the uncomprehending stars, and nurtured wild tales of frost demons and Great Carbuncles and flying saucers . . .

Bonjour Rogi!

I started violently. "Est-ce *toi*?!"

Arrange for the Metapsychic Congress to have its last supper on the mountain.

"Hah! And should I tell them who decreed the final squandering of their treasury?"

You will be able to convince Denis that the site is suitable. Your coercion is more effective than you think. After he has agreed and all the arrangements are in train . . . yes, you may tell him about me.

"Grand dieu—you can't mean it!"

Be subtle. Choose your time well. Perhaps you can tell him that you have long since accepted me as a minor delusion—a harmless unconscious projection of hope. Of *reasonable* hope, not one forlorn on the face of it.

"You haven't been around here for a long time, mon fantôme. We Earthlings have made a botch of it!"

Perhaps . . . Tell him anyhow. Tell him that he is right in clinging to the ethic of nonviolence and service. Tell him he is wrong about wanting to retreat to a low profile. The Mind of Earth must not fragment but coadunate—grow and flow together in a sublime metaconcert of goodwill, a renunciation of selfishness that coerces the Intervention of the Galactic Milieu at long last!

"Now?" I cried. "When it's all fallen apart? You've got a weird sense of humor."

The Ghost said: Your nephew Denis can scan your mind and apperceive the reality . . . if you yourself believe it to be true.

"Go away," I whispered, looking out over the western valley. "Leave me in peace. I'm only an old fool and no one listens to me, and there isn't a hope in hell that Denis or anyone else would take such a fairy tale seriously. Extraterrestrial redeemers are an old-fashioned aberration to psychiatrists like Denis. Jung even wrote a book about it! It's the perennial human desire for a fairy godmother or a deus ex machina to save us from our mortal folly—and I *don't* believe in it. So there!"

The invisible thing seemed to sigh in exasperation. It said: I hoped it would not be this way. Obviously it *must* be. Le bon dieu, il aime a plaisanter! Always the humorist . . . So! Tell me Rogi: Do you still have the Great Carbuncle?

"The key ring?" I blurted. Digging in my hip pocket, I pulled out the silvery chain that held my shop and apartment keys. The little red-glass ball of the fob winked in the powerful sunlight. "This thing?"

That thing . . . At the Congress, when the moment seems appropriate, you will once again urge Denis to unite his colleagues —and the Mind of Earth—in prayerful metaconcert. As a token of your serious intent invite him to scrutinize the Carbuncle with his deep-sight.

"Just like that!" I laughed bitterly. "And how will I know this magic moment?"

The Ghost said, rather ominously: It will be self-evident. Do it without fail. And now, au revoir, cher Rogi. We may meet again soon!

A deathly chill smote me. I gasped, and my breath exhaled in a white cloud, and I realized that the temperature of the air had fallen precipitously. Stumbling, I turned to the sliding glass door behind me and hauled it open, flinging myself inside as if the frost-demons themselves were on my tail.

The manager of the chalet was there, and he said, "Oh, there you are, Mr. Remillard. When you didn't stop in again at my office, I thought you might have left—"

"We'll have our banquet here," I said. "I've made up my mind. Let's go to your office and draw up the contract."

"Wonderful!" he said. "You'll be glad you made this decision."

"Somebody will be," I growled, and followed him back upstairs.

The following week I drove to Concord, where I had made an appointment with a consulting gemologist. He was understanding when I said that I'd like an appraisal of the Carbuncle while I waited—and watched. But as it happened, I was out of luck. He rather quickly ascertained that the chain wasn't silver, but a platinum-iridium alloy; it was also easy to determine that the flawless, transparent ball was not glass, but some other substance with a hardness of ten on Moh's scale.

"Now, ordinarily, that would suggest that we have a diamond," the gemologist said. "But a blood-red diamond would be fabulously valuable, and no person in his right mind would polish one into a spherical shape rather than facet it. So this may be some very unusual synthetic with a similar thermal conductivity."

My mind had gone numb. "Yes. That's probably just what it is. An old friend of mine gave me this. A chemist. Dared me to find out what it was. I think this is his idea of a practical joke."

The gemologist said, "To tell what this stone is, we'd have to do a crystallographic analysis with special equipment. That would run into money and take a while."

"No, no," I protested. "Why don't you just put down on your appraisal the bare facts you've told me. No monetary value of the stone, of course."

"Well, if that's what you want. You know, if this really were a diamond, it'd weigh upward of twenty-five carats. Because of the rare color, it'd likely be worth a couple million."

I forced a laugh. "Well, the joke's on me, isn't it? . . . Now how much do I owe you?"

The fee was fifty dollars. I paid it gladly, and tucked the appraisal paper into my wallet and the Great Carbuncle into my pants pocket. Then I went back to Hanover to wait for the third week in September, when the last Metapsychic Congress was scheduled to begin.

I didn't say anything to Denis about the Family Ghost, not even when the Carbuncle seemed to burn a hole in my pocket. The Ghost was welcome to make a fool of me if it could; but I was damned if I would make a fool of myself.

29

BRETTON WOODS, NEW HAMPSHIRE, EARTH
21 September 2013

SWIFTLY, BEFORE ANY EARLY RISERS WHO SHARED ILYA AND Katie's apprehensions could spot him and detain him, old Pyotr Sakhvadze slipped outside the grand hotel into dawn silence. He hurried across the dry lawn, noting that the absence of dew probably signified that rain was on the way. The sky was bright with a high overcast. It would be too bad if lowering clouds spoiled the view from the Summit Chalet during the banquet that evening, but a bit of thunder and lightning might actually liven things up.

Here and there among the beds of chrysanthemums and the formal evergreen plantations lay incongruous masses of litter—broken placards, torn banners, scattered leaflets, some beer and pop cans and snackfood wrappers—mementos of the crowd of antioperant pickets that had invaded the resort grounds last night. All throughout the week-long Metapsychic Congress there had been small groups of Sons of Earth demonstrators parading outside the main entrance of the complex; but several hundred had shown up on Friday evening, and the hotel security force had finally had to call in the State Police to clear them out. Pyotr's grandson Ilya had been quite alarmed at the sluggish response of the local authorities. He had warned Pyotr not to go outside alone on the final day of the Congress, when even more serious confrontations might be expected. However, the old man had no intention of forgoing his morning constitutional. The antioperants, he reasoned, would hardly be up and about at six in the morning. They would be sleeping off the Friday-night fracas and doubtless renewing their energies for a more climactic face-off tonight.

Abandoned placards blocked the pathway and Pyotr flicked them aside with his walking stick, *tsk*ing disapproval of the impudent sentiments. WE ARE HUMAN—ARE YOU? one sign inquired. Pyotr chuckled at another that proclaimed SUPERBRAINS INVADE YOUR INNER SPACE! By far the majority of the professionally printed placards echoed the Sons of Earth chant, "Off With the Heads"—which was often abbreviated in a sinister fashion to "Off the Heads!" The meaning of one slogan, WHERE IS KRYPTONITE NOW THAT WE REALLY NEED IT?, eluded Pyotr completely. He was relieved when he came to the turnoff at the X-wing pad and was able to head into the thick woods along the little Ammonoosuc River, which threaded the resort grounds.

Down by the brawling stream there were no traces of the demonstration. Sugar maple trees were just beginning to turn color in that amazing North American fashion that was—typically!—so much more spectacular than any Europe or Asia had to offer. But Pyotr was really hoping to rediscover another tree that he had taken note of ten years earlier, during his first visit to the White Mountain Hotel. On and on he walked, without catching sight of it, and he began to fear that it had perished, perhaps toppling into the river during a spring freshet. But no . . . there it was. A solitary mountain ash laden with marvelous great bunches of scarlet berries, the very image of the beloved ryabina trees of Pyotr's native Caucasus.

He paused and contemplated the scene with a full heart. The rushing stream, the magic tree, the mighty mountain looming darkly to the east—all so reminiscent of his old home that it made him want to weep with the loss.

No, he told himself, and forged on. What a fool you are, Pyotr Sergeyevich! You have lived ninety-nine years and you are still vigorous and in control of most of your mental faculties— meager though they be—and you have a safe home with your loving grandson Ilya in Oxford, and a wealth of memories and experiences to share with your great-granddaughters. You are as fortunate as the patriarch Seliac Eshba—even though not so tranquil, or so wise.

The path turned south, away from the river, and passed along the boundary of the resort's beautiful golf course, through an open area where the long rampart of the Presidential Range still hid the sun. The air was utterly calm. No birds sang and no civilized noises intruded upon the immense quiet. It seemed almost as if the entire New Hampshire countryside were holding its breath in anticipation.

Pyotr paused with his eyes lifted. The disasters had been many, but they had come and gone as surely as the seasons turned. In the future lay fresh perils, especially for his dear Tamara and the other operants now engaged in the struggle for power in Moscow. What would the simple Seliac think of such matters! Would he offer another homely metaphor from the abiding Earth as a symbol of hope? And why must it always be hope, rather than fruition? Must the small-souled and the evil always appear to triumph while the peace-lovers were left with only their dreams?

He walked on, brooding, toward a small pavilion where he thought he would sit and rest for a time; but the peculiar air of psychic tension was growing, together with a small but persistent pang just behind his forehead. He stopped again, rubbing his eyes, and when he looked back toward the mountain he stiffened and uttered a gasp of shcok.

The rocks of the vast slope shimmered in green and violet, and the crest of Mount Washington seemed crowned with a golden tellurian aura.

Pyotr thought: It can't be! These land-forms are ancient and stable. Surely they don't have earthquakes in New England!

He waited, frozen in place, expecting the tremor; but no seismic movement occurred. Instead, it was his mind that seemed to tremble on the brink of some stupendous discovery. What was it? He strained toward the insight that the mountain seemed to hold out to him, his eyes fixed on the brightening skyline—

And then the first dazzling limb of the sun topped the range, and he was momentarily blinded. He cried aloud, and when he could see once again the hallucination of colored light had vanished, along with the mysterious pregnant tension that had enthralled his brain.

"Usrat'sya mozhno!" he cried. His knees threatened to buckle and he barely caught himself from falling. Leaning heavily upon his walking stick, he hobbled toward the little summerhouse. In his frustration and vertigo, he did not notice that the place already had an occupant.

"Dr. Sakhvadze—is something wrong?"

A tall man who had been sitting in the deep shadows started up and took him by the arm, guiding him to a bench. Pyotr peered at him and recognized Denis Remillard's uncle, an enigmatic personage who acted as the Congress liaison with the hotel, but otherwise had little to do with operant affairs.

Pyotr sat down heavily, pulled out his pocket handkerchief, and mopped his face. "A little bad spell. Nothing physical. I am sensitive, you see . . . to certain psychodynamic currents in the geosphere."

"Ah," said Remillard, uncomprehending. "You're sure you'll be all right?" He displayed a miniature telephone unit that he had taken from inside his jacket. "I can call the hotel and have a golf cart brought out. No trouble at all."

"No," said Pyotr sharply. "You needn't treat me like an invalid! It was only a passing metapsychic event, I tell you. It shook me up. I'll be all right again in a moment."

"Just as you say," Remillard murmured, tucking the portaphone away. "You're abroad rather early, Doctor."

"And so are you," Pyotr retorted. Then, regretting his brusqueness, he added, "I felt particularly in need of a ramble today, to set my juices flowing and sharpen my wits. There are a number of important papers and talks being delivered that I am anxious to take in—most particularly Jamie MacGregor's demonstration of the prototype bioenergetic-field detector. Auras of all types are of great interest to me. And of course, there is tonight's banquet to look forward to—"

"Along with other unscheduled diversions."

Pyotr eyed Remillard with trepidation. "You think there will be serious trouble?"

"Some kind of trouble. We're doing our best to make certain that it's not serious."

"One would think that in a great and powerful country like the United States, such threats to public order would not be tolerated."

Remillard laughed shortly. "We have a saying: 'It's a free country.' And it is, Dr. Sakhvadze—for better and sometimes for worse. The Sons of Earth and the other antioperant crazies can demonstrate against us to their heart's content just as long as they don't trespass on the private property of the resort. They got a little overenthusiatic last night, and a few of them ended up in the slammer, but the mob was still unfocused. Disorganized. What we're afraid of is that another element may be moving in—a more professional type of troublemaker."

"Why don't your EE operatives investigate and forestall these —these—"

"Goons," Remillard supplied. "I'm sure that New Hampshire is doing its best. And my nephew's people have an informal group of EE watchdogs keeping an eye out. But it's the old problem in EE surveillance, Doctor—given a limited number of pEEps, where do you look?"

The old psychiatrist rose to his feet. "Quite so. Well, I think I shall go back to the hotel. It would be prudent of me to return before my grandchildren miss me. The demonstration last night was very worrying to them. They warned me not to go out alone."

Remillard still sat on one of the benches, tossing a key ring with a colorful fob from one hand to the other and frowning thoughtfully. "They're quite right to worry. It was a nasty moment when the pickets broke through the outer line of security guards and charged down the hotel driveway. The mental vibrations scared the hell out of me, I can tell you . . . It was really a primitive kind of metaconcert, that mob mind. A mass mentality with an identity and a will of its own—just for those few minutes, until the impetus faltered and the thing shattered into individuals again. Thank God there weren't more than a couple of hundred out there . . . I couldn't sleep a wink last night after it was over."

"And so you came out here."

Remillard nodded. "A long time ago I worked for the hotel. This little shelter out on the golf links used to be one of my favorite thinking spots." He flipped the key chain high, snatched it out of the air with one hand, and stuffed it into his pocket. "But I guess I've thought enough for this morning! Time for breakfast, and then I'll have to make arrangements for a special power-source for Professor MacGregor's doohickey."

"Shall we walk back together?" Pyotr suggested. "Then I will have complied with my grandchildren's directive at least partially, and they will have no occasion to scold me."

Remillard hauled himself up and stretched. "Those young fussbudgets give you a hard time, you just send 'em on to me! Let's go."

Pyotr laughed. "Fussbudgets! Doohickey! What a colorful language English is."

"I don't know that those words are English, Doctor—but they're sure Yankee. Just like me."

Pyotr's eyes gleamed. "Yes . . . I do recall now that you are a native of this region, Mr. Remillard. Perhaps you will be able to tell me whether or not there are ever any earthquakes hereabouts?"

"Why, yes. We do get one, very rarely."

"I knew it! I knew it!" Pyotr exulted; and then at the puzzled expression on the other man's face, he apologized. "I will explain my strange question in just a moment. But, please—first I have one other urgent query: What is kryptonite, and why do the Sons of Earth covet it?"

Rogatien Remillard exploded in laughter.

"But it was on the placards of the demonstrators!"

Still chuckling, Remillard asked, "Have you ever heard of Superman?"

"Nietzche's famous Übermensch? Most certainly."

Remillard regained his composure with some effort. "Not that Superman. Another one, a kind of American legend."

"I have never heard of him, no. But I would be most interested to learn about this folkloric hero. I presume there are mythic analogs to the operant condition in the American Superman's tale?"

"I never really thought about it that way—but I guess there are."

Together, the two of them started back to the resort hotel, with Rogi telling the story slowly and carefully so that the old man would be sure to get the joke.

"The Gi! Of course it was the Gi," Homologous Trend said. "One is most vexed with the silly things! What *did* they think they were playing at?"

"No real harm has been done," said Asymptotic Essencc. "Let one's tranquillity prevail. There was only a minimal matter-distortion effect. One doubts whether any seismograph in use among the Earthlings would have been able to record the anomaly at all."

"How in the world did they do it?" Eupathic Impulse was more intrigued than appalled, now that it was plain that no calamity had taken place.

"The phenomenon was generated by an empathy spasm of the collective Gi conscious," Noetic Concordance explained, "that took place as they commiserated with the aged Earthling's poignant meditations. The harmonic passed from the mental lattices to the consonant geophysical ones, setting off the tremor. One notes that the *reverse* of the phenomenon is common enough. Trust the Gi to come up with a unique twist."

"Trust them to come up with arrant nincompoopery," said Trend. "One is strongly inclined to excuse the Gi Fleet from further participation in this convocation. Given the delicacy of the approaching climax, the consequences of its lapse could have been extremely serious."

"The Gi are contrite," Essence said. "They have taken our rebuke to heart. They pledge that they will henceforth control the racial tendency to emotional ebullience."

"They'd jolly well better," Trend declared, "or they can watch the finale from the backside of Pluto! Don't they realize that Unifex is in the process of exerting Its ultimate influences? As It draws the skeins of probability taut, the slightest skew off the median may confute the solidifying nodes."

"Surely not," Eupathic Impulse protested. "Not on the very threshold of Intervention!"

"The resolution rests now with the operant Earthlings," Trend told the other three, "and possibly with the great Interloper Itself, whose ways remain as mystifying as ever. The rest of us are permitted only to watch and pray. Join with me, fellow entities, to remind the fleet of this solemn fact."

The four Lylmik minds projected the thought, using the imperative mode; and it was affirmed by each and every one of the invisible starships hovering expectantly about the planet Earth—ships of the Krondak Polity, the Poltroyan, the Simbiari, and even the penitent Gi—summoned from every part of the 14th Sector of the Galactic Milieu in hopes of hearing the Intervention signal that only Atoning Unifex might utter.

Together with the great living cruiser of the Lylmik Supervisors, the convocation of exotic vessels numbered twenty thousand seven hundred and thirty-six.

* * *

The main dining room of the hotel was crowded for breakfast, but because most of the guests were operants who exerted effortless subliminal compulsion upon the hard-working waitrons, things ran very smoothly. None of the service personnel realized that they were being gently coerced. Nevertheless, because their minds were in a receptive frame, they were able to visualize the needs of the patrons even though they themselves were normals. There were no miswritten orders, no tables that were neglected while others were overserviced, no perfectly cooled cups of coffee topped off on the sly by overzealous pot-wielders. There was not even much noise, since the delegates who had gathered for this final day of the Metapyschic Congress did most of their conversing on the intimate telepathic mode—cool and smiling on the outside while they voiced their apprehensions or complaints mentally.

Rogi came into the dining room after seeing Pyotr safely to the elevator and waved off the maîtress d'. "Thanks, Linda. I'll just join my family." *But send somebody pronto to take my order I'm starving to death there's a good kid . . .*

Lucille and Denis and their oldest three children were well into their meal as Rogi slipped into the empty chair at the big round table near the window, sitting between Philip and Severin. A waiter appeared at once and Rogi ordered oeufs dans le sirop d'erable and hot sourdough bread.

Yucko!

The telepathic critique slipped out of the mind of ten-year-old Severin as the rest of the family greeted Rogi verbally. Lucille looked at her son and the boy gave a start and sat up very straight. He said, "I beg your pardon, Uncle Rogi. It was rude to make such a comment."

"De rien." Rogi smiled. "Eggs in maple syrup are an old-fashioned Franco dish. Even though they aren't on the menu, the chef knows well enough how to prepare them. When I was a child my Aunt Lorraine used to make them for us on special occasions . . . when our spirits were in need of a lift."

"It's that kind of a day," Denis conceded.

"The vibes," Philip observed, "are mucho malific."

"And two carloads of deadheads just showed up at the main gate to start picketing!" Severin added.

Lucille said: Sevvy. How many times must I tell you not to use that epithet particularly in vocal speech when there are normals about who may hear you . . .

The little boy sighed. "I'm sorry that I used the insulting expression," he mumbled; but his farspeech, imperfectly directed to his two older brothers, belied the apology:

Well they *are* dead from the neck up and they hate our guts and right this minute do you know what they're hollering at the delegates coming in from the other hotels? they're hollering FREAKS&HEADS! FREAKS&HEADS! YOUR MA SHOULDA KNOWED YOU WERE BETTER OFF DEAD! so who's really the deadhead huh? maybe we are to let 'em get away with that shit we should do like the Russians and show 'em what Heads can do to defend themselves if Assholes mess with us—

Denis said: *Severin.*

Severin said: Oops.

Philip and Maurice, their eyes on their plates and their barriers in place, sat very still.

Denis said: Severin your Mama and I felt that you were mature enough to come to this Congress to participate in the life of the adult operant community at this crucial stage in our evolution. Some of the input you've experienced here is positive and some is negative but all of it should nurture mental growth.

"Yes, Papa," Severin said. But I just wish there was some way we could *make* the normals stop hating us *make* them like us for their own good and ours too—!

"Learning to like someone," said Severin's oldest brother Philip sententiously, "as opposed to the spontaneous goodwill experienced between compatible personalities, may take considerable time and require a large expenditure of psychic energy. Tolerance is particularly difficult for normals—who lack the insight faculties that we operants tend to take for granted. Normals almost invariably form value judgments according to prejudicial or superficial criteria."

"For example," Maurice chimed in, "a normal would look at

Severin and see only a scowling young pipsqueak with egg on his tie . . . whereas we, using metapsychic perceptions, can scrutinize his very soul and realize that beneath his unprepossessing exterior lurks a truly depraved little pillock."

I'll get you guys! Severin declared.

Boys! said Lucille.

Rogi laughed. "Yes, they're boys, all right."

Denis glanced at his watch. "Professor Malatesta's symposium on psychoeconomic vector theory starts in five minutes in the Gold Room. Philip and Maurice—you won't want to be late."

"No, Papa." Still chortling mentally, the pair bade courteous farewell and sauntered out of the dining room. At sixteen and fourteen, they were both already taller than their father. Philip was doing postgraduate work in bioenergetics at Harvard. Maurice, winding up his B.A. requirements at Dartmouth, was toying with the notion of taking a degree in philosophy before entering medical school.

Rogi said to Denis and Lucille: There was an ugly undertone in that little bit of by-play among the boys. I think all three of them are scared silly.

Denis said: You're right of course.

Lucille said: None of them has ever had to face such a concentration of enmity before. You know what an operant sanctuary Hanover is. Philip's had a few disagreeable experiences at Harvard but that place is really too hypercivilized to permit any serious incidents. This encounter with the Sons of Earth in all their deep-dyed yahoo splendor has shaken my babies rather badly. One's first meeting with hatred en masse is apt to do that.

Rogi said: You might want to consider sending the kids home.

Denis said: The security people will keep the situation under control. The boys will have to face situations like this sooner or later. They may as well do it with the support of their mental peers.

Rogi said: Even Sevvy? Denis he's *ten!*

Denis asked his son, "What do you think about going home from the Congress a little early? You've had five days' worth. Phil could drive you and Maury to Hanover—"

Severin's face crumpled. "And miss the banquet on top of the mountain? When it might even *storm* up there?"

Denis tried not to smile. "I was concerned that the unpleasant aetheric nuances from the demonstrators might be upsetting."

Severin glumly stirred his cold scrambled eggs with a fork. "I can cope, Papa." ... But those ol' Sons better not mess with me!

Lucille said, "If you do stay we'll expect you to behave like an adult, Sevvy. An operant adult."

"I promise to do my best, Mama."

"Good. Finish your breakfast then." She glanced appealingly at Rogi, posing a mental question: Would it be too much trouble for you to keep him with you for a while? Both Denis and I must sit on a rather boring panel.

Rogi said, "If you two would like to abandon us, feel free. Sevvy and I will take our time eating and meet you later."

The waiter arrived with Rogi's meal as Denis and Lucille left. The boy showed immoderate interest in the big dish of eggs poached in hot maple syrup. They were accompanied by a goblet of freshly squeezed pink grapefruit juice and a smoking-hot loaf that sat on its own miniature breadboard. Rogi smacked his lips and tucked his napkin boldly into his collar. He turned the loaf on its side and sawed off a couple of aromatic slices, passing one to Severin.

"Look here, young man. Your food's gone stone cold and I've got more than enough for the two of us. I know these oeufs look weird, but they smell good, don't they?"

"Yeah . . ."

Without another word, Rogi divided the eggs and showed the boy how to moosh them up and eat them with a spoon while sopping the bread in the delicious mess. Severin was delighted with this confounding of bourgeois table etiquette. He tied his own napkin around his neck and fell to.

"I've got an idea for when we're done," Rogi said. "I have to help the building engineer fix up the big downstairs meeting room for Professor Jamie's show-and-tell at one-thirty. We'll bring in high-voltage power cables from the transformer room and set up an auxiliary board for the demonstration. You want to help?"

"Wow, yo!" said Severin, through a mouthful of eggs.

Rogi said: Keeping busy is another good way to damp the bad vibes. At least I've found that it works.

You mean you got the fantods too?

Doggone right. Off-key goblin bassoons whooping in the pit of my stomach and thousand-leggers skating up the back of my neck.

. . . Some of those Sons out there really *would* like to kill us.

I know Sevvy.

Would you let 'em? Rather than hurt them in self-defense?

The Ethic you've been taught tells you the answer.

I know the Altruism Ethic I want to know what *you* would do.

I'm just a primitive sort of head not in the same league as you and your parents and the other giantbrains at this Congress—

Answer me straight don't futz me like a little kid!

Nonviolence is a wonderful ideal but dangerous it's amazing that so many people do opt for it. Me I don't think I'd have the strength.

If those militant doodoodomes aren't *fought* they get worse!

The dilemma will probably remain academic thank God.

No but the whole thing really bothers me a lot I've tried to understand Phil&Maury say they believe AltruismEthic just like Mama&Papa but *I can see into their minds* and they're not sure either.

Lord I believe help my unbelief . . .

Sort of. The Ethic does seem right from the point of view of alloperantstogether because it's noble you know it catches the attention of the normals FatherAndy calls it moral suasion but it's not something you have to do is it *I* don't see what's wrong with the Russian heads saying they'll defend their country mentally what good would it do them to be noble and a beautiful example of nonviolence if they all *died*?

Tough question. If you ever find a good answer Sevvy tell me.

* * *

As Lucille and Denis passed through the crowded lobby she said: Let me just stop at the newsstand for a moment before we go on to Vanderlaan's panel . . . Good heavens! The entire portico of the hotel is swarming with police!

Denis said: The hotel security chief is calling in virtually every off-duty officer in northern New Hampshire—and a few from Maine. It will cost us a bundle but I authorized the expenditure.

. . . Even though none of the pEEps detected any unusual activity?

Especially because they didn't.

Lucille said to the clerk in the hotel boutique, "I'll take this little package of aspirin. And do you have a PD of today's *Pravda* in English?"

"American or Eurasian format?"

"American, please."

"I'll call it up in a jiff," the girl said, turning to her register console.

Denis said: I told you I'd excurse to Moscow and check with Tamara late tonight.

Lucille's tone was irritable: Quick reassurances don't tell me enough. I want the background. The differing viewpoints.

There's nothing we can do to influence events over there. If the operants win they win and it will probably be more of a disaster in the long run than if they are forced into exile.

"Cash or charge?" inquired the clerk brightly.

Lucille handed over her credit card. "Charge."

Denis said: If the Red Army and the Party survivors agree to a coalition with Tamara's operants it will only be one based on force . . . coercion to control a panicking population or to intimidate the enemies of the state.

"Eight sixty-three, please, no sales tax in New Hampshire but we have to add excise for the plaque-disk of that particular newspaper. May I have your thumb here? Thanks a bundle—and you have a lovely day." The clerk handed over the purchases and Lucille tucked them into her purse.

A lovely day! she reiterated ironically. The loveliest sight I can imagine at this moment is the National Guard rolling in the gate ready to camp on the golf course . . . But instead there are more demonstrators showing up I don't even have to EE outside to know it I can feel their thoughts mindlessly massing: *Off the heads off the heads off the heads . . .*

Denis reached out and enveloped her in redactive comfort. The chanting faded, along with the small headache that had plagued her since rising. Delegates arriving from the other hotels swarmed all around them, heading for the different function rooms, but they were soundless, and even their movements seemed diffident and ghostly.

Denis said: You are not to worry. By evening it should all be over. We'll dine among the thunderclouds with serene minds and the conflagration of ions will wipe out all remnants of the haters' farspeech leaving us in peace.

You really don't think the demonstrators will try to follow us up the mountain?

No. They'd have to use the Carriage Road and the State Police are prepared to barricade it at the first sign of trouble. We'll have to endure their taunts throughout the day and there may be a few skirmishes if the pickets try to sneak onto the grounds again but there's no danger. You want proof? Jamie's daughter Katie claims to have the Sight you know and when I spoke briefly to Ilya this morning he said his wife sees nothing but great things happening today . . . Now all we—"Damn," he said out loud. "My pager."

Full-sensory reality claimed Lucille with painful suddenness. Denis pressed the stud on his watchband that halted the persistent prickling, then studied the message crawling across the Omega's digital strip.

"I'm to call the President," he said.

Lucille stared at him in blank dismay, then burst out: Don'tyouDAREgotoWashington you're the Chair of this affair you have to SPEAK tonight I won'tdoitforyouthistimedamnityou can'tgoyouhavenomorecleanshirts!

He kissed her cheek. Don't worry. Go to our panel. And try not to let anybody catch you reading your newsplaque during the dull bits."

Then he was off for the hotel manager's office and the secure landline that had been set up for a certain contingency.

Kieran O'Connor turned up the gain on the painkilling device that had been spliced into his nervous system, hating himself for the cowardice at the same time that he welcomed the wondrous semiorgasmic numbness that suffused his lower body, releasing him. It was ten minutes until noon and time to pull himself into shape for the showdown with Victor. Fortunately, that wouldn't take long.

Forgive me Black Mother soon I will return. Dam dham nam tam tham dam dham nam pam pham.

His farsensory faculties returned and he was once again able to experience the crashing waters of Upper Ammonoosuc Falls as it ramped and plunged over shiny granite ledges and boiled whitely through the monstrous potholes it had drilled in the tough bedrock. A blustery wind had sprung up that ripped the cascade's mists into furious wraiths that would have soaked any tourist brave enough to venture onto the small observation platform. But nobody was there. The parking lot of the modest roadside park was empty except for the silver Mercedes in which Kieran O'Connor sat alone.

He had rented the car at Dorval Airport in Montréal and driven it to this specified meeting place, along Base Station Road not far from the Mount Washington cog railway's lower terminus. He was thankful that all but thirty-five of the 345 kilometers of the drive had been on pilot-stripped auto-routes or freeways, giving him a chance to sleep off some of the jet lag. In order to foil the Justice Department surveillance team he had traveled from Chicago to New Hampshire via Seattle, Krung Thep, Bombay, Johannesburg, Fiumicino, Gatwick, and Montréal—shedding the last pEEp agent in the chaotic concourses of Aeroporto Leonardo da Vinci. He was certain now that none of the government investigators would be able to trace him to this Congress—much less uncover his connection to Victor Remillard or the local branch of the Sons of Earth. The only potentially weak link had been Shannon—and just as Kieran had anticipated, she had been painstakingly discreet since betraying her pathetic dupe of a husband. Even more than her father, she wanted no hint of Victor's involvement with the O'Connor empire to come to the attention of the Attorney General.

Kieran's eyes filled, surprising him, and he realized that for the first time he was mourning her loss. It should have been the daughter to inherit the night, not the daughter's daughter. But Kali would have her jest . . . *O Mother of Power, forgive her as you forgive me.*

She would be coming, even though he had forbidden it, eager for the final treachery. So be it. *Devouring Mother I would give her to you myself if I could. But I dare not waste the least spark of my dwindling powers. Please understand. Dam dham nam tam—*

"Are you asleep?"

Kieran opened his eyes. Victor Remillard was standing beside the closed window of the Mercedes. His dark wool Melton storm coat and close-cut curly hair glittered with mist droplets. A large orange van belonging to the New Hampshire Highway Department blocked the entrance to the waterfall's parking lot.

Kieran pressed the window button. "You're on time. I presume those are your wheels."

"The way the cops have the resort area sewed up, I figured something official might come in handy. Especially later."

"Everything's in order?"

"I told you it would be and it is. But you're not getting any details, Kieran."

"I don't want them . . . It surprises me, though, to perceive that you plan to oversee the operation personally. Aren't you concerned about being recognized?"

Victor laughed. "I can fuzz my identity. You mean you can't?"

"The late Fabulous Finster, a valued associate of mine, once attempted to impart the technique to me. But I just didn't have the knack. I've had to make do with other mental expedients." The old man's shadowed eyes lifted and barely reined coercion flashed in their depths. "I thought I told you to meet me here alone."

"I need Pete Laplace. He knows every back road and abandoned track in these parts and I've got other things to do besides study road maps. I'm running most of this goddam hit word-of-mouth and message-to-Garcia. No farspeech, no electronics. Not until the tail end, when it'll be too late to stop us."

"You've made the arrangements for my participation?"

"Yes. But I think you're crazy as a fuckin' bedbug."

"Never mind," Kieran said amiably. "Humoring me in this final matter will have no effect at all on your part of the operation. But it's an old Irish custom to join the dance if you've paid the piper."

"Which brings us to fork-over time."

Kieran picked up an attaché case made of black lightweight metal and passed it through the window. "It's not locked. You'll wish to program the locking device and the built-in security mechanisms after checking the bona fides of the instrument of transfer with your people at Chase Manhattan. But I assure you that everything has been arranged as we agreed. My assets will become the property of your dummy Canadian corporation upon the completion of certain legal formalities at—at four o'clock this afternoon. Sixteen hundred hours. You see—I trust you to fulfill your part of the bargain."

"What about the Big Cherry?" Victor prompted. "And the last condition?"

Kieran lifted one hand in a reassuring gesture. His smile was pained. "I told you that my final request wouldn't be difficult for you to fulfill—and a fair exchange for the access code to the override system of Zap-Star."

"Well?"

"My daughter Shannon is at the White Mountain Hotel. In spite of my strictest orders to the contrary. She expects you to kill me, as you agreed to do in return for her favors. What I want you to do is show her the documents and the gigadisk data that are in the case I gave you. Get into the hotel computer and let her see the corporate transfer confirmed. And then, use the computer to confirm your access to Zap-Star as well—but without revealing the access code to her. Then you may question Shannon tactfully on what role she plans to play in tonight's operation . . ."

Victor's gloved hands tightened on the metal case. His mind was an impregnable fortress. "Why?"

Kieran began to laugh, but then his body convulsed and he groaned through clenched teeth and fumbled desperately inside his coat. Victor could see that the old man's shirt was partially unbuttoned and a flattened plastic control mechanism with numerous electrode wire was taped to his upper chest. For a brief interval Kieran writhed helplessly, until his fingers reached the device's key-pad. He summoned maximum analgesia and fell back in abrupt relief.

Presently, Kieran said, "Sorry. Your question—?"

Victor's face was expressionless. "I don't understand why you want me to confirm my—my takeover to your daughter. It's only what she expects."

"Tell Shannon that she never really had any secrets from me. Tell her that I knew all along about her duplicate mind-screen and had access to her secret heart. Tell her she was free only in her fantasies. My pathetic little girl! I was sadly mistaken about her and it nearly cost me my—my life's goal. But I was shown another way . . ." *Thank you Mother thank you dam dham nam tam—*

Victor demanded: *What do you mean what the hell are you saying and WHO IS SHE who is that?*

"My Mother. I pray her mantra." Kieran's eyes closed and he lay limp against the soft leather seat. The rain had finally started and plump silver pearls danced among the lesser misty splatters on the waxed hood of the Mercedes. Kieran said, "Go away. Do the things I've told you. Shannon's reaction will show you what my last request of you is. The Mother has compassion on my weakness and pardons me from having to do the job myself. And she doesn't need me to bring the final Blackness, either. It will all happen as it must happen. Dam dham nam tam tham dam dham nam pam pham . . ."

"The access code! Is that it? The mantra?"

Kieran's eyes opened and blazed. *Will you do as I say with Shannon?*

"Yes." Victor's mind opened to confirm the truth.

Kieran nodded slowly. "Another thing . . . She also fantasizes that her child Laura is yours. Disabuse her of that at the end, will you? It will bring home the point. You may want to take Laura away from Gerry Tremblay and bring her up yourself . . . Or perhaps you won't. You don't want to share, the way I did." The eyes closed again. Kieran's face was yellow-gray and he breathed slowly through his open mouth. "I loved her, though. I loved them all. But not you and that's why you are my heir to the night."

Victor reached out with his coercion, exerting it with delicate care: *Kieran. Don't sleep yet. You must tell me the access code. The satellite access code. Tell me.*

Yes yes this is the phrase without any punctuation FOR BEHOLD HENCEFORTH ALL GENERATIONS SHALL CALL ME BLESSED the key to bring about the final death of energy the final dark . . . I must sleep now but I'll wake in time to see it through it's all right now Mother I've done it now rest . . .

The mental image. Victor saw it again in the instant before Kieran slipped into unconsciousness. It was a great wheel of black petals with fire at the heart, held within the belly of a barely perceptible female figure. But Victor Remillard had never heard of Kali, and so all he did was swear in French as the vision faded.

Then he opened the door of the Mercedes and brought the window up. He closed the door, locked it, and left Kieran O'Connor to sleep beside the thundering waterfall until the operation began at 1930 hours that evening.

Shannon Tremblay attended Jamie MacGregor's lecture as openly as she had the other Congress events that interested her, confident that a severely tailored suit, eyeglasses with tortoiseshell rims, and a short black wig hiding her auburn hair rendered her unrecognizable. The concept of a mental signature, a personal thought-pattern as distinctive as a fingerprint, was quite unknown to her; and so she was badly startled when someone called out as she left the meeting room:

"Oh, there you are, Shan. Would you let me have a word with you before you go on to the next round of papers?"

It was a tall, balding academic, a man she had never seen before, and she regarded him frostily and said, "You've mistaken me for someone else," and would have walked on. But coercion took hold of her and forced her to turn and accompany the man into an alcove, and she did not dare protest and call attention to herself.

"I've been looking all over the hotel for you," the man said. For a split second his ascetic face flickered and another underlying set of features took its place.

Victor!

The coercive grip tightened to the point of pain and she whimpered.

"Use regular speech," he ordered in low tones. "Your telepathy has always been incompetent in focusing along the intimate mode."

She winced at the pressure. "Let me go, damn you! What do you *mean* by accosting me—"

"You're supposed to be in Cambridge."

She reseated her glasses and turned away from him. "I can go where I please."

"So you couldn't resist being in on the kill, eh? Never mind if somebody spotted you and put two and two together! Don't you realize this place is swarming with FBI and Justice Department agents?"

"They're not looking for me," she retorted. "They're looking for Daddy—or his known associates. Daddy disappeared three days ago, you know. *I* was the one who put two and two together and deduced that he must be on his way here, to this final Metapsychic Congress. It was the perfect occasion for him . . . and for you. Of course I wanted to be on the scene for the finale." She lifted her chin with a triumphant smile. "Are these Sons of Earth militants your idea? What will they do—try to burn down the hotel? The old place is a real tinderbox. I'm staying at the Horse & Hound in Franconia, so feel—"

"Shut up," he hissed. "Do you think this is all some entertainment put on for your benefit?"

She laughed softly. "For both our benefits." Then her expression hardened. "Daddy has made the deal with you, hasn't he!

You arrange for some convenient Sons-of-Earth-sponsored disaster to befall this hotel full of operants, and he says he'll hand everything over."

"That's right."

"You're a fool if you trust him. He'll never give up his power until he's dead, and he won't die until he's ready to. The doctors can't understand how he's been able to survive this long—but I understand! He wants to offer a holocaust of operant minds to appease some horrible fantasy, and if you help him he'll find some way to finish you off with all the rest. You'll never get the best of Daddy unless you kill him. I told you that at the beginning."

"Your father will die tonight." Victor held up the black metal attaché case. "And he's already turned over everything to me—including the access code for Zap-Star."

She gasped. "I don't believe it! He's lied to you."

"There is that possibility. Which is why you and I are going to check things out before my big production number goes any further."

He took her arm again and guided her up a wide flight of carpeted stairs to the main lobby. They might have been colleagues chatting familiarly after a long separation.

"Did Gerry know you were coming here?"

"Of course not," she said. "He knows better than to question me about my affairs."

"What's he doing these days—househusbanding? Baby-sitting, perhaps?"

"Pulling his head together before going to work for a Boston branch of Carns, Elsasser, Lehmann, if you must know. He took it hard when Griffith kicked him out of Roggenfeld Acquisitions."

Victor chuckled. "Too timid to swim with the sharks, I heard. How are you two getting along these days?"

"Gerry is civil, and he's afraid of me, and there are times when I'm certain he's hiding some ghastly secret—but my redaction is no good against a trained operant like him, and I've never been able to pry it out. You'll have to. Afterward."

"How does Gerry get along with your baby, Laura? The kid's

about nine months old, isn't she? And big-brained?"

Shannon said coldly, "Aside from his little character defects deriving from overweening ambition, Gerry is a decent sort of man. He knows Laura isn't his, but he doesn't hold it against her. He's kind. He's certainly more interested in her than you seem to be—"

They had passed out of the lobby into the executive offices of the hotel and now paused before an unmarked door. Indicating mentally that Shannon should keep silence, he opened it and stepped inside. It was a suite of rooms that obviously housed the computer functions. A young man in shirtsleeves working on a sheaf of print-outs looked up in surprise and opened his mouth— then froze as Victor's coercion took control of him. Without saying a word, the young man got up and led Victor into an inner room where the equipment was kept. Victor said:

Your work for the day is finished. Go home now without speaking to anyone. You will not remember having seen us.

The young man turned on his heel and marched out, closing the door behind him.

Shannon said, "What are you going to do?"

Victor had seated himself at the manual console and began to rap expertly on the key-pads. The display said: CHASE MANHATTAN BANK DATACEN. GOOD AFTERNOON MR REMILLARD. PLEASE BEGIN UPLOAD.

Victor took the thick plastic gigadisk out of the attaché case and slotted it. Then he waited.

Shannon's eyes were glued to the display screen, which now said: WORKING. She whispered, "He couldn't have. I don't believe it." And then the screen said: TRANSACTION VLNX2234-9-21-2013 PRELOGGED AND READY FOR FINAL EXECUTION 1600 HRS. DO YOU HAVE INSTRUCTIONS?

Victor typed: PRECIS.

And the computer obliged.

Shannon gave a strangled little joyous shriek. "It's true! He's done it! My God, it's totally unbelievable!" She would have thrown her arms around Victor, but his coercion flicked her back as casually as an insect. "Wait. We have to confirm the other."

Thanking and dismissing the bank, Victor retrieved his disk and replaced it in the case. Then he typed out a certain telephone number with a northern Illinois area code. The screen said: YOU HAVE REACHED A PRIVATE NUMBER. PLEASE INSERT ACCESS CODE.

Victor typed: FOR BEHOLD HENCEFORTH ALL GENERATIONS SHALL CALL ME BLESSED.

The computer said: ENTER.

Victor typed: DIR.

The computer said: ZAP-STAR OVERRIDE 1MARY.KOC. THIS COMMAND FILE IS VALID BUT NOT OPERATIONAL UNTIL 12-25-2013 AT WHICH TIME THE ZAP-STAR SYSTEM COMES ONLINE. DO YOU HAVE INSTRUCTIONS.

Victor typed: NO. GOODBYE. And then he erased all record of both the calls, using an old hacker's trick, and turned in the seat to face Shannon.

She said, "It's true. He's capitulated completely . . . unless he plans to cheat you some way at the last minute—"

"I don't believe that he does."

"Then," she said, "all that's left to do is finish him off."

"*And* the Metapsychic Congress."

"Oh, there's no need for that! Only a paranoid like Daddy would believe that the mass murder of a couple of thousand leading operants would leave people like us with a clear field. What about all the rest of the heads in the world? If we kill this lot, others will eventually take their places. No . . . Daddy's famous 'edge' is obsolete, and so is yours, Victor. You should have seen the apparatus that Professor MacGregor demonstrated at his lecture! It was the first aura detector. All it does is shine a beam of something-or-other at a person and analyze the reflection—and it can tell whether or not that person is hopelessly latent, or suboperant, or operant. And it even quantizes the degree of operancy! One of the subjects MacGregor used in his lecture was the ten-year-old son of Denis Remillard. Would you believe the boy sent the analyzer right off the scale? . . . So you see, with a gadget like this available, it just won't be possible for people to keep their operancy secret. Even casinos will install these things—"

"There are other edges," Victor said.

Shannon looked at him mutely, her mind incredulous. Finally she said, "You can't mean it!"

"I'd call Zap-Star the ultimate edge. Of course, it wouldn't be used in the clumsy death-ray scenario your father dreamed up. Its use would be very selective."

"But it's not *necessary*, Victor! Any more than killing these operants is necessary. Once Daddy is dead you'll have all the power and wealth that any man could want—"

He shook his head. Slowly, he rose from the chair and came to her. "He said you disappointed him. You've disappointed me, too."

She didn't try to flee. Proudly, she said, "I see. You don't need people the way Daddy did. You're self-sufficient. You don't need—or love—anyone but yourself, do you, Victor? Not me. And certainly not our child."

"Laura is not my child. We've never had physical intercourse. You were quite right to call me self-sufficient."

"Good God. Not yours . . ." Her eyes were fixed on him as the truth of it slowly broke through. "Yes, I see. You're impotent."

Victor laughed at her. "Not in any way that really matters. Not the way your father is now, powerless because he still loves you. He asked me to tell you that you were never really free of him. He was always able to penetrate your double screen. I suppose he let you keep the illusion in hopes that it would shore up your ego. Keep you from suiciding."

"And it suited his plans when I came to you." Her eyes had gone dull. "Of course. He had to manipulate both of us. He must have known he could never bond you . . ." She straightened, proud again for a moment. "Neither of you will use Zap-Star, you know. The government knows the system is penetrated."

"All they know is what you—and my brother Denis—have told them. I'm willing to gamble that the President won't be able to stop the system's activation on schedule. Not on the word of two dead heads."

His farsight roamed the area, then lit on a small storeroom that opened off the computer room. He compelled her to follow him to it, opened the door, and flicked on the light.

"This will do. No one will come in here so late on Saturday afternoon. It won't matter tomorrow."

She said, "You aren't going to do it quickly."

"I have some time to kill," he said, laughing, and took off her black wig so that the long flaming hair tumbled out. Her face and mind were calm. Eventually he would give her what she wanted.

He asked her to kneel, and she sank down without protest. Then he cupped her head in both hands and pressed her against him, and stopped her heart for the first time.

30

FROM THE MEMOIRS OF ROGATIEN REMILLARD

FOR MORE THAN A YEAR, SINCE DENIS'S INTERROGATION OF Gerry Tremblay, government investigators had sought in vain for hard evidence that would connect Kieran O'Connor to the sort of grandiose conspiracy that his daughter had accused him of perpetrating. It was easy enough for EE adepts to search his offices and his residence—and the presence of the elaborate satellite uplink equipment was duly noted, but conceded to be quite legal. The heavily guarded data bank beneath the O'Connor mansion undoubtedly held the key to the mystery; but EE adepts could scrutinize its library of disks until doomsday without knowing what they contained. No search warrant could be served because no probable cause of felonious action could be demonstrated, and U.S. law forbade "fishing expeditions" as unwarranted invasions of privacy.

One of the Zap-Star battle-mirrors was plucked from orbit and taken to the ON-1 habitat for examination. A problematic chip was indeed found, one that was unauthorized in the original specifications. However, engineers of the O'Connor satellite consortium maintained that the component was entirely innocuous, designed to improve guidance system response to groundside commands. If the chip did contain an override, the thing had been hidden with surpassing cleverness and would probably display its true colors only when activated by a coded signal.

One could, of course, haul in each and every one of the 130 non-Chinese battle-mirrors and—using exquisite care—remove the dubious chip. The fix would take approximately four years and cost $7.2 billion, and in the meantime the independently operated Chinese units would remain fully operational.

The allegation of conspiracy was based thus far only upon the unsupported word of Shannon O'Connor Tremblay. Denis's mind-ream of her husband had yielded only tenuous confirmation—and that legally inadmissible. Subsequent investigations of the O'Connor empire had turned up no evidence whatsoever of any Zap-Star conspiracy—and precious little else that was even remotely actionable. The only taint was a distant one: back in the 1980s certain O'Connor subsidiaries had been strongly suspected of laundering Mafia funds. But this had never been proved and the Mob was dead and gone, while these days the O'Connor organization seemed guilty only of the immoderate gobbling of smaller corporate fry...

At least that had been the status of the government's investigation up until 20 September 2013.

On that day, an alert bureaucrat in the Securities and Exchange Commission took note of a routine notification of a transfer of assets from an American conglomerate to an obscure Canadian holding company. The SEC woman was struck by the enormous size of the transaction, and even more interested when she recognized the conglomerate to be a key-stone of the intricate O'Connor organization. A fast check with Montréal (Canada having less of a penchant for financial confidentiality than the U.S. at that time) yielded up the name of the man behind the dummy corporation. The SEC woman informed the Attorney General and he informed the President of the United States—who in turn called up Denis to inquire why his younger brother Victor was being handed control of virtually everything that Kieran O'Connor owned.

"I told him I was just as flabbergasted as he was," Denis told me. We had met at the conclusion of MacGregor's lecture, and now he and I and Lucille stood in the back of the nearly deserted hall talking the thing over. Naturally the President has asked his people to brief him on Victor; and he had been dismayed to discover that the Nobel laureate's family harbored a sheep who, if not exactly black, looked decidedly grubby around the edges.

And was a familiar of Kieran O'Connor's daughter.

"I'll give Baumgartner credit," Denis said. "He called me himself and he was straightforward about Victor. He told me that the government had a file on him dating way back to when Vic and Dad first started Remco. Tax fiddling, and later on some quashed indictments for interstate transportation of stolen property. The feds have never been able to get the goods on Vic, primarily because no one would testify against him. Lately, he's seemed to be clean—but the feds looked him up again after Shannon sprang her blockbuster. Naturally she was investigated with her father, and her relationship with Vic muddied the waters considerably. I was approached last spring and asked to mind-ream both Victor and Shannon. Of course I refused."

Lucille and I said nothing and kept our thoughts to ourselves.

"Now the President has personally appealed to me to interrogate them mentally—especially Shannon—to find out whether the threat to Zap-Star is real. If I can get confirmation from Victor, it will preclude the possibility that Shannon is suffering some delusion."

"But why do the feds think Vic would know anything about it?" I asked.

Denis said, "Because Kieran O'Connor has terminal testicular cancer. If he's passing his empire to Vic, as the Canadian connection seems to prove, he's probably passing the clout along with the assets."

"Christ!" I said. "*Vic* with a handle on Zap-Star?"

Denis said, "O'Connor evaded both EE and normal government surveillance and has disappeared. As far as the feds can tell, Vic is innocently at home in Berlin. Shannon Tremblay was traced to this Congress. The agents are certain she's here in the hotel."

"And the President wants you to find her," Lucille said, "and turn her inside out?"

"That's about it," said Denis.

"It's monstrous!" she exclaimed indignantly. "The whole thing is incredible! That wretched woman corrupted Gerry for some squalid motive of her own, and then when he was caught in the Coercer Flap she invented this other thing—"

Denis silenced her. "All I know is what was in Gerry's mind. *He* doesn't believe she's deluded. His impression—the impression of a trained psychiatrist—is that she is eminently sane in spite of a neurotic love-hate relationship with her father. Deep in his mental core, Gerry recognized that Kieran O'Connor was a paramount metapsychic manipulator, a man who had used his powers for self-aggrandizement all his life. The Zap-Star net wasn't Gerry's province. He knew O'Connor's consortium built the guidance systems for the net and he had a kind of instinct that it figured in some scheme that the old man was cooking up. That was the only verification I could give the President after my ream of Gerry. It was sufficient to launch the full-scale investigation, which yielded nothing . . . up until now."

"So where do you go from here?" I asked.

"I did a quick farscan of the place," Denis said. "I have Shannon's mental signature—in a rough approximation, I'm afraid—from my mind-ream of Gerry. I swept the hotel from top to bottom and found no trace of her. For what it's worth, I found no trace of Vic either! But that doesn't mean they're not here. Vic's a devil of a screener and Shannon's probably no slouch either. I'm going to go very quietly to the top scanners attending the Congress and ask their help in watching out for both Shannon and Vic. They may let their guard down."

"You're not thinking of confronting your brother—!" Lucille was aghast.

"I'd rather not," Denis replied dryly, "but there seems to be little choice. If he shows up, I'll play it by ear. But I don't think he will show." He looked at his watch. "By now, he's the new owner of O'Connor's billions, with more profitable ways to occupy his time."

"And Shannon Tremblay," I said archly, "is probably helping him get in the mood to romp through the money-bin."

Lucille said, "If the government agents tracked Shannon today, they can track her another day and take her into custody for your interrogation. Denis, you will have fulfilled your promise to the President when you notify the other scanners to watch out for her."

I could see that my conscientious nephew was mulling this over, trying to decide whether to remain in the hotel on farscan alert rather than join his colleagues at the banquet, where he was certain to be distracted by his own speechmaking—to say nothing of the emotion-charged atmosphere.

Impetuously, I said, "Look. My farscan hasn't much range, but I know every nook and cranny of this old place. Pass me Shannon Tremblay's mental signature and I'll spend the rest of the afternoon and the evening combing the hotel from cellar to rafters. Hell—I'll get a passkey from Jasper Delacourt and search the place physically when the delegates are out. I'd rather do that than go to the banquet anyhow. Farewell speeches depress me and thunderstorms rattling around mountain peaks make me nervous. Any old backpacker will tell you the same."

Denis eyed me doubtfully. "Uncle Rogi, if you should find Shannon—or, God forbid, Vic!—you are to do *nothing* except notify me telepathically."

"I swear!" said I, rooting in my hip pocket. I dangled the talisman and clapped my right hand over my heart. "I swear by the Great Carbuncle."

All day long the Sons of Earth pickets, a couple of hundred strong, marched up and down Highway 302 in front of the resort entrance. They chanted and flourished their placards and banners, and now and then numbers of the more dedicated lay down on the driveway when shuttle buses brought in delegates who were lodged at other hotels in the area. The police didn't bother to arrest the lie-ins; they just toted them out of the way and deposited them very gently in a handy culvert flowing with storm runoff. Along about dusk, when the big X-wing transports came in from their base at Berlin, a band of more determined activists tried to infiltrate the resort grounds by moving through the forest that lay between the hotel and the cog's Base Station Road. Police detection equipment sniffed the invaders out before they had penetrated two hundred meters. A SWAT team of State Police rounded up the antioperant commandos, who were armed with nothing more lethal than paint-pistols, and removed them to the hospitality of the county jail over at Lancaster.

By the time the delegates were ready to depart for the Summit Chalet, the heavy rain had discouraged all but a handful of die-hard demonstrators out on the highway. I had completed my search of the hotel's lower reaches and was just coming up to the main floor when Denis transmitted a mental hail:

Uncle Rogi . . . We're almost ready to leave for the banquet I presume and pray you've found nothing.

In the boiler-room was a poker game that I was strongly tempted to sit in on and in one of the empty salons a delegate from Sri Lanka and one from Greece were interrupted in the midst of researches into comparative metanooky. There is no sign of Mrs. Tremblay and no sign of Vic dieumercibeau'.

None of us has sensed their presence either. Lucille's probably right when she says they cleared out long ago if they were ever even here I've notified the President he gave me a goodwill message to read at the banquet one could almost believe he was sincere . . .

Buck up mon fils. Go have your feast my only regret is not getting to see the boys tricked out in black tie.

[Image: Interior X-wing skybus. Dim flashes of lightning through rain-streaked small windows. Multiethnic delegates in formal dress settling into seats. Whispers and apprehensive giggling. Lucille smiling white-faced TWO GAWKY PENGUINS

*STRAPPED IN ON EITHER SIDE OF A SMALL CHUNKY
ONE.]* There. I'm sorry they don't look more cheery.

Mille merde Denis what a glum and qualmish crew all you
need is a band playing "Nearer My God to Thee" Go! Go! It will
be all right! Follow your damned gleam my son Follow the Great
Carbuncle to the uttermost height!

Au revoir Uncle Rogi.

Standing there at the head of the stairs in the fast-emptying
lobby, I heard the first of the X-wings take off for the mountain
summit. It was full dark outside and the rain was only moderate,
with faint growlings of thunder. On top of Mount Washington the
weather was bound to be worse; but the transports were so reliable and sturdy that they could have made the trip safely in a
hurricane. The storm would provide a piquant contrast to the
luxurious surroundings and the good food. After the banquet they
could all gather around the four fireplaces in the chalet's main
lounge and promise to mend their battered ideals. With a little bit
of luck even Tamara Sakhvadze far away in Moscow would soul-
travel to the festivities and take heart . . .

Well, it was time for me to renew my futile quest. I checked
my watch and noted that it was nearly seven. The business offices of the hotel would be nearly empty now, as would the delegates' rooms. The only dense collections of people would be in
the hotel kitchens, where the cleaners were still at work, and in
the two bars where a few media types and other nondelegate
hangers-on had gravitated. The hotel's Security Chief, Art Gregoire, came in the main entrance shaking raindrops from his
jacket and spotted me.

"Hey, Art. What d'ya say?"

"Is that you, Roj? Thought you'd be up at the big feed."

"Got business to take care of. Things looking okay?"

Gregoire shrugged. "Once we get the folks up the hill, we
figure it's pret' near all over. Only a handful of half-drowned
pickets left. Me and my gang'll keep an eye on the X-wing pad
and cruise the hotel to make sure no loony-tune tries to torch 'er.
The county mounties and the rent-a-cops went into town to grab a
bite and dry their socks. We need 'em, we know how to get 'em."

"Any action over on the other side of the mountain—by the Carriage Road?"

"State fuzz says there ain't diddly. Nope, the Sons've given you heads a free pass tonight. You lucked out with the rain."

He went off to scrounge supper in the kitchen and I headed toward the executive offices to get on with my search. As if Shannon Tremblay would be hiding among the file cabinets . . .

I stood outside the manager's office with my eyes closed and let my scanning ultrasense rove into the nearest rooms. There was no trace of any mental emanation on the operant "band" and no clearly farsensed vision of normal people lurking about, which I would have perceived had any operant been deliberately suppressing his aura.

But there was something.

I unlocked the computer center with my passkey and turned the lights on in the windowless rooms, and at that moment I heard a noise—a faint scraping sound—and realized that it came from the storeroom on the far side of computer operations.

I tried to farscan through the storeroom door. I couldn't.

Rooted to the spot, I probed the mysterious obstacle. Behind the wood and plaster lay psychic energy of an appalling absorptive kind. It was not a barrier—the little room was filled with it, and it was opaque and magnetic and colder than death.

I think I knew at once that he was inside. I tried to give telepathic warning to Denis—to anybody. But as I uttered the mind-shout I knew it had gone no farther than the boundary of my skull. I walked without volition down the neat rows of desks with their VDTs and data cabinets and posture chairs and stood before the closet, waiting for the door to open. In there was insanity and a lust that had no relation to any natural human appetite. In there, something had hungered and fed and still hungered. Even though it wore the shape of a man it had metamorphosed into something altogether different—and done it by its own will.

A barely heard click. The knob turned and a long shadowed streak grew as the door swung inward. Not a single beam of light from the computer room penetrated that palpable blackness—but nevertheless, I saw Victor holding her. Both of their bodies were lit with a flickering blue-violet halo. Only his lips were bright, drinking the final dying scarlet radiance from the four-petaled energy-flower that seemed to be imprinted at the base of her spine.

Then it was finished.

The devouring darkness vanished. Room light shone on Victor, who regarded me without surprise and beckoned me to come closer and admire what he'd done. It was as if he knew I would recognize the pattern as the evil opposite of Ume's fulfillment of me. He was fully clothed in a gray suit, but every stitch had been burned from the corpse of the woman who lay at his feet. The body was charred and crackling, and up the spine and on the head were seven stigmata of white ash, marking where he had fed from each psychic energy-font in turn—beginning with the most rarefied and continuing to the root. I had no doubt that in place of Ume's joy there had been excruciating pain.

"There'll be more," he told me calmly. "Only I won't have to exert myself in the burning. It's interesting that you understand. I want—I want to know more about what it *is*. I think you may be able to tell me. Am I right?"

"Yes." *No no no no . . .*

Victor laughed. "Come along with me and watch."

In my nightmare, I followed him docilely out of the hotel. We went without being challenged to one of the hotel parking lots at the north end of the grounds, where a highway department van stood in the shadows. The rain had nearly stopped but there was still a good deal of lightning flashing in the east, in the direction of the mountain.

I was dimly aware of another man sitting behind the wheel of the van. It was Pete Laplace, who had worked at the cog during my years at the hotel. I got into the back of the van and we drove off.

Vic said, "The boys ready to take off on sked?"

"Ready as they'll ever be," said a dour Yankee voice. "Poor stupid bastards." He cackled, then swore as the van hit a pothole and lurched. We turned to the right and I knew we were on the back road leading to the cog base station.

"We're going to take my Uncle Rogi along with O'Connor," Vic said. "You three old gaffers ought to enjoy the fireworks together. You get steam up okay?"

"I know what I'm doin'," the oldster snapped. "Just hope t'hell you do, Vic. Still say you shoulda gone in the airyplane."

"Not on your life, Pete. That mob of heads claim to be pacifists, but you don't catch me betting my ass on it . . . Slow down, dammit. We're almost to the Upper Falls turnoff."

My personality seemed to have fragmented. One portion was howling in panic-stricken horror, while another quite calmly submitted to Victor's continuing coercive hold, acknowledging him as my master whom I would serve without question. And then there was a third psychic chunk. This was the smallest and shakiest of all, stomped to a frazzle and nearly buried in the mental cataclysm that had overwhelmed me. This part of my mind told me to hang in there and wait for my chance. It was the damn fool part of my personality, so of course it won out. I've often wondered whether other heroes were made that way, too.

The van made a sharp turn and screeched to a halt. Vic and the poisonous old party climbed out. When they returned they were supporting a tottering form. Far be it from the richest man in the world to ride in the back of a muddy van, so they strapped him securely into Vic's seat, and my nephew came back to sit silently with me while we traveled the last few kilometers to the cog railway base station.

The place was dark as the inside of your hat, without a sign of life. But one of the antique engines had its firebox aglow and the steam up, and its smokestack threw sparks on both sides of the track that sizzled as they hit the puddles. Old Pete clambered into the engine cab, and Vic and O'Connor and I got aboard the unlit coach that traveled ahead. No blast on the whistle marked the train's departure. It simply hissed like a fumarole, clanked, and set off chugging and rattling toward the cloud deck that hid the summit.

Victor and O'Connor ignored me completely as they conversed on the intimate telepathic mode. I discovered only one of the infamous secrets that the dying old villain passed on to the hungry young one. God only knows what other bizarre thoughts they shared. They were both madmen by any civilized standard, and yet sane enough to recognize and still embrace the evil that their minds created. They were not mistaken, not misguided or deluded; they were only terribly and mysteriously bent and I have long since given up trying to understand them. The little train climbed valiantly into the sky, taking one to death and the other to oblivion. I could only huddle in my seat, half frozen now that we approached the tree line, praying that one of the unsuspecting operants in the chalet above us would turn his mind downward, penetrate the dense granite bulk that blocked line-of-sight view of this part of the track from the summit, and sound the alarm.

The coach tilted more and more steeply and the little engine undertook its most severe challenge—a trestled section called Jacob's Ladder with a grade of more than thirty-seven percent. My night-sight, dimmed by Victor's coercion, saw that O'Connor was clinging like a limpet to the seat in front of him, a grimace of what I took to be excitement distorting his wasted features. We had been passing through dense cloud ever since beginning our ascent of the ladder; but now we broke free as we approached the Westside Trail crossing and there were sudden flashes of lightning from the towering cumulus massed to the east. In another moment it would be possible for us to see the Summit Chalet silhouetted against the skyline . . . and the people in the chalet would have a greatly enhanced chance of farsensing us.

But Victor's elderly henchman knew his stuff. The deafening clatter of the cogs gripping the steel rack between the tracks diminished to a portentous clickety-clack, then stopped as the engine ground to a halt. The smoke cloud, blasted by high winds, raced uphill ahead of us. Surely someone would see it—

"It doesn't matter now," Vic said. The locomotive clunked and wheezed and in a moment the rear door of the coach opened and Pete thrust himself in, grumbling about the chill.

"This is it, Vic. Get 'em up here damn quick before we're spotted."

"Higher!" Kieran O'Connor croaked. "I want to see the chalet go!"

"Shut up," Victor said. "Look there—to the north."

O'Connor keened: "Aaah!"

"Now you can get 'er rolling again, Pete!" Victor's voice was triumphant. "Our own X's are on their way in!"

The old man dived for the rear door, which was still open. And at that moment Victor's hold on me eased as he broadcast some powerful farspoken command to the approaching aircraft. I flung myself from my seat, rolled downhill toward the door, and was outside feet-first and tumbling down among the frost-encrusted granite boulders before Vic could stop me. Somewhere in my trajectory I had smashed into that aged rascal, Laplace. I heard his wail echo thinly among the crags, then cut off abruptly.

God—now what? Uphill! Keep as much rock as I could between me and that young devil, Vic, and yell my brains out:

DENIS!   DENISTHEY'RECOMINGFORTHECHALETIN AIRCRAFT!   DENISDENISFORGOD'SSAKEVIC&O'CON NORHAVEARMEDAIRCRAFTATTACKINGCHALET—

I hear you Uncle Rogi.

Coughing and gasping with the cold, I toiled upward over the rockfield. Behind me, I heard the engine give a mighty chug, then start uphill once again. Vic had probably taken the controls himself. There were two X-wings and neither of them had navigation lights. Up above the cloud deck, there was enough fitful moonlight shining between the thunderheads to show the planes approaching fast around the shoulder of Mount Clay; but they weren't gun-ships, they were ordinary domestic transports, half the size of the ones used to ferry the Congress delegates up the mountain.

DENIS THEY'RE GOING TO LAND! STOP THEM! ZAP THEM SOMEHOW USE CREATIVE METACONCERT!

I heard for the first time other minds—hundreds of them—but the lightning-fast moral debate was incomprehensible. The pair of X-wings hovered nearly over my head, their roaring drowning out the howl of the wind. Only my continued scrambling kept me from freezing.

DO SOMETHING! I pleaded.

Another mind-voice, one of surpassing power with a signature that was completely unfamiliar, said:

Together! Hit them together! Let me show you how . . .

A white fireball soared against the sky, arching over the crest from the direction of the chalet. It struck the central boss of the X-wing rotor housing on the lead aircraft and seemed to be absorbed soundlessly. But the sudden drop in the noise level was the aircraft's engine cutting out.

That's the way! Join with me again. Together . . .

NO! another voice pleaded, and I knew it was Denis.

A second ball of psychocreative energy flew up like a meteor and zapped the other X-wing. Both ships were in uncontrolled descent, windmilling with the deactivation of their engines. They pranged in not more than five hundred meters away from me, down the northwestern flank of the mountain. There were no explosions and no flames, and although my ultrasenses were impeded by trauma and the intervening crags, I knew that the occupants of the aircraft had survived and were pulling themselves together to begin a ground assault.

I cried: DENIS THEY CRASHLANDED YOU DIDN'T KILL THEM—

He said: I never tried. Most of us didn't.

I was scrambling uphill as fast as I could. Fortunately, at that point there was a footpath along the right-hand side of the cog track. As I came out of a hollow I saw the train again, chugging slowly along the skyline and trailing its spark-shot plume of smoke.

VICTOR IS DIRECTING ATTACK FROM COG! HIT THE TRAIN!

I heard laughter in the aether: *Yes. Hit the train. Together with me now!*

Another bolide arose. This time I saw it materialize just above the chalet roof and move purposefully in a flat trajectory toward the little train. But it faltered in flight and began to wobble, and instead of hitting the engine it bounced along the roof of the coach and then dove down onto the track ahead. There was a sharp flash. The coach bucked and slewed and fell off to the side. The sound waves reached me moments later—a detonation followed by a prolonged grinding crash as the coach left the track and toppled onto the icy boulders. The engine had slammed on its brakes. It screamed to a stop before reaching the damaged section of track and stood silhouetted against moonlit thunderheads on the skyline above me. Its firebox glowed hellishly and the rising gale blasted smoke over its trailing tender. A figure jumped from the engine cab.

UncleRogiDUCK!!

I did—just in time. A bullet fweenged off a rock a few centimeters above my head. I had completely forgotten the crashing X-wings and their complement of armed thugs. The warning had come from little Severin, who now told me:

They'recreepingup onyoutheyhaveinfraredGETOFFTRAIL!! I'llhelpcreatedecoybodyglowCOMEUPMOUNTAINHURRY!! SLEETSTORMCOMING . . .

I said: Putain de bordel de merde!

Sevvy said: You can say that again.

Another bullet struck, far off the mark to my left. Bruised and shivering, I resumed my climb uphill.

31

MOUNT WASHINGTON, NEW HAMPSHIRE, EARTH
21 SEPTEMBER 2013

VICTOR REMILLARD GRASPED THE OLD MAN BY THE COAT LAPELS. The head lolled and there was a bleeding gash across the forehead. But Kieran O'Connor was alive.

"What the *hell* did you think you were doing?" Victor shouted. "I should—I should—"

Kieran's eyes opened and he smiled. "You should kill me. But it's totally unnecessary. Let me warn you, however . . . one touch of probe or coercion, and I'll never answer your questions. And you do want the answers, don't you?"

They saw one another in the shadowless eeriness of mental vision and ignored the strengthening wind that whistled through the broken coach. Victor was aware for the first time of a deathly stench emanating from the body of the dying man. Through the open shirt, he could see that the telltales of the painkilling mechanism had gone dark. No agony he could inflict on Kieran O'Connor could surpass what Kieran had already freely embraced.

"You took charge of those operants when Denis wouldn't." Victor was accusative. "You knit them together in some kind of mental unit and squeezed out those globs of energy that downed the aircraft and derailed the train."

"The procedure is called metaconcert," Kieran told him. "An idea quite foreign to *your* mentality. I wasn't at all sure that I could work it. With my own people, the results have generally been unsatisfactory. But these fully operant minds . . . marvelous!"

"You fucking old bastard! You shot down my men—tried to kill them!"

"Nonsense. The craft are engineered to soft-land in case of power failure. Only the incompetence of your pilots and the rough terrain caused the damage, and most of your people were uninjured."

"Then *why*?"

Kieran indicated the Summit Chalet, blazing like a jewel box on the mountain above them. "They needed teaching, these silly pacifists. A revelation of their own power. The Russian operants have already learned the lesson and so have a few other groups. But these idealist leaders resisted the inevitable. They were too much influenced by your brother and MacGregor. An aggressive metaconcert was unthinkable for such minds—until they were given suitable incentive."

"We'll knock them out! Your scheme—whatever the hell it

is—can't work. The main vanguard of the local Sons of Earth took out the State Police barricade at the same time that the X-wings took off from Berlin. They're coming up the Carriage Road in trucks and four-wheelers right now. Even if that bunch in the chalet has called for outside help, it can't get here in time . . . and you won't pull your metaconcert trick again."

Kieran was chuckling soundlessly, his breath forming small puffs of vapor in the freezing air. He said: Of course not it's no longer necessary NOW THEY KNOW HOW they are consecrated to the Mother without realizing it O Her jests O Her infinite wisdom behold the final generation shall call Her blessed—

Victor let go of the old man's coat. Kieran slumped back against the cracked windowpane, eyes closed, breathing in raspy bursts. Victor said, "I'm not going to waste any more time listening to your crazy shit. Whatever scheme you cooked up—whatever way you planned to use me and my people—it's not going to work. I'm calling off my men from the X-wings and we're getting the hell off this mountain. The Sons can watch their own asses and take the blame—"

The mind-tone was wheedling, tempting: Don't be a fool my boy do you want your brother Denis to get away? And the other American operants the ones who will perfect MacGregor's aura-detector and use it to bring down you and your associates oh no oh no here they are together never again such a golden opportunity . . . I've had my moment. Now I leave the rest to you.

"What is the rest?" Victor raged. "You bug-fucking old devil—what have you *done*?"

The mortal stench was now almost unbearable. Victor shrank away in the frigid darkness, braced himself against the tilted seats, heard the first rustle of sleet strike the coach's metal skin. He couldn't stay here any longer. His inside man at the chalet was supposed to have sabotaged the delegate transports. Could one of them be repaired? They could still make the hit and get out before—

His racing thoughts were interrupted by the old man's voice, suddenly strong again. "I thought I would be the agent of destruction. And then it seemed that you would be Her deputy. Now at the end I see the truth—that humanity will destroy itself without our impetus. Even these superior minds! We are all children of the Black Mother dam dham nam tam tham—"

The voice dwindled away to an exhaled breath. And then Kieran O'Connor's eyes flew open in thunderstruck surprise, and he screamed and died.

Denis Remillard gripped the lectern. He had to coerce them into silence, then plead with the ones who had left the main dining room to return.

He said: *You must not leave the chalet! The temperature has dropped below freezing and another storm front will be here any minute. Please! Come back to the dining room and we'll decide what's to be done . . .*

Jamie MacGregor, wearing a borrowed parka, came striding through the disheveled banquet tables. "Every one of the fewkin' air-buses is out of commission. Someone got to 'em while the crews were eating in the lower lounge. Some of the handier delegates are outside trying to fix things, but it looks bloody hopeless. There are cars belonging to the chalet staff, but not nearly enough to evacuate all of us—even if we managed to get past those buggers who're on the way up . . . Is help on the way?"

"Not from the police," Lucille said. She and most of the Coterie were gathered around the speakers' table. "The officers who had staked out the road on the Pinkham Notch side of the mountain were ambushed by the Sons. There's no way the police on the western side of the mountain can reach us without aircraft."

Denis said, "The President said he'd send an FBI special team—but it has to come all the way from Boston. The Governor's called out the National Guard. It will take two hours to mobilize."

"Bloody hell!" Jamie exploded. "Why don't they roust out the Marines or the Army Antiterrorist Unit?"

Lucille said, "Because this country doesn't handle riots that way."

The Scotsman snorted. "This is no riot, it's a soddin' siege—"

"Jamie, please." Denis's knuckles were white as he continued to grip the sides of the lectern. *We don't have much time. We must decide what we are going to do.*

Young Severin Remillard, unnoticed in the press of anxious adults, piped up: "The only thing is to keep on like before—like Uncle Rogi and that other guy said—and clobber the sonsabitches!"

Lucille took the boy firmly by the shoulder and turned him over to his older brothers.

The Coterie turned away, returning to their seats. Other delegates who had dashed up to the observation turret or to other parts of the mountaintop convention center returned to the dining room as Denis had requested. Some sat at the tables. Others stood around the perimeter of the huge room, their farsight probing the exterior darkness. The clouds had thickened again and freezing rain ticked against the thick glass in the western lobe. The corps of servers and the white-clad kitchen personnel, normals all, huddled in a separate group.

Presently, Denis spoke into the microphone: "Ladies and gentlemen, we have called for help, and it is on the way." There were murmurs and scattered applause from the normals; but the operants were under no illusions. "It now seems clear that there are at least two forces of domestic insurgents belonging to the antioperant Sons of Earth group advancing on this building. About sixty are coming from the two crashed X-wings on the western slope. More than a hundred more are on their way up the Carriage Road on the eastern side, traveling in light trucks and cars. The motorcade seems to be equipped with rifles, shotguns, and small arms. Many of them are under the influence of one thing or another. They can be characterized as a run-of-the-mill lynch mob—and aside from blocking our escape down that road, they offer a very minor threat to our safety."

A voice yelled: "Du gehst mir auf die Eier, Remillard, mit diesem Scheissdreck! What können wir *tun*?"

"He's right! What *are* we going to do?" another voice shouted.

"That other lot from the aircraft aren't minor! I pEEped automatic weapons and at least one grenade launcher—"

Again, unwillingly, Denis coerced them to silence.

"Please listen . . . The airborne group *is* heavily armed. They have explosives with them as well as heavy weapons, and the only reason they aren't outside the chalet already is the sudden change in the weather . . . and they've temporarily lost touch with their leader. For those of you who don't already know, that leader is my younger brother, Victor."

The room vibrated with a blast of wind. Some of the chalet workers were whispering among themselves.

Denis said, "The real instigator of the attack is a man named Kieran O'Connor. Many of you know him as a pillar of the multinational military-industrial complex. O'Connor—like my brother—is a powerful natural operant who has concealed his metafaculties and used them to his personal advantage. For years O'Connor has worked secretly to destroy the operant establishment—not only because we might expose him, but also because peace isn't profit-generating to his line of business. Our globalism threatens him, just as it has threatened fanatics and dictatorships all over the world . . . just as it seems to threaten good people frightened of fellow human beings with higher mindpowers. And the normals *do* have good reason to be frightened, as long as operants such as Kieran O'Connor or my brother Victor exist."

A Chinese delegate, Zhao Kud-lin, exclaimed, "This is precisely why operants must be politically active—to ferret out and deal with such vermin!"

There were some murmurs of agreement. An anonymous mind-voice shouted: *Let's stop this palavering and whomp up another concert Denis! Come on pull us together again and let's start picking the deadheads off!*

Denis said, "It was Kieran O'Connor—not I—who led some of you in the aggressive metaconcert that downed the attacking aircraft."

Sensation!

A woman delegate cried: "Then three cheers for Kieran Warbucks!"

"No! No!" others shouted in dismay. "Shame!"

Denis said, "Kieran O'Connor knows we're divided in our attitude toward psychic aggression. I don't believe that his primary intent is to trap and destroy us here. He really wants to discredit all operants everywhere in the eyes of the normals by forcing us to abandon our Ethic. Some of you who joined his metaconcert probably reacted instinctively against a perceived danger. Others . . . did not. But we must all understand that we face the most critical choice of our lives here and now. We represent the operant leadership of the world. We will have to choose whether to adhere to the Ethic that has inspired us ever since our first meeting in Alma-Ata—or to do as certain of our fellow operants have already done: use our minds as weapons . . . I say that if we do this, even in this situation of obvious self-defense, the normal people of the world will ultimately condemn us as inhuman, a race apart, a monstrous minority too dangerous to share the planet with."

The audience was still. Momentarily, the lights flickered. A few people cried out, then fell silent again as the illumination steadied.

"Make no mistake," Denis said quietly, "we could very easily die in support of our principles. But I believe there are two honorable courses open to us. The first is simply to wait for rescue, utilizing what passive defenses we can muster. The second is to unite in a very different form of grand metaconcert—not only embracing those of us here, but also every other operant that we can summon telepathically from all corners of the world, *and even the normals*. Yes! I believe that we must try to gather them under our aegis as well. The focus of our grand metaconcert must be our enemies, the enemies of peace and tolerance everywhere. But we won't try to destroy them or even to coerce them. We'll try to reach their hearts."

Out of the stunned hush, Jamie MacGregor's voice was imploring. "But could it work, lad? It's a brave notion—but could it possibly move them?"

Denis had lowered his head. "I don't know. I don't even know if we can put together this type of metaconcert. In aggression, mind-melding is easy. Mob rule! But this other kind . . . demands that one surrender part of one's individual sovereignty to the whole, and to do so leaves the mind vulnerable. I myself find the idea of metaconcert frightening. Invasive. I've only conjoined with my wife, whom I love more than life, and with my uncle, who has acted as a father to me. I don't know whether I would be able to do it with all of you or not. There's a potential for damage—very serious damage—to the coordinator. But I've decided that I'm willing to try, if this group asks me to do so. If it chooses to uphold the Ethic."

Denis lifted his eyes slowly and swept the room. "Of course, you're quite free to choose the other way. I know you'll want to think it over. But please don't take too long."

Victor had managed to rally most of his scattered force in the lee of the Gulf Tank, a landmark next to the upper section of the railway where the cog locomotives once took on water. Sleet coated the old wooden structure with glistening rime and whitened the rocks; but little of it stuck to the huddling men, who were dressed in electrically heated suits and helmets.

The most telepathically talented of the attackers had eavesdropped upon Denis's speech, and when it was over the aether clanged with their contemptuous laughter.

Victor shouted into the roaring wind, not caring who heard: *A prayer! That's what they want to zap us with boys! Not mental lasers or great balls of fire but a goddam prayer!*

When all except a few stragglers had assembled, Victor got down to business. He projected a mental map pinpointing their location—some six hundred meters from the chalet as the crow flew, if one would have dared on such a vile night. The disabled transport aircraft that had carried the delegates up the mountain and the twenty or so vehicles belonging to the restaurant staff were in a sheltered bowl on the other side of the summit. One small squad of men would go around the north slope, secure the vehicles for the group's escape, and dispose of any persons in the vicinity. The five-man demolition crew, which Victor planned to lead himself, would advance on the western side of the chalet under cover-fire from the rest of the force.

"You guys get up two, three hundred meters from the building, and make like the Battle of Gettysburg. Never mind trying to hit anything. Just fire high and fire a lot so those heads don't have time to think about anything but their precious skins." Victor projected a farsight view of the western half of the building, which jutted shelflike above a small precipice and was supported by stout piers anchored in bedrock. If these were undermined, the entire structure would topple downhill into the vast gulf of Ammonoosuc Ravine.

"Once I'm certain the charges are placed right I'll activate the timers," Victor said. "And then I'm going to yell *go-go-go* over the helmet intercom, and telepathically too. You hear that, you haul ass for those cars. You'll have ten minutes from the shout. Whatever you do, don't mind-yak to each other—especially about the explosives! Remember these are heavy heads inside the building and they can use your thoughts to target you if they change their minds about doing a pray-in. Everybody understand?"

They muttered into their helmets. A few of the men, wearing older models with low wattage, were already having to scrape ice from the visors.

One querulous voice asked, "Vic—you *sure* we can get down the mountain with that other bunch coming up? Seems to me—"

Victor cut him off. "We got us a shit-trip. Nobody knows it better than me. But if push comes to shove we can walk off this rock-pile six different ways. Anybody starts wetting his pants better think hard about the one million cash he won't be getting if he screws up. I'm gonna come through this thing and so will you if you do what I told you. Now get going!"

32

FROM THE MEMOIRS OF
ROGATIEN REMILLARD

AS I ROBBED THE BODY, I CURSED MY LATE ADVERSARY FOR
being built like an ape instead of a proper beanpole.

This meant that his electric suit would have to be slit around
the upper inseams and crotch in order to fit me—a mutilation
that fortunately did not damage the thermal wiring—and the em-
barrassing fore and aft gaps filled in with a ludicrous loincloth
rigged from my cut-up jacket. His high moon-boots closed the
ankle gap nicely, however, and once I had turned up the suit's
heat full blast, pulled on the warm gauntlets, and settled the helmet into place, I was no longer at imminent risk of death through
exposure, an expedient that had seemed all too likely before I had
encountered this straggling mercenary and chopped him across
the back of the neck with a sharp wedge of granite.

I had managed to bash my head and bruise my left leg severely in my escape from the train. The injuries, together with the
arduous scramble that had preceded my ambush of the mercenary, had reduced my mental faculties almost to zero. Not only
was I dead beat and only slowly recovering from hypothermia,
but I was emotionally torpid—certain that nothing I could do
would be able to help the twenty-eight hundred operants trapped
in the chalet above.

I had no farsight and I had no farspeech. The helmet was
equipped with the usual intercom radio, but to use it would only
alert Victor and his minions. I could expect my neurons to revive
as I thawed out—but the storm was intensifying, and with the
increased wind velocity and precipitation the atmosphere was becoming loaded with wrongo ions. Trained operants could project

their thoughts through such muck, but hardly the likes of me.

I knelt to study my victim's weapon. It was thickly glazed with ice and unfamiliar in aspect, resembling a cross between a large electric drill and sections of the chromed exhaust system of a small motorcycle. I hadn't the faintest notion where the trigger might be, and the thing's weight was formidable—no doubt the reason why the desperado had fallen behind his companions, only to be dispatched by me in very cold blood. I decided to give further armed combat a miss and concentrate on saving my life.

I began to work my way across the slope in a southerly direction, having a vague notion of outflanking Victor's force and approaching the chalet obliquely by way of the main portion of the Appalachian Trail. On my left, the chalet blazed with lights, and I thought: Boobies! Don't you realize you're sitting ducks? Blackout! Blackout!

But then I realized the foolishness of my futile shout. Victor and his operant henchmen were not handicapped as I was; with their farsenses, they could perceive the chalet as readily with illumination as without it. I was the booby, as usual.

I crept into the teeth of the wind, more often than not going on my hands and knees over the icy, boulder-strewn mountainside. My mind drifted back to the time so long ago when I had been marooned in the Mahoosucs in another storm, only to be rescued —if I really had been—by the Family Ghost. O ingenious figment of my imagination! Where are you now—off on some interstellar jaunt? Or given me up as a bad job?...How could I blame you, Ghost? I disobeyed your orders. There I was, at least three times feeling the irresistible compulsion to tell Denis the tale of the Great Carbuncle, and on each occasion cringing at the banality of it...

O Ghost, you picked a loser. You told me I would know the appropriate moment to urge Denis to unite his colleagues and the Mind of Earth in prayerful metaconcert. And if this isn't the moment, I don't know what it is! But here I am and there Denis is, and Lucille, and their three boys, and all the rest of the good-guy operants, and I've blown it, and so have you.

Ghost, mon ami, let me try to make small amends. I will pause in the shelter of this blasted crag (since I'm in need of a breather anyway) and at least attempt to fulfill your esteemed orders. I will squeak into the hurricane and perchance le bon dieu in his mercy (if not you in yours) will bring a happy ending to this comedy:

Denis! This is your Uncle Rogi. Listen my son. I have been told to give you an important message. Unite the minds of your colleagues in a metaconcert of goodwill. Renounce violence. If you do this beings from the stars will no longer shun our poor planet but will come and be our friends ... This sounds incredible? Bien entendu! Nevertheless I have been told many times that it is true. Denis! Do you hear me? Answer if you do.

I waited.

The first thing that happened was that every light in the chalet went out.

The next thing was that all hell broke loose.

Victor's men began to fire at the building with their automatic weapons from a long line of attack strung across the slope just above me. Tracer bullets stitched the curtains of sleet with scarlet smudges. I heard the sound of smashing glass, then exploding grenades. The howl of the wind was almost drowned out by the racket of the weaponry and I crouched in numb horror for several minutes—and then unaccountably felt infused with fresh energy and impelled to get moving.

I came upon some kind of trail. My impaired night-sight showed me the cairns quite distinctly, together with the slightly less rough rock surface that passed for a designated pathway on the Spartan slopes of Mount Washington. The shooting was really nowhere near me, but to my left. I began to move rapidly uphill, and the trail slanted away at an angle that put the wind at my back. I judged that I was probably approaching the chalet by one of the steep short cuts that gave access to the summit from the southwest. The thump of grenades had stopped, although fusillades of bullets continued unabated. I was moving up a gully and could no longer see the tracers. I had no idea whether Vic's troops were advancing or standing pat.

Then the gunfire became muted by the lay of the land, and once again I was acutely aware of the hundred-voiced wailing of the mountain wind and the hiss of freezing rain. My personal aether was a tangle of ionic chittering and sibilance, as meaningless as static on an untenanted radio frequency. I heard nothing from Denis, no Ghostly reassurances, only my ragged breathing and the pounding of my pulse. Slipping and sliding on the ice, I climbed upward. My semiexposed rump, with its inadequate covering long since soaked through, had lost all sensation. My legs worked automatically. I had some vague idea, I think, of coming up beneath the overhang of the building and working my way around to the service entrance.

The ground began to level out. I was in an area of enormous jagged rocks, heaped around the massive concrete pillars that supported the western side of the chalet. My farsight provided a faint grayish view for a radius of a few meters. Beyond that was blackness.

Until I saw the blood-red glow.

A frisson of dread passed through me. Had Victor set the chalet afire? But the patch of radiance was too small for that . . . and it moved. Heaven help me, I thought of the *real* Great Carbuncle, that will-o'-the-wisp of Mount Washington folklore that lured stormbound hikers to their doom. But what would it be doing flitting about the foundation of the chalet? The bulk of the building now loomed above me, every windward surface plastered with a heavy crust of rime. I could dimly farsense that most of the western windows were broken. There were no telepathic thoughts to be discerned.

The magnetic carmine gleam drew me toward it. The worst of the sleet was behind me now that I was beneath the overhang, but there was a kind of frozen fog swirling through the cavernous dark that disguised the source of the red glow until I was nearly on top of it.

Suddenly, my ultrasense went off like an alarm clock, telling me that the thing I had perceived wasn't a light at all. It was an operant's aura, and the mind generating it was powerful, pitiless, and all too familiar.

I saw Victor.

He was recognizable in spite of the cold-weather gear he wore, unscreened and heedless, ablaze with anticipated triumph as he strapped the last of three packages of explosive to one of the piers of the chalet. Before I fully realized what he was up to he had finished the job. From a nearly empty backpack laying on the ground he took a device like a pocket radio, flicked switches, and tapped out some code. Then his voice was loud in my helmet phones:

"Go-go-go!"

The gunfire stopped, and at the same moment there was an abrupt lull in the wind.

Victor turned and saw me standing there, not ten meters away. My mind was paralyzed by his coercion even before I realized that he had spotted me.

"It took you long enough to get here," he said. Carefully, he tucked the little electronic gadget into the pack. Then he came for me. He didn't say another word, didn't transmit a farspoken message; but I knew what he was going to do. During that trip up the mountain in the cog, Kieran O'Connor had passed on to Victor the terrible secret of mind-bonding. Kieran had used his body as a tool. Victor wouldn't have to. The ultimate result on me would be the same . . . and if I refused him I'd finish up as Shannon had, incinerated as my psychic energies revitalized this creature that had once been a human being.

Victor had taken his helmet off and cast it aside. His eyes were like bore-holes into lava. And I thought, Jesus, I can't let him take me and I *won't* be a martyr. I'm going to try one last out-spiral—

Victor stopped.

Deep within the mountain was a sound, a slow and swelling vibration. The rocks around us began to shine with a barely perceptible greenish fluorescence and there were clashing tinkling chiming noises everywhere as their ice coating fractured like glass. The terror and hopelessness I had felt was wiped from my mind and in its place came an uncanny sense of warm benevolence: a beckoning bright calmness. Victor seemed to be feeling it, too. His raging aura dimmed and he flinched as if he had been struck, then looked frantically about. The expression on his face was one of a furious, perplexed child. Poor Victor! Something seemed to urge me to reach out to him, to show him where help lay. But I was too old and too wary and I resisted—

The phenomenon cut off as abruptly as it had begun. The banshee wind, carrying thick snowflakes this time instead of freezing rain, smote us with renewed vigor. It had gone pitch black except for Victor's red halo. I cringed before him and before the storm and heard him laugh.

"So that's the best they can do, is it?"

Then he was coming at me again. One blow of his fist knocked my own helmet off, and then he clamped my skull between hands like the jaws of a vise. The deadly eyes! My vision was a flaming blur and my heart leapt behind my breastbone and I shouted *NO* and summoned my body's core-energy and made it spiral around and around and around and out...

Victor was lying there at my feet. He had no aura but he breathed. His face was dark, bruised profoundly. His gloved fingers made small scrabbling noises in the icy detritus.

A voice said, *"Quelle bonne rencontre."*

I gave a violent start and looked behind me. Someone was coming through the blizzard, carrying a powerful halide lantern that threw vivid orange reflections on the wild scene. I recognized Victor's villainous old sidekick, Pete Laplace, and would have ducked away—but my psychocreative zap had so drained me that I was incapable of moving a muscle. Pete limped up, shone his lamp briefly on Victor, then unwound his Ragg wool muffler and stuffed it under my nephew's head.

The vibration in the mountain started up again.

Old Pete looked about, smiling thinly. As the rocks went phosphorescent he scrambled over to Victor's backpack and began stomping all over it. I heard breaking noises along with a fresh chorus of glacial tinkling.

"That's enough of *that*," old Pete declared. "Now let's see if those folks upstairs and their brain-pals around the world and a few other souls on this perverse little planet have got what it takes."

I felt once again the pervading flood of calmness; but its joy and serenity no longer invited me—they passed me by. I experienced it but I was not really a part of it. I seemed to see faces—the delegates, Lucille and the children, Jamie, Pyotr, members of the Coterie; and I saw others whom I knew were elsewhere—Oriental and Slavic faces, blacks and Latins, natives of America and Australia, the hawk faces of desert tribes, urbane Europeans. There were Caucasian elders and suboperant schoolchildren from the Indian plains, academics, operant peace officers, scientists, government officials. I saw Ayeesha, the kind Syrian nanny of the Remillard household. I saw Jamie MacGregor's grandmother. I saw Tamara Sakhvadze, weeping, with her grown children Valery and Anna. I saw Gerry Tremblay. I saw Elaine . . .

So many of them in free coadunation, operants and normals, and Denis extended to his uttermost mental limits holding and guiding the prayer. I could not hear what they said. It had nothing to do with the stars and everything to do with Earth. It was not my prayer, nor was it affirmed by every mind on our proud and stubborn and foolish world. But it sufficed.

Old Pete came up to me, reached out, and seemed to take something that I had. He said, "Come on," and headed out into the open. The thunderous vibration was gentling and the wind fell so rapidly that by the time we were out from under the chalet and heading along the down-slope trail toward the south the air was dead calm and the snow had dwindled to a few drifting flakes. Pete had left his lantern behind. The sky was oddly bright, and when I stopped and looked back at the chalet I saw that the entire structure was clothed in auroral brilliance.

"This is far enough," Pete said. He held something up above his head with one hand. I saw it was the Great Carbuncle.

"You!" I said.

The thing flared like a nova, blinding me. I felt someone take my gloved hand, slap something into it, and press the fingers shut.

"You can have it back now. But take good care of it. This is only the beginning, you know. Au 'voir, cher Rogi."

When my vision returned he was gone, and the New Hampshire sky was filled with the thousands of starships of the Galactic Milieu, and the Great Intervention had begun.

FINIS
VINCULI

EPILOGUE

HANOVER, NEW HAMPSHIRE, EARTH
26 APRIL 2113

ROGATIEN REMILLARD LOOKED AT THE LAST WORDS ON THE DISplay of the transcriber, hit both PRINT and FILE, and then treated himself to a luxurious yawn. The cat Marcel, sitting at his elbow on the battered deal desk, pricked up its ears and stared alertly at an empty corner of the bookshop's back room.

"Is that you?" Rogi inquired of thin air.

Naturellement!

"Checking up on me, eh? Well, I've finished this bit. Don't think it was easy, even with your help."

My congratulations on a satisfactory job.

Rogi grunted. "Let me ask you a question or two off the record. Were you responsible for Vic not killing me when I found him and Shannon at the hotel?"

No. He wanted you. In spite of all his power, he was an ignorant man. He hoped, pathetically, that you would somehow be a mentor to him, as he perceived you had been to the young Denis.

Rogi shook his head. "Too damn psychological for me . . . Another question: Were you always Pete Laplace?"

I assumed the personas of living humans when it was convenient, setting them . . . aside until the guise was no longer needed.

"Did you do that kind of thing very often?"

I confess, it did tend to become habit-forming! You must try to understand that, at the beginning of my direct participation, I was unsure how much adjustment of the probability lattices would be required of me. Meddling by an incorporeal Lylmik seemed marginally riskier than manipulations done in human disguise. In time, I came to realize that my doubts were merely prideful resistance to the promptings of the Cosmic Afflatus. My actions, though quite freely willed, were demonstrably preordained in the larger Reality, which is mystery. Keeping this in mind, I just got on with it.

"And even enjoyed yourself!" Rogi's tone was accusing.

The Ghost laughed: We Lylmik take our Olympian pleasures where we may. I assure you they are few and far between.

"I'll just bet," said Rogi sardonically. Then he asked, in a more serious vein, "What really happened to Victor? In retrospect, I don't hardly see how I could have zapped him without your help. I was just too far gone."

I helped.

"Why didn't you kill him outright instead of trapping him inside his skull? My God, he was blind, deaf, deprived of all tactile sensation and every metafaculty but self-awareness. And the poor bastard lived another twenty-seven years."

The tenderhearted may regard cerebral solitary confinement as too harsh a purgatory for any entity. I assure you that, for a mind such as Victor's, it was not. He was vouchsafed a period of reflection . . . just as I was. Unfortunately, *his* final choice was the wrong one. Priez pour nous pécheurs, maintenant et à l'heure de notre mort.

Rogi sighed. "Well, I'm going to take a vacation before I start in on the next part. Yours. Get in a little skiing before spring strikes with a vengeance. Might go to Denali. That was one of your favorites, as I recall."

The Ghost was chuckling. Marcel flattened his ears as the printed paper pages in the transcriber's receiving rack riffled, as though flicked by an invisible finger.

The Ghost said: So you are quite sure now, are you, that you know me?

Rogi nodded complacently. "Haven't figured the why of it— much less the how. But I guess I'll worm it out of you eventually along with some other parts of the story that always mystified me a bit." He cut the power to the transcriber, stood up, and stretched. "I'm outa here and up to bed."

The Ghost said: Good night, Uncle Rogi.

Rogi said, "Good night, Marc."

THE END OF

INTERVENTION

APPENDIX

THE REMILLARD FAMILY TREE

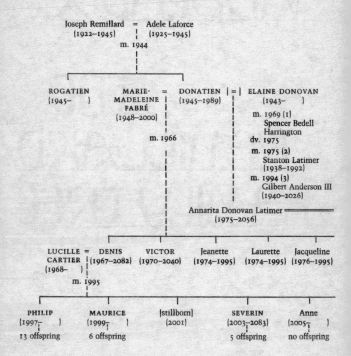

Joseph Remillard = Adele Laforce
(1922–1945)   (1925–1945)
          m. 1944

ROGATIEN   MARIE- = DONATIEN | = | ELAINE DONOVAN
(1945–   )   MADELEINE (1945–1989)   (1943–   )
                FABRÉ
                (1948–2000)   m. 1969 (1)
                                            Spencer Bedell
                                            Harrington
                        m. 1966   dv. 1975
                                            m. 1975 (2)
                                            Stanton Latimer
                                            (1938–1992)
                                            m. 1994 (3)
                                            Gilbert Anderson III
                                            (1940–2026)

                        Annarita Donovan Latimer
                        (1975–2056)

LUCILLE = DENIS   VICTOR   Jeanette   Laurette   Jacqueline
CARTIER (1967–2082) (1970–2040) (1974–1995) (1974–1995) (1976–1995)
(1968–   )
         m. 1995

PHILIP   MAURICE   (stillborn)   SEVERIN   Anne
(1997–   )   (1999–   ) (2001)   (2003–2083) (2005–   )

13 offspring 6 offspring   5 offspring no offspring

THE REMILLARD
FAMILY TREE

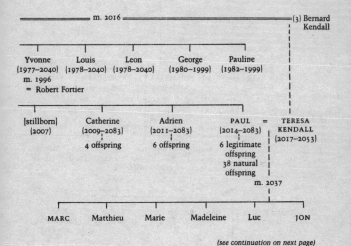

	m. 2016				(3) Bernard Kendall

Yvonne (1977–2040) m. 1996 = Robert Fortier	Louis (1978–2040)	Leon (1978–2040)	George (1980–1999)	Pauline (1982–1999)	

[stillborn] (2007)	Catherine (2009–2083) 4 offspring	Adrien (2011–2083) 6 offspring	PAUL (2014–2083) 6 legitimate offspring 38 natural offspring m. 2037	TERESA KENDALL (2017–2053)

MARC Matthieu Marie Madeleine Luc JON

(see continuation on next page)

O'CONNOR GENEALOGY

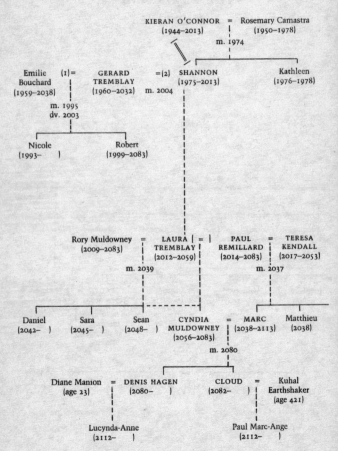

KIERAN O'CONNOR = Rosemary Camastra
(1944–2013)   (1950–1978)
m. 1974

Emilie   (1)=   GERARD   =(2) SHANNON   Kathleen
Bouchard   TREMBLAY   (1975–2013)   (1976–1978)
(1959–2038)   (1960–2032) m. 2004

m. 1995
dv. 2003

Nicole   Robert
(1993–)   (1999–2083)

Rory Muldowney = LAURA | = | PAUL   = TERESA
(2009–2083)   TREMBLAY   REMILLARD   KENDALL
                 (2012–2059)   (2014–2083)   (2017–2053)

m. 2039   m. 2037

Daniel   Sara   Sean   CYNDIA   = MARC   Matthieu
(2042–) (2045–) (2048–) MULDOWNEY   (2038–2113) (2038)
                               (2056–2083)

m. 2080

Diane Manion = DENIS HAGEN   CLOUD   = Kuhal
(age 23)   (2080–)   (2082–)   Earthshaker
                                              (age 421)

Lucynda-Anne   Paul Marc-Ange
(2112–)   (2112–)

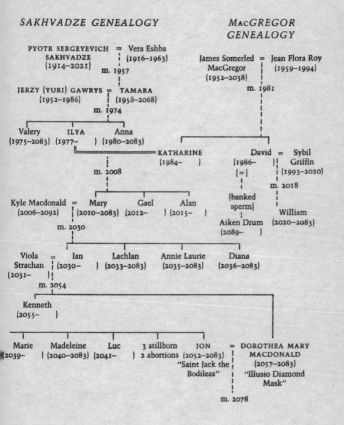

SAKHVADZE GENEALOGY

PYOTR SERGEYEVICH = Vera Eshba
SAKHVADZE (1916–1963)
(1914–2021)
m. 1957

JERZY (YURI) GAWRYS = TAMARA
(1952–1986) (1958–2068)
m. 1974

Valery   ILYA   Anna
(1975–2083) (1977–   ) (1980–2083)

KATHARINE
(1984–   )

m. 2008

Kyle Macdonald = Mary   Gael   Alan
(2006–2092)   (2010–2083) (2012–   ) (2015–   )
m. 2030

Viola   = Ian   Lachlan   Annie Laurie   Diana
Strachan | (2030–   ) (2033–2083) (2035–2083)   (2036–2083)
(2031–   )|
m. 2054

Kenneth
(2055–   )

Marie   Madeleine   Luc   3 stillborn   JON
(2039–   ) (2040–2083) (2041–   ) 2 abortions   (2052–2083)
                                                      "Saint Jack the
                                                      Bodiless"

MacGREGOR GENEALOGY

James Somerled = Jean Flora Roy
MacGregor   (1959–1994)
(1952–2038)
m. 1981

David   = Sybil
(1986–   )| Griffin
[=] | (1993–2020)
         m. 2018
(banked
sperm)
              William
Aiken Drum   (2020–2083)
(2089–   )

= DOROTHEA MARY
  MACDONALD
  (2057–2083)
  "Illusio Diamond
  Mask"

m. 2078

ABOUT THE AUTHOR

JULIAN MAY's short science fiction novel, *Dune Roller*, was published by John W. Campbell in 1951 and has now become a minor classic of the genre. It was produced on American television and on the BBC, became a movie, and has frequently been anthologized. Julian May lives in the state of Washington.

Julian May's

SCIENCE FICTION SERIES:

The Saga of Pliocene Exile